Beyond *the* Moon

Beyond *the* Moon

Beyond the Pain. Beyond the Darkness.

VELDA BROTHERTON

FOYLE
PRESS

an imprint of
OGHMA CREATIVE MEDIA

OGHMA

CREATIVE MEDIA

Foyle Press
An imprint of Oghma Creative Media, Inc.
2401 Beth Lane, Bentonville, Arkansas 72712

Library of Congress Cataloging-in-Publication Data

Names: Brotherton, Velda, author.
Title: Beyond the Moon/Velda Brotherton.
Description: Second Edition. | Bentonville: Foyle, 2019.
Identifiers: LCCN: 2018955386 | ISBN: 978-1-63373-403-6 (hardcover) |
ISBN: 978-1-63373-404-3 (trade paperback) | ISBN: 978-1-63373-405-0 (eBook)
Subjects: | BISAC: FICTION/Women | FICTION/Romance/Contemporary
LC record available at: https://lccn.loc.gov/2018955386

Foyle Press trade paperback edition January, 2019

Cover & Interior Design by Casey W. Cowan
Editing by Greg Camp

The Vietnam war officially ended
Saturday, January 27, 1973

For many it never has.

*This book is dedicated to those veterans who remain
haunted by that war, and those who love and care for them.*

ACKNOWLEDGEMENTS

MY THANKS FOR making this book possible go to many people. To my late husband Don for his encouragement through the years. To the many members of The Northwest Arkansas Writers Workshop, for their support throughout many years and many books before this one finally saw the light of day. To my late friend Dusty Richards, who pushed me so hard to become published in the first place. To my daughter Jeri Henson for her hours of love and understanding. To Casey Cowan of Oghma Creative Media, who took a chance on this book when nobody else would. And last, but not least, Greg Camp who edited this tome with patience and a smile which I know must have been difficult to maintain at times. Each of you made me a better writer.

Our Fathers being weary
laid down on Bunker Hill;
And tho' full many a morning,
Yet they are sleeping still,

The trumpet, Sir, shall wake them,
In dreams I see them rise,
Each with a solemn musket
A marching to the skies!

A coward will remain, Sir,
Until the fight is done;
But an immortal hero
Will take his hat, and run!

Goodbye, Sir, I am going;
My country calleth me;
Allow me, Sir, at parting,
To wipe my weeping e'e

In token of our friendship
Accept this "Bonnie Doon,"
And when the hand that plucked it
Hath passed beyond the moon,

The memory of my ashes
Will consolation be;
Then, farewell, Tuscarora,
And farewell, Sir, to thee!

...Emily Dickinson, 1851
"Sic transit gloria mundi"

P A R T
ONE

...Yet they are sleeping still,

ONE

OCTOBER, 1985
VA HOSPITAL, ARKANSAS

THE HOSPITAL CORRIDOR formed a tunnel Katherine prayed would take her straight back home. She did not dare turn and run, for Doctor Spencer blocked her way, and she had nowhere to go but the sunroom.

"He's just over there," Spencer herded her with competent, clean hands. Perhaps psychiatrists had a thing about that, a symbolic washing of their hands to absolve all guilt.

She grasped at such ridiculous thoughts in an effort not to look toward Spencer's patient, who was still merely a shadow seated against the brilliant backlight of the tall windows. Bright bands of October sunlight spilled through the glass, bent up and over huge pots of ficus and fern to puddle on the sparkling tile. The squeak of her worn suede boots sounded much too loud as she approached the man in the wheelchair.

"Though I don't approve of tags," Spencer had said earlier in his office, "you should know the difference between a psychotic and a neurotic."

"Do I have to?"

Spencer interrupted her reverie. "Katherine, this is Glen Tanner. Glen, this is Katherine Kelly." Then he moved away, the coward, and left her to handle the awkward moment. Tanner obviously wasn't going to help any either. Too soon. Way too soon to care about someone else's wounds. Her own had scarcely healed. Picked at, they still bled.

"Glen loses touch with reality." Why did she continue to recall the worst of what Spencer had told her this morning in his office? Was losing touch with reality psychotic or neurotic? Why did it make a difference? Either one was still crazy.

Whatever, she couldn't remain here staring everywhere but at Tanner, so she raised her head, tossed back an errant strand of hair, and met his gaze.

Nothing could have prepared her for the encounter. His brown eyes glittered golden in the sunlight, as fragile as fine crystal. In that brief first moment, they were all she saw. Multifaceted slivers of agony gleamed back at her. Not as if from a physical hurting, but more like fragments of a vicious emotional rape. She recalled the image of an injured hawk captured by well-meaning saviors. Its eyes, the color of Glen's, had that same expression as it alternately quivered in fear and lashed out in fury at all who offered help. Ultimately, the beautiful bird gave up, but the eyes never lost their hatred and despair.

Like his. Dear God, like his.

She forced herself to murmur a greeting and glanced at the canvas on which he'd been working. Much like the samples in Spencer's office, yet she gasped and pinched her mouth to prevent crying out. Looked away, then back again. The painting was hauntingly grotesque. Gray dripping trees set off cold blue figures in all manner of poses, mouths wide in soundless screams, some with no eyes, no arms, legs torn and scattered.

Others held gory remains. Babies, women's breasts smeared over the entire canvas beneath great globs of blued crimson that had to be blood. In this man's world there was no sun, no color but one, no hope of redemption.

Damn that Spencer for exposing her to this. Hadn't she gone through enough when Stan died? She refused to cry anymore. To keep from doing so, she gazed out the windows at the shaded, rolling green lawn, fallen leaves scattered over it like bright quilt scraps. Finally the trembling stopped, and she rubbed her damp palms on the legs of her jeans, lifted her shoulders, and turned back to meet that amber gaze. She felt as if they had taken hours to appraise each other, and Glen still hadn't acknowledged either the introduction or her greeting.

Someone had to do something, so she offered her hand without saying a word. He fumbled with a brush, laid it down, and reached for her, grabbing hold as if to halt a downward spiraling fall, his skin cold. The cracking voice startled her.

"I'm sorry. I don't remember your name."

She leaned forward to repeat it as if he might be hard of hearing and saw with dismay the white jagged scars around both his wrists. Without realizing what she was about to do, she touched them with trembling fingertips, and he captured her other hand, too. She had no time to move. His clinging in silent desperation kept her bent over, his breath on her cheek, her nose filled with the smell of shampoo in his shaggy blond hair. She glanced around for Spencer. He was gone. In his place stood an orderly who rocked on his feet. Heel, toe, heel, toe, arms clasped behind his back. The dour expression told her nothing except she was on her own unless attacked.

Unfamiliar odors of disinfectant and illness trickled into the atmosphere of forced normalcy in the airy room. No matter how many easy chairs they placed in careless precision, nor those fancy plants or lamps or books, this place was for suffering. It was for dying. Escape was her only thought, but this man held on to her, wouldn't let her go. If he had let go at this moment, though, she could not have left. Not after a glimpse at his hopelessness.

To break the somber mood, she smiled, felt like one of those circus clowns with its joviality painted on in thick colored grease. Such an awful lie. Dimples winked on in his cheeks, then went out. The eyes for that mere instant gave her a peek at his soul before disconnecting. A splatter of sunlight revealed scars on his face. Thin lines as if someone had tried to erase them but had not quite succeeded.

Look away, she told herself.

Do not stare at him.

The silent conversation had gone far enough. Though the painting horrified her, she locked her gaze there. It was easier than to think what had been done to him.

"How long have you been painting these?"

His voice, when he managed to use it, sounded ruptured, each word spoken low and soft and broken. "Who knows?"

"Are you from around here? Arkansas, I mean."

An expectant, hopeful reply. "Yes, around here. A long time ago."

Spencer had told her Glen needed someone to care about him, care about what he did, and what he hoped to do. Could she be the one? He ensnared her, this frail and damaged man. She should never have entered this room if she hoped to leave unscathed. Besides, as long as he held her hands in his icy grip she could not think of pulling away.

"I paint, too," she said. "I have a studio in Cedarville." Her voice caught, and she cleared her throat, went on. "That's where I live. Maybe I could join you here once in a while. We could paint together."

For an instant, she hoped he'd say no and let her off the hook. But it wasn't going to be that easy, for even if he did, neither she nor Spencer could let that be the end of it. It was too late. She was trapped by his need.

"Paint nightmares, do you."

His voice more a flat statement than a question.

She jerked away from the anger and bitterness in the question, and he turned loose of her as if from the same reaction.

She fought to keep the conversation moving.

"Sometimes artists do paint their nightmares. But then there's also what comes from the soul or what we see out there." She gestured toward the huge oak trees beyond the window, their leaves dancing toward the ground in graceful beauty. Turned back to the painting before him. "You're too talented to continue to paint these."

His eyes widened, glistened with moisture, and she feared for a moment he would burst out crying. He didn't, so she relaxed and sat in a chair near him. On a table at his side, the paints, a jar of cleaner and pots of linseed oil and thinner among the messy tubes, all exuded a comfortable familiarity, an aroma that eased her tension. The palette held three splashes of color. Umber, blue, and crimson. Beside them, mocking in its purity, roiled a snake of titanium white.

Painting was all that had saved her sanity following Stan's death, and it could be a great catharsis, just smearing paint on a pure white canvas. She understood this man's need to do so, but what was coming from his damaged soul endangered his wellbeing. Easy to see why Spencer thought she could help him. But why had he thought she would? When she glanced back at Glen, he stared at her, and she knew the answer to that.

"If I came back next week, could we paint together?" she asked.

His gaze never wavered, as if he were waiting for something more from her. Unable to meet the challenge, she glanced away.

His question was abrupt. "Do you have bad dreams?"

A closer look revealed deep creases around his mouth, making him appear older than his thirty-one years, and a rumpled scar doctors hadn't quite been able to fix tucked under his jawline.

"Of course, everyone does." Night after night until she had almost gone mad. Stan falling, her trying to catch him, tumbling after him.

"Do they?" Searching eyes dug deep into her soul, asked if she lied.

Reach out to him, Spencer had advised, and he'll respond.

Glen's pale fingers, two permanently bent at the knuckle, moved minutely into a patch of afternoon sunlight on the arm of the chair. So she took the hand in hers, again startled by the deadly coldness of his flesh. Her heart jerked painfully when he turned his luminous eyes toward her, eyes that overflowed with questions she couldn't decipher, much less answer.

In a voice falsely bright, she said, "We'll start by doing some sketches. I'll come back next week. This fall weather is lovely. If it's a nice day, we'll go outside and do some charcoal drawings."

"I don't go out." The voice frozen over like puddles in January.

"Doctor Spencer tells me you're going home soon. You'll have to go out then. Might as well start now as later."

Until that moment, she hadn't realized she was still touching him. Without replying, he turned his hand over under hers and squeezed her fingers. His expression denied something. What?

Encouraged by what little adverse reaction he'd shown, she said, "Paint something for me this week. Not like that." She gestured at the easel. "Something cool, soothing, peaceful. Whatever comes to mind."

"There's nothing left in me but that." So softly spoken she barely heard. He jerked from her touch, shouted something she couldn't understand, and she leaped backward. He pounded his chest until she feared he would shatter apart. Pointing first at the painting, then at her, he went on in a flat monotone of denial. "I don't want you coming back here. There is no peace in here. It won't work." A fist clenched over his heart.

What did he mean no peace in here? "It will work if you want it to."

"Since when did what the fuck I want matter?"

The ragged whisper tore through her. The guard stopped rocking on his heels and stood alert, ready to move. She blinked away sorrowful tears. How could they think of letting him go home like this? She needed badly to say the right thing, something that would make this man accept her.

"His sister is a good woman," Spencer had told her, "but she's so sorry for him, so sympathetic she brings out the very worst, his own self-pity. Treats him like a child. He has to be made to fight back, to stop laying all his problems out as excuses for not doing anything constructive with his life. A therapy we can all live with. He must learn to deal with reality again. Something has to work, or he is lost."

Glen closed his eyes and rubbed his thumbs aimlessly on the arms of the wheelchair, producing a muted squeak, pulling her from her reverie.

"You want to sit here and waste away, I guess that's up to you."

He raised his fine sandy brows. For a moment, she could see an urge to retaliate flash over his features. He settled for continuing to glare at her, as if he were studying an idea he'd not yet considered.

Before she could lose her composure, she rose. "I'll be back next Friday, then. See you. Okay?" The silly fluttering of her fingers faded with the babbling words, and she escaped before her rubbery legs dumped her to the floor.

She hadn't felt so bereft since Stan's funeral eight months earlier.

Spencer leaned against the wall just outside the sunroom, his face one of eager anticipation. She didn't disappoint him.

"I don't think I can do this. What do you expect of me, anyway? My God. How in hell could that happen to him?"

"Prisoner of war camp. More than nine years, best we can figure."

"War? What war?"

"Vietnam."

"That war's been over a long time. Surely he hasn't been like this all those years."

"Oh, no. He'd be dead if he had. In fact—"

"Damn you, Spencer. If you tell me what I do here is a matter of life or death, I'll punch you, so help me." She sucked in a breath. "How? Tell me about it, and I'll try to keep my big mouth shut."

"An intriguing promise." He gave them both a chance to relieve some pressure with smiles. "Let's go get some coffee and sit. It's a long story."

"And you want a chance to think up enough embellishments to hook me."

He didn't deny the accusation.

They strolled together, his hand scarcely touching her bare elbow. She could feel Glen Tanner's eyes boring through her shoulder blades, but didn't turn around.

The psychiatrist's office was much like the man. Rumpled, disjointed, and comfortable. She sat in a chair from which he'd removed a magazine on horses and a *National Geographic*. He sank into the deep cushions of a couch opposite her.

"Usually I have different seating arrangements, but I expect this will probably work out just as well." He stretched out his long legs, crossed at the ankles, and scrunched in the corner.

"Well?" She sipped from the Styrofoam cup of bland coffee.

He did the same. "Ah, yes. Vietnam. He came home in '83."

"But I thought—"

"Ah." He touched his lips, dark eyes glittering at her. "Hear me out as you promised. It will do no good for this to go further than this room. In fact, it wouldn't be the wisest move on your part. Do you understand what I'm saying?"

She nodded and reacted by holding a finger over her lips. This was all too histrionic for her taste, but she waited.

"There is an organization based in California. No names are necessary. They are in and out of Asia on a regular basis. In fact, most of them are Laotians, and they are experts at what they do. For enough money or other considerations, they, shall we say, perform rescue missions. They ran across Tanner crouched in a four-by-four foot cane cage hanging in a tree in the forest. Like a goddamned animal. Evidently, the group who had him had been scared off before they could drag him along. By that time, he wouldn't have been doing any moving on his own. He had been tortured on a regular basis. Kept alive as a chip in the politics of bargaining with the United States. Perhaps they abandoned him for expediency's sake. Things were warming up over there on this MIA thing. Anyway, these mercs decided to lift him out along with their original objective, a Senator's son-in-law.

"Tanner was a navy chopper pilot, and he went down during a dust-off mission that went awry. It was presumed no one came out of it alive, and they all were classified MIA. After he was expatriated, they kept him in a hospital out on the coast for several months, patching him up as best they could, then quietly put him on a plane and sent him home to his sister. It rated a small notice in the local paper, but it sounded as if he'd been in hospitals for a long period of time. Vague stuff that raised no questions.

Uncomfortable, she shifted, stared at Spencer, then through the glass into the sunroom where Glen continued to smear paint on the canvas as if she had never interrupted him.

Dear God. Nine years kept in a cage and tortured. That would destroy anyone.

"Anyway, the Tanner family owns a farm outside Cedarville, and he lived there, oh, up until a little over a year ago, managing somehow to get through the days, though I gather from what his sister told me, some of them were hell and all his nights were one continuous nightmare. One night, he lost it. Became that man in the cage trying to kill his captors. Julia called the sheriff only because she didn't know what else to do. After a night in the county lock-up, we got him. He just shut down. Quit walking, tried to quit eating and sleeping, got hold of a blade from somewhere and slit his wrists.

"Then, out of the blue a couple of months ago, he asked for paints, canvas, brushes, and a wheelchair. God only knows what prompted it, but he started painting. At first, he couldn't even sit up without being tied in. He ate and exercised and turned out those hideous canvases, as if trying to tell us something, send us a message. One he couldn't bear to speak aloud. If we could somehow keep him at it, make him want something more, goddammit, anything....

"He has to have been tough as hell to come this far, and I can't let him down. But I'm at my wit's end. We've never treated anyone with his history of captivity and abuse. The results go far beyond post-traumatic stress syndrome. Someone has to help him—"

"And you think that someone is me?" Incredible as it sounded, she could do it. Give him an outlet. A blank canvas on which to express himself.

"Professor Endlebeck says you're a damn fine artist and teacher, a sympathetic human being. Says you minored in psychology and sociology."

"Spencer, don't push it. Endlebeck didn't say that about the sympathetic human being. He never would have said such a thing. Besides, we've known each other a long time. Would you believe all that about me?"

"It's you who doesn't believe it." He smiled, but behind it was a silent, morose plea.

For a moment, she couldn't think of a thing to say, stuttered into something. "I—uh—I thought you doctors didn't get involved with your patients." She tilted her head, studied his dark eyes for a moment. "You love him, don't you?"

"If I had a son… something like this… my God, I would hope… it's difficult to get someone to care about themselves if you don't care yourself. Yes, I love him. It begins with giving a damn, then moves on. The bravery of someone like him is unbelievable. I abhor what happened to him while he was still just a green kid. If I could help just one like him, if you could, Katherine. I promise you more satisfaction than you could possibly dream of… just to see him smile. Once."

She stared at the cuffs of his brown slacks, slid her gaze up the long, gangly figure, the jacket with its leather elbow patches, the features that were all extreme unto themselves. Eyes too large, nose too long, lips too thick. He was trying very hard to hide a smugness that should have angered her, but didn't.

The bait was cast, and the bastard knew she couldn't help but bite.

"And all I have to do is come here once a week, help him with his paintings, steer him away from those monstrosities?" She cast a quick look through the glass.

"Well, that and after he goes home let him come to your studio as a private student. They have the money to pay whatever you care to charge. That isn't the problem."

"Don't you *dare* suggest all I care about is getting paid for this." She started to rise from the chair, and he held up large hands in supplication.

"Hey, we all have to make a living. I get paid, too. So cool down, Kate."

"Katherine. My name is Katherine. Don't call me Kate. You don't know me that well."

"And only your dead husband called you Kate." He watched her over tented fingers. "So what do you care about, Katherine Kelly? Stan's been dead eight months, and what do you care about this very minute? Why do you continue to exist? What is your purpose?"

"You're a real son of a bitch, you know that?"

"Why? Because I know my job?"

"No, because you're so damned self-effacing about it."

"Well, that would indeed be the day." He laughed, a strained laugh, and she made herself join him.

A while later, standing outside in the parking lot, she stared up at the windows in the three-story brick hospital, gleaming in the golden dusk. Which room was Glen's? A puff of wind blew her shoulder length hair across her face, and she shoved it back angrily. Like everything else she'd let go since Stan's death, the sandy strands were unkempt. There were smudges under her eyes from a combination of lack of sleep and crying too much. Every morning she gazed upon herself in the bathroom mirror and did not know the woman who looked back at her. A woman of forty who looked much older. God, she would soon be forty-one. And she was a mess, but up until this moment she hadn't really cared.

Stan had loved her hair, used to tousle it, sometimes at the most inopportune moments when she was concentrating on painting or studying for an exam. And she would get exasperated and push him away. So impatient then. Probably because she waited so long to get her education and felt as if time were passing her by. Then, when she had it all, came the cruelest of jokes. God declared she could have everything she wanted but happiness. In retaliation, she eradicated God from what remained of her life.

For a long time after that, she hadn't wanted anything. Did she want this? Away from the influence of those wounded eyes and

Spencer's suspicious manner, she wasn't sure if she could come back the following week after all.

She wheeled her blue and silver van in a wide circle and left the parking lot.

TWO

THAT NIGHT KATHERINE fell easily into her old habit of loung-
ing on the fur rug in front of the fireplace, loose afghan pulled around
her feet while she sipped at homemade elderberry wine and conjured
up fantasies of Stan.

Her parents had died within six months of each other when she was
barely eighteen. By the time she was nineteen, there was Stan, taking
over where they left off. Caring for her, soothing her heartache when she
found she could not bear children, encouraging her in her mid-thirties
to go back to college and finish her education.

Dragging herself away from the memories, she stared through the
burgundy liquid at the dancing flames, then took a long drink, savoring
a bite that edged the wine's smoothness. Why was everyone she loved
dead? Their desertion had left her incomplete, unfinished, with no ambi-
tion or desire. To answer Spencer's question, she had no purpose.

From the shadows of the darkened room came the voice she had
known so well for so long. "Come on, sweetheart. Time for bed."

"Oh, Stan. Oh, dear God, Stan. Why did you leave me?" Again with the tears, as if that would solve anything. When the only reply was the bright snap of the burning hickory logs, she banked the fire and trudged upstairs to bed.

The nightmare was long in coming and jerked her awake, her body bathed in perspiration. Men, thousands of them, screaming to get out of the gray jungles in which they were caught. Their mouths, open and silent, emitted gouts of torn organs. Their cries soundless because no one listened. How could she bear to return to that hospital and Glen's bleak world? She drew in a ragged breath. How could she not?

Sunday morning she carried her easel and paint box down the hillside past the studio to the creek. The bright, cerulean blue sky and the hills flamed in colors cried out to be captured on canvas. But her mind remained as dry and crackling as the leaves under her feet. Before she finished the preliminary sketch on the canvas, she knew the painting would be no good. Still, out of stubbornness, she kept at it until the light faded and a damp chill tumbled down on her from the mountains. Before gathering up her things, she scrubbed across the wet surface with a turpentine-soaked rag. Rivulets of thinned colors ran to the bottom and dripped onto the ground.

Everything she did that week bespoke of an inexplicable anger. By the end of her classes on Thursday evening, she was exhausted. She hadn't slept and had eaten little all week, but she would go to the hospital tomorrow. It wasn't a decision she felt comfortable with, but any other would have been intolerable. Guilt over things left undone never rested easy with her.

After the last student left, she remained in the studio. Sat alone in the room among the things she most loved, inhaling the oily odors. The spacious workroom bubbled with Stan's laughter, something she had not heard since his death. What an odd thing. Until now all she had remembered were her own regrets at things she failed to do. Like telling him goodbye or how much she adored him. Now, he was laughing?

He built her the studio, put in the skylight, and patiently resealed it after every rain until it quit leaking. She could still see him standing on the sturdy worktable, calling down to her, calling her Katie darlin'. He had always called her that, as if it were one word.

She jumped up, gazed around the room at the paintings on the walls, at the easels and paint-smeared rags, and somebody's empty Pepsi can overturned on the long table. Shrugging wearily, she walked out the door and closed it behind her.

THREE

SPENCER PEERED UP at her through his eyelashes. "You look...
um, well, *terrible*, Katherine."

"I appreciate that."

He fluttered his fingertips over the desktop, a nervous move that sent
a few papers flying.

"How do you find anything in that mess?" She dropped into the
chair across from him.

"Bet you've got nice legs."

"What?"

"I said—"

"I heard you."

"If you'd wear something besides jeans, they'd show."

"You sound angry. What are you so mad about, anyway? You wear
that same ratty brown jacket day in, day out."

"How about some properly placed outrage?"

"About what? I'm not sure I—"

"Yes, you do know what I'm getting at. You going to mourn in silence the rest of your life, or scream and stomp and cry, then get on with it?"

She straightened, drew her feet under the chair, crossed her ankles, and flashed him an icy stare.

He smiled. "I like you, Katherine Kelly. Always have."

She tilted her head, let the anger flow away. Not sure she could return the compliment, she said nothing.

"You're gutsy. You just don't know it yet."

Despite herself, she laughed. "What kind of doctor talks like that?"

His merriment joined hers for a moment, but then he sobered. "Glen didn't think you'd come back."

"Oh?" She picked at a fingernail. "I'm not sure I thought so either."

"Don't try to lie to him about your motives."

"That would be hard since I'm not sure yet what they are."

"I know you're not, but you will be. And Katherine?" He stood and went to a window. She watched him and waited. When he turned, he was serious. "He's strangely perceptive or maybe just overly suspicious. Of pity, of pretension. All you really have to do is care and show it; otherwise he'll see right through you."

She picked up her case. "That I can do. Just tell me one thing. What's the difference between pity and compassion?"

"Pity is feeling sorry. Compassion is doing something about it." Spencer looked quite pleased with himself.

She waited until she left the office before muttering aloud, "Thinks he's got a two-for-one sale." The doctor had subtly taken her on as an unofficial patient, but that didn't upset her. What did was the idea of facing Glen and those mournful, accusing golden eyes.

Two elderly gentlemen sat across the sunroom from Glen, playing checkers in front of one of the windows. The soft murmur of their voices followed her across the room. His back was to her, and he sat so still he might be asleep. His overseer slumped on a couch against the wall, concentrating on a magazine. He looked up at the sound of her footsteps, put down the magazine, rose, and went to the wheelchair. The two men spoke in muted tones for a moment, then Glen turned the chair slowly toward her.

He may not have expected her, but he was quick with an angry greeting. "Come back to get another look at the crazy guy, did you?"

She set down the case, took the chair the orderly had placed near Glen, and lay her hand easily on his arm. Thin flesh corded under her touch.

"Why are you angry with me?"

He refused to look at her, glared instead at her long, narrow fingers, the unpolished, bluntly cut nails, then put his other hand over hers. The touch was wary and insecure, his words a challenge. "I didn't do the painting you wanted."

"It's okay. You'll do it next time."

"Will I?" Again, that defiance.

She tilted her head toward the hovering orderly. "What's his name?"

"Harry. He's your bodyguard."

"I thought he was yours."

"Mine? I don't…." He peered at her broad grin. His dimples winked on and off in an almost smile.

If that smile ever reached his eyes… but that was just another if to cloud her life. Probably his, too.

"Harry is going to take us somewhere we can work, aren't you Harry?" It amused her to catch the somber-faced man off guard. He fussed around with the magazines for a minute before starting toward them.

She laid her case in Glen's lap and signaled Harry to lead the way. "I'll push," she told them both.

"I can do it," Glen objected.

"Be a gentleman and carry my books." She laid them carefully in his lap, afraid she might break him, and maneuvered the chair out the double glass doors, following Harry onto the back lawn.

They moved beneath giant oaks along a curving blacktop path. It sloped gently. Halfway down the incline a sycamore had dropped huge, curly leaves that crunched underfoot. The air smelled bright and clean, with only a smidgeon of the town's industriousness. At the bottom, they came upon a small creek that murmured over its rocky bed. The largest of several oaks clung to the edge of the opposite bank, its mammoth roots jutting out above the water. The tree must have stood as a sentinel when the Union soldiers marched through over a century earlier. Warm sunlight filtered between half-naked branches to form patches of yellow across an old wooden bench that faced the stream.

Harry sat on the far end, leaving the other end free for her. Glen handed her the heavy case, his strength surprising her. She set it down. No one said anything, and the moment hung there, untouchable and precious. A small gray squirrel darted down the tree across the way. Holding its tiny feet as if praying, the animal stared at them with bright eyes. The silky tail twitched, once, twice, again.

With an unnatural ease she laid her hand on Glen's arm, and together they watched the squirrel until it leaped high into the trees and raced away, scolding.

In the deepening silence, she became conscious of the warmth of his skin under her palm, the slight movement of muscles and tendons as he reached and took a strand of her hair between thumb and fingers. He held it a moment, then caressed the curve of her cheek, cupping his palm over her ear. Without moving she turned her eyes toward him. Her breathing was shallow, her heartbeat thundering. She should be afraid.

But this man she scarcely knew looked at her with eyes full of wonderment, and she smiled.

"What's your name?" His tone sounded puzzled.

"Katherine." Her breath trembled.

His fingertips trailed across her cheek, like a butterfly tasting honey. He didn't speak or alter his expression. A ripple passed through her, and she closed her eyes for a moment of sheer and unexpected pleasure. He took his hand away, suspending it in front of her breasts. She glanced at Harry, who nodded his head and continued to watch as if they were specimens in a lab.

Lower lip caught in her teeth, she waited for Glen to move or say something. He reached toward the top button of her blouse. A muscle across her back twitched, yet she remained immobile. When his cool fingers contacted her warm skin, he licked his lips, and she did the same.

"May I call you Katie?" he whispered.

Her breath drifted out when he took his hand away, and for a brief moment, she wanted him to touch her, slide his hand under the fabric, and hold her aching breast in his palm.

Katie? Katie darlin'.

Only Stan called her Katie.

"Yes, call me Katie." Maybe that would chase away the ghosts or, at the very least, soften the loneliness.

His eyes were moist and bright and aimed at her, and she wanted to shout at him not to look at her that way. She couldn't help him, not with the dark foreboding questions he never asked but questions always present.

With a businesslike gesture, she picked up the case and snapped it open, took out pads, pencils, short fat pieces of grainy charcoal, and a large red eraser.

"Time we got busy."

He accepted the proffered materials and opened the tablet to a glaring white page. They sketched in silence, the scratch of the charcoal across the paper loud above the faraway traffic sounds. She made long heavy strokes over the page, capturing the magnificence of the great trees and the soft contour of the ground beneath. When she finally looked up to see what he was doing, he sat staring at her. Without a word, he handed her his sheet of thick paper. He had done a full-page study of her face. Fine hair blew gently around high cheekbones, one strand across the small nose. He had captured her round chin and long neck. The lips were soft but unsmiling, and she glanced from under half-closed lids, as if expecting something wonderful to happen at any moment.

He had made her beautiful, and she couldn't believe he saw her like that. There were no crow's feet, no smudges beneath the eyes, no puffiness at their corners. She might have been twenty instead of forty.

She took the drawing. "Really very good." That was inane, but it seemed to satisfy him.

After she shared her sketch with him, he began another of his own. She watched the horror grow on the paper, his face drawn tight while he struggled to capture what was before him. All he found were the tormented memories pouring from the charcoal like oozing sores. Tortured and deformed faces grew from within the shadows of skeletal trees. His breath caught in his thin chest like growing sobs. The air around her shoulders turned frigid, the branches of the trees danced in a macabre ballet. She snatched the charcoal from him, slipped the paper from his fingers, and ripped it in half.

He sat there a moment staring at his empty hands, then gazed through her and asked, "Are you going to leave now?"

"No. No, it's okay. But I'm cold, let's go inside."

He nodded and the expression on his face, even his restless body lan-

guage, told her he thought she was lying to him. He must think the minute they reached the safety of the hospital, she would abandon him. Her
heart jerked in her chest. Just as he had been abandoned over there so
long ago, if what Spencer said was true. So she didn't rise, but remained
sitting there to reassure him everything was fine. Desperately he blurted
an explanation she found quite unnerving.

"I can't get them out of my mind, you know. They all just keep dying
on me. I couldn't hear their screams over the noise of the chopper, but I
can hear them now. Doesn't make sense, I know."

She hugged herself and shivered.

"Cages don't always have bars, do they, Katie?" He reached out and
touched her. She flinched.

Where had all this come from? His compulsive need to speak of the
horrors? The deep insight he had into his own hopelessness? As quickly
as the mood had come upon him, it was gone. He smiled at her. Not a
good smile, not at all. It gave her the chills.

"I was going to paint you a chocolate ice cream cone until I decided
you weren't coming back. That's why I didn't do the painting. Is it okay?"

The agility of his mind-jumps evaded her, and it took a moment for
her to remember she'd asked him to paint something cool and soothing. His asking if it was okay placed them in a peculiar relationship of
student and teacher. Or did it go deeper than that? Was he asking his
captor to give him permission to do something? She had to turn away so
he couldn't see the tears in her eyes.

"It's okay," she finally managed in a hoarse voice.

"All the other guys wanted steak and French fries, things like that,
but I craved chocolate ice cream. All I wanted."

All the other guys? For God's sake, how many were there left over
there to rot? She glanced up, saw he was waiting for her to say some-

thing. "What do you want now?" She hoped for a simple wish she could somehow magically grant.

"Chocolate ice cream." Mischief lit his eyes. A brief promise that perhaps he would recover after all.

She gathered their things and stuffed them into the worn, paint-smeared case, set it once more in his lap, and took him back, Henry trailing along behind like a patient dog.

They were inside before Glen spoke again. "Do you have to go now?"

With no place to go, she could not lie to make her escape, so she didn't. "No, I don't have to leave yet."

A smile almost reached his eyes, and she marveled at the joy it gave her.

"Talk to me, then. Tell me things."

Harry left them in a secluded corner of the sunroom and went back to reading his magazine, as if he'd never been interrupted. She sat on the low couch, and Glen rolled the chair as close to her as he could, touching her knees with his. Unabashed, he reached for her hands, held them while she talked, clasping them together over his knees.

He needed to eat more, his bones lay just beneath the flesh.

"There are movies we can watch at home on our television sets. And we sent the first Space Shuttle up in 1981." His eyes widened, but he said nothing. "Elvis died in 1977."

"Hound Dog," he murmured, then stopped her, fingers squeezing her hands. "I want to know about you."

"Like what?" This was not supposed to get personal, but it was rapidly doing so, and she was frightened in a way she hadn't expected.

"Family, friends, what you do."

"No one, nothing. I don't do anything."

He fingered her gold wedding band, rubbing at it so it turned round and round on her finger.

"He's dead," she whispered. Stan left me. Stan's gone.

But she'd never said aloud simply he's dead. Perhaps because the words were so final, so empty of future and hope and security. In the back of her mind, the thud of a door closing. She collapsed to her knees on the floor beside him. He held her head in his lap, patting her back clumsily and touching her hair while she cried, a final mourning of Stan's death.

"Mrs. Kelly," someone said.

She lifted her head. Harry stood over her with a strange expression on his face. Like he wanted to pull her away from his patient. His charge.

"They're serving supper. He has to go now. I'm real sorry."

Maybe he thought they were being intimate. Strange, foolish man.

The room was lit against a closing darkness. How long had she been here? She sniffed and wiped her nose with the back of her hand. When she stood, Glen held on to her hand with a firm grip. The weakness of the moment had overcome her stoic reserve, leaving her feeling damn stupid. She was ready to leave, but Glen wouldn't let go. Harry tried to get behind the chair, and Glen turned on him.

"Just a goddamned minute." Chords stood out on his neck, his face turned red. "We're not through yet."

"It's okay." She caught his attention and nodded, smiled. "I have to go. It's all right."

"Are you?"

"Of course. I shouldn't… I didn't intend to do that. I apologize."

"No. It's okay." His effort at controlling the outburst was amazing.

She wanted to take time to help him adjust to what had happened between them. Make him understand. But Harry insisted on inserting himself into the moment, his dark eyes impersonal and unreadable.

"I'm coming back here next Friday. I'd better get a painting, or you'll get an F. Got it?"

Glen snapped a mock salute and let her fingers slide from his other hand. "Yes, ma'am."

In the parking lot, she sucked in the frosty night air. She could still feel his touch, his hand on her back comforting her. This man who had nothing to live for, with eyes haunted by the horrors in his own personal valley of hell, had reached out and cared for her pain. An almost forgotten sense of clean pleasure flowed through her. She might not yet be free of her grief, but at least she was being offered a chance. But was it at Glen's expense? Would he now carry her sorrow as well as his own? Somehow she would have to fix this.

FOUR

THE FOLLOWING FRIDAY, Katherine nosed the van into the parking space at the hospital with renewed anticipation. She hadn't experienced the feeling in a while and had forgotten how it felt to look forward to something. What a meager something, too. A man who might or might not be sane and a doctor who was using her for his own purposes. Just how much did Spencer really know about treating this type of delayed stress syndrome? He admitted to being at a loss.

She'd read a lot in the past week in magazines and newspapers. The more prevalent PTSS became, the newer and fancier the names given the syndrome. Men, seemingly well adjusted, flashed back to vivid traumatic experiences in Vietnam. There were the extreme cases such as the veteran who sat down at the Vietnam Memorial in Washington, D.C. and blew his brains out. Reading about it was certainly upsetting, but coming face to face with someone like Glen triggered a more emotional reaction.

Inside, she asked Dee Dee, the gum-popping, smiling receptionist to put a package in the freezer in the nurses' lounge until she finished with

Spencer. The young girl took the brown paper sack. "Gee, Mrs. Kelly, you look kinda different today. What'd you do to yourself?"

Katherine patted her hair. "Like it?"

"Yeah, pulled up like that shows off your face, makes you look younger. This is cold. What's in it?"

"Chocolate ice cream." She headed for Spencer's office.

After rapping, she entered to find him standing at the window, his shoulders hunched. He was wearing a tan sweater with his cocoa slacks. Without turning, he greeted her bluntly.

He must be pissed at her for breaking down in front of Glen. "Before you jump all over me, I want to tell you I'm sorry about what happened last week. I shouldn't have done that, am not sure why I did. I realize it might have upset Glen, and it won't happen again."

"You're babbling, and it's...." He broke off in midsentence when he turned around and caught sight of her. "What in the hell have you done to yourself?"

"Well, you said I should stop wearing jeans. So I thought I'd start by doing something with my ratty hair and putting on some makeup. It isn't too much, is it?"

He laughed. "Now if we could get you out of those jeans and into something more... less... more feminine."

"You gonna try?"

"Young lady, are you flirting with me?"

"It had occurred to me."

The gangly, reticent man surprised her by blushing furiously and searching for something to occupy himself. It turned out to be the papers on his desk.

"I... is Glen okay?

"Sit down, Katherine."

"Well, is he?" What if her actions had caused him to relapse?

"Relax. He's better than okay. He's acting like a young stud courting his first love."

"But, I didn't do anything that way, I don't think. Maybe I should lie on the couch, let you do that job on me you've been hinting at. I swear, Spencer, I didn't lead him on. I wouldn't."

"Just what happened last week I don't know about?"

"Nothing happens that you don't know about. Your spy has filled you in, I'm sure."

"Spy?"

"For a psychiatrist you're a lousy liar. Who me? Not me. Innocence doesn't become you, Doctor."

"Okay. But Harry's on the outside looking in. You were in there with him, obviously further in than I figured on for your first try."

"So you admit you used me."

"You let me."

"And so you're satisfied with the outcome?"

"Well, just look at you."

"I didn't mean me, silly. I meant with Glen."

"Ah, yes the young man who suddenly thinks he's in love. Smitten. And who could blame him?"

"Spencer, I'm a good ten years older than him. I don't want him to fall in love with me. It will hurt him when he realizes I can't… *we* can't…."

He tilted his head and gave her that mind reading look of his. "Can't what? Enjoy each other's company? Have a healthy sexual relationship? What exactly can't you do?"

"But he's so very damaged."

"The damaged heal or at least learn to live with who they are. We're doing everything we can to see he has a normal life, Katherine."

"What are you? A pimp? Is that why you asked me to do this?"

"Lord, no. Of course not. I'm just saying it's not such a bad thing for either of you. Let whatever happens happen and don't be so frightened to embrace life. There's good and bad, sunshine and storms in every life. Nothing is perfect. And when you can make someone like Glen happy for even one day, well then you've brought about a small miracle. Wouldn't hurt you to be happy either. Go in there and do what you're here for."

"Is he really doing that much better?"

"I wouldn't advise you to cry in his lap every time you come here, but it did give him something to think about other than himself. And the fact he did just that is a very good sign."

"What a relief. Did you see the portrait he did of me?"

"No."

"It's in my case, but I ran off last week and left it here. Figured Harry'd have it and show it to you."

"Glen has it. Assured me he would hold it for your return today. But he didn't show me any portrait."

"Under all that anger and hate, he was very kind to me. Will that rage ever leave?"

"We can only hope so. He was sacrificed and should have died. There were a lot like him, some are still over there."

"So I hear. What do you think of that?"

"Can't save the world, and we can't fight whatever forces refuse to acknowledge their existence. Political expediency wins. It always does."

"And is that sacrifice worth it? To them? To this country?"

"Who knows? The world doesn't work the way it used to. Threats are too final. You can't call a bluffer's hand when he can destroy the world if you're wrong."

"Or even if you're right, and he doesn't like it," she snapped back.

Again, he watched her without replying.

"Do we just forget the others, then? Will they survive, and do we not care?"

"Most of them are dead by now."

"But not all."

"I don't believe so, but… look, let's help the ones we can, okay? What will you two be up to today?"

"I brought him a quart of chocolate ice cream. After he eats that and I look at the painting he's supposed to be working on, we'll see. I'm still feeling him out, trying to find what pleases him."

Spencer's eyebrows wrinkled, and she hurried to explain. "He told me that's what he craved in prison, so I thought…." She broke off and gazed at his surprised expression. "What?"

"He talked to you about the prison? Christ, you got more out of him than I have in a year. Then, of course, I don't have as pretty gams as you."

"Gams? You've been watching too many old movies on TV. Try reading a book, an up-to-date one. You'll find we women prefer you admire something besides our physical attributes that stimulate your male sexual perversions."

"Oh, good Lord. Will you get out of here so I can see someone who needs me?" He waved her away with a grin. His mood had improved as well, and that pleased her.

FIVE

SHE HAD JUST stepped out of the nurses' lounge carrying the carton of ice cream when Glen came wheeling down the hall and nearly knocked her down.

"Come on, Katie. Come on." He cut a donut on the slick tile.

She ran to keep up with him down the hallway toward the sunroom. He reached the easel and rested one arm on its wide lip to wait in mock impatience. In place of the blue and white striped pajamas she'd seen him in earlier, he was dressed in a red plaid shirt and a pair of jeans. They were too big on him. There was a dab of white paint on one shirt cuff and a smear across the worn denim on one knee.

He grabbed her hand. "Shut your eyes. Tight, now." He led her blind around the easel and placed her just so. "Okay, open up."

On the small canvas a lake reflected a colorful sunrise. No sign of gray dripping trees or blood or silent, screaming faces. Never mind that it was stiffly done with little perspective. Clearly it was a major victory for him.

"It's wonderful. Great composition. I'm very proud of you."

He looked up at her with so much lost hope awash in his expression that she leaned down on impulse and kissed him on the cheek, whispered in his ear, "It's lovely."

She was temporarily embarrassed, and he backed away a bit and turned shy as if he were at a loss for words, too.

He recovered first. "You look very beautiful today."

"Thank you. I brought you something." She held out the sack.

After a brief hesitation, he took the gift and removed the small round carton of chocolate ice cream. His eyes widened, and he said nothing.

"Come on, let's eat it. I brought spoons."

In the corner of the room, seeking privacy, she fed him his first bite and he retaliated by doing the same for her. They ate the entire carton, laughing and sometimes missing each other's mouths. In another corner, Harry looked on and chuckled with amusement.

"Maybe Harry wants some."

"No deal. He can get his own. Can't you, Harry?" Glen called.

Harry smiled and lifted an arm.

She wiped at a dribble of chocolate on Glen's chin and offered it to him on the end of her finger. "Here, lick."

His lips encircled her finger, his tongue caressed her flesh, and she trembled. He watched her closely and sucked the ice cream off, then took her hand in his and held it close to his mouth. "Katie... Thank you so much."

The cold lump the ice cream had left in her stomach melted from the heat swelling through her. He was so ravaged and so needful of her caring. She feared the nearly forgotten rhythmic clutching deep down inside. She hoped it only meant she'd been too long without sex. No woman in her right mind would allow herself to fall in love with a man in Glen's predicament. Especially not a woman of her age not yet recovered from losing the love of her life. Didn't we only have one chance at that? If so, it left her feeling as if her life was over. How could one live without love?

Why would anyone want to?

Glen's hand completely enclosed hers, and his smile went all the way to his eyes, dimples winking, the irises flashing gold and umber.

"We'd better get to your lesson." She softened the words so as not to add to his burden. He pointed out places in his painting that didn't satisfy him, and they went to work.

"When you come from the indistinct muted colors of the background, do it gently, not intensely and all at once. So that way when you get to the foreground, the quality of detail you want will mean something, will stand out and give the flat canvas depth.

"You're a talented artist. I could tell that from the portrait you drew last week. All you need to learn is creating a vanishing point with color." She went on to illustrate and he watched intently, leaning so close his breath feathered across her cheek.

Time fell away into a settling, easy comfort. The whisper of his hair touching her face, the fragrance of his soap-clean skin drew her out of her lonely world. So immersed and so close together were they that she jumped when he spoke in his ragged voice.

"Did you ever fly?" He pursed his mouth and continued to blend in reflections on the calm lake.

"Yes. Stan and I… he went to a lot of conventions, meetings, things like that, and I always went with him."

"Like it?"

"Oh, yes. The first time, well, I guess I'll never forget it. A night flight from Dallas. The moon was full, big drops of water danced across the wing, touched by light, and they were rolling, clinging to the shiny metal to keep from falling. The black sky was at the same time so bright I couldn't even see the stars. It was like hanging...." She searched for the proper words, then went on, "... suspended alone with your soul in a place where there's no time, no disappointments. I've never had anything affect me quite like that, but then I was so happy."

He held the brush still and waited for her to go on.

"I don't suppose a helicopter is the same."

"Why aren't you happy now?"

She embraced the tone, welcomed it, then shrugged, and picked up a paint-smeared cloth. "Because I can't... I don't see a future alone."

He painted in silence for a while, finally whispered in a voice that barely covered the scratch of stiff bristles over canvas. "The first time they put me in a chopper, I was this stupid, gung-ho kid. I'd flown since I was sixteen and thought I knew it all. After OTC we went to aviator training." His glance darted across the room, as if searching for something dark, foreboding, then came back to her. "I was a good pilot. Damn good. You bring her down right on top of the trees, their limbs whip beneath like an angry ocean, and you follow the curve of the land like you touch a beautiful woman. Close and easy, leaving only a ripple behind."

The vivid description swept her along. She could almost see the trees swaying beneath her as she soared in imaginary flight, wondered oh so briefly how long it had been since he'd touched a woman, let that thought fly away.

"Just like a giant hummingbird." He daubed with the tip of the brush to fashion growth on the bank of the lake. "Darting in and out, up and down, testing, barely testing." His tone changed and lost its dreamy quality. "There, how's that?"

The question startled her out of the visions of his reveries. "Okay, now you're ready for some highlights. Finish that foreground."

"Hell, I thought that's what I just did."

She laughed at his utter chagrin and he joined her. "Oh, no. You're not through there yet."

She handed him a knife, showed him how to ice on brilliant touches like frosting a cake.

"Why aren't you happy?" he insisted.

This time he would settle for nothing less than an honest answer. It was funny how she'd evaded the truth herself, but yet couldn't do the same with him.

"Today I feel happy. But when I think of my life, where it's going… or not going, well." She shrugged and plunged on in a low voice. "Stan's things are still in the closets, his bureau drawers look as if he'll be home this evening. I can't seem to get past his death, like there's nothing there for me. I don't want anyone around me. Some of my students literally forced me back into teaching, or I'd be sitting in my house waiting for something—God knows what—to happen. Some days I wake up all enthused, thinking, today I'll get on with it, but my convictions last about as long as a June frost."

"Wishy-washy." He spoke lightly as if afraid of offending her.

It made her laugh, and she was grateful to him. "I suppose you're right. I wish I could want something so badly I'd do almost anything to get it. It just isn't happening."

His lack of response made her stab a glance at him. How foolish she was to voice such shallow desires to a man whose life consisted of a daily struggle just to survive the threat of the monsters dwelling in his soul. It made her ashamed, and she attempted to cover the feeling with a bantering question.

"Now that you've had your chocolate ice cream, what do you want?"

"Nothing. I learned not to want anything."

The retort was much too serious. She tried to tease him away from his pensiveness. "That surely can't be true."

"How in the hell would you know?" The curt demand startled her.

She stepped behind him to get out of range of the fire flashing from his eyes. Placing her hands on either side of his neck, she massaged at the tenseness with her thumbs. He leaned into her touch, emitted a small sigh.

After a while, "Katie?"

"Hmmm?"

"I'm sorry. Thanks for the ice cream."

"Nothing to be sorry for, and you're quite welcome." She continued to stroke his shoulders, feeling the bones beneath his gossamer skin. When the next question came, she was relieved to be standing behind him.

"Did the good doctor tell you why I don't walk?"

Her fingers halted, dug in. *Don't*, not can't.

"Because I don't want to," he snapped, as if expecting her to challenge him so they could have an argument about it.

She said nothing, took her hands away, but couldn't think of what else to do.

"Don't you want to know why I don't want to?"

Of course she didn't, but she had no control over what he might tell her, over horrible things she didn't want to hear.

He whirled the chair, banged into her with it. She didn't blink or move away. She felt herself a lump of malleable clay. This man could mold her in any direction, and she wouldn't object, nor cry out if it hurt. But when she saw the expression of infinite sadness cross his features, she forgot her own feelings and knelt down to him. She could never see what he had seen, feel what he had felt, but she so ached to stop his suffering she forgot everything Spencer had told her. She held him, let him hold her, made soothing, cooing sounds while her warm tears wet his neck and shoulder. Their anguish bound them together so neither moved or spoke.

A firm hand on her arm, a strict commanding tone. "Mrs. Kelly." It was Harry, but she didn't turn or take her attention from Glen. She shook her head savagely and clung tighter. The movement loosened the pins holding her hair and they fell to the floor, forming a jigsaw. Harry's hand grew tighter, more insistent.

"Go away," she said between sobs.

Glen strengthened his hold, clutching at her while Harry tried to pry them apart.

"That's enough, Harry." The voice, that of Doctor Spencer, came as if from far away. "Glen," he ordered.

He took a deep breath and loosened his grip. Then he said in a wild, uncontrolled way, "Hell, just when we were getting to the good part," and released her.

Climbing awkwardly to her feet, she took several steps backward and wiped angrily at her wet cheeks.

"If you wish to continue with this, Glen, you'll stop that."

"Continue with what? Look at her, Doc. Scared to death of the loony." He turned off the intense, mocking glare he'd aimed at Katherine. "Get her out of here."

His rage grew until it filled the room with a violent pandemonium. He assaulted the easel, grabbed the wet painting and slammed it across the room, then gave the table a vicious shove and spilled its contents over the floor. Oil oozed toward a tube of cadmium, while turpentine puddled from a broken jar to fill the room with its bright citrus aroma.

"I'll kill the bitch," he screamed.

Katherine, who had started toward him, turned and fled.

SIX

PURSUED BY THE image of Glen's raging tantrum, Katherine wanted nothing more than to enfold herself once again into her former chrysalis. The urge lasted until she reached Spencer's office. There she stopped, leaned her forehead against the letters spelling out his name and pounded at the wood until both fists began to throb in protest. Then the doctor was behind her, comforting her, guiding her inside and to the couch, where she curled up in a protective ball.

"Come out of the womb, and join the real world," he said.

"Stop that, you sanctimonious bastard. Just because you like being surrounded by futility doesn't mean I get my kicks that way."

"How do you get them, then?"

"I guess I don't."

"Oh, well, then. Maybe you'd better crawl back in that safe, dark place where no one can hurt you ever again."

"But I don't want to. I want to go back in there and help him, and I can't."

"And that's why you're so angry with me?"

"Yes, dammit. If it weren't for you, I wouldn't even be here."

"Ah, and of course Glen wouldn't be in there going through hell alone, either. If it weren't for you knowing about it."

She glared at him, refused to answer, and sat up. Lying there under his scrutiny put her at a disadvantage she wasn't willing to settle for.

"Let's see just how strong you are. How about it?" He studied her for a long while before she replied.

"He doesn't want me to come back. You heard what he said."

"I heard what he said. But you're wrong. He wants you back. Right now that's what he wants more than anything else in his cell of horrors."

"Then why did he say that? Do that?"

"Because, if you return after seeing him at his worst, then he can be sure of you. Right now, he's sitting in there wondering what you'll do next. He's thinking you hate him and it's all over. But, maybe, just maybe you'll come back. Maybe you don't hate him at all."

"And what does he do the next time, throw me across the room?"

"Extremely unlikely."

"Well, that's reassuring."

"So what are you going to do? It's up to you. Do you give up or come back for more? Simple decision."

"You're so damn smart."

"He's gotten more out of this than you can possibly know. He's beginning to believe there's something he can do, someone he can relate to. He's relating to you more than he has anyone else. Don't let him down now."

"Don't you lay that on me. I can't be responsible for that." She stared at him through a haze of tears. What, indeed, was she responsible for? Her own decisions, her own life, her own guilt? "I think I hate you," she whispered.

"That's okay." He smiled. "It's perfectly acceptable to hate me. It's called transference and I'll take the heat for that invisible boogey man in your closet." He moved toward her, reached down, and clasped her hand. "Go home now. Let me know what you decide."

If he was right, Glen was sitting in that empty room, wondering what she would do and if he'd see her again. Manipulating her? Testing her? Did it matter? There was no way she intended to carry that image home with her.

"I forgot my case again. I'd like to get it myself, tell Glen I'll be back. That is, with your approval."

At his smile, she snapped, "If you have to be right all the time, you could have the decency not to be so damn smug about it."

He laughed aloud and, as she left the room, cheered her on with an, "Atta girl."

An elderly man in whites with a mop and large bucket scrubbed slowly at the floor of the sunroom. The easel had been returned to its place, paints and supplies all neatly lined up on the table. Her battered case waited beneath it. There was no sign of the painting. Out of reach of the long bars of late afternoon sunbeams, Glen sat in the wheelchair on the opposite side of the room. His elbows propped on the arms, he stared at the floor. His features appeared half-formed and devoid of expression, as if he were a robot waiting for the final touches that would humanize him.

She walked carefully across the damp floor, skirting the old man, who didn't look at her. Neither did Glen, and she touched him before he acknowledged her presence. Then it was only with a tipping of his head and several jagged breaths.

"You scared me half to death," she said.

"Are you mad?"

Like a child, afraid Mommy doesn't love him anymore because he's been bad.

"Yes, I suppose I am, but not at you. What happened wasn't your fault, but it wasn't mine, either. So let's just leave it there."

"Why'd you come back? Aren't you afraid of me?"

That was a hell of a good question and one she couldn't answer. When she thought about it in the peace and quiet of her own home, she was afraid of Glen and what he might do, but here with him, the possibility he'd do her harm seemed remote. Yet he'd called her a bitch.

"I'm not a bitch."

"Of course you're not."

"That's what you screamed at me."

"Oh, no. Not you. Ellie. That slut." He ground the words through clenched teeth.

"Who's Ellie?"

"If I could. If I could. I'd kill her. You don't know, you can't know the meaning of the word bitch unless you know Ellie."

His outburst wound down, and he went limp, arms lying in his lap, palms up and fingers forming loose claws. She had stepped back imperceptibly and wanted to say something to calm him, but he had shut her out and stared down at his hands, no longer aware of her.

After a moment, she fetched her case and walked away, footsteps echoing a lonely tapping rhythm against the slip, slap, slop of the old man's mop. Later, she'd find out who Ellie was and why Glen hated her so much. Right now all she wanted was to escape, go home, and crawl into a hot bath, then bed.

SEVEN

THE NEXT MORNING, before she could actually breathe on the mirror for proof she was alive, Katherine discovered there was no coffee or bread or milk in the house. Grumpily, she dressed and drove to the store. Cedarville lay in the vee of a small valley about two miles west of her home and across a busy highway that bypassed the town twenty years earlier. There wasn't much left of the place, but struggling residents kept it alive as a better choice than city living. There was a school, a post office, a small library only open twice a week, a tiny city hall, and a general store. A mini mart and the volunteer fire department sat out on the highway. Around and about were churches of just about every denomination except Catholic. In other words, it was a typical southern mountain village, overlooked by culture and progress, the residents not at all worried about what was missing. After all, thirty miles away was the university and all that went with it. Only a hair too close for comfort was the consensus of opinion.

The town boasted a well-informed gossip network. She thought about that on the short drive. How much of the Tanner family's business was common knowledge? She parked and climbed rock steps to the elevated sidewalk fronting the few businesses that made up Cedarville. A bell jangled when she opened the massive glass and wood door of the general store.

Three men stood in the shadows at the back of the high-ceilinged room, all carrying on a lazy conversation with Sam Jenson, the third-generation owner. They each greeted her politely, tipping well-soiled hats and murmuring, "Mornin' Miz Kelly." All except for Sam, the owner, whose shiny bald head tipped slightly in her direction while he used her first name. They were country gentlemen, and she was a widow. Southerners had invented the salutation *Ms.* long before the rest of the world even considered the possibility it existed. They just spelled it differently. Whether it carried the same connotation was definitely questionable.

"Been up to?" Sam produced her usual hunk of bacon and started cutting. She couldn't resist buying it whenever she came into town.

"Visiting at Veteran's hospital. Do you remember Glen Tanner?"

He tore a section of paper off the roll and slapped the bacon on the scale. "Well, now, let's see."

A bearded man in the corner spoke up. "Weren't that Tanner feller, no that was Tomlinson."

"How old of a feller is he?" Sam asked. "My daddy had a friend name of Tanner."

"No. Glen was in Vietnam. He and his sister have a farm around here somewhere. I'm not sure exactly where."

"Oh, yup," the older of the three men spat square, straight, dead on in a three pound coffee can sitting on the floor. "The feller went over there and come back short of a full load? Used to call it shell shock. He the one?"

Before she could answer, the subject was launched full-blown, and she wasn't sure she wanted to stay to listen. But Sam took his time with wrapping the bacon, and though she strolled around getting her supplies and piling them on the counter, she couldn't help but hear.

"They all come back doped up. You know that's where most of these hippies come from that drifted in here back in the early seventies, doped out of their skulls."

"Tanner? Wasn't he the one middle of the night he's screaming and yelling and breaking out windows and his sister called the deputies? It was told had he a gun he'd a killed that old gal and maybe a deputy or two."

Sam wormed his way back into the conversation. "He was a nice boy. I know the one now. Always was a good kid. Folks was killed, and that old maid sister of his raised him. They live about five miles out Number Ten. They kept that farm with a little help from some shirttail relations. That's what happens when they get in the army and lay around with whores and smoke dope. Come back thinking the world owes them a living."

He shoved the wrapped meat across the counter, caught the expression on her face, and said, "Sorry, ma'am. This feller, he may not be that way at all. He kin of yours?"

Cheeks flaming, she paid for the purchases, jerked up her sack, and escaped. At the van she tossed the groceries onto the front seat and climbed in. "Bastards," she muttered and backed out with a screech of tires.

"But you started it, old girl, and you got what you went for." Bad habit, talking to herself. Needed to get a cat.

She drove too fast up the twisting lane to the house, tires spitting small rocks that hit the undercarriage of the car with sharp thunks. A rambling split level ranch sat halfway up the south side of the slope. Huge windows along the southern side reflected the sunlight, and framed the southern ridge of mountains and the valley and creek below. She jumped from the van and slammed the door with a great deal of vehemence. And why was she once again so angry? Since that damned Spencer had called and asked her to take Glen on as an art student, she'd spent a lot of time angry.

She went up onto the front deck and in the door to the country-sized kitchen. Coffee came first, then she slapped bread in the toaster and a few slices of bacon in the toaster oven. The home she and Stan built together had never seemed so empty. They'd lived here twenty years, long enough the cedar beams across the open ceiling and the knotty pine above had turned a dusky gold from age.

The toaster popped, snapping her back to the present. She buttered the bread, layered bacon on each slice, poured herself a cup of coffee, and went out to sit on the deck. Birds soared over the valley below, their shadows darting across the pasture. The air was crisp, and she breathed deeply, cleansing away remnants of her morning encounter. If that was the real world, she had no more place there than Glen. And Spencer's opinion wasn't infallible by a long shot. But what was she to do? Continue to do nothing that mattered, leave no footprints. Stay hidden away here in her hillside home with Stan's things surrounding her, reminding her of her loss?

Now that he'd pried her out of here, Spencer thought her in need of psychoanalyzing and had set about getting inside her head. Trouble was, he could be right. She'd met him years ago at a University event, and sometimes thought he was a little bit in love with her, though he'd never said so. But she was ready to accept that Stan was no longer a part of her life. As to whether that first step would make her strong enough to take the next one, only time would tell.

Armed with a second cup of coffee, several large plastic bags, and cleaning supplies, she climbed from the main floor to one of the two bedrooms. The one she and Stan had slept in, the one she hadn't been in except to remove all her things the afternoon after his funeral. Eight months of neglect had left corners cobwebbed. Bunnies dusted beneath the bed. But it still smelled of him, of his aftershave, the powder he used in his work boots, even a faint scent of the Lava soap for scrubbing grease off his hands after working on the tractor. The tractor that had killed him.

The mirror threw back a reflection of scowling intensity, but she ignored it and went to work clearing the dresser top. She kept his harmonica and the cat's eye cuff links she'd given him for Christmas one year when French cuffs were in style and he'd owned one white shirt that sported them. With her left hand, she reached to close the jewelry case. Light glimmered on the gold band she still wore on her third finger.

She turned it round and round, then slipped it off, placed it in the case, and stuffed that in the back corner of a bottom drawer. Its removal left a band on her skin that would not vanish. Tears filled her eyes, and she cried, soft at first, then, throwing herself onto the bare mattress, great sobs sent pain racking through her chest until there was nothing left but dry heaves. Each breath dragged in the musty smell of the long-unused mattress. Time to air it out and move back into this room. Make it her own.

At last sober, she went in the bathroom and washed her face, then back to the bedroom to drag curtains off the windows and clean the room. Stan's clothing went into bags for the church rummage sale.

It wasn't as if she didn't love him anymore or wanted to forget him. He would always be with her like that mark on her third finger, left hand. She picked up his picture.

"All the time I thought I couldn't live without you, but it's really that I can't live with your ghost. It's killing me." She put the photo with the small collection of his things. Memories of a lifetime stored away in one drawer, but etched in her mind forever.

After hours of purging herself, she showered and plopped down in front of the fireplace. Thoughts of Glen tumbled into the blank spaces and she couldn't let them go. Who was Ellie? And why did he hate her so? A girlfriend or wife, maybe. Perhaps she sent him a Dear John letter. That would be enough in his situation, locked up with no longer a tie to someone he loved. Would he ever leave that place and return home to live some kind of normal life?

How in God's name could she continue to see him weekly and not fall prey to her feelings of compassion that could well lead to a big mistake? For a long while, she watched the fire.

There was nothing else she could do, for if she deserted Glen now, she wouldn't be able to live with the guilt. Compassion means doing something about it. Spencer's words, but some she had taken seriously at the time. Still did.

EIGHT

THE NEXT DAY—her first as a single, self-reliant woman—a letter arrived to challenge those untried strengths.

The single page missive was from the Valley View public art gallery. The board included Professor Endlebeck, one of her former instructors at the university, the man responsible for recommending her to help Glen. Now he and the directors hoped she would submit a few paintings to be juried for a display of local authors' work.

Every morning for the remainder of the week, she drank her three cups of wake-up coffee and glowered at the letter lying open on the table. Showing her own work was something she had always resisted as she considered teaching more her forte. If all it took was guts, she'd give it a whirl, but placing her work at the mercy of judges invited failure and rejection.

And she wasn't sure she was willing to risk that.

Friday morning dawned rainy. She hated to drive in the rain, a damned good excuse for staying home, and by this time she was looking for a way to avoid facing Glen. But guilt over that wasn't something she wanted to feel, either. Too many negatives rolled about in her head, and depression set in. She dressed and climbed in the van. Maybe it wouldn't start. She turned the key. It came to life with a purr.

Fog hid the mountains, skirted the highway, and floated over the car, leaving her lost and alone, driving to town. The steady drone of the wipers relegated her confused thoughts into a band that marched around in her head, cymbals clashing, drums beating. The situation at the hospital, her unexplored feelings for Glen, what he would do when he left the hospital, that damned letter folded in her purse. All crowded around begging for attention. And the largest one loomed like a dark cloud. Could she allow him to come to the studio where they'd be alone? Or was she too frightened of him and herself to try that?

She entered Spencer's office, fingering raindrops from her hair and peeling off her soaked windbreaker.

"Raining?" he asked.

In no mood for banter, she put a quick end to it. "Cut the crap. Who's Ellie? And what did she do to Glen?"

"You know, when you come in here, I feel as if I should be holding a lance and wearing a suit of armor. Is that what is known as coming straight to the point?"

"Ellie."

"Was his wife."

"Dammit, Spencer."

"She has nothing to do with this."

"The hell she doesn't. He wants to kill her. You practically gave me your blessing to make out with him, if that was what it took. And all the time he's married. I may be old fashioned, but that stinks. Where is she, anyway?"

He leaned backward in his chair. The ratty corduroy jacket gaped open, a button missing from his shirt. She'd never known if he was married, but from the shape of his clothing he obviously was not. What kind of a wife would let her husband wear a shirt to work with a button missing? Odd to think of this in the middle of her irritation with him.

"Ellie lives in Joplin, I believe. And they are divorced."

"Are you sure he knows that? Married or not, how could she just not be here when he needs a connection so badly? How in God's name could she let him go through this alone?"

"He doesn't want her here. You heard him, he hates her to the point where he wants to kill her."

"Could he? *Would* he? Dear God, Spencer. This is the kind of thing I need to *know*. What else haven't you told me?"

He eyed her for several moments. "What you're really asking is could he kill just anyone. Perhaps you."

"The thought crossed my mind." She was so mad her teeth clenched over the words. "Why?"

"Why what?" he asked.

"Why does he want to kill her?"

"It's interesting you didn't ask me… ah, never mind."

"I hate that never mind business. Did you not finish because I'm too dense to understand, or I couldn't deal with it, or it just wasn't important?"

"Are you afraid of him, afraid he might try to hurt you, kill you?"

"I need all the facts. I didn't, probably still don't, have all of them." She stood and went to the window where she watched fat raindrops drizzle down the glass. Her breath steamed up the pane until she couldn't see the drenched grounds beyond. "I'm not sure. In the dark in my bed, I worry about it, but in there with him I don't. He could have killed his sister, though, couldn't he?"

"Where did you hear that?"

"Cedarville, at the general store."

"Gossip, that's all."

"Uh-huh. So, why does he hate his wife?"

"From what little I can gather, she sent him a Dear John letter. He got it just before he went out on that last mission. Said she didn't love him anymore and was divorcing him."

The information shifted Katherine's concentration of fury from Spencer to the unknown Ellie.

She imagined a young, eager Glen climbing into his helicopter, strapping in, and flying off, perhaps to die. Fear would have clogged his throat with his new and certain knowledge his wife no longer loved him or prayed for him or waited for his return.

Spencer continued speaking, and she dragged herself from the wartorn skies of her imagination back into the office. Fluorescents erased the shadows from the deepest corners, sent feelers out the windows into the dreary morning.

"… affected the way he dealt with his imprisonment. On the whole, men who had someone waiting for them fared much better than those who didn't. Glen knew he had no one depending on him, wanting him to live. He managed to survive, but it was to come back and get her. As they applied more and more torture, his hate mushroomed. Basic survival training taught him to transfer that hate from his persecutors onto someone or something else. After all, he could do nothing to stop what was happening to him, could no longer fight back.

"What's amazing is he lived at all. Man can adjust to any adversity, but he will do so only if it's just. Or, that is, if many are being subjected. If in his mind he is alone, or nearly so, and his punishment serves no purpose, he may… no, hell, he *will* break.

"We know it was the intensity of Glen's loathing, his need to retaliate against Ellie for her betrayal, that kept him alive."

Back to the window and the dreary day, Katherine asked, "What about his sister? She was waiting."

"Julia? Yes, he loves her, but that's different. She has always been his mother figure, being so much older and raising him. The death of their parents while Glen was so young is a classic basis for his type of breakdown. While his captors beat him senseless day after day, put him through God knows what emotionally, he punched away at invisible pillows, promised himself he'd survive to pay Ellie back. Now, he can't go through with it, can he? Not as long as he's in that chair."

She stared at him, amazed. "So he's trapped in the damned thing by his own twisted thoughts, even if he could walk again, he won't? Dear God, how tragic."

"Are you all right with this?" he asked.

To rid herself of the fury burning inside, she paced the floor to the desk, around the chair, back to the window, and keeping her back to him, finally answered. "Oh, sure. I'm used to talking about people getting tortured. Think nothing of it." Then she forced herself to look at him through a blur of tears.

He leaned back in his chair, fingers tented beneath his chin and unwavering dark eyes on her. If he waited for her to reveal her innermost thoughts to the psychoanalyst in him, he could forget it. She refused, instead gathered up her jacket and briefcase. She might have to bite her tongue, but she would not let this interfere with what she now considered her duty to Glen.

"I'll go see him now, if you don't mind."

"I don't think you should."

"Why? What's wrong, is he sick? What?"

"No. It has finally sunk in he's going home next week, and he isn't taking it so well."

"Then why did you let me come if you won't let me see him? And how in the hell can you consider letting him go home in the shape he's in?"

"I didn't say you can't see him. I want you to calm down a bit and get some more information before you go up to his room. And as for him going home, I have two choices, and this is the best of the two. It's go home or go down to Little Rock to a nursing home. We aren't equipped to keep him here, and I've pushed his stay past the limit."

"I don't want to hear any more about what they did to him. Why can't you try drugs? I've heard there are some successful uses of drug therapy with this type of syndrome."

"Tried them. He had a bad motor nerve reaction, not too uncommon, but with his other problems, it didn't seem the way to go. Reality therapy appears to be the best, though we still are flailing around in there."

"Is that where you get on with it, rather than discussing what's in the past?"

"Been doing some reading, I gather." A corner of his mouth turned up.

"Enough to learn it's all guesswork."

His grin became a laugh. "Too much reading is bad for you. Freud would turn over in his grave at some of the things we're discovering. And, of course, it is guesswork. We do what we can, and most of the time we succeed a little. We stumble a lot. We're dealing with something we don't fully understand. It's incomprehensible when the mind short-circuits. Usually we can figure out why, but we can't always fix it. Post-Traumatic Stress Syndrome is one thing and difficult enough to handle, but this... this is much more than that."

She gazed down at him, tried to probe beneath the professional mask, saw nothing but indomitable patience. "May I go to his room now?"

He nodded. Her hand touched the door handle. He called after her, "No pity now, be firm. He has to leave this place. Soon. And Katherine?"

She waited.

"You never did answer me. Are you afraid of him?"

"No, I'm not afraid of him."

"Perhaps," he concluded and rose, "he brings out the motherly instinct in you."

Damn him. He'd waited until she was off-guard and thought the interview was over before getting to the real heart of the matter. Truth was, she'd considered that possibility herself. To cradle a man against her breast, comfort him like a child, was as much to fill her own needs as his. Women nurture, men protect. Yet the awful truth was that nothing so simple could purge Glen of his demons.

"Bite your tongue. I know I'm older than he is, but have a heart."

They both laughed, and she welcomed the release of tension.

NINE

IN HIS RUMPLED whites, Harry waited outside Spencer's office and led her upstairs to Glen's room. The orderly wasted no time on conversation. Did he possess much of a vocabulary past the dozen or so words she had heard him speak?

Then he pushed open the door, and she forgot Harry. Glen lay in the bed with his back to her, the wheelchair nearby. The other bed was empty. There was a bar above Glen's head he could use to move himself around. She went to a straight-backed chair between him and the rain-washed window. His eyes were open, but he made no acknowledgement of her presence except a quick blink when she said his name.

It was so quiet in the room when she sat down beside him, she heard his shallow breathing, the beating of his heart. Surely, that had to be her own, thumping beneath the heavy sweater.

He spoke gruffly, startling her. "God, I hate the rain."

She rose and closed the drapes, leaving the room to the mercy of shadows and the yellow glow of his bed light.

When she turned, he tried to smile at her. "I'm glad you came."

The words broke through her reserve, washed away her doubts like a floodtide. The words trapped her and she sensed no escape. She moved to the edge of the bed, bent, and kissed the papery skin of his cheek. At her touch, he wept great racking sobs that tore from his throat. He didn't turn away, just clenched his fists on top of the striped spread and bawled. As she had done earlier in the week. And she gave him what she had so desperately wanted and received from him then.

She lowered herself to the bed and gathered him close, buried her face in the hollow of his neck. Rocking, murmuring soothing, unintelligible words, she held him. He wrapped both arms around her and held on much like he had that first day they'd met, hanging on to keep from drowning, or perhaps from flying off the edge into total darkness. His tears ran into her hair and across her face, branding her forever with his torment.

After a long while, he grew silent, and when his breathing settled, he spoke, each word touching her cheek.

"Sometimes it rained for months at a time, and we were always wet. We were out in the swamps, before they took us up north to Laos. They built these cages under water, so we could be locked there when we were being punished. Sometimes if they just took the notion. I can remember looking up through the cracks in the wooden docks and seeing their feet, the butts of their rifles. When my head would get to falling down in the water, I put my fingers through the cracks to hold myself up."

He dragged in a deep breath, and she kept her eyes closed. She didn't want to hear this, but he needed her to. To hell with Spencer's reality therapy. Compassion was not the same as pity. She would do what this man needed.

"They beat my hands with the rifle butts until they were bloody and I turned loose."

"Oh God." She sobbed and silently begged for him to be able to stop reliving it. She couldn't assimilate sitting here in the strange glow of man-made lights, warm and dry, while the rain slithered down the window panes, and he spoke of a time and place out of her comprehension.

"Katie, I'm sorry. Please, it's okay," he whispered, his breath hot against her skin.

"No, it's not okay. It never will be." She raised her head, smoothed a lock of damp hair from his forehead.

"It was a long time ago. I should have let it go by now."

"Oh, sure. Forget it and get on with your life. God, the arrogance of some people, especially doctors." The corners of his lips twitched into a half-grin, but she was off and running. "I'd like to see how they'd handle something like that, I sure as hell would. You've got more guts than all of them put together, those bastards who sit down and write out all their little remedies to cure mankind's ailments.

"Is this our art lesson for today?"

His question forced her to relinquish the remainder of her fury and they laughed together, not heartily, but a release nevertheless.

Finally, he said, "I'm sure glad you're on my side."

"You damn well better believe I am."

"And they can all go to hell. Right?"

"Straight to."

He gazed at her. "I think you mean that."

"Yes, I do." She willed him to believe her, tried to give him something strong and total to hold to. After all, she had experienced how wretched it was to have nothing or no one to hang on to. She could give him that, if nothing else. "Now, what's this I hear about your going home?"

"I'm not sure I'm ready. And I worry about my sister."

"Oh? What's the problem?"

He shrugged and shoved away from her, letting his arms drop to the mattress, his features closed down.

"Come on, don't do that. Remember, I'm on your side." She reached for his hand, but he jerked it away.

"What are you really doing here, anyway? You go home. Go home where it's safe. Here it's safe for me."

"Safe?"

They weren't different at all. Both wanted only to be free from failure. If he went home where there were no regimented controls, he might fail. "You can't stay here forever, can you?"

"I asked you what you're doing here."

"I'm not sure I know what you mean."

He enunciated slowly, as if speaking to an idiot. "I mean, you just keep coming back. Every week, coming back. Once you get me snared, then you'll leave. You can't possibly get anything out of this."

"That's where you're wrong."

"Then tell me why you come here."

"Because I'm selfish. I need to stop feeling sorry for myself. I need to know my existence is worth something to someone, to you, and finally myself. It's truly a selfish act. I'll admit that. It's more for me than for you. And besides," she finished in an effort to put a humorous note into the conversation, "you're one hell of a guy. Great personality, life of the party."

"Ah, Katie, I'm thirty-one years old and already used up. I've spent the last twelve years in a place you never knew existed. I'd rather you never knew any more than I've already told you. Don't waste your time or that great sense of loyalty on me. You'll only be disappointed."

She laid a palm on his cheek. "I don't think so."

He tucked his thumb under the tip of her chin. "Too bad I didn't meet you a long time ago. Then I could have fallen in love with you, Katherine Kelly."

Through a mist of tears, she studied him. Me, too, Tanner, me, too. Aloud, she joked, "You saw that in a movie."

"Nope. I made it up, I swear." He gazed into her eyes. "And I meant every word of it."

"I'm flattered, really I am. You wouldn't want to do that though. You'd only be disappointed. But I'm not going anywhere," she hastened to add, lest he think she meant he was right about her leaving him. "Now, tell me your plans for getting home. Need a ride?"

"I've got wheels."

"More than these, I hope." She gestured toward the wheelchair.

"Oh, yes. These go sixty miles an hour."

"Better watch that stuff. It's not legal now, you know. Then you'll be going home alone?"

He shot her a sharp look. "Why not?"

"Nothing. It just seems so anticlimactic, so ordinary for such an exciting thing."

He grabbed her hand, his grip popping the bones in her fingers. "I'm scared shitless, Katie. But I have to do this myself. Get in the car and drive down the highway, just like it was an ordinary day, and go to the farm and move back into my old room like nothing ever happened. I have to do it that way or not at all."

"Can you... I mean, don't you need some help?"

"I'll have some, but I don't need much. I can take care of myself. You don't think they just send us guys out into the cruel world without teaching us how to take care of ourselves, do you? Shame on you. Why, we're veterans. We fought for the freedom of this country."

The cynicism seeped through his obvious efforts to keep it light.

"No, no, don't do that, please." She pulled his hand to her lips, kissed it.

"Sorry. Didn't mean to upset you. You suppose I could stop by your studio and see you sometime?"

"I certainly hope so. We have to make arrangements for you to come once a week to paint."

"Sure. I meant, if it's okay, and you could give me directions, maybe the day I go home I could stop by for a minute. Look the place over. Say hi?"

He needed to be connected, to retain this tie they had formed, despite any of his earlier objections to her presence.

Misunderstanding her brief hesitation, he said, "Hey, it's okay. I understand. You're probably busy with classes and everything. I had no right to impose on you. You're not taking me to raise. I don't want you to think you are. Maybe we'll get together when you decide on a schedule for my class. That's to be one on one, right?" His voice rose in pitch.

"Glen, stop it." She touched his shoulder.

He batted his eyes several times, looked around as if confused as to where he was. "Stop what?"

"Don't play with me like that. You don't have to test me or doubt me. I do have classes, and though I'm sure the ladies would love a visit from you, it might be better for you if you came when no one else was there."

"Loonies do have a bad habit—"

"Dammit, don't do that." She trembled and clutched his arm.

"I'm sorry. Seems like I say that a lot, but I am."

"No apology necessary. Just calm down. You're getting upset over something you should be looking forward to. I'm going to leave you my phone number, here on the table." She scrabbled around in the drawer, found a pen and paper, and wrote as she continued to talk. "When they tell you what day, you call and we'll set it up. If you can get away early enough, we can have lunch together at the studio. Morning classes finish at eleven and I don't have any more until two in the afternoon. Now, my friend, is that satisfactory?"

"Just one more thing."

"What?"

"If you've got a hug left over, I sure could use one about now."

"It just so happens I need one myself." She settled into his outstretched arms, put hers around him.

So thin, so frail, this man who had once been a big, tough fighting man. Reduced now to insecurities, fears, doubts. It made her so angry she could scarcely contain her feelings. What would become of him? How could he possibly survive the memories she could not even guess at? There was no way in this world or the next she could do anything for him.

PART
TWO

...In dreams I see them rise,

ONE

WHEN GLEN CALLED a few days later, she promised him a sumptuous lunch if he cared to stop by the studio on his way home to the farm. He sounded high strung, what the kids called wired.

Shooing the last of her students out right on time, she sat before a painting and picked up a brush, stepping into the scene. She was still there, entranced by the laddering on a dew-sparkled spider web deep in the woods, when a car horn sounded.

Dropping the brush in the jar of cleaner, she grabbed up a paper towel on her way out the door and wiped at her smudged fingers.

A bright red Buick hardtop sat in the drive. An arm rested in the open window. The noonday sun flashed against the windshield, so she couldn't make out his face until she went to the car. He wore a matching red shirt and jeans that looked new and stiff and uncomfortable. Who had bought them for him? The wheelchair was folded behind the driver's seat.

"Wheels for my wheels," he said, as if he might have a frog in his throat.

"It's beautiful. You look good," What a foolish thing to say. He actually looked like he was scattered and needed gathered up, the rare beautiful smile not in evidence. "I made sandwiches, ham and cheese with lettuce and tomato. A jug of lemonade. Cookies, too, from my very own kitchen." She sounded as scattered as he looked.

"That's great for my first non-hospital meal. Everyone gone?" His grin was sheepish, forced, as if to say he knew his reluctance was dumb, but what the hell?

"All gone. We'll be alone. Come on, get out and come in. I…." She reached for the door handle.

"Go on in. I'll be right there." An order issued with military curtness.

She'd never seen him drag himself from one place to another. He probably felt awkward about it, perhaps even a bit defensive. Hands on her hips she put on a stern, reproachful look, but turned and went inside. Better to let him do it his way, not push and shove at him until the pressure matched everything else in his life. She shut the door, leaned her back against it, and waited.

What if he fell? What if he was lying out there too proud to call for help? No, give him time. A little more at any rate, then peek out and see.

A tap sounded on the door.

"Who is it?

"Katie, let me in."

"Katie? Don't know a Katie."

"Come on, I'm starved."

She opened the door, waited to see his expression before laughing. He grinned, still having trouble getting it all the way to his eyes.

"Won't you come in, sir?"

The chair bumped over the threshold, and he paused to look around. "Hey, this is nice."

"And messy." The long workroom was a massive clutter of paintings hung and stacked against the walls, many displaying various stages of talent and completion.

"All your students'?"

"Most of them. A few of my own successes and failures are here and there, too."

The waist-high table running the length of the twenty-foot room was cluttered with multi-sized canisters of brushes, piles of rags and turpentine in peanut butter jars. She had tacked the portrait he drew of her on the wall, and he contemplated it in thoughtful silence. He turned his attention to a painting of a dark-haired girl in a burgundy cowboy hat. Her hands, covered with matching gloves, rested beneath her chin. The face was unfinished, with just the suggestion of eyes and lips brushed in lightly.

"I'm impressed. This is marvelous," he said.

"She did that in one session. Turned a blank canvas into the beginnings of a perfect likeness. Here's the photograph she's using." She handed him a billfold-size, color picture. "The girl's a brilliant talent."

"Maybe she has a brilliant teacher."

She shrugged. "I don't know. Here." She picked up a childish attempt at a copy of a landscape, green leaves resembling bananas. "This one doesn't understand the simplest nuances of color and composition. What do you think about her teacher, if we're to judge that way?"

"Sloppy, terribly inept. Shall I go on?"

She had him laughing and wanted to keep it that way. But his face was so thin it appeared like the painting, not finished yet, the eyes too large for its well-formed structure. She threw her hands up. "Help, help. I've had enough. Let's eat."

They went into the office, a small room with only a desk, a chair, and a couch. She sat in the big comfortable chair she and Stan had discarded when they refurnished the house. The matching couch stood against the wall where Glen inspected the contents of his fat sandwich. She poured two glasses of lemonade from a Thermos and handed him one.

He raised it in a toast. Before he could think of one, she said, "To you and everything you can be."

"And you and everything you are," he said without hesitation and clinked glasses with her.

She couldn't stop searching his eyes as they drank, then put down the glasses. For a long time she sat, their gazes locked, until she feared the bread would turn to arid dust around them. Hadn't she known all along she shouldn't have him here? Here where she felt the deepest, darkest, most terrible loneliness. It was more than that, though. Something passed between them, beyond her compassion or his nervousness. Something basic, a bonding both tender and desirous of understanding. Yet she knew better than to ask him to worry about such things. His strength was being taxed just holding himself together one day at a time. She shook her head, hard and fast. Fantasies, yearnings of a woman too old to be so foolish.

"Eat before it molds." Picking up hers, she took too big a bite.

He laughed, a harsh false sound. They were both nervous, but her laughter joined his in a tinkling arpeggio that seemed to please him. He began to eat then, making noisy smacking sounds to show his appreciation of the juicy, dripping concoction.

Nothing much was said until he finished the last bite and, ignoring the napkin, licked his fingertips.

She gave up after a few nibbles and sipped at the tart lemonade.

"Always makes me nervous when the cook doesn't eat her own fixings." He laughed easier, still not completely letting go. But he would, he surely would.

"I like your studio." He took up the napkin and finished the job of cleaning his fingers and mouth.

"Stan built it for me, but I designed it."

"Tell me about him. Your husband."

Pale yellow sunlight filtered into the room and embraced them. With a napkin, she wiped at a smear of wet paint on her jeans to put off a reply as long as possible.

"I met him at a rodeo. Fourth of July weekend." Once she began, it was surprisingly easy to share a private part of her life with him. Somehow, she was not surprised. She smiled at the memory, her thoughts drifting into the brazen humidity and excitement of that long ago hot day. "We were sitting next to each other. He hit me with his big old hat. Guess he just got too excited by the bulls or something. We were pretty well acquainted by the time the rodeo was over. I was nineteen years old, he was twenty-seven, and I was immediately smitten, as the saying goes. We both were, I guess. As far as we were concerned, we'd found who we were looking for. Six months later we were married."

"And you loved him? Always?" He swallowed noisily.

"Oh, yes. Except on the days I hated him."

He gave her a sharp, biting look.

"Oh, don't look so vicious. Every married couple goes through that. We hated each other once in a while. But it never lasted past our first goodnight."

"Never?" Small and tight, the question held disbelief.

For a moment she tried to remember any time their anger had held overnight. "Never."

"How… can you talk about how he died? I'm sorry, it's just I want to know everything about you. Even what you think while you're brushing your teeth or cutting your toenails."

Though the statement startled her, she did not want to admonish him for making it. He was trying to care for someone besides himself, and she had to allow that. "All that personal? You may be sorry. But I wish we didn't have to be so serious. Couldn't we…?" She peered at him, the sun cutting across the high plane of his cheek, and decided to answer his question. It might be good for both of them.

"It's okay if you'd rather not talk about it. I just thought—"

"A tractor turned over on him. I don't know how long he lay there before someone found him. I—uh—he…." She cleared her throat and tried again. "He was dead, and we didn't get to say goodbye. And that's all, forever and always all." She tugged at the front of her oversized sweatshirt, blotted at her eyes with one sleeve, and tried to form a sickly grin. She'd gotten through it without breaking apart. A good sign.

"And now? Are you doing better?" He remained out of reach, but she felt him touching her, with his gaze, with his caring. Her heart lurched painfully.

Don't do this, Katherine. Don't fall in love with the pieces left over from this shattered man, this young man, this man who may need more than you can give. Worse, don't mistake compassion for love.

Do *not* hurt him.

"I'm fine," she finally managed.

"How did that happen? How did you get fine?" He whispered the question, gazed at her, the sunlight flashing in his remarkable eyes.

She wanted to tell him it only just happened. That he had held her and let her cry when no one else had bothered. But she didn't say that, for she could so easily fall in love with him and was terrified of that admission to herself.

"Oh, I guess it's just time. Like they say. I'm ready for the rest of my life. Eager for it."

His gaze broke, and he appeared to be angry. "Goddammit, Katie. Why didn't I meet you twenty years ago?"

"Cause you were only eleven, silly," she blurted. What in the hell was she going to do with all this desire bubbling up in her like an artesian well? And him appearing to match it.

"Eleven. That was an eternity ago, wasn't it?"

"And, too, it was only yesterday."

He grabbed the wheels of the chair, moved toward her. He was going to touch her, and she didn't know what to do about it. Certainly not run away from him. Damage what little was left of his psyche. So she remained watchful and still while he put out his hands and took hers, kissed the palms. She trembled and gazed into the closely cropped curls on top of his bent head.

"Go easy, dear sweet man. Everything's going to be fine. You. Me. Let's just give it time." Damn, why did she keep saying such stupid things?

"Don't worry, Katie. I don't expect anything. You need a whole man, not a broken one. Just wanted to touch you, that's all. Don't worry."

"I'm not worried. You're not broken, just a bit bent. Aren't we all, in one way or another?" She smiled at him, and his face exploded in a most beautiful expression that lit his eyes, dimpled his cheeks, and made her want to cry. Want to touch his face with her fingertips.

"Would you come out and meet my sister?"

With no hesitation, she took the next step. To hell with it. "Yes. Yes, I'd like that."

There was nothing to be done but just go with it, see what happened. She was so damned tired of being careful, being alone, being circumspect. Missing Stan, missing love, missing sex. Dammit. Tired of all of it.

"Tomorrow night, after supper?"

"Yes,"

There was that boyish grin, that gorgeous expression that said he felt alive. God help them both.

TWO

A SILVER-HAIRED stock dog barked and ran from under the porch when Katherine climbed down out of the van. She patted the silky coat and headed across a neat lawn, the dog scurrying around her legs and watching her with mismatched eyes, one pale blue and one dusty beige.

The house was old but well kept, with a long screened-in porch across the front and a native rock foundation. It had probably been painted once, but the rough boards were now a weathered, sturdy gray. They looked better that way, set the place in harmony with its surroundings so it looked as if it had grown right out of the land on which it sat. Sprouted and grown up much like the surrounding oak and maple trees.

In the doorway appeared a thin woman in a limp, faded dress who spoke in a low-pitched drawl, first to the dog, "Sparky, behave yourself," then to Katherine, "Sorry about him, he's always pinin for company. You must be Katherine Kelly. I'm Julia Tanner. Glen's been lookin for you for at least an hour now. I want to thank you so much for comin."

Julia dropped her gees with an accent that caressed words in a love affair with the language. She was one of those ageless women who, because they affect a severe dress and hairstyle, look middle-aged all their adult lives. In fact, she was only a few years older than Katherine. Yet her hair was gray and twisted into a tight knot at the back of her head, and she wore stocky-heeled black, lace-up shoes. She regarded Katherine openly with eyes much like her brother's. But where Glen's held devastation and bewilderment, Julia's reflected a mild suspicion. She wasn't prepared to like this usurper, but would still remain polite. At least for the moment.

Inside the compact living room were old-fashioned floor lamps that glowed against the early twilight. Overstuffed furniture vied for space with tables of several vintages covered with crocheted doilies, tidies they were called, and a television console over which a white fringed scarf was draped. A new wood-burning heating stove made the room too full, yet there was no sense of clutter. Hard to tell how Glen could maneuver his chair through the room. An aroma of spices and perking coffee mixed with the sweet smell of burning wood.

Like so many others, the Tanners had refused to change their way of life when their earning powers increased with the growing poultry business in the state. They lived much as they had when row crops and peddling eggs, milk and the like were their only source of income. Possessions mattered little.

Glen came rolling through a door across the room, eyeing Katherine.

"Thought there for a while he was a goin to come lookin for you," Julia said, her words directed at her brother with a childlike fondness Katherine found unnerving.

He wore a bulky green sweater and the inevitable jeans, and he looked more robust than he had in the hospital atmosphere, but he appeared nervous. Katherine wasn't doing much better, standing in the middle of the room facing him, both grinning like idiots.

"Tell her to set." Julia walked past him into another room Katherine supposed was the kitchen.

He rolled around in short little bursts to make his way. "You heard her. Set." He motioned her to a mammoth chair. By the time she lowered herself and folded her denim-clad legs to one side, he was next to her, the wheels shushing over the patina surface of the bare oak floor.

The absurdity of the situation might have called for levity, but she didn't think so, and obviously neither did a sober Glen. Their smiles had been replaced by solemnity.

"She's been after me all day to watch my manners, and I hope you'll forgive her. She's really very sweet and kind. Just not used to strangers coming around. Especially to call on her baby brother, who she protects fiercely."

"I take it you're not, either. You're acting like I'm here to foreclose on the farm or something." Something about the way Julia's eyes would not rest long on Glen made her nervous. The woman had, after all, had him carted off to jail.

"It's strange having you here," he added. "I mean away from the hospital. Hell, it's strange having myself here. I don't know what to talk about." He moved to one of the large windows, clipping a table corner, and pulled the filmy white curtains aside to gaze at the lowering night shadows. The haunting call of a hoot owl drifted into the stillness of the house, set a background for the slow rhythmic ticking of a grandfather clock in another room.

"Well," she said. "We could discuss art or the weather or the price of chickens and eggs." Or I could ask why you can't have a place of your own. Wisely, she kept that to herself.

"We could go for a stroll in the moonlight. It's coming up over the mountain—the moon, I mean."

She rose. "Yes, I'd like that. If you think we won't get on a snake."

He regarded her with wry amusement, as if to be afraid of snakes was beyond his comprehension. "I'll just tell Julia."

"I trust she isn't coming with us."

His quick glance was sharp. Ready to pounce.

Oops, don't criticize big sister.

She smiled. "As a chaperone, I mean, not to kill the snakes."

It took him a few seconds, but then he laughed, a hearty sound that brought Julia through the door with a frown.

"We're going for a walk," he said, then laughed some more, took Katherine's hand, and faced his sister.

"Well… all right. Why is that funny?"

"A joke. She told a joke, that's all." He turned toward Katherine. "Come on, let's go. We'll be back but don't worry about us. She's not afraid of snakes." He laughed again, and Katherine joined him.

"Don't you forget, I baked a spice cake. You'll want it warm with coffee. And Glen, don't you take a chill, now. The nights are gettin wet and cold."

Still grinning, he turned loose of Katherine's hand and went ahead of her to the door, grabbing a jacket off a hook as he went out. She hurried after him before Julia could admonish them anymore, as though they were two teenagers. Funny, though, that's how she'd felt when she first entered the house.

At the edge of the porch, he paused, slipped into the jacket. "You'll have to back this thing down the steps. There's no ramp." A sharp-edged remark. Must've been a fight over that at one point.

"Then you always have to have someone get you off the porch?" Saying that before thinking how it sounded embarrassed her. "I'm sorry, I didn't mean that the way it sounded."

"You're right. Julia says I don't need to be traipsing around by myself."

With a deep sadness, she took the back of the chair and lowered it down the steps. That was the same as keeping him prisoner. It was beginning to look as if he had good reason not to want to come home. She would talk to Spencer about finding him some place of his own, or at least suggesting it to Glen. On second thought, starting to manage his life was probably a bad idea.

At the bottom, he whirled the chair easily on the smooth path and followed it around the house toward a gate. She trailed along behind, warning herself to bite her tongue before she said anything untoward. A rosy saucer moon spilled frost over the rolling pastures.

"It's lovely out here," she said. "Imagine living on top of a mountain."

The gate squealed on rusty hinges when he shoved it open. "Five hundred acres cleared to pasture. Rich in fescue as it is, it'll graze a right smart herd of cattle. A big improvement over row cropping. We got the chicken houses first, then it made sense to fertilize the fields from the houses and raise cattle, too. Most every farmer out here does that. But I'm just prattling. You live here, expect you and your husband did the same."

"Well, no. Stan had cattle and horses. I sold them off, and now I rent our pastures out to neighbors and sell hay as well."

"You don't ride?"

"No, I was always so busy at the university and with private classes. I never really got acquainted with horses. Stan bred and raised them to sell. He didn't ride either, but hired someone to break them from green."

They approached the barn, a black hulk against the night sky. Two figures came through the darkened doorway and started across the field, casting elongated, wavering shadows on the moonlit ground. Each raised an arm in greeting and went toward a cabin below the chicken houses. Glen returned the wave.

"That's Luke and Mark, Uncle Rob's boys. They've worked here more than ten years now. Since I… left home."

The miniscule pause didn't break into the contentment she felt listening to him speak. It was an orderly, normal conversation, gentle on her ears. They started up a rise past several low broiler houses strung out to the right, curtains drawn almost closed against the chilly evening. She imagined the twenty-thousand chickens in each going about the business of growing to fryer size.

The wheels of his chair sank a bit in the soft earth, and he had some trouble keeping it moving. She stepped behind him and gave him a hand. "Who takes care of the chickens?"

"I haven't met them. Jake and Lou Emerson. Julia got them while I was in the hospital. They were back-to-the-landers, what some folks called hippies. Then they found out they needed money to live, even in Arkansas. They live over there in that trailer house." He gestured and fell silent. They moved on.

Just past the crest of the slope, they came upon the pond, a silvery mirror with stars twinkling on the surface. He drew in a satisfied breath. He obviously liked it here.

"Nice isn't it? There's no place for anyone to hide."

He did say the weirdest things sometimes, but she kept quiet. He felt like talking, and she was content to listen to his pleasant voice.

"When I was a little kid, Uncle Rob brought me up here to the pond to fish. Luke and Mark were just babies back then. Uncle Rob and my dad were real close, even though Dad was a lot older. They were around most of the time, especially after the accident. Uncle Rob had his own place, his own family, but he helped out where he could until I was old enough and even after that. Now I think of it, that was the best part of my life."

She came around beside him, dropped to her knees on the carpet of grass. A breeze blew up, teasing her hair across her face. When she reached to brush it back, he touched her hand with his fingertips.

"I want to tell you something," he murmured. She leaned toward him to hear. "I want you to know this because of the way I feel, the way I think you feel. It would be unfair if I didn't tell you. Every time I get ready to die, something stops me. Some hellish desire, I'm not even sure what. But it isn't a desire to make my life better. I was supposed to die over there, that's why I went back the third... the last time. To complete the circle. I'm sorry I didn't. I look at this pond and think that would be a good way to finish it. They say after the first panic, drowning is peaceful."

Heart kicking painfully against her ribs, she grabbed his hands, willed him to turn away from the gossamer surface and look into her eyes. "Don't say that, please don't even think it."

"Katie, you don't know. I hope you never do know what I'm feeling."

"I do know that I care what happens to you. And I know, dammit, that you care about me, too." Her eyes filled with tears, her nose and throat choked up until she couldn't speak.

"I do, but don't you see, I don't dare care about anyone anymore. If I did, believe me, I would care for you. I can't. When I was over there, at first all I wanted was to live through it and come back home to... to.... Then by the third tour, each time I crawled in that chopper, it was to die. I've never been able to do that, have I? Not even when the fucking thing crashed. Everyone but me dead. Who can live who needs so badly to die? In the camps, when we found out the war was over, America had gone home and left us there, we were obsessed. First with denial, then with anger. For a long time those feelings kept us from giving up. We finally admitted no one back home gave a damn if we ever came back. Then all the stink and filth, the pain and terror became a constant. A day-by-day life. Some of us got too stubborn for our own good. After a while it was a grisly contest to see who could endure the most punishment."

A frenzied intensity lay just beneath the words, and she stopped him the only way she could think of. Could not let him go on here in this peaceful place. She hugged him into the hollow of her shoulder. An awkward move because of the arms of the chair. Still the hug muffled his words.

"Listen to me. You can have a life. You can. A piece of something pure and wonderful. All you have to do is try. Please, please, don't do this."

He sighed, turned so his lips touched her cheek. They were soft and warm against her cold skin. After a moment when she didn't move away, he broke the contact, but didn't pull from her caress. "You try so damned hard. I'm afraid it won't be worth it, for either of us."

"For the first time since Stan died, it will be worth it. I want back the feeling of loving and being loved. Of caring for myself and someone else. My heart has shriveled. For this moment, Glen, does it matter if what we do is for you or for me or just for the moment?"

She detached herself from him. He was a statue. Nightglow touched the planes of his face and deepened the scars and depressions. Stars twinkled in the depths of the pond as if dumped there by the bucket-ful. The cold earth wet the knees of her jeans, and his hand trembled in hers when she slowly placed it on her breast. He closed his eyes, took slow, deliberate breaths, and moved his palm over her hardening nipple. A hot core of fire blazed out of control deep down inside her. She rose languidly, keeping her gaze pinned on his, golden reflecting moonlight and something else she couldn't define. It was restful, though, maybe even hopeful.

One by one, she unfastened the buttons of her blouse, let it slide from her shoulders to reveal her bare, shivery flesh. She glanced down to see what he would see. Her nipples stood dark against her moonlit skin, upturned, rigid, eager. Between her legs throbbed a dam, a hot need for him. But she didn't remove anything else, simply waited for his response. She stretched, arms uplifted, watched him while she rubbed her palms down over her breasts. Watching him watching her. His eyes glazed with passion, he licked his lips, but didn't move to touch her.

Was she doing the wrong thing here? Could she hurt him or help him? And what about what she might be doing to herself? With a muttered curse, she pushed the warnings away. To hell with it, to hell with it all. He needed a reason not to jump in that pond, and she needed a reason to start her life over. So she took his hands in hers and placed them one over each breast, closed her eyes, and waited for him.

He moaned down in his throat, but made no move, just kept his palms firmly over the mounds of her breasts. Finally, she opened her eyes. Twin trails of silvery tears ran unheeded down his cheeks.

"Oh, sweetheart, I'm so sorry." She brushed his cheeks with her thumbs. "I would never hurt you, I didn't mean to… to make you so sad. I wanted you to enjoy touching me, that's all."

He shook his head, pushed away from her, the chair rolling a foot or so before stopping. "I can't. I want to, but I can't. The thing I want most in this world this very moment is to lie with you in the frosted grass. Take off all our clothes and wrap our arms and legs around each other. But I can't. I hope you aren't angry with me."

"No, it's all right. Everything is okay. I am not angry with you. I could never be angry with you, unless you talk about harming yourself again. Promise me you won't do that. Promise me now." If her voice was too harsh, she couldn't help it. The idea of him throwing himself in that pond terrified her.

"Katie, I have a hard-on." Surprise colored his voice.

"Well, I guess that's to be expected. For an old broad, my breasts are quite amazing."

He was silent for a beat, then he started laughing. When he could finally control it, he said, "No, I mean, I have a hard-on, and I haven't… shit—dammit, I don't know how to talk to a woman, and I don't think I could fuck one if I tried."

Kneeling beside him, staring at him, the words slammed hard into her chest, knocked the breath out of her. She'd been seducing a man who hadn't, couldn't, didn't want…. "Oh, Glen, I do apologize. I really had no idea."

"I don't know why the hell you're apologizing. If I could get up out of this chair, I'd probably break my abstinence record for damn sure."

She thought about that for a few seconds. "I could help you out there, if you'd like."

"I'm afraid, but if you tell doc any of this, I'll deny it ever happened."

"That would be best, but could I ask what you're afraid of?"

"You know, Katie, it's been a long time since I've been around women other than Julia, but I think you must be the rare type who says what she thinks without thinking first. Let me see. I'm afraid I might fail to follow through, I'm afraid I might not fail to follow through. How's that?"

"You never have to be afraid of anything with me."

"What if I told you I'm afraid that in the middle of this fucking business, I might go stark raving mad? I might hurt you, then what would you think?"

"I don't believe that, not for one minute."

"Well, I think we'd better go back to the house before Julia sends the National Guard out looking for us. But I do want to thank you again for this miraculous occurrence, though I'm not sure how comfortable I'm going to be for the next few minutes."

"Your own fault. You turned me down when I said I could take care of it for you."

"Put on your blouse and push, woman, before I change my mind and take you up on it. I smell spice cake."

"Okay. Let's go."

Inside the warm kitchen she sat at the kitchen table with Glen and his sister and ate large chunks of fragrant, raisin-filled spice cake and drank strong black coffee. "If you feed him like this he'll soon put on some weight."

He made jokes about how fat he was already, and everyone teased him. Beneath the banter and laughter, she felt his steady gaze. Julia saw it, too, kept looking back and forth between the two of them. Wonder what she would say if she knew what they'd been up to out by the pond, or at least what they had discussed being up to.

Later Julia dragged out a family album. Glen withdrew to the window to stare into the inky night, while she pointed at a photograph of a football player in uniform. "That's Glen, his senior year. He was a live back or something."

She gazed at his image captured in the album. A much younger and happier time. He was looking at someone behind the photographer, posing as only a teenage boy can pose. Long hair blew in the wind, and he was beautiful even then. She placed her fingertip lightly on the cheerful features in an attempt to experience the total abandon, the joy of living trapped there. Julia's sullen gaze fastened on her face. The woman resented her.

Trying to keep her composure, she studied the photograph on the opposite page. A boy, almost a man, athletic, muscular, and so damned young. Not suspecting for a moment what lay in wait for him just around the corner. In jeans and a white tee shirt, his arm possessively around a tiny, dark haired girl. Under the picture the words Ellie and Glen. That was her. The absent wife.

The bitch.

Julia flipped the page. Katherine glanced toward Glen and saw he was staring at them morosely. On the page, in the center, all alone, a five by seven of Glen, hair shorn, looking excited but terribly vulnerable in his Navy uniform. All of eighteen years old. The rest of the pages were empty. The end of his life. Julia closed the album and glared at her as if it were her fault, all that happened after that final photograph.

Without a word, she left the room. Katherine couldn't contain her feelings a moment longer.

Tears poured down her cheeks. Glen worked the chair through the muddle of tables and chairs back to her side. "I wanted to make love to you. I wish I had."

She did, too, and that surprised her. "You didn't tell me why you can't. Is it because of the chair… because you can't walk."

"Not really," he answered and left it at that.

She experienced a sudden, unreal panic, a need to flee this house of misery and mourning. Run away from the reverberations of memories and his absolute futility.

"I have to go now. Come back to the studio."

He made no reply, and she fled, unable to remain a moment longer.

Outside in the van, engine idling, she stared at the lone light in the front window of the old house. Mixed with her urge to escape was a strong desire to go back inside and take him in her arms. If she had been younger, less experienced, in that time of life when love is everything, she would have done so.

But love could demand so damned much, and love denied could cause so much damage. She wasn't equipped to handle it. And if she tried, she could very well hurt him much more than she had by walking out on him tonight.

One day, she would have Spencer explain to her the difference between compassion and love, but doubted he could tell her.

THREE

AFTER A LONG, torturous weekend while she roamed through the house and took long walks, Katherine remained undecided. How foolish could she be even to consider loving Glen when they both were so vulnerable. When his frail emotional condition could not possibly sustain such a relationship. And her still struggling to let go of Stan. But walking and talking to herself did not solve her problems. She would enter the judging at the art gallery. Perhaps one forward step now and again would be enough to keep her life on an even keel. She filled out the registration form and dropped it in the mailbox during one of her forays around the property.

Accustomed to going on foot to the studio, she donned a heavy sweater and set out Monday morning. Overnight, the underground spring that kept the road wet most of the year had frozen in a thin crust of ice that crackled underfoot, a warning winter was at hand. But not there yet. The rising sun spread warmth over the fields and nibbled away at a scattering of frost. The day would be a pleasant one, after all. She drew in sight of the low-slung building and stopped dead in her tracks. A green and white pickup sat in the drive, and Julia stood under the porch roof. So much for having a good day. What in the world did the woman want? It couldn't be a friendly visit.

The woman's dour expression kept Katherine from saying anything. She unlocked the door and let Julia precede her, clicking on an overhead light and closing the door.

Without preamble, Julia said, "Hope I'm not botherin you. I know I got no right to be here, messin in Glen's life, but—"

That was for sure. "Is he all right?"

"If you could call it that, I suppose he is."

She was in no mood to pussyfoot around. "Is something wrong?"

"Yes. Yes there is something wrong."

"Did you call a doctor? What is it?" Her hand shook when she opened the Thermos and poured coffee into two cups.

Ignoring the steaming brew, Julia rounded on her. "You're a goin to hurt him, hurt him bad. He can't give you nothin, and you sure can't give him nothin. What do you want with him?"

Katherine let out a long breath of relief. At least he was okay. "I don't want anything from him, and I certainly have no intention of hurting him."

"Maybe not, but you will all the same. I saw the way you two was a lookin at each other, and it don't have nothin to do with paintin those purty pictures, neither. Now he says we're goin to fix him up a room out on the back porch, and you're goin to come out there for a while. You goin to do that?" Julia peered at her as if nearsighted.

That was news to her, but be damned if she'd admit it to Julia. If anyone was hurting Glen, it was this ignorant woman. "If that's what he wants." She said it more to annoy Julia than anything else.

"You'll do just about anything he wants, won't you?"

"But you won't," Katherine shot back. "You keep him penned up in that house, so the only way he can leave is if you allow him to. It would be better if he came here."

"I don't think he's ready to be a runnin around all over creation. And he sure ain't no artist. You feed him that nonsense? Reckon it was you arranged for that sinful car, too. Everyone knows what red stands for, and it fixed so he can go drive it hisself. Come runnin over here to you any old time."

"Painting is therapy prescribed by his doctor, you know."

"Therapy," she spat. "Foolin around in his britches is what you call therapy?" Her eyes, so much like Glen's at times, took on a malevolent gleam. "You hope to do evil, wicked things. But what you don't know is he can't do nothin like that for you."

Coming from the prim woman, the suggestion was shocking. Not something she cared to argue about, either. "Does he know you're here?" Katherine bit her tongue to keep from yelling and screaming obscenities at her.

Julia shook her head. "What could a woman like you want with a cripple, anyway? You're purty enough to get you a whole man." Her voice was ugly and distraught.

Damned if she'd hold her temper a moment longer. "Don't call him that. Good God, can't you see what that kind of thinking does to him? He's not a cripple, he just needs things other people don't. And you're not giving them to him. Do you have his room equipped so he can care for himself? I'll bet not, seeing you never built a simple ramp so he could come and go."

Julia's face turned crimson. "What do you know? What do you understand? Turn him loose to do God knows what, maybe burn down the house or someone else's. He's crazy, you know. He could kill you or lots of other people. Why don't they keep him in that place where he can't get out and hurt anyone?"

So, Julia really was afraid of having him at home, despite her odd stance. "He will not kill anyone, and he's not crazy. I'm tired of being told I don't understand. Who am I, Mary Poppins?"

Julia glared holes in her, seemed about to spit or worse.

How could she possibly get past such set patterns of beliefs? This woman's values left no room for explanations. So this sister of his would tend to him as if he were helpless, hopeless, and dangerous. Soon he would retreat within himself and wouldn't have to roll that chair into the pond to kill himself. He had such potential for breaking free.

She would call Spencer; see what she could do about getting him away from this pitiful woman to somewhere he could recover. And while she was at it, they would have a long talk about the advisability of this attachment Glen was forming with her. Not to mention the way she felt about him. A woman her age ought to know better, and that was what he would tell her. But he set up the entire thing, and she needed more of an explanation than he'd given.

There was no use in trying to explain to this woman that Glen felt he had to atone for surviving by remaining in that chair with no hope for a life. That his nightmares drove him to despair.

"Julia, please, you must try to understand he has a chance for recovery. Give him that chance."

The woman shuddered on the verge of collapse. Katherine led her into the office, seated her in the large chair, and carried the cup of coffee to her. After a few sips, Julia placed the cup on the side table and stared off across the room. And when she began to speak again, Katherine dropped onto the couch, rested her forehead in one hand. Thought of the smiles and laughter she'd coaxed from Glen the night before.

"You should a seen him when he come home. I went to meet the plane. I just got this phone call, out of the blue, tellin me he would be on it, to come to the airport. I didn't even know he was alive no more. Do you know how I felt? No, course not. Anyway, he come down the steps—they let me stand right there by the plane—and he was wobbly and so skinny and his hair was fallin out and his eyes looked like they was thousands of years old. Someone had to help him, or he would've tumbled right down those steps."

Katherine squeezed her eyes shut against the images.

Julia slumped in upon herself, a gesture that deepened the lines webbing her face, and took another quick sip of coffee. "He had scars all over his face. They'd fixed him up some out in California, but you could still see where the stitches had been. Give him some teeth, they'd been mostly knocked out."

Katherine clutched her temples between thumb and forefinger until pain shot through her head. She couldn't speak.

"He looked at me like he didn't know who I was, and when I put my arms around him, it was like holdin on to a bundle of straw. All crackly and full of funny smellin air."

Tears erupted from Katherine's eyes, and her throat closed until she could barely ask Julia to stop. The word came out a croak.

"Oh, no. You want to understand, you want to know. You're goin to hear it all. They sent him home from the war twice before, sent him home, and he'd stay a while, acting wild and like a stray dog running off all over the county doing God knows what. Pretty soon he'd up and go back, like there wasn't nothing here for him. Do you know what that did to me? Then he went to that prison, and I thought he was dead. All those years, I thought he was dead. My baby brother and not even a body to bury. Then, out there at the airport, when I put my arms around him and he just stood there all blank around the eyes, I remember thinkin, dear God, he hasn't come home after all. He's still over there in that jungle. Might as well be dead."

If she had to listen to much more of this, she was going to scream.

Julia stopped as if she were finished and neither of them spoke, just sipped at the cold coffee and stared off out the window. If Katherine had the strength, she would stop her, but she couldn't.

Julia went on, determined to continue. "I took him home and I took care of him." She smacked her thin chest. "Me. You understand? All he did was what I told him to, just like when he was a baby. Sometimes I couldn't bring myself to make him do anything but eat and sleep and get back his strength."

And now, Julia wanted it to stay that way. Glen would have to be stronger than his sister if he were to overcome her destructive influence. And Katherine doubted if he were. He would need help, and she wasn't sure if she was up to that, or if he would allow it from her.

"But Ellie, what about Ellie?" she finally asked.

"That one," Julia sneered. "After it was in the paper about him comin home, she called a few times. I never let her talk to him, though. He would go crazy at the mention of her name.

"I reckon they loved each other once. Kids, crazy in love, they were. She married him 'fore he left the last time. But she was flighty, and when he left, she just run around with anything in pants. I tried to do something about it, but I couldn't. She was a bitch in heat, that one was, and men just flocked around her."

"When did she divorce him?"

"She just up and left one morning a couple months after they called him missin. Why would she stay married to a dead man?"

"But then after he came home, wouldn't she have…?"

"Never heard about it if she did."

Drawing a long breath, Katherine sagged against the back of the couch. Thank God, the woman was done at last. What else could she say to her?

But Julia wasn't finished. "One night he started screaming and having the most god-awful fit. I couldn't stop him, he just… they had to take him away in handcuffs. I've been crying ever since. Now, he's back home, this time in that wheelchair, and I reckon that's where he's going to stay. I want you to leave him be."

"He's a grown man. He'll have to tell me that himself," Katherine said.

If Julia hadn't shown up this morning, Katherine could well have decided not to see Glen again, either in a professional or social way. It was a good thing Julia didn't know that, because she was determined now to see he tore himself away from her. If he didn't, he could soon become as good as dead.

FOUR

FRIDAY KATHERINE RETURNED to the Tanner farm, this time for her weekly art lesson with him. The one she would not have known about had it not been for Julia telling her about his plans to fix up the back porch for a studio. She took along her teaching supplies, but mostly she wanted to make sure he was okay. There wasn't much else she could do. Spencer couldn't see her until the following Monday, so she didn't have a leg to stand on officially. But she would follow through on her rash statement that Glen would have to tell her to leave. She didn't look forward to another confrontation with Julia. He came to the door, and she breathed a sigh of relief. He looked ill kept, raggedly dressed, but otherwise okay.

"Hi, I'm glad you came. Julia said you wouldn't."

Okay, she wouldn't say what came to her mind. Not a good idea to get between these two. "Well, I'm here. Where do you want to work?"

"Out on the back porch. I cleared some of the junk out and made room for us. There's plenty of light."

He led her through the living room and kitchen, wheels bumping against corners of furniture, and out the back door to a long narrow screened-in room with plastic nailed all around to keep out the cold. Good thing the sun was shining, but come winter, this room would be too cold. If he were to continue, he would have to come to the studio. And he should be allowed to paint in his own room where it was warm. Well, she would tackle all that later.

He acted as if the other night had never happened, and so she didn't mention it either. He was wearing a sweater with holes in the elbows, that might have come out of a ragbag. Oil paint stains were hard on good clothing, so she disregarded his ratty appearance.

They sat beside the east windows in the sunlight, each working on a charcoal drawing of a herd of white-face cattle grazing in the pasture around the pond. An eerie mist rose in lacy tendrils from the water's surface, reminding her of their time spent there.

He grunted, pulling her away from the reverie. "Help. They look like giant ants or something from outer space."

She took the powdery stick from his fingers, curved a few lines, lengthened a figure, and showed him how to improve the composition.

He protested when she handed him back the charcoal. "That's not what's out there."

"Artistic license. Learn to see what you want, not what is. It won't move from your brain to the paper if you don't use some imagination."

With a solemn expression, he continued to work. She watched him for a while, saw his drawing seemed to be progressing well, and began to sketch him in quick studies that soon filled a large page.

Then she had an idea.

"Could I have that picture album Julia and I were looking at the other day?"

"What for?" He kept his eyes on the paper, but the movement of his hand halted in mid-air.

"I just want to do some sketches."

"Of me?"

"Yes, if you don't mind."

His glare left her feeling a bit uncomfortable, but he gruffly acquiesced and told her to holler up Julia who'd fetch the album for her.

She didn't want to holler up Julia. She remembered where the woman had put the album and went to get it. On her way back through the kitchen, she found Julia standing there, arms folded over her breasts with a stony stare that followed her out onto the porch. Neither said a word.

Between checking on Glen's progress and filling pages of her sketch pad, the morning flew, and when Julia poked her head through the doorway and announced dinner was ready, Katherine glanced over, surprised.

"I brought something, thank you." She continued to draw with fierce concentration, not wanting to sit down at the table with brother and sister.

"Well, Katie, that's silly," Glen said. "Can't you just come in and sit with us? I mean, it doesn't make sense for you to eat out here by yourself. Right, Julia?"

His sister didn't reply, and Glen looked from one to the other. "What the hell's going on here?"

"Please don't curse, Glen. There's nothing going on."

"No, nothing," Katherine echoed.

"Let's all get in to the table and eat." He wheeled past Katherine, stopped and reached out to take her hand. "Come on," he urged.

It was difficult to say no to him, and that was strange, since no one had ever been able to tell her what to do, least of all a man.

It wasn't an enjoyable meal, and she was glad when it was over and she and Glen could escape to their work, leaving Julia to clean up the mess.

Katherine didn't offer to help. She hadn't wanted to contribute to the dirty dishes in the first place. Papa used to call her mule-headed, started calling her that when she was no more than ten years old. And she hadn't changed much in that respect. A definite flaw in her personality.

Back in their seats, she took another look at Glen's sketch. "I think you should transfer that to a canvas and have a go at painting it."

He sorted through some canvases he'd obviously stretched earlier, and they settled on a size, then propped it on his easel. He squeezed out some paints onto a palette, said, "I don't know what's going on between you and Julia. I'm sorry if she upset you. I feel guilty she gave up her life to raise me and keep a roof over our heads. It's made a dour old woman out of her. But she loves me and I love her."

"I'm sure she doesn't want you to feel guilty about her sacrifice." There, that must have sounded suitably kind, though she didn't mean it to be. It satisfied him, though.

She watched him sketch in distant mountains for a background to his original sketch. After a moment, he tossed down his charcoal and tugged the ratty sweater off over his head. "Getting hot in here." He poked a finger through a hole in the front of his tee shirt. "All my clothes are nearly as old as I am. Guess I need to buy some new ones someday." He tossed the sweater aside and turned toward her.

She smiled. "I'd be glad to take you shopping someday, if you'd like."

"I don't know. Julia usually buys my clothes."

Well, then she ought to get buying.

She again bit her tongue and kept quiet.

"Is something wrong? You haven't said much since we finished eating. You could at least say uh-huh once in a while so I'd know you were alive."

She kept her eyes on the sketch of Glen in his football uniform. "I'm sorry, I guess I really don't know what to say."

"Because?"

"The other night. I want to make sure I didn't give you the wrong idea."

"Forget it. It didn't mean anything."

She eyed the firm line of his jaw, the set of his lips as he concentrated on his drawing. A woodsy aftershave mixed with the heat from his body surrounded her. How did some men manage to smell so good, so sexy?

"Why did you do it if you're now sorry?" His words were sharp, angry.

"I didn't mean I was sorry. I enjoyed it. I just didn't want you to get the wrong idea. You didn't exactly object."

"Hell, no. Who would?"

"That was a lousy thing to say."

"It was a lousy thing to do."

"No, it wasn't. It was quite enjoyable, at least for me."

"That's twice now you've said it was enjoyable. Is that why you did it, for entertainment?"

"No. You know that isn't true. I wanted you," she whispered.

"I didn't hear you."

He had heard her perfectly well. "Dammit, I said I wanted you. I wanted you, and you enjoyed it, damn you. I know you did. And quit yelling at me."

"I'm not yelling, *you* are," he said in a calm voice.

Anger still running rampant, she did what she so often could do. She said something she didn't intend to say. "I'd do it and more if you'd give me a chance." The words silenced both of them.

His jaw worked furiously, and he stared at her. "Well, shit."

The reaction startled her, and she jumped up. "What's wrong?"

He stuck out his chin at her, and she had an urge to punch him one right on its beautiful tip. Instead, she unclenched her fists, took a deep breath, and glared at him.

"I told you nothing could come of it. Why would you want to keep trying? To torture me or yourself?"

"Why are you doing this? I don't understand why you're so upset." She started across the space between them, but he stopped her with an upraised hand.

"This isn't going to go any farther. I want you to leave, now." He turned the chair so his back was to her.

"Why? You're a good looking, virile man and I'm at my sexual peak, so to speak, so what is wrong with this?"

"Jesus, if you aren't the most stubborn woman I've ever met in my entire damn life."

"And just how many women would that be?

He whirled around, face twisted into an ugly mask. "One was quite enough, thank you very much."

There she was at last. Ellie, thrown out between them like an insurmountable barrier. Instead of fleeing, she went to him, knelt on the floor, and tried to hold his rigid hand that grasped the rim of the wheel. He remained stiff and unyielding.

"I'm not Ellie. I am not."

"Get away," he shouted, shoved at her, and jerked the chair out of her reach. She fell forward, then caught herself.

Julia came to the doorway, thin lips turned up in a grin that looked more like a snarl. "What's going on out here?"

Katherine glanced at Glen, who refused to look at her. "Nothing. I'm leaving." Discretion kept her from venting her anger, more at the woman than at Glen.She went into the studio, tossed her supplies into the carrier, and hurried from the house, seeing neither brother nor sister. For a while, she pounded on the steering wheel. When she could finally drive, she started the van and shifted into reverse.

Glen sat at the window, watching her.

"Dammit, dammit, *dammit,*" she shouted and sped away, tires spraying dirt into the warm afternoon air.

FIVE

THE NEXT DAY, searching for a scarf, Katherine found the gun. A blue-black Colt .45 lay in the drawer of the bedside table and had done so for a lot of years. But after Stan died she forgot all about it. The weapon in her palm set her to trembling. This gun was made solely for the killing of another human being.

Her shakes progressed to tears, which angered her. How could she be so weak, and why couldn't she stop crying? Must only be partly grief over losing Stan. The rest somehow was bound up with what was going on between her and Glen. She just wished she knew what that was.

The telephone rang and she nearly leaped off the bed. The pistol went back to its nest in the drawer, replaced in her hand by the receiver. She mumbled out a hello.

"Spencer here. Thought I'd call to see how things are going."

"I made an appointment to see you Monday."

"Oh? You know I don't look at my appointment book, especially over the weekend. What's up?'"

"I don't want to talk about it over the phone." Yeah, how would it sound saying I tried to lay him, dared to enjoy it, and he took offense and kicked me out?

This was one hell of a state of affairs for a grown woman.

"Why don't you come on in today and see me? And please don't drive like you're acting or they'll be scraping you off the edge of a mountain somewhere."

Without replying, she hung up, shoved the table drawer shut, and took off. She was nearly to town before she realized she had neither driver's license, money, nor a coat. All she had with her were her frustrations and a need to box Spencer's ears, which would cause her great delight. What the hell was she going to do now?

Spencer waited patiently while she blurted out a somewhat coherent story of what had happened. Sometimes he was infuriatingly patient. All he did was shake his head occasionally and scratch at his chin. Nothing fazed the man, even when she got to the naked part. Well, half naked.

"Now," he said, when she finally wound down. "I suppose you expect me to tell you why it happened."

"No, I want you to tell me I didn't do the wrong thing. I don't want to hurt him or cause him to… oh, dammit, Spencer. Say something; tell me I didn't do the wrong thing."

"You did not hurt him. Right now, you're hurting, but only because you think you hurt him. What does that tell you?"

"Oh, shit, don't use that psychobabble on me."

"Okay, don't get more upset. You are getting reactions out of him; he's telling you things he hasn't told anyone else. That's good for him, and if it hurts you, well, hell, Katherine, you're a strong woman, and like you said, you're all grown up. So let's put on our grown-up panties and face this. The more you get him to talk, the closer he comes to beginning his recovery. He may already have begun to face what's all bound up inside him when he blew up at you."

"Are you sure, 'cause he looked furious."

"But he didn't throw things or threaten to kill himself or anyone else, did he?"

"No, of course not. And I didn't tell you about that sister of his and what she said."

"Julia isn't my concern."

"She should be. She's keeping him prisoner. They don't have a ramp on the porch. He's not allowed to be self-reliant at all. He can't get out of the house unless she allows it. She helps him do everything. I wouldn't be surprised if she doesn't go into the bathroom with him. Can't you do something about that?"

"Not me personally. I can make some calls. Get someone to remodel the place so he can live there comfortably."

"You're not listening to me. She's crazy and dangerous, and he loves her too much to see it."

"I think you're overreacting. I know she seems a bit odd turned, but she loves him. I don't believe she'll hurt him."

Infuriated with his attitude, she turned on him. "If anything happens to him while you play God, so help me. You used me like a pawn, like this was a game. Telling me to care, just care. Well, I do care. Damn you, now what do I do?"

"Keep in touch with him, let him know you're there, and get on with your life. Do you love him?"

"Of course, but not... shit, how do I know? I don't want to, because it's so damn complicated, and I've only ever loved one other man like you mean it. Right now I want simple and easy and—"

"Alone," he finished.

"What good would it do if I did love him? He won't talk to me or see me since yesterday. And just what do you mean, alone? As if I had a choice in the matter, as if I wanted it that way."

"Well, of course it's up to him to make a decision about that. He has to start taking some responsibility for his own actions and quit hiding out, just like you do."

"Wouldn't it be a good idea if he could heal some more before you put that on him? A lot of brilliant men disagree thoroughly with your pet reality therapy. Rap sessions, getting everything out in the open, is getting very popular." She refused to defend herself against his accusations concerning her own choices. This was about Glen, and she aimed to keep it that way.

"See you've been reading again."

"So what if I have? And just what makes you so much smarter than anyone else?"

"Nothing, but I'm his doctor. I'll decide on his treatment. I want what's best for him, just like you do, like Julia does."

"Only one problem with that. None of us agrees on what is best for him. When I left he was a wild man. I'm surprised she hasn't called you."

"Julia will handle him."

"That's what I'm afraid of. Besides, it was you who told me she pitied him too much to be good for him."

He held up a palm. "Okay, Katherine, arguing is getting us nowhere. Just relax. He knows he's worth your caring because you let him see that. Now, even if he has to give you up, dammit, he qualified for life. Believe me, either way it goes will be better for him than what he had."

"You didn't hear him tell me he couldn't care for me because he couldn't trust women. He made a reference to Ellie. Don't fool around with me. I don't trust you."

He gave her a beatific smile. "I knew I was right about you."

Mouth open, she stared at him, raised her brows in a silent question.

"You never once asked about yourself, what this was doing to you. Aren't you just a little angry for what you think I might have done to you?"

"I suppose so, but I can take care of myself. I still don't think you had any right to play with his life this way."

"He had no life when I started. I can't erase what's happened to him. The best I can do is help him find something to live for."

"And you offered him me?"

"Not really, you did, and I'm wondering if you aren't pretty well fed up with your mourning weeds and being alone by now. Who's your best friend? Who do you pal with? Take in a movie or go out to eat or hit a bar or rodeo with? God, woman, did you die with your husband?"

She smiled at him. "You might ask Glen, but apparently not. You can be a real bastard, can't you? I don't think that's very professional, and it's certainly none of your damn business."

"I'm sorry, I didn't intend to upset you. I asked as a friend, not as a professional, because I care about you. I'm frankly worried. It's my belief we all do what we want to do. The problem is many of us tend to blame other circumstances or people for our choices, when it's really our own inadequacies at work.

"Now, I'm going to make some phone calls and get someone out to the farm to do some upgrading. You try to make up with Glen… that is, if you want to. I wouldn't pretend to tell you what to do. Still friends?"

"I'm still too angry to say. I'll let you know."

His laughter followed her down the hallway to the front entrance of the hospital.

Confused, Katherine resorted to an escape she hadn't practiced since Stan's death. She went shopping. At a local western clothing store, she chose some brushed denim jeans and several shirts for Glen, then topped off the purchases with a silver-gray Stetson with an iridescent feather band. At the counter, she charged everything to an old account that had been inactive since her husband's death. Playing with one of the tags, she noticed the size. Stan's size. Oh, well, if they didn't fit, she could always exchange them. On the way back to the van, she stopped at the window of another clothing store to admire a green, sheer knit dress that clung seductively to a mannequin. Inside the shop, she changed into the dress and eyed herself in the mirror. The scooped neck showed a bit too much cleavage and the dress hugged her hips as it had the dummy's. It made her look ten years younger. At least. She charged it without looking at the price, already wondering why she bought the thing when she had no place to go.

SIX

THE TELEPHONE RANG late Saturday night. She pawed her way to the extension phone on the bedside table and mumbled "Do you know what time it is?"

"Katie?"

She sat up. "Glen?" He sounded wired.

"I'm sorry. Katie.... Can you come get me? Now. I—"

A click and dead air.

She spoke his name, slammed the phone into its cradle, slipped out of bed into jeans and a sweatshirt, poked her feet in tennis shoes, and raced downstairs and out the door. Keys were in the car, she didn't bother with her purse. Something was badly wrong. That crazy sister of his had done something to him.

The van fishtailed its way out the gravel road, up the long winding lane to the Tanner farm where she skidded it to a halt, taking forever to cover the distance. Shutting off the lights, she leaped out. Stopped dead. No lights on in the house at all. Down below the barn one window in

Luke and Mark's cabin glowed. The moonless night was so dark, she'd fall and break her damned fool neck. On her knees on the van seat she scrabbled around in the glove compartment, came up with a flashlight. Following the beam, she ran across the yard and up the steps.

Without stopping to knock, she eased the door open, thanked God country folk didn't lock their doors, and slipped inside. This could get her shot if Julia waited somewhere in the dark. She let the door click shut and paused. It was so quiet in the house the tick of a clock echoed. She tilted her head. Listened hard. This time there came a long humming moan from off to her left. A hallway led into that part of the house, probably the bedrooms, and she followed the flashlight beam in that direction. For some reason she didn't quite fathom she did not call out, but rather went looking for who or what was making the sound. It was coming from behind the door on her right. Ear against the wood panel, she turned the knob and pushed. The hinges creaked, and the moaning cut off. Inside the bathroom the noise of a shower running.

"Glen?" she whispered. "Is that you?"

The moan turned into a guttural no, repeated several times. The lancing beam hit on the closed shower door. With one hand she yanked it open. A naked man lay coiled in the corner. The shower was running a cold spray, and an aluminum and vinyl kitchen chairs lay on its side.

Good God. That *witch*.

She shut off the taps, dropped to her knees in the standing water, and touched his icy shoulder. It was Glen, both arms wrapped around his knees, head buried against his thighs.

"Sweetheart, you're freezing. What happened?"

He tried to crawl up the wall, jabbered the word, no, some more.

"Glen, it's me, Katie. You're home. You're okay."

"Katie. What are you doing…? Shh, don't let them get you. Run, run."

"Glen, you're home. You called me on the phone. I came to get you. Did you fall? Where's your chair? Your sister? What's going on?"

He made that shushing sound again, but he did relax a bit. "I can't walk. They've done something to me. Run away, Katie."

At least he knew she was there. "No, sweetheart. You're okay." Which he definitely was not. She put her arms around him, the beam of the flashlight climbing the wall to the ceiling. God, he was so cold. She had to get him out of there and under some blankets.

"Can you help me?" he whispered. "Before they come back?"

She couldn't lift him or move him. "Yes, yes I will. I'll go get Luke and Mark. I can't lift you."

"Don't you leave me, too. You can't do that. Please." Then, deep down and God, so frantic. "Please do not leave me."

"Okay, you're right, of course. I won't leave you. Can you move at all? Help me get you out of this water." No way could she reach the light switch without leaving him. That she could not do.

Tucking the flashlight under her arm, she hooked both arms under his shoulders and managed to drag him out onto the bathroom floor. The tiles were slick and wet, so she made it into the hallway before she slumped down, unable to drag his dead weight any farther. He broke away, hauled himself along for a few feet, then began to crawl as if the devil pursued him. Another few feet, and he collapsed in the open doorway of a dark room. That was as far as he could go, though his nails continued to dig into the floor. He was wild, and she needed to settle him down. There had to be a light switch on the wall somewhere, but when she did find it and flip it, nothing happened.

"Lay still, I'm going to find some blankets. Just a second, I'm not going far."

He made no sound, and she stumbled around him. Inside was an empty bed. She pulled the blankets off and rushed back to roll him up in them. His fingers twined around her wrist and hung on, so she collapsed on the floor beside him and bundled him into her arms. When he began to quiet a bit, she said, "Where's the phone? I need to call an ambulance for you."

"No, no ambulance. They'll take me to jail. I don't want to go to jail. Katie? Not yet. Not yet. I'm not hurting anyone. I'll be okay."

"Do you know where you are?"

His head nodded. "I had a flashback, that's all. I know where I'm at now. Katie, how did you get here?" The shivers trembled his voice, but he sounded stronger all the same.

"You called me. Don't you remember? Where is Julia?"

"I don't remember. I don't know."

"I'm going to get you out of here. You could have been badly hurt or taken pneumonia, lying in that cold water like that."

"I'll be all right. Just… can you just hold me for a while?"

Unable to resist, she brushed back his wet hair and kissed his temple, held him, rocking gently until he stopped shivering. She couldn't leave him lying on the floor, and she couldn't get him in the bed, either. His breathing evened out. Thinking him asleep, she eased his head down into the padding of blankets and found the bedroom telephone. But when she lifted it off the cradle, it was dead.

Someone had unplugged it or cut the wires. She prayed for the first and followed the wire from the back of the phone to the wall. Using the flashlight, she located the jack and plugged the line back in. Good God, what was going on here? Had Julia lost her mind? And where was she?

Spencer answered on the fourth ring. "He doesn't want me to call an ambulance. Says they'll take him to jail. Julia is not here anywhere I can tell. If she is, she's gone deaf. I can't get him to my van by myself. I want you to call an ambulance. He is not violent, so don't you dare let them bring the sheriff or truss him up when they get here. You hear me, Spencer? I just want him out of this woman's house, as quickly as possible."

"Okay, Katherine. You've convinced me. This isn't good. I'll get there ahead of the ambulance so I can sedate him, and we'll take good care of him."

"I'm going with him."

A long sigh, then, "I'll take you. I'll handle everything."

She hung up without saying goodbye and went back to sit on the floor with Glen until Spencer arrived.

If Julia showed up, she just might throttle her.

Luke and Mark came running, followed Spencer inside. "Saw all the commotion. Not used to all these vehicles coming up here," Luke said. "Can we help? Is it Glen?"

"He's going to be okay. He had a flashback." Be damned if she'd go into detail about Julia's part in this. He wouldn't have flashed back to that cell they kept him in had it not been for her. If she had her way, the woman would never come near him again.

"Hold him still, Katie. I want to do this as easily as possible. He could get excited and cause a ruckus."

She nodded and unrolled enough of the blanked to expose his arm. "It's okay, sweetheart. Doc is here now, and he's going to take care of you. I'm going with you."

There was no response.

Spencer located a vein and slipped the hypodermic needle in. Glen didn't flinch. He grew heavy and relaxed in her arms in just a minute or so.

"Goddamn her, Spencer."

"Hsst. He'll hear you. Just be calm and hold him until the ambulance gets here."

"The lights are all out. I think she shut them off. She must've put him in the shower and left him there under the cold water. My God, who does something like that?"

"I don't know. A better question, where is she?"

The lights all came on, blinding her.

"She is right here," Julia said, moving toward them from the kitchen. "You going to put him where he belongs now? Before he hurts someone. I can't take it anymore."

Had she not been holding Glen in her arms, Katie would've clocked the woman. Knocked her flat out on the floor. Instead, she gritted her teeth and glared at her in silence.

"Julia, would you get his wheelchair and any belongings he has here?" Spencer's voice held an edge no one would dare ignore. "He'll need to take them with him."

"What's she doing here?" Julia asked, sneering at Katie.

"Just get his things, Julia."

She nodded and skirted Katie and Glen, went to the closet where she took a few hangers of clothing out and tossed them on the bed. Her heels thunked across the hardwood and down the hall to another room where she fetched the wheelchair, piled his clothing in it and rolled it into the living room.

Glen shivered and groaned, and Katie held him close. "Sshh, sweetheart. Everything's okay."

In the distance, a siren wailed. "It's about time. He's still very cold. Make sure they warm him up. May I go with him in the ambulance?"

Spencer shook his head. "No. I'll take you in if you want. You're too upset to drive."

"I guess. Besides I don't have my purse or anything. I came so fast when he called."

"I'll take you. I can bring you back home when you're ready."

The ambulance cut the siren when it started up the lane. In a moment doors slammed, a low conversation and three EMTs came inside. Flashing lights painted patches on the floor. Luke had been waiting at the door, and he led them into the small bedroom. Katherine lowered Glen's head onto folds of the blanket and moved out of the way.

"Strap him down," Spencer ordered. "I've given him a sedative. Hang an IV drip and I'll follow you to the hospital."

"Oh, hey doc. Didn't recognize you there in your tightie whities," one of the men said, gesturing toward Spencer's sweat pants and shirt. "Straight to Vets then?"

"Yes. Come on, Katherine, let's get out of here."

She rolled the wheelchair out on the porch and off the steps. Spencer opened the trunk of his car and fitted everything in. "Stuff looks like it came from Goodwill," he muttered. "Might as well have burned it."

"I bought him some clothing the other day, but I don't want to leave any of his stuff here, even if it is rags," she said, climbing into the front seat of the big Chrysler sedan and leaning back against the luxurious leather seat. "God, I'm tired." She sat forward. "All his art work and supplies."

"We'll come back and get them later. Close your eyes and relax. I asked the boys to take your van to your place so we wouldn't have to come back here for it.

"Thank you so much for coming without asking any questions."

He keyed the ignition. "I know you, I trust your judgment. Should have done so this morning. I just could not imagine Julia hurting Glen. In fact, I don't really think she is aware she hurt him."

"That's a crock of shit," Katie said. "For a psychiatrist you're sure a bad judge of character."

"I've been told that, and it's probably true."

"She put him in the shower, turned the water on him, well water that is freezing this time of the year, and took away his wheelchair, cut the lights and phone, and walked off and left him. What did she think it would do to him? It's a wonder he didn't go out of his mind, considering what he's already been through."

The rest of the way into town, he said nothing, and she dozed in the comfortable seat until he pulled into his parking space at the hospital, the ambulance circling around to the emergency doors.

A row of empty chairs near the cubicle where they took Glen looked inviting, and she sank down to wait for Spencer to come out. She would not leave the hospital, would stay with Glen, and Spencer had better not give her any lip about it at all.

He didn't. Once they had Glen tucked into warm blankets, they wheeled his bed down the hall to a ground floor room that was empty. She and Spencer followed. When the nurses stopped their fussing, she got hold of the only chair in the room and started dragging it toward his bed. Spencer helped and said nothing when she sank down and took Glen's free hand in both hers. His other arm was tied down to prevent him thrashing and tearing out the IV.

"He'll be all right," Spencer said in a low tone. "You could come back in the morning."

She glared at him, and he raised his shoulders in defeat.

She kept her voice to a whisper. "You started this, now you let me finish it. He called me. That's who he has."

"I'll tell the night nurse you're staying."

"Thank you."

She scooted the chair closer to the bed, laid her head on the mattress, and closed her eyes, never releasing his hand.

The sun shone through the windows when she awoke. Glen was still sleeping. Spencer must have given him another shot. She brushed a fringe of hair off his forehead. The light made the thin scars visible on his cheeks and throat. The Navy had done a good job of stitching him back together.

She lifted his hand, touched the white line that ran up the inside of his forearm, then kissed him.

He jerked. His eyes flew open, panic streaking through them like jags of lightning. She cupped his face in her palms, then lay her head on his shoulder.

"It's a dream, that's all. Just a dream. Go back to sleep."

"Katie? I thought that might be the dream."

Spencer came in, stood on the other side of the bed without saying anything.

Raising a bit, she kissed Glen. Couldn't stop reassuring him. She was so angry, so afraid what this might do to him. Unchecked tears poured onto his face.

He rubbed at her cheeks with his thumb. "Oh, don't cry Katie. I'm so sorry. I can't stand to see you cry." He snaked his arm around her and pulled her close. "You're drowning me in tears. Were you here all night?"

Spencer replied for her, since Glen had tucked her into the curve of his shoulder. "She sat right there in that chair all night and held your hand."

"Come here," Glen said. "Come on. This bed is big enough for both of us." He straightened his legs to make room.

She glanced at Spencer, and he nodded. Without a word, she crawled onto the bed and nestled in against Glen.

Spencer pulled the sneakers from her feet, set them on the floor. "I'll tell the nurses not to disturb you two. You both need some sleep. I'll be back later today."

The shades along the bank of windows made a swishing sound, cutting out the sunshine. The lights went out, and the door shut with a chuff. Head pressed against Glen's chest, his arm wrapped around her, she relaxed her exhausted body and closed her eyes.

Opened them when he murmured her name like a question.

"Mmm?"

"Know what I remember? The first thing?"

She was almost afraid to ask. "No, what?"

"You. I don't remember getting out or coming home or being here. I just remember looking up one day and seeing you sitting beside me out there by the creek. The sun made your hair all shiny, brighter and more beautiful than anything I thought was left in this world. I touched it, and it felt like silk. Your skin was like satin." He rubbed absently at her cheek. "You were making me draw, and I didn't know why or how we got there. But none of that mattered as long as you didn't go away. I would have done anything you asked me to. I thought you were an angel and I'd died and gone to heaven."

A choking sensation filled her throat. She most certainly didn't feel like an angel. Tucking the covers around them, she kissed one corner of his mouth and curled against him.

"Go to sleep, sweetheart," she whispered, but he already had.

SEVEN

THE SMELL OF food woke her. Her stomach growled. Out in the hallway metal trays, dishes, and silver rattled. She shifted a bit against his still body, felt something.

"Uh oh," she said under her breath.

His whisper came from under the covers. "Katie? You know that hard on I had the other night?"

"Yes."

"I've got it again, but first I gotta pee. Can we do something about it?"

Chuckling, she slipped from the bed, dug around until she came up with a urinal. That chore accomplished, she set it on the table and crawled back in beside him.

First, she wrapped her fingers around him. "Now, where were we?"

"Ah, woman. Do you know how long it's been? Couldn't you just... I mean. Oh, shit. I need...."

"I'm sorry. I thought that's what you wanted."

"It'll do, but...."

Something broke inside her, and a craving for him poured through her. She needed him as much as he needed her. She shed her jeans and sweatshirt, all she wore, then slipped beneath the blanket and snaked one leg over his hips. "Like this?"

So easy, so perfect, they fit as if they were meant for each other. She took him in, began to move, her insides quivering and hammering to the rhythm.

He grabbed her and shoved his hips up tight against her. "Ah, good God almighty. So fucking fine." The heat of his release filled her, and she vibrated from the inside out. Saw stars where there weren't any and thought she might faint from the pure joy of it.

He went limp beneath her. "Oh, Lord, I forgot how sweet a woman is."

She bent forward, her naked breasts on his chest, covered by a ridiculous hospital gown tied in the back so she couldn't get it off him. She sat back, which evoked a sharp cry from him. "You okay?"

He made a funny little humpfing sound.

At least he was still alive. She tugged the gown up to bare his stomach and as much of his chest as possible.

"Can't talk right now," he said.

"Know what you did?"

"Yeah, let's do it again."

"Doofus." She laughed, wiggled about to tease him. "Did you know you moved your legs to make room for me in the bed?"

"That's good." And in that moment he was hard inside her again, his heat and heartbeat like an explosion that touched every single part of her that cared. That wanted him, that hungered for his love. That sent her bone-deep crazy.

His free hand covered her breast, his mouth enclosed the other. "Oh, yes, keep doing that. It feels so good." So he did, setting her hips to moving again. He let go, tried to reciprocate. But flat on his back, one arm strapped down, the other hanging on to a breast, he couldn't do much in return.

"More, sweetie, more," he said, and when she did, he spilled inside her, crying out with sheer pleasure. "Dear God, dear sweet God." Dragging her back down to place his mouth on her breast. Sucking, licking, tugging. A pure enjoyment of such a simple pleasure.

"Well, aren't you something?" Again she wanted to tease him, to let him know what they were doing was fun.

He let her breast go. "I don't know what to do next. Remember I'm making up for lost time." So out of breath he had to gasp in air between words.

"And doing a fine… oh, my, you are a young stud, aren't you?"

"Shit, shit, shit."

"What is it, Glen? What?"

"I just forgot how fucking good this feels. Makes me sorry I missed it all this time."

She grinned. "Seems I did, too. Just keep doing that, if you don't mind. You're touching parts I didn't know I had."

"Mmm. Hang on. Here we go again. Seems I'm gonna have to do a hell of a lot to catch up."

And she found out what he was doing. Difficult to believe he could keep going like this, but she didn't want to slow him down. Orgasms felt so much better than she remembered, and she was having one after the other. He had not forgotten how to please a woman.

"Glen? Glen?"

"What? What?"

"Go back and do that some more. Yes, there, there. Don't stop." For a man with one arm strapped to an IV, he had some delectable moves.

"I may have to stop."

"Why? You okay?"

"Fine, but I'm falling off the bed."

"Not good." She scooted off him, took his hand, and wrapped her other arm around his waist to pull him back onto the mattress. "Hold on."

"Doing my best."

"I've got you, sweetie." Not wanting to miss anything he might yet have coming, she curled her leg over him, settled in once more. Hoped this wasn't going to end anytime soon. It was like shooting over the stars and soaring back down, over and over.

"Indeed you have. I think I'm in love."

"And here I thought we were just having fun."

"Well, I am, are you?"

"Yes indeed. Uh, okay, once more, then I have to rest."

"Aw, Katie. Why?"

"I'm old, remember?"

"One more time. Uh-oh."

"What?" she asked. "You okay?"

"Not sure. It's not working. I think I may have reached the end of my endurance."

Silence, then giggles and wiggles, and she was lying beside him, his arm around her.

"Well, that's not bad for your first time, kid," she said. "Don't worry, you'll do better next time."

He laughed, a sound she reveled in. "I'm just out of practice."

She lay there on his arm for a long time, trying to imagine what it must be like for him. Nine years of torture and doubt and pain and no one to care, then he's thrust into the arms of a crazy sister who tries to finish the job of destroying him. Maybe if she held him close enough, she could drive those memories, if not away, then at least to the dark recesses of his mind.

"Glen?"

"Can't just yet, sweetie."

"No, I gotta go."

His arm tightened, his voice serious with an edge of panic "No. Please don't go.".

"Just the bathroom. I promised I would stay with you, remember?" She kissed him on the mouth. "It's okay. You know what? You're going to be okay. I promise. Now let me go before I get your bed wetter than it already is."

After she finished, she wet a wash cloth with hot water and brought it back to him. "Want me to do this?"

"Yes, I would enjoy that a lot."

While she cleaned him up, she thought about him crawling across the floor at his house, and later moving his legs in bed. When she'd mentioned that to him earlier, he changed the subject. Granted they were hotly involved at the time. She would speak to Spencer about it.

"I'd better dress and see if we can get something to eat. I smell food."

"Sounds good."

Slipping into her jeans, she asked, "What did you do? I mean did you miss sex? Did they let you have a woman now and then? Did you just take care of it yourself?"

"It was... I mean, at first I had wet dreams sometimes, but after a while, when things got so bad, I lost all desire for sex. Concentrated on staying alive. It was all I could do."

She stood, holding her sweatshirt in her hands, unable to move, to imagine nine years of hell like that, after serving three tours in a war that was itself hellish.

"Katie?" He touched her, gazed up into her eyes. "Please don't cry for me anymore. I don't want that."

"I'm sorry. I don't mean to, but the tears just come. Spencer says I'm grieving Stan's death through you, and I do apologize. I wish there was something I could do, something more."

"You're doing it, but just stop crying. You and I... well, I don't understand what the hell is going on, but I feel connected to you. I'm inside you, even when I'm not, if you know what I mean. I will not tie you to me, though. That's not fair to you and sure wouldn't be fair to me either. But I can't help the way I feel about you. You made a promise to me last night I don't expect you to keep. You were trying to help me in the only way you knew. And this day has been unbelievable. This is truly my first time to have sex in nine, no twelve years, and you made it fucking-A."

"Fucking-A, huh. Well, it was pretty damned wonderful for me, too. And I'll decide who I want to be tied to. Okay? I want to stay with you, see you through your recovery."

"Why? I don't understand why. We didn't even know each other a few weeks ago."

"Because I feel we are all responsible for what happened to you and the guys like you. We let it happen, and even now most don't even care. But I care. And beyond that, I care for you. So you need to let me do this. If I feel like it's getting to be too much, well, then we'll talk. But I will not up and leave you. And that's still a promise. You can't make me take it back. Now, if I don't get some food I'm going to faint."

"Go, go. Bring back. I'm starving, too."

Dropping the sweatshirt over her head, she slipped her arms in and opened the door.

Spencer stood at the nurses' station desk, a clipboard in his hand. "Well, look who's back. How's everything going?"

"Don't you dare smirk. I hate that 'I knew it all along' look you get. So smug. We're starving. Can we get something to eat?"

He nodded. The aide standing nearby said. "I'll go get two trays for you. It'll be a little while."

"Thanks." She gestured toward the door. "I'll just go back in there with him until it comes."

Spencer glanced up. "How's he doing? If he's awake, I'd like to come in and talk to you both for a few minutes."

"Fine. Come on in. I'll just tell him. You might want to know he can move his legs when he's not really thinking about it."

His eyebrows raised. "Interesting."

She went back into the room. "Do you want the bed raised so you can sit up and eat?"

"Yes, please," he said. "I hope they let me up tomorrow. I'm not hurt or anything."

How much of last night did he remember? Maybe Spencer would ask. She flipped the handle from under the bed and turned it until he was sitting. "Spencer's coming in. You can ask him, but I think they probably will."

The door whished open, and the doctor entered. "Well, you look a lot better than you did last night," he said. "Do you remember what happened to you?"

"No." He reached out, and Katie took his hand, leaned against the bed.

"Nothing at all?"

He glanced at her. "I remember being wet and cold and her wrapping me up in a blanket. Nothing before or after that until I woke up with her holding my hand. I'm not telling you what we did later."

She punched him on the arm. "Behave yourself."

Spencer chuckled. "I don't need to be told—I can imagine."

"I doubt that," Glen said. "Unless…." His gaze slid from Spencer to Katie and back again.

"No, I haven't had the pleasure, I'm sorry to say," Spencer said.

Heat flared across her chest and face. "You two stop that right now."

Both men laughed. "Yanking your chain," Spencer said.

"Yeah, but what's he doing?" She glared at Glen.

"The same," he said and smiled in that rare, beautiful way he had.

Spencer glanced from her to Glen. "We're trying to get a place for you to live, but most of the apartments are filled right now."

"What has to be done to make a place qualify?" Katie asked.

"Well, doors wide enough to accommodate the wheelchair, facilities lower so he can reach things, bars on the walls in the bathroom, a shower he can get in and out of by himself."

Katie shuddered, thought of the overturned kitchen chair and no way for him to get up off the floor when he fell. A chill embraced her shoulders.

Spencer glanced at her, nodded. She knew what he was thinking for she'd been thinking the same thing.

"How long will he be in rehab here at the hospital?" she asked, for that was one thing Spencer had explained. Glen would work with a physical therapist who thought he might get him back on his feet.

"Maybe 'till Christmas. It depends on how he responds."

"Hey. Could you quit talking about me like I'm not in the room?"

"Sorry," Spencer said and laughed. "Bad habit. I want your doctor to examine you in the morning, make sure you don't have any broken bones. We'll disconnect the IV this evening and you can get some more rest tonight. Unless she—"

"Spencer, stop that." Katherine peered at Spencer. "So then if I applied to qualify for the housing, that side room on my house could be fixed up for him by the time he's ready to leave?"

"Hey, wait a minute. You aren't going to be my nurse or caregiver. I won't tie you down like that. You have your classes and all. I have a question. Why can't I go back to the farm? What's all this rehab for two months, then a place in town? I don't even like town."

Spencer took over. "By the time you leave, you won't need either a nurse or a caregiver. We're getting you prepared to take care of yourself. It's time you had your own life. It was a mistake to send you back to the farm to be cared for."

He had skated around telling Glen what Julia had done, and she was glad. It would break his heart.

Spencer addressed her. "I don't know about the room out at your place. They'd have to come out and look at it. Normally they want a fully equipped apartment so he can do his cooking and a bathroom, an outside entry."

"I understand." She smiled up at Glen. "And I want you to have a place of your own. A life of your own. I'd like to be a part of it, but that's up to you." She kissed his hand, then leaned forward and kissed his mouth, a quick touch. His eyes glistened, and she turned away to keep from crying herself.

"Well, let's begin by installing you in a rehab room, closer to the gym and swimming pool. After you finish your supper, which ought to arrive momentarily, we'll do that. Doctor Radnor will see you first thing in the morning, check you out, and make sure you're healthy. I think this young lady ought to go home and get some rest, don't you? Tomorrow's Monday, and she has classes."

Glen nodded, if reluctantly. "Tomorrow's Monday? I must've lost a day or two. Katie needs to get back to her life. I don't need babying." She wasn't sure she liked his tone of voice, as if he'd turned off something that had been there only moments before between them.

The door opened and the aide came in, carrying one tray loaded with enough food for both of them. She arranged everything on the swing around table so it sat before Glen. "I guess you can divide this up any way you like. I'm sure there's plenty here."

They thanked the young aide, and she beamed at Spencer, then left.

"I'll take you home anytime you're ready, Katherine," Spencer said.

Katherine and Glen began a discussion over who got what on the tray, and Spencer slipped from the room.

EIGHT

GULF WINDS BLEW in warm rains through Thanksgiving. Days were crisply pleasant and nighttime temperatures barely dropped to freezing.

Katherine called Glen or visited him twice a week when she had free time from her art classes. He appeared frustrated with the rehab, but Spencer assured her that was not unusual. He wasn't walking, though every day his therapist took him to the gym and put him on his feet between bars, and he dragged himself across and back. That just proved his arms were stronger. He swore he could not move his legs nor support himself. Yet each time she saw him his physique had grown stronger. He put on weight, his chest and upper arms thickened, his belly tightened. She teased him about becoming Mr. Universe.

Glen turned down her invitation to come for Christmas. She wasn't sure why, but it hurt her nevertheless. He'd grown more distant recently, but she'd put it down to his failure to walk again. She'd promised not to leave him, and he was the one who withdrew. She felt bereft and lonely. Spencer tried to bolster her self-esteem, but she was having none of it.

A terrible loneliness had crept around her while she wasn't looking, forcing her to reconsider Spencer's insinuations she was hiding out. For the past week, she'd had no classes. Closed for the holidays. Like her, closed. All her students were involved with their families. A few had dropped by with gifts, then whirled away amidst clouds of aromatic bayberry and spice cake and unbearable merriment. Nothing remained to keep her company except her desires, and they raced in erratic circles that eluded her grasp.

The morning of Christmas Eve dawned clear and beautiful, and Katherine found herself shrouded in self-pity, so lonely she ached with it. She crept around the house in a fuzzy blue robe, feeling as if everything around her had died and left nothing to nourish her soul. She fetched a basket, filled it with snack foods, apples, crackers, cheese, cookies, dressed in sweats and a parka and stomped down to the studio. At least there, she could work and keep her mind and hands occupied. Forget it was a holiday where families gathered and exchanged love.

While she built a fire in the cast iron heating stove, she discussed aloud the advisability of getting a cat to talk to. One-way conversations with herself offered little stimulation, and somehow she could always anticipate the answers. At least cats had a way of conversing with their humans.

The sketches she'd done of Glen at the farm lay scattered across the desk, and she rifled through them. Damn but she missed him. What was he doing this Christmas Eve? She trudged to the storeroom for a canvas, came back with one, prepared a palette, and applied blobs of color in broad harsh strokes as if the demons of hell drove her. The effect startled her senses. Streaks of vermillion splashed with vibrant blues, madders harsh under eruptions of Payne's gray. At last she turned away in disgust, leaving the paint-filled brush to dry unheeded. She couldn't even prepare a background for the portrait she'd hoped to create.

She drank cup after cup of coffee, wandered around straightening supplies, stacking and re-stacking blank canvases, cleaning and arranging brushes, and lining paint tubes in a neat row on the work table. Daylight faded into an ashy dusk, and she finally quit her dithering to sit and nibble morosely on the food she had brought. She'd done a fine job of feeling sorry for herself with no solution in sight.

She raised a cup of cooling coffee, the last from the Thermos. "Merry Fucking Christmas."

Unaware of how long she sat there, she grew cold. The fire had gone out. In the other room, stacking wood on the glowing coals, she raised to open the damper. A car moved slowly down the road. The clock showed a few minutes after ten, and she went to the window. The car had gone. In the moonless night, floating crystals shimmered in the glow from the yard light, sparkling in a fairy-like dance. Along the fencerow stark branches threw back icy reflections, rigid and still against the winter sky.

In the silence, the hollow chunk of a car door. She held herself as still as the night, afraid to think or hope it might be Glen. But who else would come this late? Be sensible, why would he come at all? Obviously, he did not want to see her anymore. It was someone lost, or a student seeing the light on and stopping by at the last minute to wish her a Merry Christmas. If Glen had come, what would she say? Or how would his presence make her feel?

When she could wait no longer, she went to the door and opened it. There would be no one. It was her over-active imagination and wishful thinking. But he was there, coming across the grass, head down while he concentrated on pushing at the wheels of his chair. The crystals landed in his hair, giving him a shimmery appearance. The light behind her formed a path leading him to her. Knees too wobbly to hold her up, she leaned against the doorframe, heart thumping painfully.

In the instant it took him to cross the concrete slab, she admitted what she'd known for some time. She not only loved him, she adored him, craved him, needed him. Practical considerations or being sensible and acting her age were cast aside. All the arguments, self-doubts, and warnings drifted away like the disappearing puffs of her breath. In a breathy silence she stepped back from the open door to let him in. Trembling with anticipation. Waiting.

He didn't speak right away, and now that her own decision was made, she was afraid of why he had come. She shivered from the blast of frigid air, then, feeling foolish, hugged herself against the tendril of apprehension that touched her and was gone. He held out one hand, said her name. Pushing the door closed, she placed her fingers in his, and he guided her around and pulled her into his lap.

"I couldn't stay away any longer. I miss you way too much. Need you more."

She leaned against the cold of his face. "I love you." It was said before she could consider that she ought to wait, not put him on the spot in case he didn't feel the same.

"Ah, Katie. You're sure, are you? Because I love you like crazy. Like fucking crazy. And I'm sorry for the way I've been. I wanted so much to walk into this room and tell you that. It hasn't happened, and I'm so sorry for so many reasons. Saddling you with this...." He pounded on the arms of the chair "...it's so unfair. And all the other shit muddling around in my brain. You deserve so much more. But I... I guess I'm selfish, because I want you so much I can't breathe when I'm not with you. I can't even think straight. Please forgive me for doing this to you."

In her grew a mixture of disappointment for him and an indescribable pleasure at this wonderful new discovery. "It doesn't make a difference, I love you so much. I've been miserable without you."

His hands like blocks of ice clutched at her back and he buried his face against her breast.

"You're so cold you're shaking. Why didn't you wear a coat?" She rubbed his chest through the thin shirt.

Untangling herself, she rose and ordered him into the office where she helped him from the chair and onto the couch. In the storeroom, she gathered blankets and returned to curl up beside him, wrapping them both snugly together.

She hesitated to anticipate his true motives for coming here. He wanted her as much as she wanted him, for he touched her hungrily in all the intimate places where no man had been save Stan. He said he loved her, needed her. But how far did he want to go with this? She was ready to live with him, marry him, whatever he wanted, just to be with him.

His warming hands slid under her sweatshirt, the tips of his fingers tracing her skin as if reading Braille. "Until you, I'd forgotten what a woman felt like, tasted like." He took her mouth to his. Warm and moist and sweet. The tip of his nose made an icy dot against her cheek. "Smells like." He sniffed her playfully, nibbled at her skin from jawline to the lobe of her ear.

She shivered, remembered making love on the narrow hospital bed. She dismissed all earlier thoughts and unbuttoned his shirt. Her hands roved over his chest, circled the nipples, and smoothed at the scars laced in ridges across his skin. For an intense moment filled with hatred, she ached to get her hands on whoever had caused him such irreparable harm. Twist their heads off, do dreadful things to them, as they had done to him. Yet such destructive forces accompanied that kind of thinking.

"We need to go on from right this minute," she said. "Spencer said it and it's so true. From now on to forever, with no looking back."

Glen didn't say anything, he appeared to be content to hold her and explore what he could get to without taking off her shirt.

His hands felt so good, his fingers long and graceful, except for the two that had been broken and not reset,

"Katie?"

"What?"

"I don't know what's going to happen to us. Do you? I didn't want to do this to you. Ask so much of you. I tried so hard to stay away and let you be free, but I couldn't. I just can't give you up."

Her deep sigh of relief ruffled his hair. "I'm glad you didn't. I've missed you so much. No one ever knows what's going to happen. Even in the best of worlds nothing's a sure thing, I was coming to you if you hadn't come here, so you see it wouldn't have mattered. Together we're bound to be stronger than we are apart. We'll handle whatever happens."

In a low voice he said, "One day you may wish you'd never set eyes on me, but I love you, and I want you never to forget that, no matter what happens." He hugged her so fiercely she grunted and wondered for a split second just what he might mean by that.

A dark shadow darted over her and was gone.

NINE

WRAPPED IN HIS arms on the couch, she had almost dropped off to sleep when he said, "What time is it?"

"I don't know. My watch is under here somewhere. Why?"

"Doesn't matter. I brought you something, and I wanted to wait until it was officially Christmas to give it to you, but I can't stop thinking about it." He shifted, dug in a pocket and came up with a small box.

Dumbfounded, she untangled her hands from under the covers and took the gift, opened the box and gasped. A ring with a swirling circlet of diamonds that winked and glittered around a center stone took her breath away.

All she could say was, "Oh," over and over again.

"Let me put it on for you. Which finger?" He touched the mark from her wedding band. "This one?"

With a series of mute nods, she let him slip it on the third finger of her left hand.

"It's not near what you're worth to me." He slid the golden ring snugly over her knuckle. The freewheeling circle of diamonds danced, throwing sharp darts of color against the ceiling. He glanced at her. "Aw, please don't cry." He rubbed away her tears with both thumbs. "I can't hardly take that."

Attempting a smile, she asked, "It's too soon. Isn't it too soon?" The look on his face told her she was wrong, as far as he was concerned. "Okay. I love it, and I love you, so to hell with too soon." He smiled, dimples and all. "What would you have done if I didn't love you?"

"Besides dying, you mean?" he asked, then shrugged. "Put it on your right hand, and we'd have been fast friends forever. I didn't mean that about dying. I know how much that frightens you. I swear I didn't mean to say that. I promise I will not try that again. Ever. I've given it a lot of thought. If you can love a beat-up relic like me, the least I can do is think enough of myself and you to show you some respect."

What an odd thing for him to say. She threw her arms around his neck and wept. He gave up trying to shush her and held her until she finished. Later, she snuggled into the curve of his arm, drew the covers over both of them, and lay quietly. It was a long time before she realized he was asleep.

Carefully she rose, lifted his legs onto the couch, placed a pillow under his head, and tucked him in with a kiss on each cheek. The action brought a feeling of total contentment that frightened her with its power. Too much hope could tempt the fates, and they just might slap her down once again. She'd lost one man she loved. She couldn't bear to lose another.

She left him and went to fill the stove with wood. Returning, she removed the cushions from the chair, laid them on the floor beside him, and went to sleep there, her hand resting on his arm so she could feel the warmth and heat of his presence.

A harsh buzzing awoke her. The phone. She sat up, reached to the desk, and picked it up. It was cold, the sun just coming over the mountains to paint the sky in pale wintery shades of blue and pink.

"Yes? Who is this?" Christmas day. No one calls on Christmas day but family, and there was none.

Except....

The woman's voice grated. Hang up on the bitch. After what she did to Glen, she dared call here?

"What do you want?"

Glen raised his head and peered at her. He mouthed, I love you. She only halfway listened to Julia's rant.

"I want to speak to my brother."

"I'm sorry, he's not here."

"You're lying. I know he is."

She stared at the phone a moment, then reached behind and pulled the jack out. Let her glance slide back to Glen whose somber expression flew apart. He tried to rise, cried out, and fell backward onto the couch.

She ran to him.

"Fuck," he yelled and arched his back, fists bunched in knots.

"Oh, God, what is it?"

His mouth was drawn tightly over his teeth, but the muscles in his arms and back relaxed. "Shit," he gasped. "I don't know."

Beside him on the couch, she rubbed his back.

After several deep breaths, he gave her a reassuring nod. "Better. It's better now."

"What happened?"

"I'm not sure." He panted, wiping away sweat from his forehead. "Like someone was burning me, like when they... damn." He massaged one thigh.

"Your leg hurts?" She spread her fingers alongside his, helped him rub the tight muscle.

He lay back, closed his eyes. Sighed once and began to talk in that voice she'd grown used to, the remembering one. "They kept us in cages most of the time, like animals. They'd tease us with food, see how we'd react, then when we were almost starved, they'd burn us when we went for a scrap of moldy bread."

She continued to stroke his leg and let him talk. Every word tore another chunk from her.

"I lay there on my face in the stinking mud." He was someplace else now, not in the cage, and he gazed at the ceiling intently for a moment, then put the back of his hand against his forehead. In the dim light, she saw the white jagged line that ran a few inches up his arm.

He began over. "I lay there on my face in the stinking mud. Men groaned, I could hear one choking. They were dying all around me. Then I heard, far away, a sound I knew, and I raised to look. An A-4 roared across the paddies throwing up a rooster tail, smoke trailed as she moved away. God, it was beautiful. I remember thinking the pilot was crazy. But then who wouldn't be when beauty and life and death and ugliness had been wrapped up in one package."

His hand dropped to the pillow, and with a deep breath, he closed his eyes. She watched him for a long while, hand moving over his thigh, but he didn't move. When he did, he seemed all right, though he was pale around his eyes and lips.

"We could run you to the hospital. Make sure you're okay."

"On Christmas day? No deal. Shit, there wouldn't be anyone there, anyway. Besides, I'm fine now. Just one of those reflexive things, I guess."

She sank down beside him, caressed his face, then leaned forward and kissed him. His lips responded, and she put her arms around him, a bit frightened about what had happened, but he seemed okay now. In spite of herself, her mind wandered to what he'd told her. In cages like animals. How had he survived? How had anyone? And worse, where were the others still left behind? Dead by now? She couldn't imagine the horror and despair. And the god-awful truth that men were still over there made it even worse to imagine. What was wrong with this country?

"Who was that?" he asked. "You didn't seem very happy."

He must not have heard her remark that he wasn't there, so she lied. They had never told him about what Julia had done to him. Spencer said he would either remember it or he wouldn't, and so there was no need to mention it.

"A wrong number. Some kid wanted to talk to his grandpa. Hope he gets the right number." She shivered. "Let's go up to the house. Spend Christmas with me. That is why you came, isn't it?"

"Thought maybe I ought to go see my sister."

Oh, shit. Now what? Tell him the truth and hurt him, ruin Christmas and much more for him?

"I haven't seen her since…" He tilted his head, frowned and studied her. "…funny I can't remember the last time."

"It was that night… when I found you in the shower. Honey, I hate to tell you this, but your sister…."

"My sister what? *She* did that to me?" Dawning of the truth must have hit him like a bullet to the stomach. She thought for a moment he would flash back, but he held on. Muttered, "My God, Katie. No."

"I'm so sorry. Spencer says she thought she was doing what was right. She was afraid you would—"

"Go crazy again. She doesn't understand. This shit has been so hard on her."

"She asked us to take you away. She was afraid."

His expression was one of anguish, and she hugged him tighter. "I love you so much, Glen."

"So did she… once." He stiffened, drew away from her. "Loved me, raised me, took care of me." His shoulders heaved, and he covered his face with both hands.

All she could do was put an arm around his shoulders and let him cry. At last, he allowed her to pull his head down against her chest and hold him. What would she have done had he pushed her away?

"Poor Julia," he finally said.

She kept quiet. Poor Julia indeed. The woman could have killed him and appeared to have no remorse. "Spend Christmas with me. I'll cook. I know that isn't too reassuring, but I can manage to make something good." She pulled his hands away and kissed his forehead, each cheek and then his lips. "I'm all alone, you're all alone, and it doesn't make sense when we can spend it together.

"Okay, sounds good," he said. "Sorry about that. Just hit me all wrong. Yes, let's go up to your house. I'd like to be with you today."

"Let me set the electric heat so the water doesn't freeze down here. Need help?"

"What? Oh, no. I can manage." He glanced at her. "How'd you get down here? I didn't see the van."

"I walked down, but I'd like to ride back up with you, if it's okay."

"Sure thing."

Since the revelations about Julia, he'd been so formal with her. Katherine hoped this wouldn't hurt him so much he'd crawl back into his shell. That would be a tragedy after he'd come so far in the past two months.

At the house, she had him back his car up near the door so that when he got out he wouldn't have to cross the gravel drive. Turning her back to him, she took her time opening the door to give him a chance to get into the wheelchair. They were going to have a talk about his hesitancy to let her see how he handled himself, but now wasn't the time.

Inside, he took a look around at the rustic décor. "This is nice. I like the way you rocked that entire wall where the fireplace is, all the way to the roofline. The open beams are beautiful, and I like the hardwood floors." He rolled around through the living room and into the country kitchen. "Wow."

She put her hands on the back of the chair to halt the jerking motion. "Glen, please stop."

He didn't look at her. "Stop what?"

"Whatever this is. If you're angry at me about Julia, just let me know. I can take your anger, but not this... this condescension."

"Oh, hell, I'm not angry with you, Katie. I'm just disappointed you and Spencer kept it from me. Is there anything else you're not telling me? Like maybe I acted crazy out there?"

"No, I held you in my arms, and you were fine. Sweetheart, you were so fragile. You could have died if no one had found you, and we didn't think you should have to deal with that while you're working so hard to rebuild your life. You've had to deal with being abandoned by your country, your wife, and now your sister. It's just too much."

"Fragile? Katie."

She dropped to her knees beside the chair. "I couldn't bear to see you hurt anymore. I just couldn't. You are not... were not fragile. Poor choice of words. You are probably the toughest man I've ever known. It's just that you've struggled so hard. I guess I wanted to protect you. If that was wrong, then I'm sorry."

"If I'm so tough, why can't I get up out of this chair? I swear to you, I want that more than anything. I want it so you and I can have a normal life. Please believe me."

"I do believe you. I really do. The diagnosis doesn't mean you consciously do not want to walk. It means your brain can't connect with your being able to walk. You were kept in a cage for so many years. You keep working at it, and one day the connection will be made."

She laid her head in his lap. "Want to see the room I was telling Spencer about?"

"Yes, sure. But listen, Katie. If the day comes when you can no longer take... well, you know, and you feel just like Julia, please let me know. Please don't just walk away. I couldn't take that, but I will understand if you talk to me about it. This stuff is not easy to deal with."

"I'll deal with it, because I don't want to lose you. How's that?"

He laid his hand on her cheek. "I'm going to work as hard as I can to get over this."

"Okay, enough of that. Let's look at your room." She rose and took him past the round dining table through a door that led off the kitchen to a sunroom on the west side of the house. It was bright and warm. "Stan built it and put in all the windows to warm the house during the winter. There are lots of plants out here now so it looks like a greenhouse, but those can be hung in other places. See, there's a bed. I've been sleeping down here 'cause I couldn't bear to sleep in our bedroom. He built a washroom along the back so when he came in from working he could clean up there. It also has a walk-in shower and commode besides the deep sink. We could easily put bars in there and fix the shower so you could access it. Also, we can hang a bar from that beam above the bed so you can move around, get in and out of bed without help." She paused, studied his expression of enjoyment. "Not that I mind helping you at all. It's just I know you'd rather be independent."

He moved around under the hanging plants, a purple bougainvillea trailing blossoms.

"Smells good in here. Nice and bright, too. Must be hot in the summer, though."

"No, we have those roll out awnings along the outside wall, plus there are a lot of trees that help keep it cool. And we could put in an air conditioner if it's still too warm." Amazing how badly she wanted him to move in here where they could be together. But would he want that? Perhaps he wasn't yet ready to share his life with her.

"I still have rehab three times a week. I'd have to drive in."

She laughed. "Well, you could be like everyone else who prefers to live in the country. It'd be like driving in to work and back, only you'd just have to do it three times a week."

"Well, that's a thought, isn't it? But we need to talk about some things you'd have to deal with... I mean, I'd be ashamed to ask you to—"

She rose from the floor. "Let's go in the living room. I'll build a fire, and we can talk there."

The dry wood was soon crackling. The fan came on, spreading warmth through the room. She sank into a nearby chair and reached out to him.

He went to be beside her, taking her hand in both his. "Now—"

"Wait, I have something to say before you tell me what you're ashamed of. There is nothing you would need from me that you should be ashamed of. You are a hero, a brave and gentle man, the man I love. There is nothing I wouldn't do for you, and I'm sure you feel the same way about me. Don't you?" She peered at him.

"Of course, but—"

"But nothing. Tonight we are going to crawl in that bed out there in the sunroom and make love. I've never been with any man except Stan, so I don't have a whole lot of guys to compare you to, but I have to tell you, I look forward to another night with you. I can't wait to see what you can do when you don't have one arm tied down."

"What will you do if I have to piss in the middle of the night?"

"Stan broke his ankle once."

"That's interesting, but what's the point."

"When he had to piss, as you so quaintly put it, in the middle of the night, he figured out he could cut the top off a gallon milk jug and set it by the bed. Then in the morning, he'd empty it in the bathroom."

"Well, do you have an empty gallon milk jug?"

"No, but I can find you a substitute."

"You're so smart, think you have it all figured out, don't you?"

"I'm smart enough to figure most stuff out."

"Okay, this one is harder. I have nightmares, often, and if you touch me or wake me, I might come up swinging. Not on purpose, it's just a reaction. How fast can you duck?"

"Guess I'll have to take my chances with that."

"Oh, God, Katie, if I were to hurt you I couldn't stand it."

"Are they bad? Isn't there anything they can do?"

"Short of a lobotomy? No, afraid not."

She cupped his face in both palms.

"Don't cry, please. Just don't cry." His own eyes were moist, the firelight reflecting in their gold streaks.

"I'm doing my damnedest not to, but this is difficult."

"If I agree to stay here, you have to promise to stop feeling sorry for me. It's hard enough not feeling sorry for myself, but I work at it."

She sniffed and wiped wet eyes. "Okay, if you'll give this a try, I promise I'll try to stop crying for you. I can't help it. Just thinking of you having to go through those things makes me so sad, then I get mad, and when I'm mad I usually cry."

He grinned. "Oh, so you're saying you don't cry 'cause you feel sorry for me, you cry cause you're mad at me?"

"Of course not, silly. Mad at the conditions that allowed that to happen to you. I want to get my hands on someone, any politician would do, and squeeze the life right out of him."

"I expect I can't move in until the work is done on the room. I'll be glad to pay for that. The government paid me a lot of money for the years I spent in those cages. Nice of them, wasn't it?"

"The bastards," she said.

"The fucking sons a bitches," he echoed.

"I'll not try to out cuss a sailor." She chuckled and was happy to hear him join her.

TEN

"ARE THERE CANDLES?"

Katie turned from whipping potatoes. "There, in the bottom of the sideboard on your right. Candles? That's romantic."

He dug around through piles of linen napkins, a stash of spare dishes, and a pile of pot holders. Looked up at her with that incredible smile, dimples and all. "You sure they're in here?"

"Yep, you're getting warm. To the right, now back a bit." She tasted the mashed potatoes. "Got 'em?"

"Finally. Of course I'm a romantic, but you, my sweet, could really use a housekeeper."

"You volunteering for the job, 'cause I will hire you on the spot. I think the candle holders are up on that shelf. Oops, I'll get them." She moved quickly to his side, reached above her head, and found a crystal set.

Her breast brushed the side of his head. "Mmm. Nice." He ran a hand along the inside of her thigh. "Ooh, good."

"Look out, big boy."

"Or what?"

"Dinner will burn is what." She gave him a quick kiss on the mouth, but didn't give him time to respond, handed him the candle holders and went back to finish dishing up their Christmas dinner.

"It sure smells good in here."

"Good thing I keep the freezer stocked. I don't even remember buying that rotisseried chicken, but it sure came in handy. Wonder why I bought it."

"You knew I was coming. Do we need anything else on the table?"

She turned off the oven and removed the baking dish holding the chicken. "Wine and glasses."

He whirled in a neat circle. "Most definitely. Where?"

"I'll get the glasses, there's a bottle of wine in the pantry on the bottom shelf. I think it's chardonnay. Will that do or do you prefer beer, being a jock and all?"

When he didn't reply, she turned to see him staring out the window. "What?"

"There's a man in the yard with a gun. What's he doing? Get down, Katie. Down." He launched himself from the chair, caught her below the hips, and brought her to the floor. The wine glasses shattered all around them, flashing shards of light. Outside the rifle went off once, then twice, and Glen covered her body with his. His breath sucked in and out against her ear, he trembled, but held on. "Lay still. Don't move."

"Damn fool hunter. Deer season closed last week." He hadn't been imagining it after all.

He continued to hold on, then said, "I lost my rifle, do you have yours?"

"Glen, honey?" She tried to roll him off her, but he was determined to keep her pinned down.

"Hsst, be quiet. He'll hear you."

"It's okay. It's just a hunter. Let me up, please. Glen, let me up."

"Hmm? What the hell? I'm sorry." He pushed up with both arms and rolled off her. "Are you hurt? Did I hurt you?"

"No, I'm fine. Be careful there's glass everywhere. Don't get cut." Blood seeped from the side of her hand, and when she sat up, he saw it. "You're hurt. I'll get… dammit." He gazed up at her with a dumbfounded look in his eyes. "Could you give me a hand here?"

She helped him sit, then rose to her feet and wheeled the chair over beside him, released the arm nearest so he could get a hold and lift himself up. Once he was in the chair, she went to the door, threw it open, and shouted at the man in the yard.

"What do you think you're doing, shooting in my yard?"

"Hell, I aimed away from your house. They's a whole herd out yonder."

"This is private property. Please leave now, or I'll call the sheriff."

"You don't need to get so huffy. I'm a going."

Glen pushed her aside and shouted, "Hey, asshole. Next time you come around here with a gun get ready to get shot at."

"Glen, no. Don't—"

"What? He's trespassing. Gonna get himself shot or shoot somebody."

She shut the door, and the man, who had whirled to glare at them, trotted down the hill toward the road. A moment later, a truck roared to life and took off.

"Well, that was exciting." She hugged herself.

"Hey, sorry," Glen said, and took her hand. "Get a paper towel, and I'll clean up your hand. Is it bad?"

She stuck it under the faucet and turned the water on. "No, it's not bad." It burned, and she pulled a paper towel off the rack above the sink and handed it to him.

"Let me see."

"It's just a flesh wound." Because he sounded so worried, she lightened her tone.

After he patted on it awhile, the cut stopped bleeding.

"Come on, sweetie, it's okay. Let's eat before dinner gets cold."

He remained silent as they cleaned up the broken glass and finished putting the food on the table. She poured the wine and lifted her glass.

He sat still for a moment. "And that's what it's like to live with me. You still sure you want me here?"

"I have a toast. Get your glass."

He picked it up, and she raised hers, "Through sickness and health, for better or worse, together forever."

She hoped he didn't think she was being too mushy.

"Okay, but you're getting the raw end of the deal."

They clinked, drank, and then started eating.

"Yeah? Well, just wait until you're seventy and I'm eighty, see who has the raw end of the deal then."

He ignored the remark and picked up his plate. "I need more of those mashed potatoes and gravy. And another slice of breast meat. I've always been a breast man, myself."

"My amazing breasts, in particular?"

"Of course."

"Want more bread while you're at it?"

"Sure." He winked, reached out a hand.

Relieved they had made their way past the frightening incident, she took herself another slice of bread, buttered it, then passed the butter to him. "Sorry I'm not a better cook."

"Sorry? This is the best meal I've had since I left the farm."

Abruptly, before that subject could be opened, she said, "I love a man who likes to eat."

He shoveled a forkful of potatoes dripping with gravy into his mouth. Swallowed, then added, "As good a reason as any. So happens I love a woman who isn't too picky who she loves."

After dinner, he helped her carry the dishes to the kitchen and stacked them in the dishwasher after she scraped each one clean.

They went into the living room and settled in front of the fire, each with another glass of wine.

"Hey, I forgot your Christmas present." She set down her glass, ran to the closet, and took out two gold wrapped, beribboned packages. "Sorry I didn't have a tree to put this under." She set them in his lap, and he placed his glass beside hers.

His face lit up when he unwrapped the box containing the silver gray Stetson and immediately screwed it on his head. Then he ripped the paper off the jeans and shirts. "Wow. How'd you know my size? These are great. I was dreading going shopping, but I was just about naked."

"I noticed. As for your size, well I thought you would probably be putting on some weight, so I bought a size larger than the jeans and shirt you wore home from the hospital. Hope they'll fit."

They finished their wine, and he sighed. "This has been my best day in a long while, despite my little showing in the kitchen earlier. Reckon I'd better get on back to the hospital before they send out a search party."

"Oh, I didn't know you had a curfew. I'd hoped you'd stay the night."

He studied his knuckles, restacked the jeans and shirts, then glanced at her. "Better not. I don't want you to have to take care of me, Katie. And nighttime is the worst. There are things… I wonder if maybe I ought to get someone to do those things until I get to where I can."

"No," she said, louder than she intended. "I don't want someone taking care of you who doesn't really care for you like I do. Oh, that didn't make sense, but you know what I mean. Dammit, why are you so stubborn about this? I've told you and told you—"

"And I've told you. You're not going to be my nursemaid."

"You are the most exasperating man I ever met."

"And how many men have you got to know well enough to know that?"

She stared at him a moment, sitting there in his fancy new hat, glaring at her with those gorgeous eyes, perplexed and frowning, and she giggled. Like some damn teenager.

He tilted his head, stared back at her, then grinned and said softly, "Did we just have our first fight?"

"No," she said. "We just had our last fight. Now, let's go take a shower and go to bed."

"The hell I... let's take a shower?"

"Yep, let's. I think I've got a chair upstairs you can use, and I'll wash your back if you'll wash mine, and even some other parts, if you so desire."

"You know what?"

"What?"

"A man would be a fool to turn that down."

"You damn well better believe it."

The shower lasted until the hot water ran out. Starting with his hair, she dried him briskly, double folded the towel in the seat of the wet wheelchair before helping him into it, then pulled a dry towel off the rack and handed it to him.

"Now dry me, and don't miss anything."

One thing led to another and they barely made it to the bed.

"I sleep nude. How about you?" she asked.

"Oh, me, too. Of course. Always."

Nothing in her life had prepared her for the joyous free feeling of lying deep within his love. An eternity would not be long enough for her to hold that sensation. She would never let him go. The rhythm of their movements matched her soaring thoughts. If she opened her eyes, she would see sparks crackling into the air from their bare skin, lighting the room like fireflies on a summer night. And it was the end of the world, it was the beginning of the world, all exploding in a blinding flash of passion. Nothing mattered but that very instant.

She came down slowly, as if awakening from a dream, and he lay beside her on one hip, his fingers working through her hair, and his head propped on his other hand so he could see her face.

"Honey, I wish…." His voice soft, trailing off into the darkness.

Fingertips over his lips, she silenced the wish. "Hush. No wishes, no more. Not now. They've all come true right here, right now. Put your arms around me, and hold me. I won't lose you. We're—"

He quieted her with a tender kiss while love flames leaped within his half-closed eyes.

Before he fell asleep, she snuggled up against him. "You need anything, you wake me, you hear? What is it you military guys say, 'I've got your back?' Well, I have. And there's a jug just under the bed on your side, in case you need to piss."

"My God, Katie, I love you."

Arms wrapped around her, he fell asleep.

ELEVEN

SOMETIME IN THE dark of night, Glen howled, his body bowed double, sending her rolling away. Before she could scramble back to him he convulsed.

Immediately alert, shaking so hard she could scarcely do so, she dialed the operator and asked for an ambulance. She had no idea what to do for him, other than make sure he didn't hurt himself. The ambulance took twenty minutes to get there, and she died a thousand deaths. The convulsions eased off before they arrived, and she was able to hold him. When boots pounded across the porch, she yelled at them to come in. Since hers was the only light, they'd had no trouble finding her.

The EMTs went to work on him immediately. The tall gangly one recognized Glen from the previous call out at the Tanner farm. "Same thing, ma'am?"

"No, not at all. He had some kind of terrible pain that bowed his body, then he went into convulsions. Can you take him to Vets hospital?"

"Yes, ma'am."

Whatever they did for him quieted him, and he reached out blindly, called her name.

"I'm right here. May I take his hand?"

"Let us get him settled in the ambulance. You can ride along and keep him calm, if you'd like."

"Yes, please. I'll put on some clothes." She had managed to throw on a robe in the middle of all the uproar, so she hurried into the jeans and sweatshirt she'd discarded when they showered. "What do you think is happening to him? He was doing so well, but he did have a pain earlier Christmas Eve. It lasted a few minutes, and he said he had a burning sensation in his legs."

"Hard to tell. He's stabilizing now, so let's get him loaded up."

He mumbled her name again.

"Come along then," the EMT said. He followed the stretcher into the back of the ambulance, then reached out to help her in, and seated her next to Glen. She gathered his hand in both hers.

"I'm here, sweetheart. Hang in there. You'll be okay."

He didn't answer, but his hand squeezed hers.

It began to rain before the doors were closed, sheets of water that could turn to ice at any moment, it was so cold. Maybe they'd make it to town before the highway froze over. The heavy semi traffic should keep it clear, at least for a while.

She barely controlled herself, peering into his pale features. So still, so drawn. What could be wrong?

At the highway, the ambulance slithered up onto the pavement and barreled down the road. Sitting in the back, blind to their route, she imagined where they were as they rocketed along. Ages, years, eons passed before she sensed the turn off Highway 71 and through the gates of Veterans Hospital. The siren wound down, the back doors were jerked open, and she was jostled outside so they could unload the stretcher, drop the legs, and race him through the emergency room doors.

Spencer was there, the shoulders of his corduroy jacket wet, and his hair gleaming with drops of icy water. She'd never been so glad to see anyone as she was the laconic doctor. He nodded at her, said, "Wait here, please. I'll talk to you in a moment. Doctor Radnor is waiting. Be right back."

He followed the stretcher through double doors that swung closed, leaving her standing there, forehead against their cold metal, fists hard balls at her waist. Perhaps she was losing her mind, for she noticed the strangest of things. Her jeans, wet from the knees down. Her bare feet. Wet footprints along the hallway floor. Muddy boot prints left by the EMTs.

Oh, dear God, help him, she prayed and rubbed at her goose-pimpled flesh. Despite God's abandonment, praying was all she could think of to do, so she kept it up, eyes gazing at the floor.

Please don't take him away from me. Don't you dare.

Spencer's black Oxfords halted.

She raised her head, terrified, forced back a sob, and held on rigidly to a tiny shred of sanity.

He gave her a weary smile. "Been a long, hard night, hasn't it?" He studied his clipboard, nodded.

She had no energy left to scream at him, so she waited.

"Doctor Radnor wants to run some tests in the morning. Meanwhile, Glen is sleeping, and everything is fine. He'll be all right, Katherine."

"Spencer," she uttered in a ragged voice.

He took her hand. "Come on, stay with me a moment more. How long has he been having this pain?"

"Christmas Eve, but then he said it was gone. Who knows? Then we're in bed, both asleep, and he screams, and his body arches almost double. Then he goes into convulsions." She clutched at his sleeve. "What's happening to him?

From the speakers. Code Blue, Code Blue. Room 177.

She clawed at him.

"No, Katherine. Not him. Settle down."

"Someone is dying." Helpless to stop the panic. On her feet. Nurses hurried along the hallway. Not him, but someone. She should care. She did care, yet she thanked God it wasn't him.

Spencer took her by the shoulders. "Hang on. People die in hospitals. That's what some of them come here to do. Not Glen. He's here to live. Stop it, now. Listen to me."

Dizzy, close to passing out, she sank back in the chair.

"He's perceiving pain that, medically, isn't there. Oh, he hurts, but like his other problems, it's his brain trying to make connections it hasn't made in years. I'd guess he's fighting a battle between functioning again or shutting down all the way. When did you two get back together?"

"He came out Christmas Eve, gave me a ring, he stayed the night, we spent the day together. Had Christmas dinner. Made love. Then this." She gestured wildly.

"I know it's hard to believe, but the pain is actually a hopeful sign. I don't suppose it would do for you to try to go back home in this storm. He's in ICU, so you'll have to use one of the couches in the waiting room. I'll see you tomorrow."

"Bye," she muttered at his retreating back. "Could walk home, I guess." A giggle warned she was close to hysteria. Deep breaths. Take deep breaths.

Only those waiting to die or waiting for someone else to die were left awake. Shiny hallway underfoot, bare feet squeaking, she went in search of an empty couch and curled up on it.

Lush grass, green and cool, stroked her bare skin as she ran through the warm-bath glow of a spring sun. Glen ran behind her, calling out, laughing. He caught up, grabbed her around the waist, and dragged her down into a bed of clover, sending bees swarming. His mouth on hers, his body welded against her.

His life, his love, hers to cherish.

Someone shook her. Coffee perking. Grease getting hot.

"Wake up, Katherine. Come on, wake up."

Her eyes opened to the frowning countenance of Doctor Spencer.

"I gotta tell you. That outfit is by far the nicest thing you've worn here to date."

"Stuff it, Spencer. It's not funny. How is he? Is Radnor here yet?"

"We took him out of ICU and Doctor Radnor is running some tests. I thought you might want to go down and get some breakfast, clean up a bit. We'll let you know something as soon as we can."

After a hurried breakfast she didn't taste, she returned to the waiting room. No one was around, so she crept down the hall until she came to a door standing ajar and heard Spencer's voice. She padded up to peer inside. A nurse had given her some hospital slippers so she didn't feel quite so ratty.

"It'll be up to him now," an unknown voice that must be Doctor Radnor said. "Depends on how he gets along with the therapy, but I think this fellow is trying his best to recover." He patted Glen on the shoulder. "Work hard, young man, and I'll keep in touch with your therapist."

Though she couldn't see Glen's face through the narrow crack, his voice came through clear. "I intend to, sir. Thank you."

Unable to contain herself any longer, she burst into the room. Two doctors, a nurse, and Glen all turned surprised looks her way.

"Sorry, I couldn't stay away."

Grinning, Glen held out a hand, and she pushed her way to his side. "Some people will do anything to get attention." She kissed him on the cheek. Last night's fear escaped from her, left hollow spaces that immediately filled with joy and relief until she thought she would burst.

"When you finish here, Katherine," Spencer said, "I'd like to see you in my office." The succinct request sent a niggling of apprehension through her, but she pushed it away. He'd not ruin their happiness with his dramatic attitude.

It was almost noon before she kept her appointment with Spencer, for she found herself unable to leave Glen's side. Exhausted, he finally fell asleep. Her own clock was running down, and she fell into the chair across from Spencer's desk.

Not one to beat about the bush, he hit her between the eyes with his announcement.

"Ellie's called the hospital three times since Glen went home."

"What has that to do with me? What am I supposed to do about it? I don't understand what difference it could possibly make to Glen and me."

"She'll find out he's back. Someone, one of the nurses, will tell her. I just thought under the circumstances, you should know. What are you two planning?" He gestured at the glittering ring on her finger.

"Well, that's something I wanted to speak to you about. Glen wants to stay with me during his therapy sessions. He likes the room, and it can be remodeled for his needs. He wants to travel back and forth." She smiled. "He's going to pretend he has a job. No different from many of us out in the boonies who work in town."

Spencer studied her, drummed his fingertips on the desk. "You are aware of his feelings about Ellie. They are divorced, but that doesn't change anything in his mind. And I doubt the Veterans Administration would approve your place for the work."

"Neither of those things matter. You put me on this road, Spencer. What did you think would happen when I began to work with him?"

"I didn't expect you to fall in love with him."

"No, but you knew he would become dependent on me. Don't tell me you didn't."

He held up both hands. "Okay, I'll admit that. He needed someone he could trust, and apparently, he trusts you. Who wouldn't? He's telling you things he never has told me. But back to Ellie. She won't go away."

"I don't care. He does not want to hear her name, let alone see her. And he and I both have the money to do the remodeling. We don't need the VA's approval unless it would somehow affect his getting his therapy here."

Spencer let out an explosive sigh. "Katherine, are you sure of this? I mean it's a big step, and he needs expert help until he recovers."

"Yes, we had our first and last fight over that. I can learn how to take care of him. I refuse to let someone—a stranger—take care of him when I can do it. While he's in therapy, I can learn what I need to do for him."

"But you fought over it?"

"Not that much. He said what he thought, I said what I thought, and that settled that."

Spencer laughed. "Yes, I'll just bet it did. Does he know how stubborn you can be?"

"He's learned." She rose from the chair. "I love him. I want to help him. You know I can do it."

"You're sure it's love and not compassion—pity?"

"I know the difference, Spencer. Of course, I'm sorry as hell for what happened to him. But it goes way beyond that. I'm not ignorant, and I'm not a kid."

"What about your art classes? And the exhibit? You'll need to prepare for that."

"How did you know about that? I haven't told anyone except Dr. Endlebeck I'd accepted the invitation to enter my work to be juried."

"Endlebeck told me. We are both so pleased. I'd hate to see you give that up. You could grow to resent Glen."

"I can do both. He is anxious to become self-reliant. I want him to feel good about himself again. Besides, he wants to continue with his own art. He's talented, and he can work with me when he's not in therapy."

Spencer gave up that tack. "I can see you're set on this."

"I think it's time you explained what I should expect, what Glen will have to go through now. How much recovery Radnor expects."

"The next few months will be crucial. He may go through several of these attacks similar to what you witnessed last night. Physically, we could expect nearly complete recovery, except for the damaged leg, but there's no telling when it comes to his mental state. A healthy man his age, even though he has remained inactive, it would be safe to say that in six months with hard work, he can be on his feet walking, maybe not unaided. When he returned, he was walking some, but the leg, hell, they really ripped it up to keep him from running. At first, it'll be worse than a baby learning to walk. He'll want to give up a thousand times. It won't be easy. And he'll need you more than ever. You'll have to give him everything you can. Are you sure you want to do this?"

"Of course. I can continue to paint. It's not like he's a helpless invalid. He's been at my place for two days and nights, and we managed quite well."

"You have not considered his emotional condition. I can't make you any promises. He lived for a reason, and that was to come back to get Ellie for what she did to him. You might make the difference. Hell, I wish I could say for sure."

"And you wonder if I can handle it?"

"No, I'm sure you can. But not with her threats hanging over your every move. He'll have to face that sooner or later. You can't continue to shut her out, because she does exist, and I don't think I can stop her doing what she wants if she takes a notion."

"You mean, she might be able to control Glen's treatment?"

"No, of course not. They are legally divorced, but she can cause a lot of trouble, if she's a mind to, and it seems she is."

"Give me her telephone number, address, whatever. We'll see about this. I'll take care of it. When is his first therapy appointment?"

"His therapist is off for the holidays. I'll have him call and set up Glen's appointments as soon as he returns."

"Do you think he'll have any more of those attacks?"

"He could, but now that he knows what's going on, probably not. Doctor Radnor can tell you how to handle that, since you're going to be Glen's caregiver."

"Okay, I'll go sit with him until the doctor can speak to us about it. Then I'm going to take him home with me where he belongs. Wait. I don't have the van. I rode in the ambulance with him."

He came out from behind the desk. "I'll take you both home. Katherine, are you absolutely sure of this?"

"Yes, I am. Thank you, Spencer. I appreciate all you've done for him, for us. You've gone way beyond your call of duty."

"Glad to do it. I'm very fond of both of you. Let me know when you're ready, and I'll get someone to take any appointments I might have."

PART
THREE

...Until the fight is done;

ONE

AFTER DOCTOR SPENCER dropped them off and declined an invitation to come in for coffee, she got Glen settled and he fell asleep within minutes. She continued to lie beside him for a while, then eased her hand from his and went upstairs to her bedroom to make the phone call she did not want him to hear.

On the other end, the telephone buzzed monotonously. She wanted to hang up before anyone answered. After all, what could she say to this woman? God, she was so nervous she needed a written script. Before she could put the phone in its cradle, a slurred, impatient voice questioned a hello.

"Ellie Tanner, please." Her voice wobbled and she cleared her throat.

"Yes, this is me... I mean, that's me. Who is this?"

"You don't know me. I'm calling for Doctor Spencer at Veteran's Hospital. It's about Glen Tanner." Every word poured out before she gulped audibly.

"What about him? Did he die?"

The bitch sounded hopeful. "No, just in case you were worried. However, his doctors feel it's very important to his recovery that you break off any contact. He does not want to see you; in fact, the idea upsets him greatly and could hinder his recovery. I hope you'll consider what he's been through and leave him be." Get a life, you bitch.

"Just who are you, anyway? What is this all about? What did you say your name is?"

Katherine paused. She wasn't about to give her name to this woman she'd learned to hate without even meeting her. "I didn't and it doesn't matter. I've delivered the message. Do you intend to leave us alone?"

Harsh laughter rolled through the wires. "I get it. You must be nuts. Taking up with a loony just cause he's got money." A long pause while she sucked on a cigarette, blew out the smoke. "It is the money, isn't it? That old prune of a sister of his die or something? Glen inherited everything? Well, you can plain forget it. I'm getting a share for being married to that loony, even if we are divorced. You hear me? You hear?"

Katherine squeezed the receiver and closed her eyes. "I think you'd better remember you deserted him while he was in Vietnam. You can forget getting a thin dime."

"Hear that he's mad as a hatter. Can't even write his name, the way I hear it. Besides, I didn't leave him, he left me to rot with that pruny sister of his. Jesus, him and his precious duty to country."

Quivering with rage, Katherine slammed the phone down. So much for that. She wadded the paper with Ellie's number and address on it in her damp palm, started to throw it away, then dropped it in the drawer of the bedside table. Maybe she could cool off enough to try again. If Ellie caused any trouble, she would have no choice.

Glen called to her, and she ran downstairs, stuck her head in the room she already thought of as his. "You okay, sweetie?"

"Sorry to bother you. Were you going to sleep in here tonight?"

"Sure. Until we get the room equipped, it would be a good idea, don't you think?"

He was very still for a minute.

"Is something wrong?" She snapped on the light, went to the bed.

"Do you feel like talking for a bit? I can't seem to go back to sleep."

"Of course." She had changed out of her damp clothes into a warm velour gown, and she crawled across the mattress and lay down next to him. "Would you like to turn over?"

"Yes, please."

She helped him roll onto his side facing her and went into his arms. "There, is that better?"

"I know you must be tired." He sounded worn out himself.

"Not too tired to talk or anything else you might like to do." She kissed him and snuggled her head against his chest.

"Afraid even my hard can't get on tonight. Wore it out or something."

"Or something is right. You've had quite an adventure. It'll be back." She waited for him to go on. He certainly had something on his mind and was having a tough time saying it.

"God, I hope so."

"Sweetheart, if you're worried about what happened, don't be. You heard what the doctors said. I know this was scary, but it's a good sign."

"Do you really believe that? I feel like I've fallen down a bottomless pit and can't climb out. Every time I start doing well, something happens. I think they're sugar coating this whole thing. I don't think I'm going to get better. I'm afraid I'm getting worse."

She leaned back to look him in the eyes, cupped a hand around the side of his face. "No, that's not true. Don't let those thoughts get ahold of you." He closed his eyes. "Look at me. Listen to me. You are getting better. Spencer told me you could be up and walking within six months. That this attack tells them you're overcoming whatever was holding you back. Honey, is there something specific that's bothering you? Tell me."

"I'm wondering… don't take this wrong, Katie, but I'm thinking I ought to go back in the hospital for the therapy. I don't want you to have this burden."

She started to object, but he put his fingers over her mouth. "No, hear me out. You can come see me anytime you want, and I can work through this without worrying I'm causing you to give up your life, your plans. Honey, I saw the letter about the art exhibit. You need to concentrate on turning out some paintings, and you can't do that with me hanging around always needing something."

Tears filled her eyes, leaked out and ran down her cheeks. If he did this, he would never come home. Never. And she would lose him. Worse, he would lose himself into that black hole he spoke of. No, she would not let this happen.

Who would hold him at night when he panicked?

"Don't cry, Katie. That's not fair. You know I can't…." He snugged her back up against his chest. "Oh, hell. Don't cry, don't cry, please don't cry." A mantra that broke her heart. "Don't you see, I have to do right by you. I love you so much, and if I become a burden, cause you to give up what you've always wanted, you'll resent me. I know you will. You have to let me do this my way."

She sobbed against him, tried to stop, but absolutely could not.

Until she realized he was crying, his sobs jerking his chest.

"Oh, no. Sweetheart, I'm so sorry." She sucked in a breath. "Please, I didn't mean to make you unhappy. I want you here with me, but if this is what you absolutely need to do, then, well, I'll do whatever you want. But please promise me something."

He raised his head enough to kiss her. "Anything, I'll promise you anything. What is it?"

"That you'll get well and come back to me. That I can come see you, anytime, all the time if I have to. Will you promise me, cross your heart promise me that?"

"I'll do my damnedest."

"No, that won't do. You have to promise."

"Katie?"

"Yes."

"I promise, cross my heart promise."

There was no way she could stand to let him go. It would kill her inside. How could she paint or breathe or live without him? Worse, not knowing from day to day how he looked or felt or smelled. Not seeing that smile that lit her heart.

Love was like that, wasn't it? All encompassing. Cruel. Delicious. Impossible. Demanding. Dealing with never seeing Stan again had been all she could manage. Now Glen was asking her to agree to what could be the same thing.

But she had to do it for him, because he needed it to be this way.

"When do you want to go? Your therapist won't be back until after January first. Will you stay with me until then?"

"Yes, I'll do that. Thank you. I know this is the best for both of us."

She couldn't manage a reply, nor could she fall asleep, so she held him close until he relaxed and began to breathe evenly, then she slipped from the bed and went into the living room where she curled up in her recliner and stared dry-eyed out the window. It had started to snow, big fat flakes that floated through the light shining out the window into the night.

So achingly beautiful.

By morning, a few inches of snow covered the deck and yard. She opened the front door and breathed in the cold, wet air, then went into the bedroom to be there when he woke up.

After breakfast, they bundled up and went out on the deck. Snow was so rare in this part of Arkansas as to be an event to celebrate. She gathered a handful and rubbed his face in it, then dodged his own attempt at throwing a snowball at her. They said very little, except an occasional pointing out of something beautiful. When he began to shiver, they went back inside where she made hot chocolate, carried it into the living room, and they settled in front of the fireplace.

She did not want to mention his leaving, and it seemed he didn't either, so she made a big dinner.

At the table, he gathered a napkin across his lap, looked over the platter of fried chicken, baked sweet potatoes, biscuits, and salad and said, "You keep this up, I'll get fat. Please pass the chicken."

While he ate, she played with small amounts of food, but didn't really taste the few bites she took. Somehow, she had to get past this feeling of despair. She wanted what he needed for himself. But in the dark of night, when he was terrified of a nightmare, who would hold his hand? Who would kiss him when he awoke panicked and drenched in sweat? Thinking he had awakened in that damned cage. Somehow, she had to push these thoughts aside. He'd gotten along without her for a year locked up in that place, he could surely make it through six months, especially if she visited him often. At this moment, watching him enjoy his dinner, that seemed like an eternity. She was afraid it would be for him, too.

He was still so very tired from the events of the previous day that he wanted to take a nap after he ate. She went with him, helped him get settled, then lay down beside him, took his hand, and stared up at the ceiling while he slept. Gave herself a long talk about her own strengths and made up her mind to stay strong, no matter what.

The week flew by. They spent all their time together, talking, making love, sitting on the deck in the bright sunshine that quickly melted the snow and warmed the air. Being together. Preparing for the time when they wouldn't be.

New Year's Eve they retired early, made love, and fell asleep spooned together. It might have already been 1986 when he awoke shaking from an intense nightmare involving some of the men still trapped in their cages in Vietnam. The experience of such a horrific dream often made him come awake ready to fight, to hump through the jungle in an effort to rescue them, to climb mountains or fly again.

Expecting a session of wild, intense loving to burn up the resulting adrenalin, she kissed him and held him a moment.

He caught his breath, then told her a dreadful tale. "They left him in the cage with me after he died. Going so silently, I didn't know until later. Much later. And in the heat, the flies, the stink. I begged, but they wouldn't take him away. He rotted." He sucked his breath in and out.

"Stop now. It's over." She touched his lips, then found them with her own. Gently, carefully, lest he go back there.

At last he stopped trembling, expecting what would come next. Ready for it. He turned to her, gripped her shoulders, and captured her mouth in a fiery kiss. What he wanted, what he could not do himself, she could, and so she pushed him down, crawled on top, and straddled him. Took him roughly inside and rode him hard, his hands on her hips to urge her on until he came with a shout of despair and triumph.

For a long time after, she lay on his chest, his heart hammering in her ear, until it slowed. "Okay? Better now?"

"Yes. God, yes. You understand, don't you?"

Of course she did. Understood why he needed sex, not love, after such a debilitating experience. The human condition. She'd studied enough psychology to understand that. Fear, an adrenalin rush, screwed up the mind. Titillated the body. Often a near death experience brought on the same reaction. She dare not remind him it would be their last time to make love for a long while. Yet he knew that, for he held onto her as if he might fall off that precipice he talked about so often. What would he do without her? What would she do without him? She was terrified of the answer.

New Year's Day they discussed everything they could think of to keep their minds off the next morning when he would return to the hospital and begin his rehab. His bag was packed and waiting near the door. He would leave his car with her, which meant he could not come home unless she picked him up. The van waited outside. Everything was ready, but she could not get up from the breakfast table.

He rolled the chair backward, forward, backward again, his gaze on her. Anxious.

"I know, I know. It's time to go." Still, she nursed her coffee until the last sip grew cold in the bottom of the mug.

"Katie?"

Without looking at him, she rose, went to the closet, and took out his coat, then hers. Hands shaking, she held his while he shoved an arm in, then wrapped it around his back, waited for the other arm. It was like saying goodbye to her world, a thing she had done ten months ago and now was forced to do again. Did he know what he was asking of her? Of himself? Did he have any notion? She wanted to scream the questions at him, but remained silent, put on her coat, and went to the door. Opened it for him, picked up his bag, and followed him out into the cloudless morning. A slight breeze dried the tears on her cheeks, and she kept her head turned so he wouldn't see them. Vowed not to shed another. It was over. Done. Damned if she would cry anymore. Fed up, tired of it. There was no God, or if there was he was one hateful bastard.

She turned onto the highway before Glen spoke. "Katie, you'll come see me like before? Once a week on Friday, when you don't have classes."

"I'll talk to Spencer, get your schedule. I may have to come in the evenings. You'll probably be tied up all day every day. I'll check on weekends. If you're off then, maybe you can come home with me on Friday evening. I can take you back on Sunday evening. Would you be willing to do that?" The words all spilled out over each other. Idiotically, she blathered.

He watched her for a while. Without looking, she knew he stared at her. "Katie, I'm not punishing you. I'm trying to do what's best for both of us. Of course, I'll come home with you anytime I can get free. Anytime you want me."

"I know. I know you aren't punishing me. I'll want you… always." She shut up and drove, unable to say anymore without breaking down. He was going off to fight a battle without her. A battle she wanted so badly to help him win.

"And I'll always want you." He looked out the window, said no more.

In the deep shadows of the red brick buildings, snow patched the hospital grounds, but the parking lot and walkways had been cleared. She pulled into an empty slot, dragged his chair from the side door of the van, and opened and positioned it the way he wanted. He lowered himself easily, and before she could grab hold, raced it up the ramp to the sidewalk. She helped push up the steeper ramp to the front door and inside they went to the check-in station. Spencer's office door stood open, and he came out to greet them. Probably watched them arrive through the front windows.

"I think this is a good decision, Glen." He nodded her way. "Good morning, Katherine"

"I want to talk to you later," she said.

His eyebrows raised. "I've called Harry. You remember him? He'll take Glen to his room and get him settled."

"Fine," she said, leaned down, and kissed Glen. "I love you," she whispered, then turned and went into Spencer's office. She closed the door behind her so she wouldn't have to watch him wheeled away out of her sight. Damn Spencer. Damn them *all*.

TWO

OVER HALF AN hour passed before Spencer returned. She had left the window and sat in the chair facing his desk when he came in.

"Well, he's in good hands. His therapist is Mason Harrington. I'm sure you will meet him later. They are getting acquainted as we speak."

"And is he going to be at his bedside when he has night terrors or those hideous dreams that drive him into a panic? Is he going to crawl in bed with him and hold him until he goes back to sleep?" She had wanted to curb her temper, show him she was a grown woman in control of her emotions, but that hadn't worked out.

"Katherine, I am so sorry I set you up for this. It was not my intention at all."

"Oh, that's good. Don't answer my questions. So just what was your intention, Doctor?" She slammed the last word at him.

"Actually, it was and still is to help Glen. He is my patient, and I'm sorry I let you get involved at all. It was probably not wise, but you have made it possible for him to come this far. Had it not been for you, he would still be a shadow of a man painting out his horrid memories of blood and gore. Or he could possibly have died out there on the farm in that icy shower his sister set up. You should be pleased with your part in his ongoing recovery. Now why don't you put your shoulders back and tackle the next phase with as much courage as you've shown so far? And stop feeling sorry for yourself. You have a life, too, you know. It's time you got on with it."

"He is my life. And you want me to go on without him? Asshole. Just because you've never loved anyone, don't understand what it means."

He batted his eyes, and turned away for a moment before returning her hard glare.

"I'm so sorry you feel that way." He picked up a pencil and began to play with it, passing it between his fingers, one by one, back and forth like a magician with a coin.

She stared at his long, immaculately clean fingers until her anger began to die. He said no more, waited on her to respond. "Okay, Spencer. Do you have any words of advice for the emptiness I feel?"

"Yes, I do. Come visit him regularly. He'll finish around 4:30, eat his supper, then he'll be in his room until bedtime. I'd suggest you come around 6 p.m. And I also suggest you get to work on those paintings for the spring art show. That, along with your classes, will keep you occupied so you can stop pitying yourself and enjoy life again. Haven't you grieved enough?"

"You're a real smartass, you know that? I thought I had, until this."

"He can't recover living with you where all his whims are cared for."

"You saying I coddle him?"

"No, you care for him. He needs to learn to care for himself. Until he does, he won't be completely whole."

"He thinks he's coming back here to stay. That he's getting worse. I tried to tell him different. That's why he really came back to the hospital, so I wouldn't have to care for him, as you so sweetly put it, while he grows worse. Helpless again."

"Ridiculous nonsense. Mason will soon put that notion out of his head. What are you going to do today?"

"I have an afternoon class, then I'm going to go up to the house and collapse. I may sleep for twelve hours. Tomorrow, I'm not sure yet. I'll wander around and figure something out."

He rose, dropped the pencil on his desk. "Katherine, stay busy, and how about you wait until Friday evening to come visit him? Then you can come as often as you like, but let him know when it will be, would you? We can't have him looking for you when you aren't coming."

"Will you tell him I won't be back until Friday? Or should I?"

He studied her for a long time. "Maybe you should. He's liable not to believe me."

She followed him on rubbery legs down the hall to the very end room where Glen and Mason Harrington were discussing his impending therapy. They stopped talking when Spencer opened the door. He gestured to Mason to leave the room with him, and they both stepped out, leaving her standing there, Glen staring at her.

"He said I could come and tell you I won't be back until Friday 'cause they want you to get adapted to your schedule first."

"Come here, Katie," he said softly.

She went to him, knelt beside the chair. He held her head in his lap for a long time, then lifted her chin, and kissed her. "It's going to be all right. I'll be fine."

Mutely she nodded, and kissed him once more. "If you need to talk to me, call me, even if it's the middle of the night. You hear?"

"Yes, I hear. I will. And I'll see you Friday. Right after supper?"

She stood up, moved out of his reach. Clearly, the rules of her visits had already been explained to him.

"I forgot to ask Spencer if you could spend the weekends with me."

Glen shook his head. "I already asked. The first month or so I'll be at it seven days a week. Maybe after that, Mason said. Depends on how I come along." He smiled at her, his eyes as flat as river stone.

Somehow, she managed to return his smile, then backed out the door, closing it between them, pressing her forehead against the wood and sucking in deep breaths. Spencer took her shoulders, turned her around, and accompanied her to the front doors and out to the van.

What a fool she was. This should not be so difficult. She was stronger than this. It must be because of her fear he would not do well without her. Or perhaps she was afraid he would not need her anymore, and wouldn't love her.

God, she was a mess.

Time to straighten out. She drove home listening to R&B on a local station, even managed to hum a few bars here and there. Parking the van in the carport, she hurried into the house, hung up her coat, and set to cleaning Glen's—no, that wasn't right—the sunroom. She stripped the bed, put on fresh sheets, blankets, and a bright coverlet, tossed the linens in the washing machine, cleaned the bathroom, dusted the floors. Still not satisfied, she began on the rest of the house, including the bedroom where she and Stan had slept. She would sleep there from now on.

By the time her students began to arrive that afternoon, she had cleaned the studio and chosen a few of her paintings to consider for the art show. She would have to paint several more. Her sketchpad lay on the table. She flipped through it to the studies she'd done of Glen in his football uniform the day he and she worked out at the farm. She would group this one with him in his flight uniform, then another of him now in the foreground. Call it "Life of a Warrior." And she would start on it the very next morning.

Which dawned sunny and warm. It no longer appealed to her to plan every moment of her day. She would do anything she pleased, be open to whatever new ideas came along. After breakfast, she grabbed her camera and a sweater, ran down the hill to the art studio, and spent a couple of hours setting up shots that would represent her best work to date. The photos she would send to the committee for jurying. Then she propped a 2'x3' canvas on an oversized easel, applied a coat of white, and while it dried, worked on preliminary sketches of Glen. Her first student of the day knocked on the door at 3 p.m. and she glanced up, surprised she had worked through lunch without pause, a charcoal rendering of the football hero all but finished on a background the varied colors of his eyes. She threw a cover over the canvas and went to the door. That evening she called Ellie Tanner again, this time adamant they meet.

Ellie agreed and said she would be at the Signpost Bar at eight o'clock Saturday night. Katherine could meet her there or not, whatever she wanted. She had no idea how she would approach the woman, except to make it clear that she stop her interference in Glen's life.

The work caused the week to pass, if not quickly, at least smoothly. After morning classes on Friday, she walked back to the house, laid out what she would wear that evening for her first visit to Glen since he had gone, and turned on the shower. For a long time, she stood there staring at the water steaming in the cubicle. She was showering next to the room that had been his. Did not remember leaving her bedroom.

When she was finished, hair wrapped in a towel, she lay across his bed and fell asleep, dreaming she kept chasing after him in that field of flowers, but could never catch him. The long slant of a setting sun across her face awoke her, and she sat up, startled. Confused, her hair a mess wrapped in the towel. Barefooted, she padded across the living room and upstairs where she dressed in a blue pants suit and wrapped her hair into a loose knot at the back of her head.

The clock read 5:10 when she grabbed her purse and coat and a foil package of cookies she'd baked the day before. It was a twenty-minute drive to the hospital, so she stopped at Braums and bought a strawberry milkshake for herself and a chocolate one for Glen. She hadn't eaten since a muffin for breakfast, but didn't care. Didn't feel hungry.

It was a quarter to six when she walked into the hospital, bypassed the nurses' station and went straight to his room. Funny Spencer hadn't stopped her.

Glen was lying in bed, covers pulled up under his chin, eyes closed. She settled in the chair beside him, set his milkshake and cookies on the table, and studied his features. He looked tired, drawn. She leaned forward and kissed him lightly. He shifted, drew a deep breath, and continued to sleep.

"Probably hadn't ought to wake him," a voice said from the doorway. She turned to see the tall, broad figure of Mason Harrington, his shaven head gleaming from the overhead lights.

"Is he all right?"

"Yeah, he's fine, ma'am. Working hard wears him out. Meds put him to sleep."

"Meds? What meds?"

"That's private information, ma'am." He hesitated before the ma'am, like he wanted to call her something else.

Her gaze locked on his, she laid her hand on Glen's chest. "I brought him chocolate ice cream. His favorite. I'm sure he would want to eat it before it melts. He can go back to sleep. The nights are long for him as it is."

"Go ahead, then. Wake him up, if you can."

Definitely a challenge.

Anger boiled in her chest, and she rose from the chair, sat on the edge of the bed, and kissed him. His eyes fluttered open, and he peered up at her.

"Hi, sweetie. How are you?" She whispered so the nosy Harrington, hovering in the doorway, couldn't hear.

"Hmmm?" Glen peered at her through slitted lids.

"It's me, Katie. Wake up. I brought you chocolate ice cream."

"Katie?" His voice, thick with sleep or something else. What had Spencer or maybe Radnor prescribed for him?

"Yes, darling. I'll turn up the bed if you want your ice cream."

"Uh-huh." Though he struggled to wake, he remained groggy.

Despite that, she turned the handle until he was sitting up, opened the milkshake and stuck the spoon down into the thick mixture.

Because his arms were still under the covers, she spooned up a small bite and fed it to him. Like a robot he opened his mouth, closed it, swallowed. After a few bites he appeared to become more alert.

"This is good," he said.

"He shouldn't be eating that. He's already had his supper." That damned Harrington.

Her hackles raised, and she was ready to do battle. She turned and stared up at the huge, bald man. "He's not on a restricted diet, is he? He still needs to gain some weight. This'll help him. Is Doctor Spencer here?"

Mason shook his head. "He's at a convention in Little Rock. Won't be back until Monday."

"I see. And what about Harry. Is he around?"

"Off tonight." Mason grimaced at her.

"And I suppose Doctor Radnor...?

"In Little Rock, as well."

"I'd like some privacy with Glen if you don't mind." Her tone made it clear he'd better not mind.

He must have realized he was coming close to getting in trouble, so he nodded and left, but he wasn't happy at all. She didn't give a rat's ass and planned on having a talk with Spencer first thing Monday about the man's attitude and what kind of meds they were doping Glen with. He didn't like to be doped up all the time. Besides, coming off them tended to bring on a flashback.

"Katie, when did you get here?"

"Just now, sweetie. Want some more ice cream?"

"Yes, please. Damn food here is so bland." He removed his arms from the tangle of covers, took the large cup, and spooned up a big bite. "God, that's good. I'm so damn sleepy. What time is it?"

"A little after six."

"Fuck." Some of the ice cream dripped onto his blanket. "Missed my mouth. What is going on?"

"I don't know," she said, taking the cup and spoon and giving him another bite. "but I'm going to find out as soon as Spencer returns. I want to know what they're giving you."

"Me, too. I can't focus. Everything's blurry."

"How long have you felt this way?"

"Don't know. What day is it?"

"It's Friday. How is your physical therapy going?"

"Hell if I know. Can't remember anything much. You find out what this is, will you?"

"You're damn right I will, sweetheart."

They finished off their ice cream, using straws to suck up what had melted into the bottom of the cups.

"Brought you some cookies, too. I'll put them here in your drawer."

"Give me a couple of them now, would you?"

"Glen, are you hungry?"

"I think so. Don't remember eating supper. I must have though. Hell, they're probably giving me Jello and chicken broth."

"Surely not after a hard day's workout."

His chin dropped to his chest, he jerked. "Damn, can't stay awake. Sorry, Katie, sorry."

She brushed his hair back off his face, trailed her fingers down the line of his jaw, then kissed him, turned the bed down, settled him comfortably on his pillows, and cleaned up their mess. Something was going on here she didn't like, and she was going to find out what. But it looked like not until Monday. She hated to leave him here over the weekend without knowing more, but short of kidnapping him, could do nothing.

On her way to meeting Ellie at the Signpost the next night she would come early and swing by, check on him. Whatever it was probably wasn't dangerous. These people took good care of their veterans. It was just a mix-up between doctors' orders, she was sure. Spencer would never allow anything that would harm Glen.

Sometimes, though… sometimes doctors misdiagnosed or miss-medicated with the best of intentions. She'd get to the bottom of this. But tomorrow she had to face Ellie and talk her into leaving Glen the hell alone. The mood she was in, she might just start by clocking Harrington, then turning her wrath on Ellie.

THREE

IT WAS ALMOST seven when she returned to the hospital the following evening. Glen was not in his room. She went back to the nurses' station and asked about him.

A cute little aide checked some papers on her desk. "Um... I think he's still in rehab."

"This late? Well, could you direct me there?"

"Sure, it's right down this hallway, turn left. That hallway will put you right in the gym."

She thanked her and hurried to follow her directions. But Glen was not in the gym, either. No one was but Harry, who was folding towels at the far end. He saw her coming, kept his back turned like he didn't want to look at her.

"Harry, have you seen Glen this evening?"

"Uh—he's in lockdown." Murmured.

He might as well have hit her. "Lockdown? I don't understand. What happened?" Her insides quivered and she wanted to scream at him.

"Had a flashback. Threw a stool through the glass partition over there, according to that bulldog Mason who had to restrain him and strap him down. They put him in lockdown until he settles down."

"I have to go to him, Harry."

"Nope. No visitors."

"Harry. You know how I feel about him. How he feels about me. You let me in there, right now."

He sighed. "Come with me, and keep this quiet, you understand. You could get me fired."

"Harry, if anything has happened to him, I'll get everyone in this goddamned hospital fired. Now, where is he?"

"I said I'd take you. Don't get all upset. I seen you and him together. I understand. Believe me, I do. Come on."

So angry her head throbbed, she trailed along after him through another hall, then another, to a row of rooms with closed doors and small glass windows with wire covering the inside. Harry took a ring of keys off his waist and unlocked one of the doors, scooted her inside. "I'll wait out here. Don't be long." He closed the door.

A shadow lay in a dark corner of the room. There were no windows save the tiny one in the door that let in only a narrow strip of light. That alone was enough to send Glen into a panic. She felt her way along the side wall so she wouldn't trip over anything. Reached him and ran both hands over his still body. Straps across his chest, thighs, and ankles held him to a narrow bed. He didn't move, his chest going up and down rapidly.

The straps buckled under the edge of the cot. Fumbling with shaking fingers, she undid them. He lay motionless, not speaking.

"Glen," she said close to his ear.

"Huh." More a grunt than a reply.

"It's Katie. Wake up."

"Huh," again, then he began to stir, arms raising and falling, head lolling back and forth.

"Okay, sit up." She pulled him upright, wrapped both arms around him. "Chair. Where's your chair?"

"Corner, I think. Corner." He lisped the words so she knew he'd been doped up after the flashback.

"Okay, sorry, sweetie. I'm going to have to lay you back down until I can find it." She lowered him onto the cot. He flailed at her with his hands. "Easy, I'll be right back."

"Right back," he muttered.

Once she got him out of here, she'd have Mason's job and maybe a few more. In a hurry for fear someone would come and stop her, she stumbled into one corner, found nothing, into the other, still nothing. She rapped on the door hard. Keys rattled, and Harry opened it a crack. "Find a wheelchair for him, Harry."

"You can't take him out of here."

"The hell I can't. You can explain it all to Spencer when he gets back. Until I find out what's going on, I'm not leaving him here. This doesn't happen to him when he's with me. Now get me that chair, or I'll start a ruckus that'll bring everyone running."

He scooted away without further comment, and she went back to get Glen ready to move. Once more, she pulled him to a sitting position, lowered his legs off the edge of the cot, then sat beside him, holding him.

"Doing here?" Glen said.

"Came by to see you, sweetie. I'm taking you home with me for a day or two until we can talk to Spencer. That all right with you?"

"Katie." He was making little sense, but at least he wasn't fighting her.

Mouth so close to her ear that his breath feathered across her neck he murmured, "Sorry, so sorry. Don't know what happened."

"Not your fault. I'll have that bald-headed jackass's job before this is over." It was a blessing they'd doped him up. If not for that, he'd be climbing the walls of this eight-by-ten cell.

"I couldn't do it. Said I could. He said I could if I wanted to. I wanted to. I couldn't." He kept saying, "I couldn't," until his voice faded to nothing.

"Hush, sweetheart. It's all right."

Finally, after what seemed an eternity, keys rattled again, and the door swung open.

"Come over here and help me, Harry. I can't move him by myself and he's doped up on something."

The muted swishing of the chair's wheels told her he was coming through the dark room. Together, they lowered Glen into the seat. "Strap him in. He's almost unconscious."

He obeyed. "I'll go first, make sure the coast is clear. You keep me out of this, would you?"

"Do you have any idea what's going on here?"

"It's that Mason guy, ma'am. You know Doc wouldn't allow this. The guy isn't what he claims to be. Just a bouncer out of some club, thought he could handle these guys cause he's big and strong. Fake papers, I think. I didn't know, honest I didn't. Not until tonight, then I didn't know who to tell, what with Doc gone and all. That's why I was there folding towels, in case Glen needed me. Now you gotta not get me involved in this. I like my job here. You know I take good care of these boys, but I'm just a nurse. I ain't no licensed therapist."

"Apparently, Mason isn't either. You should've called me. I'm taking Glen home with me. If Spencer gets in touch or comes in before I can talk to him, you'll tell him I made you let me in. Threatened you, whatever you want to say, but I'm not leaving him here over the weekend. I don't give a damn if I have to kick some ass. You understand?"

He chuckled. "Yes'm, I surely do. Come on, this way, I'll have to let you out the back exit, but you can take the chair all the way around on the sidewalk against the building. It's well lit. You be careful now, you hear?"

"You, too, Harry. Thank you." She kissed him on the cheek.

He patted Glen's shoulder. "Take care, big guy. I'll see you soon."

"Is there any way I can find out what drug he's on?" she asked Harry before he could close the door he'd opened to the outside.

"I'll see what I can do and call you. Your phone number on his records?" He nodded toward Glen.

"Yes."

"Okay, go on, git, 'fore we get caught. Can you get him in the car?"

"I'll manage. Thank you, Harry."

The door swung shut, leaving her out in the cold dark night. She felt like one of those private detectives in the movies. Pushing the chair was easy, but getting Glen into the van might not be. The cold air obviously brought him around some. Halfway along the side of the structure, he said her name clearly, and she answered him.

"Where we going?"

"Home. How are you feeling?"

"How'd you get me out of there?"

"What do you remember?"

"Not much. They strapped me down, but I don't know why."

"I don't either, but I'm going to find out."

"How did you know about it?"

"Look, we're at the parking area, and over there's the van. Are you going to be able to help me get you loaded up?"

"Yep. Are we escaping?"

"It would appear so, if no one catches us."

"I'm cold."

"I know, sweetie, but as soon as we get you in the van I'll get you warmed up."

His strength amazed her, considering, and he grabbed the handhold above the door with one hand, placed his palm on the seat, and swung himself up and in with little effort.

"Good." She buckled the seat belt and shut the door, loaded the wheelchair into the back, ran around, and jumped in. She fumbled for the keys, and they were away with no one leaping out to stop them. Something she'd expected from the beginning.

She was on the highway before she remembered her appointment with Ellie. Well, that would have to wait. The woman would go home when she didn't show up.

"Are you going to be arrested for kidnapping me?" Glen asked.

"I'm not sure. I don't think so, but I do know Spencer is going to give me hell."

"You can handle him. Katie, thanks for coming for me. When they strapped me into that dark room, I blacked out. It was like being put in a cage again. I couldn't face it."

"I know, and someone is going to pay for that."

"I'll just bet they do. What are you going to do?"

"Let's worry about that later. Right now, what I'm going to do is take you home. We'll have to talk about this some more, I'm sure. I know you don't want to be there, but it's a hell of a lot better than being strapped to a bed in a dark room. I won't do that to you."

The tires swished on wet pavement. Traffic crept through the darkness, headlights flashing across the windshield, the wipers making muted passes to clear the water thrown up by passing vehicles. His silence was thunderous. Maybe he'd fallen asleep.

"Glen, what is it?"

"Don't think I don't want to be there with you. I wanted you to be free of my hang-ups. You need a life of your own, and I want you to have it."

"You need to know when something like this is happening to you, I can't have any other life. That's what loving someone means. I care more for you than I do myself."

"That makes it hard, then doesn't it?" His voice hollow sounding.

"I guess so. What are you getting at?"

He didn't say anything for a while, then, "Well, I care more for you than myself. You care more for me than yourself. How will we balance that out so we're both happy?"

"I don't know about you, but I'm happy when we're together. I know you need the physical therapy. I want you to walk and run and chase after me. I have dreams about it. But until we get this mess settled, I'm not taking you back there. You don't need to be locked up in a cell. You spent nine years locked in a cage. It isn't going to happen again. I'll take you in every day for therapy and back home again, if need be. We'll just pretend we work in town, that's all. But let's just wait until Spencer gets back, and we can talk to him. Then we'll decide together what to do. Is that okay with you?"

"Yes, I guess." He leaned back against the seat. "I'm still sleepy."

"That's okay. Go to sleep. I love you."

"Mmm. I love you, too."

The rain continued to come down, melting what snow was left on the north slopes of the mountains. She glanced at the clock. Eight thirty. Ellie would have given up by now and gone home. She'd call her again, but not until this was cleared up. The woman could scarcely do anything to Glen while he was with her, could she?

FOUR

THE DRIVE HOME seemed endless. Heavy rain turned the winding highway black as the night itself, the stripes fading to nothing. It was past nine when Katie backed up as close to the door as she could, jumped out, and ran around to Glen's side. He was still asleep, but she opened the door and woke him. If he awoke and found himself shut up in the dark, he would certainly panic.

"Stay right there. I'm going in and get a coat to put around you. You'll freeze in that stupid hospital gown."

He nodded, and she sprinted inside, grabbed the first heavy coat she could find in the closet, went back outside, and dragged the wheelchair from the side door of the van, positioned it and unbuckled the seat belt. By then she was soaked to the skin.

"Lean forward, and slip into this coat."

He obeyed, catching himself on the dash with both hands. She wrestled him into the coat. "Okay, can you—?"

Again, he followed instructions, like an automaton. After some struggling, they were inside the door and out of the rain. Water poured off his hair, and she fetched a towel from the upstairs bath, scrubbed at his head vigorously.

"You could use a haircut." An observation spoken to take her mind off what had been done to him by that Neanderthal, Harrington.

Like a child, he turned his face up to be dried. After patting the towel down across his cheeks and chin, she leaned down and kissed him, first on the forehead, then on the mouth. Still no reaction, as if his features were frozen in place. Her heart tripped, but she held her tongue.

A few minutes later, after a quick trip to the bathroom, she had him out of the coat and damp gown and snuggled beneath blankets. He had not said one word. When she went to hang up the coat, she saw it was one of Stan's. Stopping dead in her tracks, she held it close to her face, breathed in his fading scent, then draped it near the fireplace to dry. Must have missed it when she finally took all his clothes to the Salvation Army.

Hugging herself and shivering, she ran back to the sunroom, stripped out of her wet clothes, and crawled in beside Glen. He reached for her, and she took his hand.

"You okay?" she said.

"Yes. So sleepy. You're freezing. Come here."

Relieved he was coherent, she snuggled against him. "I'm fine. Go to sleep. I love you."

"I love you, too."

The next time she opened her eyes, the sun was shining through rain-washed windows, and he lay curled around her. It took a moment to realize what that meant. He was moving his legs again. She shook his shoulder, too excited to wait for him to open his eyes.

"Wake up. Come on, wake up."

His lids lifted lazily. Still sleeping off the last of the drugs.

"You turned over in the night," she said.

He stared at her for a moment, then looked down at his legs curved around hers. "You must've turned me over."

"No, I didn't. I didn't. Try to roll back over. See if you can."

Some grunts and shaking of the bed. "Nope, can't. The spirit is willing, but…. Want me to try some more?"

"No, it's okay. You're obviously doing something in your sleep you can't do when you're awake."

"Damn," he said. "That's what Mason said to me before… before I…."

"What did he say?"

"He knew I could because I moved in the bed. He saw me. Kept yelling at me. You're just lazy, you don't want to… stuff like that.

"Then I, uh, went back in the jungle, when they first captured me. I don't know what I did then, next thing I knew he had me on the floor pushing a needle into my arm. Then he tossed me in that room and strapped me down." He held her tight, shuddering. "Then you were there."

"I'm so sorry you had to go through that. It won't happen again, because you're not going back there. I have an idea, but let's talk about it later."

"Oh, yeah. How much later?" He ogled her and grinned.

"How long will it take you to make mad love to me? I've missed you."

"Me, too. Come here."

"Here I come."

"Me, too," he said.

At the breakfast table, both wearing jeans and flannel shirts, and eating Sunday pancakes drenched in maple syrup and real butter, she laid out her idea.

"All we need is the proper equipment for your rehab, right? Then we can hire someone to come here every day, and you can stay here. I'll call my friend who does handicap remodels. He can fix us up with every-thing you need. I don't know why I didn't think of it before."

"It sounds good."

"You don't sound too excited."

He shoved a dripping forkful of pancakes in his mouth and chewed. "Oh, wrong, I am excited. Whatever he doped me up with, I don't want any more of it. God, these are good."

"See, I can feed you much better here, and I promise I'll hold my classes and get the paintings ready for the show. And no more dope, ever. It'll be perfect, and we can be together."

"Where is the money going to come from?"

She stared at him for a full minute. "Is that what you're worried about?"

"Well, yeah. I'm not a gigolo, you know. I can't let you support me and buy me fancy stuff in return for my services." He grinned.

She laughed. "I ought to smack you."

"I know, I'm teasing. I have plenty of money, you know. Besides my back pay for living in that cage, Julia put money in a trust fund for me when I left home. She wanted to make sure I had everything I might need. You haven't heard from her, have you?"

"No, I haven't." She stirred a bit of pancake around in syrup swirling with butter. She hoped she never did, either, but obviously, he still felt an attachment to her, despite what she had done to him.

"Maybe I should call her."

"Are you sure… after what she did?"

"She was terrified, and who could blame her?"

"Exactly what happened out there the first time, when she called the sheriff and let him haul you off to jail?"

"I don't remember, but it must've been really bad. Maybe I tried to kill her, who knows?" He refused to look at her.

"I seriously doubt you tried to kill her. Unless you were a totally different man than you are today. Let's forget it. Eat the rest of your breakfast, and call her if you want to. I'm sure she would like to hear you're doing okay."

He hadn't a violent bone in his body. The worst he could've done was flash back to the battlefield. Even so, he never tried to fight back when that happened. All fight had been tortured out of him during nine years living in a bamboo cage hung in a tree. Poked at, cut, stomped, beaten, hauled all over three countries. She could hardly stand to think of all the things those monsters had done to him. He did well to come through his flashbacks sane.

In addition, after what Harry had told her about Mason, she was beginning to doubt Glen had thrown a stool through the window at the hospital. More than likely Mason did that to justify strapping him to that damned cot, when all along he was pissed because Glen couldn't move his legs on command. He'd said as much to Glen.

She was going to get that straightened out Monday first thing. The bastard wouldn't get away with what he'd done. When she got through, he wouldn't have a job.

"Come back," Glen said.

"Oh, sorry. I was just thinking."

"Did you work on your paintings this week?"

"Yes, as a matter of fact, I did. I took photos of those I want to enter and have a large one started. I think you'll like it."

"You have classes tomorrow. Let me come with you, if that's okay. I want to see, and I'd like to paint some."

"I'd love to have you join in. You haven't worked on your paintings in a while. It's not until one o'clock. I should be able to get everything straightened out at the hospital by lunch time."

"If I call Julia this morning, I'd like to go out and see her if it's okay with her. I think I need to get that trust fund straightened out. We're going to need the money for your project."

Katie shuddered. He absolutely could not go out there alone. No telling what the woman might do. She was certifiable. "May I go with you?"

He glanced up quickly. "You don't have to protect me, you know."

Oh, yes, I do. "I know, but after all those meds they gave you, maybe you ought not to drive for a day or two."

"Come on, Katie. Don't be silly."

"Okay. I know I'm not your mother or your protector. But dammit, she put you in a shower and turned icy water on you, hid your wheel-chair, cut the power and phones, and left the house. What do you suppose she thought would happen to you?"

He dodged as if she had slapped him, turned the chair, and went into the sunroom, closing the door behind him.

Dammit, now she'd upset him. She'd forgotten he didn't remember exactly what had happened that night. Still, he needed to know, even if it did upset him. Instead of following him, she cleaned up the dishes, loaded the dishwasher, and dug around in the freezer for something to thaw for dinner. Took out a roast, unwrapped it, put it in a baking dish, slid it into the oven and turned it on. In a couple of hours, she'd add potatoes, carrots, and onions. With gravy, it would be a delicious Sunday afternoon meal.

Then she went to his door. "I'm going down to the box to get the Sunday paper. Be right back." When he didn't answer, she called, "You okay?"

"I'm fine. Could you just leave me alone for a while?"

"Sure, sweetheart. I'll be right back."

He'd been through so much, but it hurt her feelings to be shut out. He needed his space once in a while, though. She pulled on a sweater, slipped her feet into a pair of yard shoes, and trailed down the driveway to the paper box. The trees on the mountains that rimmed the tiny valley were a feathery gray, cut by jags of deep green cedar and pine, the winter sky forming a pale blue backdrop. The creek chattered over its rocky bottom, a song to accompany the beauty of the day.

She breathed deeply of the clean air, excited about her idea for the sunroom and Glen's rehab. Maybe he'd change his mind about going to see Julia. Maybe Ellie would fall off the side of a cliff. Yeah, and maybe Spencer wouldn't tear her a new one for whisking Glen away from the hospital. Not likely, any of those. Still, Glen was home with her. Everything else could be settled.

He was still in his room with the door closed when she returned, so she sat down in the recliner to read the funnies, having no desire to know what was going on in the world when her own was so messed up.

While she was on the last page, his door opened, and he came out. Stopped by her chair. "I talked to Julia, but I'm not going out there. She is very angry with me, and I'm not sure why. Gave me the name of the bank holding the trust fund, then told me to go back to the loony bin and not bother her anymore." He took a really deep breath, and she wanted to hug him, but let him go on.

"But, I think we're in trouble. Spencer called. Evidently, someone called him from the hospital and told him you had spirited me off. No explanation other than that. Probably that Harrington. He's fit to be tied, and if I read him right, he's on his way out here. Maybe we'd better run away somewhere until he cools down." He grinned at her. "Not mad at me, are you?"

"Of course not. You have a right to your feelings. I'm sorry if what I said about Julia upset you. I shouldn't have let you have it like that. You didn't know what she did."

"Ah, it's okay. She's got worse problems than me. I feel bad for her, though. She did raise me and did the best she could. It was hard on her, and she never married. Gave her life to me, and then when I enlisted, she was a sour old maid at thirty."

She laid the paper aside. "I'm beginning to understand why you don't want me to take care of you."

"I guess that's part of it. But I sure don't think of you as my older sister."

"Glen, she's only two years older than I am. I could well be your older sister. Does our age difference bother you?"

"Babe, I'm eons older than you are. Believe me." He took her hands in his, folded them together. "And besides, you are one sexy dish."

"Dish? Did you call me babe and a sexy dish, all in one sentence?"

He laughed. "Well, I meant it as a compliment."

"And it's a good thing. But what are we going to tell Spencer?"

"The truth."

"I'll try, but since you don't remember much, how can you back me up?"

"I can lie."

"That's not a good idea. Spencer's not stupid, he'll figure that out real quick. Well, let's just go with the truth and hope Harry will back us up. He knows what happened, but I promised him I wouldn't involve him, though I'm a bit peeved he didn't do anything for you when he knew what was going on."

"He was probably afraid of Mason. The man is tough as nails. He picked me up like I weighed nothing."

"Picked you up? Why did he do that?"

"When he tossed me on the cot and strapped me down. That I do remember, though I don't recall throwing anything, like he said I did." He shrugged. "However, I'm not the best witness to the entire episode, am I?"

"We'll make sure and tell Spencer that. By the way, Harry did tell me

Mason has forged papers and that he's really a bouncer who lost his job. Can we tell Spencer somehow without involving Harry?"

"Maybe Harry will come through for you. He always did like you. Just tell Doc you heard it on the grapevine." Glen said. "Could I have the funnies? I'm way behind on Garfield."

"Oh, really? All he does is sleep. How can you get behind?" She laughed and handed him the paper.

They sat on the deck in the sunshine after eating the roast and vegetables. Glen ate three pieces of bread soaked in the brown gravy. Patted his stomach. "Gonna get fat. Is there pie?"

"Yes, smarty-pants. I baked it last night after we came home. Wait, I think there's a frozen one, I'll put it in the oven."

"What kind?"

"Oh, getting picky on me?"

"I prefer cherry, but apple will do."

"Geeze. Sorry, but I think it's peach."

"My very next favorite."

She turned off the oven and left the pie in to cool before they went out into the afternoon sunshine.

He turned his face into the warmth. "This is nice."

"Lovely."

"You know, I could be perfectly happy doing this with you the rest of my life." He took her hand. "This day, I mean, the entire thing."

She swallowed past a knot in her throat. "You are the nicest man I've ever known. You always say the right thing at the right time."

"And I mean it, too," he added. "How about a kiss?"

"Love one." She leaned toward him, heard the car barreling up the driveway as their lips touched. Prayed it was someone lost and looking for directions, but down deep in her heart knew it wasn't.

FIVE

SPENCER SPOTTED THEM on the deck through the side window of his car. He didn't smile. Oh, shit. Damn and shit. He came around the house, long legs bringing him up the steps onto the deck, a frown wrinkling his features.

Before either of them could speak, he lit into her. "I know you always have to be right, Katherine, but you have outdone yourself this time. Dragging this boy out of the hospital on a frigid, rainy night just to prove your point."

At first, she was going to let him rant and run down, but intimating that she put Glen's life in danger made that impossible. She came up out of the chair so their gazes would be on the level. "I have never done anything to hurt him. Never. And you watch your tone with me. I'm not an underling just because I did something you asked me to do. You might have checked to see why I took him out of there before you came barrel-assing out here with your mouth running. That Harrington, who by the way, is not a physical therapist but a bouncer in a bar, picked him up, threw him on a cot, strapped him down, and stuck a damned needle full of dope in his arm because he couldn't walk. And if you think that was right, well then I've totally misjudged you."

Her heart beat so fast darkness closed in around her, and she dropped into the chair, breathing hard.

Glen laid his hand on her arm. "I think you owe both of us an apology, Doc."

Spencer's face turned pale, his mouth pursed into a white rim. He lowered himself into a nearby chair. "What the hell are you talking about? He's a what? He did *what*? Glen?"

"That's exactly what he did. And if she hadn't come, I'd a been in a bad way. Shut up in that room in the dark. Not a good place for me to be, Doc. Not at all."

"All right. Both of you. Start at the beginning. Who is first?"

"Apologize to her first, Doc. I mean it, man. You can't go around treating her like that. I won't put up with it. You taking someone else's word without a thought for what she might have done. She doesn't owe you an explanation. Who the hell do you think you are?"

She had never seen him so angry.

"I apologize. I'm sorry, Katherine. I'm sorry, Glen. Now will you kindly tell me what really happened Saturday night?"

"Well, that's a little better. I suppose it's the best you can do."

Katherine patted Glen's tense arm until he settled down a bit.

She went on to relate in detail what had happened at the hospital, including Mason's treatment Friday when she took the milkshakes in. Glen added he was sorry if he really threw the stool through the door glass, but didn't think he had, suggested Spencer talk to some of the nurses. Harry, maybe?

"He drugged you? Hell, he had no right to do that. I didn't prescribe, nor did Radnor prescribe, drugs of any kind. Only a mild sedative. Drugs could cause you a hell of a lot of trouble. Probably did cause that flashback you had. I'm truly sorry this happened. You both know how hard we try to keep the hospital a safe place for vets. I'm going to look into how this man got hired in the first place."

"I promised to get everyone in the hospital fired if anything had happened to Glen. Someone may have heard me, I was so furious and loud. You might try to smooth that over a bit. But it would do for them to pay more attention to what's going on around them. I know some are scared of Mason Harrington, but that's no excuse."

"Well, by God, I'm not afraid of him. I'm going to see if he can be arrested for falsifying papers to get a job in a Veterans hospital. That could well be a Federal offense."

"I hope it is," Katherine said. "Would you like a piece of peach pie before you go? It's warm in the oven and I know Glen has been salivating since we ate dinner."

"Thank you, but I'm going straight to the hospital and try to get this straightened out."

"I could cut you a piece to take with you." She opened the door and stood back so Glen could pass through.

"That would be nice. Thanks."

"You're welcome, Spencer. By the way, we're going to hire someone to come out here and assist with Glen's rehab. I'm ordering all the equipment we'll need tomorrow."

He stared at her a moment. "I'm sure the VA will help with that. I think you could probably rent the equipment and they'll take care of a large portion. I'll look into it, if you'd like. I have no idea why I didn't think of that. I guess most people don't have the patience to do something like this at home. I mean, to help out and be responsible... well, you know what I mean." He lowered his voice. "I hope you know what you're letting yourself in for."

From inside, Glen called. "You two gonna stand out there yakking while my pie gets cold? I can't reach that blasted wall oven, you know."

Spencer and Katherine both laughed and went inside. "He can be so demanding sometimes," she said and glared right at Spencer, sending him a silent message to butt out.

Spencer took her arm. "Fix him his pie, then step out the door with me a moment. I almost forgot something we need to discuss."

Puzzled, she took the pie from the oven, a plate from the cabinet, and set both on the table. "You go on. I can handle it from here," Glen said, slipping the knife blade into the crust.

The door swung shut behind her.

Spencer thought for a few seconds, then began, "I hate to tell you this, and I didn't want to bring it up with Glen. He absolutely used to go berserk with even the mention of Ellie's name. But she came to the hospital this morning before I returned from Little Rock City. Kicked up quite a fuss looking for that 'loony husband of mine,' to quote her. Said someone had called saying she was representing the hospital and wanting her to stay the hell out of his life. You do that, Katherine?"

"Yes, I did that. I was supposed to meet her at some bar Saturday night. Then when I decided to drop by the hospital first, I got involved in the kidnapping and didn't get there. I was hoping to get her to take care of her problems without involving him. Spencer, he's doing so well. I mean, look at him. Does he even resemble the man you asked me to help back in October? And he's had several setbacks, but look in there at him. I will not let that bitch destroy him or hurt him in any way. Hell, she needs killing."

"Katherine, be careful who you say that to. A woman like her could well get killed. Then you'd be in jail."

"Oh, you know what I mean."

"You're right, but I don't like you saying you represent the hospital."

"I'm sorry, I really didn't know what else to say. What do you think we can do to get this settled? He needs her out of his life. She mentioned his money several times."

"I'm not sure. Let me get this other matter settled first, then we'll see if we can figure something out. Glen needs to continue to see me and Doctor Radnor. Will he come in once a week, do you think?"

"We'll see. I'm trying very hard to let him make his own decisions. He's been told what to do for so long, and he needs to be trusted to think for himself, even when I don't agree with him."

He kissed her on the cheek. "You're good for him, and I apologize again for crawling all over you without thinking. Do you know how good it was he stood up for you, instead of just thinking of himself? That's a huge step."

"I better get in there before he eats the entire pie and we're up all night. Oh, did you get yours?"

"Next time. I've gotta go now. See you soon. You two take care of each other, okay?"

"We are. We are."

Hugging herself against the chill, Katie went back inside. "I hope you saved me some of that," she said. Saw he had cut her a piece and placed it on his empty plate. "Thank you, kind sir."

The way he studied her, it was clear he was curious about her private conversation with Spencer, but he didn't ask.

Instead, he said, "Suppose we could take a nap now? I'm so full I need to hibernate for an hour or two."

"I'll be right there. You go ahead. Save me a spot in the bed."

After he left, she picked at the pie with her fork, her mind on Ellie and the trouble she might cause. She needed to do something about that before the woman showed up and wreaked havoc.

"Katie, you coming? I am."

"Me, too, sweetie," she said, slid her pie back in the pie pan and put it in the refrigerator, then went to join him in the bedroom. It was indeed true women in their forties were hot for sex. Must be because experience had finally taught them how good making love really feels. Or maybe it was the younger men willing to satisfy them.

Glen fell asleep afterward, but she lay wide awake, unable to stop worrying about the damage Ellie could do to his life. After a while, she slipped out of bed, went to the upstairs phone, and dialed the number on the wrinkled scrap of paper in the drawer.

She dialed and waited through fifteen rings before giving up. While there, she sorted through some of her older clothes, something she'd meant to do for a while. The pile on the bed grew, and she lost track of time until someone drove up the driveway.

Too late, she started down the stairs.

The front door flew open, a voice she recognized from an earlier telephone conversation shouted, "Where the hell is the son of a bitch? That crazy husband of mine?"

SIX

WHEN SHE RACED down the stairs, Ellie stood in the middle of the living room floor, swaying and trying to focus on her.

"What do you want? What are you doing in my house?" She grabbed Ellie by the arm, got up close, hoping Glen had not heard, would not hear. "How did you find us?"

The woman stuck her face right up in Katherine's. The smell of strong liquor nearly knocked her down. "Us, is it? Funny, you don't look like you're stupid."

"Would you kindly keep your voice down to a dull roar? What the *hell* do you want?"

"Oh, 'scuse me. I thought I made that clear." She peered at Katherine. "I want my mother-fuckin' husband, and I want him now. I need to tell him something."

From behind the bedroom door came the most horrible sound of anguish Katherine had ever heard. The door slammed open, and a naked Glen came scrambling across the floor on his hands and knees, shoving with his feet, headed straight for Ellie. The look on his face one of pure animal ferocity. This is what they had turned him into in that cage. A wild man set on tearing someone apart.

Ellie screeched, leaped behind Katherine, and grabbed her shoulders painfully. "Keep that loony away from me. I just come to talk, that's all. To talk."

Frozen by terror, Katherine stared into the golden eyes of the man she loved, a man who stared through her as if she didn't exist. She knew in her heart she could not stop him. Legs bent, he bounced to one side, then the other on all fours, in an attempt to get past her to the object of his animosity.

She turned and grabbed Ellie. "You get yourself out that door this minute, unless you want him to tear you limb from limb. Go! Now!" She shouted. Glen growled and pounced, made a grab for Ellie, knocking Katherine aside. She stumbled, hit her head on the coffee table. He almost got Ellie, but even in her drunkenness, the woman obviously saw the danger and skittered out the door, slamming it hard.

Outside, she shouted. "I'm calling the cops. They're gonna come get him. He tried to kill me. You just wait."

Glen whirled around, glanced at Katherine sprawled on the floor, and collapsed so silently he might have been struck dead.

The blow to her head had not knocked her out, but it stunned her so that for a minute or two she couldn't get up. When she finally did, she couldn't think rationally. What should she do? It would take Ellie a while to get to a phone. So take care of him first, or since he was quiet, call someone? No telling what shape he would be in when he came to.

The only thing she could do was go to him. Nothing else made any sense to her at all. If Ellie called the police, she'd need to have him in bed and looking harmless by the time they got here. With the woman being so drunk, maybe she could convince them she was hallucinating such a wild story.

She hooked him under his shoulders and dragged him across the hardwood floor, his naked body squeaking over the shiny pine boards. It took several tries and a lot of pauses to get him to the bed. When she finally did she couldn't lift him onto the mattress, no matter how hard she struggled. She dropped down beside him, began to pat his face hard enough to wake him if he was only asleep.

"Wake up, Glen. You have to get up and in the bed. Now. Please."

His eyelids fluttered, opened to reveal golden eyes, no longer maniacal, but blank of any understanding whatsoever. She draped his arms across her shoulders. "Come on, help me get you up. Push with your legs, I know you can do it. Push."

He grunted, bent his legs until his knees touched her butt, and gave a great heave that sent him upward. She pushed him onto the bed, in one magnificent effort.

"Did it, you did it. Now, under the covers. Yeah, just like that."

He folded his legs and rolled toward the center of the bed. She covered him, ran in the bathroom, got a washcloth and cleaned her face, combed her hair, then brought the cloth in to wipe the sweat from his forehead and temples.

"Good, sweetheart. You did good. Now don't say anything. Okay? Some people are coming, and I need you to be really quiet. Can you do that for me?"

He gazed into her eyes and frowned. Hard to tell if he understood or not, so she repeated it again. He nodded vigorously and held a finger over his lips.

Dear God, no telling what damage that harridan had caused to his fragile mind. At that very moment, she wanted to get a gun and go out and shoot the bitch. Maybe kneecap her. Not kill her, that would be too good for her. Taking out both her knees sounded about right.

Instead, she dropped down on the bed beside him and stroked his temples until he relaxed and closed his eyes. Damn her, damn her, *damn* her. She leaned down and kissed him, kept her cheek against his for a long time. Actually prayed, which might or might not help, depending on which god might be listening. Watching him come across the floor like an animal had been the most horrendous thing she'd ever witnessed. She hoped never again to see such a thing, but feared she would continue to see it in her mind for a long time.

Her head hurt, but no worse than her heart. She touched the knot behind her ear. No blood. That was good. Now, she was ready.

She picked up the phone and dialed the operator, asked for the sheriff's office and got hold of a deputy who said someone was in the area and could be there in a few minutes.

Out in the yard, Ellie had at last stopped screeching and paced back and forth, so drunk she evidently thought *she'd* called the sheriff.

"They'll be here any time now," she crowed, staggered against her car and waited for the sheriff or one of his deputies to show up. Never a very good liar, Katherine rehearsed her story over and over, while she massaged Glen anywhere she thought might keep him calm.

What a mess, what a terrible mess.

Siren silent, lights flashing, the deputy flew up the driveway and braked to a halt near Ellie's car. Through the window across the living room, she watched him talk to her for a while, then put her in the back of his unit. Good, he must see she was drunk.

Then he came to the door, tapped on the glass with his keys.

She smoothed her hair and clothing and went to the door. "I'm so glad you're here. That woman has been driving me nuts, running around out there screeching. I hoped she'd just go away, but she wouldn't. That's when I called you."

"May I come in for a moment, ma'am?"

"Of course." She smiled, opened the door wider and stepped back.

"Are you here alone?"

"No. My boyfriend is asleep in the bedroom."

"Asleep? Through all her noise?"

"Well, yes. He… he's just home from the hospital and took a Percodan for pain. They knock him out."

"Would you mind if I look in on him?"

"I guess that would be all right. Just please don't awaken him."

"What's wrong with him?"

"Um—uh—he's disabled from Vietnam and had some problems, so they kept him for a few days. He's back home now. Please don't disturb him. He's hell to get back to sleep, and I'll be up all night discussing the Hogs football team."

The deputy smiled. "Yeah, ain't they something, them Hogs?"

"Yes, something." Surely he could hear her heart pounding while he stared down at Glen, so angelic in sleep.

Without another word, he tiptoed from the room, and she pulled the door shut at her back, breathing a silent sigh of relief.

"I'll just take her in for drunk and disorderly and disturbing the peace. She's no business driving. Okay if I send someone after her car in the morning?"

"Yes, that's fine. It'll be okay there."

He touched his forehead with the tips of two fingers. "Good luck with him. Looks like a nice guy."

"He is, believe me, he is. And thank you for coming so quickly."

She clenched her fingers together behind her back until he disappeared down the driveway. No way in the world would this be the last they'd see of Ellie, but it gave her some breathing space, some planning time. Tempting to pack up their stuff and run, as far and as fast as they possibly could. But that would never do. Glen needed to be near the VA and his doctors, and she needed to remain close to him and here on the farm she loved so much.

Right now, she had to get back to him. See if he had any damage from Ellie's visit. She might have to get Spencer back out here, pronto. In the bedroom, she undressed and crawled up on the bed, sitting cross-legged and staring at him. For the first time since she'd laid eyes on him, she was afraid, and she hated that so much she could hardly stand it.

What if he woke up and was still that wild creature? What in God's name would she do?

SEVEN

KATIE REMAINED SITTING cross-legged on the bed, just out of Glen's reach. Every time he twitched, she tensed. Soon his eyes began to dart back and forth beneath the lids. He was dreaming, maybe having a nightmare. The result of what had just happened or something unrelated to that? She had no idea. Sweat popped out on his forehead, his facial features twisted and muscles corded in his arms he'd earlier flung out from under the covers.

Having been warned about waking him, she waited. After more than ten minutes of pure torture, his eyes popped open. He gazed around, caught sight of her. She cringed. Hold him. Go to him and hold him. Tell him everything is okay.

"Holy hell, Katie? Could you—uh?" Lying on his back, quite clearly unable to rise, he reached out to her.

Recalling the earlier terrifying incident, her heart shattered into tiny pieces. She had to hold him, touch him, love him. The images of him scrabbling across the floor, intent on throttling Ellie faded, and she rose to her knees, pulled him to a sitting position and wrapped her arms around him.

"A bad one?" she said.

"Fucking bad." His tensed muscles slowly relaxed, his breathing and heart rate slowed, but he didn't let go, and she didn't, either.

"Well, you're okay now." Dear God, could it be possible he did not remember his earlier total breakdown? What a blessing. She only wished she could forget it, but it wouldn't be that easy. He had used his legs to propel himself across the floor on all fours, much like an ape. How would she ever forget that? All she could do was pretend he was someone or something else then. Now he was the man she loved.

"What's wrong? Katie, you sound strange. Odd."

"Oh, sweetheart, I'm sorry. Just tired, I guess."

"Who could blame you? Want to get under the covers with me?"

"I'll just turn out the lights. Be right there."

She let him go without thinking. He fell backward.

"Well, shit. Sorry, I wasn't ready. Warn me next time. Hey, honey, what's wrong? I didn't mean anything. You look—uh, I don't know…."

She skittered away, shut off the lights, cracked the bathroom door open so its light could be seen, and climbed in the bed with him. Prayed that creature she had glimpsed never returned, then took him in her arms.

"I'm just tired is all. I love you so much. So very, very much."

"Me, too, you," he murmured, gathered her close, put his lips gently against her cheek, sighed, and went limp.

Asleep.

How could he do that so quickly?

Pray God he never remembered what he'd done or that Ellie had even been here. Better yet, that she even existed at all. That it could all go away. But she was no fool. Life didn't work that way.

Hey you, give him a break, please, just give him one goddamned break. And I wouldn't mind one myself. The gods remained silent.

By morning she'd slept fitfully, but had almost managed to convince herself the day before had never happened. Beside her, Glen woke slowly, stretching his arms, moving about, turning toward her with an ease that amazed her. At that same moment, while still in motion, he opened his eyes. Heart in her throat, she tried to relax in his embrace.

"Katie, what's wrong? You feel stiff as a board. Like you're afraid of me."

"No. You just turned over. You must've noticed. Your eyes were open."

With slow deliberation, he raised his head, then turned her loose, sat up. "Holy fuckin' shit. Look at that." He pulled one leg up until his knee made a tent of the blankets.

She pulled the covers away. "Do it. Do it with the other leg, too."

And he did, as simple as that.

She threw her arms around him, knocking him to his back, both of them laughing like idiots. Then she kissed him all over his face, down his neck. He caught her in a tight hold and rolled over so he was on top. One more roll, his feet kicking, insane laughter.

Like always, she cried. She cried when she was happy, and by God, she was happy. He'd gotten the break she prayed for the night before.

Propped on both arms, he hovered above her, leered down. "You know what this means, don't you?"

"Yes, yes I do. You'll be able to walk soon."

"Oh, sure, that, but something else."

"What could be more important than that?"

"I'll tell you what." He buried his face against her neck, making growling sounds, then came up for air. "It means I can be on top."

With that statement, he spread his legs, planted one on each side of her wiggling body.

"Doofus," she cried, peered downward. "Looks like it's a good thing we sleep naked."

"Get ready, I'm coming," he crooned.

"Take your time." She locked her legs around him.

He came down on her ever so slowly, going deep, deep and deeper. Pulled away. Again and again until both were on the edge of an insane desire that came like a fiery explosion. His fists clenched and unclenched wads of sheet, his chest heaved, back arched. The intensity of her orgasms set her to writhing, crying out, legs wrapped around his sweat-slick back. She would fly, maybe die, but she would never turn him loose. When he collapsed beside her at long last, she moved over him and lay her ear against his chest to listen to his racing heart.

"I never thought it would happen." His words came out in spurts, one at a time.

"You're going to walk again."

"I meant the other. Fucking like a man." He laughed, hugged her, laughed some more. His mood was contagious, sent them both rolling around in the big bed, locked together, like a couple of teenagers after their first joining.

Finally spent, they lay wrapped in each other's arms, not saying anything for the longest time.

Expression serious, he said, "Do you really think it means I'll walk? That's got to be a long way off. Harry said it will take months to get strength back in my legs. Said I had to realize it took nine years to do this to me, I couldn't expect an overnight cure. I've been home over a year, getting worse instead of better. Maybe it's too late, Katie. Maybe they're gone." He closed his eyes, shuddered all over so hard it shook the bed. "I try to remember the last time I actually walked, and I can't. There were times we marched for days, over the mountains when they moved us from Vietnam to Cambodia. But I can't remember what year that was. Sometimes they'd take us out of the cages and drag us around from village to village, tied to one another so the villagers could throw rocks at us, so we must've walked then. I walked off the plane, with help. But—"

"Don't, sweetheart. Don't torture yourself. You've had enough of that for a lifetime. Let's be happy for every step forward. I know you can't forget all that, but today is better than yesterday, tomorrow will be better than today. We have to think of it that way."

"Do you have any idea what it's like, Katie? Of course you don't. Sit in that chair or lie in the bed and wait for someone to do everything for you. Can't even get up and pee on your own. And every time you close your eyes to get some sleep, they come to haunt you, those months and years. The dead, the living. Take your pick. What do you want to see tonight? Cages? Beatings? Or maybe you'd like to listen to one of your buddies scream while they peel a chunk of skin off his back until he dies? Then maybe, just maybe, after a few months you'll know what it's like. Oh, but not really, 'cause down inside you'll know you can get up anytime you want. And wipe those nightmares out of your life, too. That it's all been pretend. Then you can start telling me how I should feel."

"I'm sorry, Glen. I didn't mean it that way."

"And don't be so fucking sorry all the time. Sorry doesn't do a thing."

She lay silently beside him, not moving, not speaking. Wishing she hadn't said anything, she understood why he was talking to her this way. He had to get this stuff out of his system, but that didn't keep her from being hurt by his words. The frustration, the hope, the lost dreams and desires. The fear this was all a dream and he'd awaken in that cage. The years he would never get back, no matter what. Spencer wanted him to forget, let it go, look only to the future, but he didn't understand, either.

He'd said himself he'd never treated anyone who had undergone what Glen had, so he was lost as to where to start.

Slowly and carefully, she lay an arm across his chest, and tucked her head against his shoulder. "I love you more than anything in this world. More than my own life, I want you to be happy. I'll do anything you need or want to see it happens. You know that."

"Katie," he whispered. "I'm terrified."

"You're going to be okay. I'm with you. For always. Nothing bad is going to happen to you, ever again."

"I wish I could believe that."

She shuddered, wished the same thing. She had to do everything in her power to keep something like what happened yesterday from happening again. Together with Harrington's treatment, the drugs, and his breakdown when he heard Ellie's voice, his mind had nearly ruptured.

"Let's get up. I'll make a special breakfast to celebrate. I have classes after lunch. Come with me, paint with us."

With a grunt, he sat up and slowly moved his legs over the edge of the bed, placed his feet on the floor. "A landmark, isn't it?" He turned to her and smiled, so beautifully she wanted to cry with happiness. The courage it took to come this far and escape those dreadful years was incredible, unbelievable.

Before she could stop him or even realize what he had in mind, he made a lurch, an attempt at standing, nothing to hold on to. Even as she scrambled across the bed to catch him, he fell forward, cracking his knees and slamming to the floor with a loud grunt.

"Oh, no, no, no!" She crawled to his side, afraid to turn him over.

He lay very still, making no sound for a full minute or more. The longest minute of her life. She stroked his bare back until he stirred, his shoulders started shaking, scaring her. It sounded like he was....

"Are you laughing?"

"That didn't work too well, did it?" He laughed some more, then turned himself over, and sat up, admittedly with a little help from her.

"Didn't that hurt?"

"Sure did. I just wanted to see if I could get up off that goddamned bed and walk away. Leave that sorry wheelchair sitting in the corner."

Her stomach turned over, her throat filled. She would not cry. Dammit, she would not. "I ought to smack you one, right upside the head. You added ten years to my life. Bad enough I'm already older than you. Don't you do anything like that again, ever."

"Aw, Katie, honey, I'm sorry."

"Aren't you the one that said sorry don't do anything?"

"Yeah, I guess I did. Bring that damned chair over here, if you would, and I'll get up off the floor and behave myself."

"You just better. You try something like that again, my heart may stop. Then where would you be?

He sobered. "Nowhere, Katie. Without you, I'd be nowhere."

Throat clogged. Again. Would she ever stop this? "Maybe we ought to get dressed. Both of us laying around in here naked as jaybirds."

He tweaked her breast. "Mmm, nice."

"Behave yourself, indeed. See how long that lasted."

"Get me that chair, woman, and I'll chase you around the house. And when I catch you, you'll find out how long I can last. You'll beg for mercy."

She left him there and brought the chair, removed the arm nearest so he could lift himself up. "Whoa, you're right. This damn seat is cold on a bare ass. Guess I'll put on some clothes."

Later, at the breakfast table where she served ham, eggs, fried potatoes, toast, and strawberry preserves along with hot coffee, he asked something that nearly did stop her heart.

"What was all that uproar last night? I must've been half asleep, but I heard someone yelling and screeching. You came in and told me to stay quiet and then I guess I fell asleep."

She could barely swallow the bite she'd taken just as he asked. "Oh-uh-some woman came up here, drunk as a skunk. I had to call the sheriff. They must've arrested her. They put her in the police car, left hers here, but I think someone from the department was here earlier and picked it up. I haven't looked."

"Wonder why she came up here? Do you know who she was?"

"I don't know anything, and he couldn't get anything out of her." God, she hated lying to him, but it was easy when she considered the consequences if he found out it had been Ellie. And worse, if he realized what he had done. Appetite gone, she leaned back and sipped at her coffee, refusing to meet his gaze.

"You gonna eat that piece of ham?" he asked.

"You can have it, I'm not too hungry. Guess I ate too much roast beef yesterday. I'm going to start calling you tubby."

He patted his flat stomach. "It'll be a while yet."

"What do you want to do the rest of the morning?"

"I thought I might take a run up the road and back." He grinned.

"You are really in a good mood today. Why don't we go for a drive out to the top of the mountain? It's a beautiful day. Maybe we could take some pictures."

"Sounds good. I'll drive."

She only hesitated a moment, remembering what she'd told Spencer the night before. That Glen ought to be able to do some things he wanted to do without interference. But what if he... what if he went off the deep end while behind the wheel of the car? No, she had to stop thinking that way.

"Katie? Where's my car?"

"It's in the barn. I'll take you to it, and we'll go from there. Then, if you want, you can bring it on up here. There's room for both in the carport. That way, you'll have it when you want it."

"Great idea. I thought you were going to object."

"No, Sweetie, I was thinking of something else, that's all. I'll just clear the dishes and we'll go."

"I'll help."

Down at the barn, she let him get out of the van into his chair, then into his car. He tilted the back of the driver's seat forward, folded the chair, and slid it behind him. It took him a while, but his expression when he finished told her she'd been right to stop pampering him so much. He wanted to do things for himself. It was hard for her, though. She was accustomed to helping him, hated to see him struggle.

When he was ready, she climbed into the passenger seat of the Buick.

"Nice car you got here," she said when he backed it out, spun the tires, and spat gravel getting up on the road.

"Yep, I like her. It feels good to be driving again. Let's roll down the windows, and let the wind freeze our cheeks until they're numb." He cranked his own down.

"You idiot." She laughed, followed his lead. "It's cold."

"Yep, but we can't roll them up until our cheeks are numb. Those are the rules."

"Okay. I can take it if you can, tough guy."

After a mile or so, she shivered, reached over and poked a finger against his cheek. "Yep, frozen solid."

"Yeah?"

"Yeah, please."

"Okay, roll 'em up."

"It's beautiful out here, isn't it? Along this road always looks like a well-kept park."

"No one lives along here to keep it cut. The deer do it. They forage on the grass, keep it mowed year round."

Soon the road climbed in long curves that carried them to the top of the mountain. With the leaves off the trees, the rock bluffs stood out along the north slope curling alongside the road. On top, a huge pond reflected gnarly sycamore trees that reached into a blue sky dotted with puffs of white clouds. Wild geese marched up and down in the pasture like a miniature bird army, pecking bugs from the grass. A few ducks quacked and dunked for minnows beneath the surface of the pond.

"Stop, stop here. I want to take pictures looking back."

He pulled over, and she hopped out, found spots from which to frame and shoot. Then she came around the car and took several of him, his arm resting in the window frame as he looked out at her. He made silly faces, then broke up laughing when she lowered the camera, stuck out her tongue, and crossed her eyes.

"Give me that thing. I want some of you, looking just like that."

She did and posed, acting silly, laughing. She took the camera and captured a few more, then pointed.

"See that pasture over there?"

"Yep, sure do."

"It's filled with wildflowers in the spring, blues and whites and purples. A sight to behold. That's where you're going to chase me, drag me down into the blossoms, and have wild and crazy sex with me. We'll teach those bees something."

"Oh, yeah, when is this going to happen?"

"By the end of May."

"God, I hope so. I'm horny now, though. Do I have to wait that long?"

"You're horny all the time. Besides the ground is soppy and cold."

"Not on the ground. You'd be horny, too, if you hadn't had a woman in twelve years. Then all of a sudden got exposed to a hot chick like you."

"Hot chick, huh? Mmm, I'll have to think about the horny part."

"You know what I mean. This conversation is getting convoluted."

"I'm cold out here in the wind."

"Get back in. It's getting late, and I'm starved."

"Good Lord, a man of many hungers." She ran around the back of the car, climbed in and turned up the heater.

He didn't start out right away, and she glanced over to see him gazing at her. She smiled, and he did, too. "Thank you for being you," he said.

She reached over and rubbed his leg. "What a nice thing to say."

"I mean it. Even in my wildest fantasies, and I had them for a while, I never imagined anyone like you."

"What did you imagine? An angelic blonde with big boobs who would keep her mouth shut and her legs open and behave herself, I'll bet. And look what you got."

He took her hand. "Look what I got indeed. A sassy old woman with big boobs." Bringing her palm to his mouth, he kissed it. "I'll never figure out how I rated you. Just want you to know that, no matter how I may grouse sometimes, I appreciate everything you do for me. More than you'll ever know."

"I'd like to crawl up in your lap and have my way with you, right here and now," she said. "You say the sweetest things. Except for one little thing."

"And what might that be?"

"My boobs aren't big."

He smiled the greatest smile in the world, and she went all trembly inside. "Big enough, sweetheart. Big enough."

He started the car, gunned it on down the road, applied the brakes, and executed a U-turn in the middle of the pavement so they were headed back.

She squealed. "Wow. Just like in the movies. What was that about?"

"The quicker to get us home so you can have your way with me. And I wanted to find out if I could still do it." He drove slowly so she could take pictures. "I had this buddy —he and I used to take our cars out to the airport at night and practice the LA U-turn, figure eights, all that fun stuff. He was in the chopper when we went down. Didn't make it."

She waited, not knowing what to say. "What was his name?"

His lips twitched into a slight grin. "Mac, MacArthur really. He hated it, said his mother would pay someday for naming him that." After a beat, he murmured. "I guess she did."

The turn of the conversation left a black hole in what had been a fun day, but he had to talk about all this, and she did understand that, even if he didn't think so.

"So what's an LA U-turn?"

"Ah, my sweet innocent. That's when you drive backwards as fast as you can, slam on the brake, and use the emergency brake to make an… altogether now…" and she joined him in saying "… LA U-turn."

Back at the house, he led her into the bedroom, stood her in front of his chair and slowly unbuttoned her shirt, slipped it off her shoulders and let it go, then undid her jeans and peeled them down to her ankles. Sitting up, he rubbed his temples, paused.

"What is it?"

"Just a bit of a headache. It'll go away. All I need is a little nooky."

"You sure?"

"Yup." He grinned, cupped her buttocks, pulled her forward so her knees were touching his legs and kissed her belly button, then slipped her panties down, kissed lower and lower until his tongue crept inside her to do wild and crazy things to her libido.

Driven to a frenzied passion, she clung to his arms, leaned back in his embrace, and let herself go. Her world exploded in lights of fire and ice, her heart slammed against her ribs, breath caught, and she slumped into his lap, consumed by an emotion all new and clean and rapturous.

He whispered huskily in her ear. "Get on the bed, Babe. Please hurry."

She pulled him and his chair around facing the bed, took hold of his belt, fell backward onto the mattress, spread her legs and pulled him on top of her, all so quickly he made a surprised sound. Fingers working, she undid his belt and zipper, reached inside to find him hard and hot.

"Hurry, hurry."

One hand encircling him, she guided him unerringly, and he plunged inside her, came with a roar she'd learned to expect. He was insatiable, as if attempting to make up for so many years of a miserable existence. Yet this time he made sure she was satisfied first.

Spencer kept telling her that anytime Glen thought of someone else's needs or comfort, it was another step toward his recovery. He'd made some more steps today.

They lay together for a while, him still inside her. He would soon want more if they didn't get up.

"It's late, and we should eat before we go down to the studio. Time we made ourselves presentable. I'll go turn on the shower and get the water hot." She smacked his butt, rolled him off her. "Get undressed." Left him there to get in the chair and join her. This was becoming the most difficult of her tasks. Not helping him. Spencer said she pampered him, and he was right, so she stood inside the bathroom and peeked out to make sure he got his clothes off, something he could do now, and made it into the chair with no problems.

He rapped on the door. When she swung it open, he was still smiling. God, he looked delicious when he smiled and popped those dimples, revealed glimpses of that beautiful young man who had marched off to war so long ago. They showered together, him sitting in the makeshift chair. She washed his hair because she enjoyed doing it, then he leaned forward, and she scrubbed his back, then handed him the washcloth.

"You're on your own now. Anything else I might do would cause a delay. We don't have time. And before you ask, no, you can't wash my boobs or any of my other parts. Not today. Get busy. Time's a wasting."

He soaped the cloth and went to work. "You're getting pretty sassy in your old age."

"Oh, that does it." She cupped her hands, filled them with water and threw it right in his face.

For a moment he froze, head down, and when he raised it, his eyes were slits, his mouth so tight it was white.

"Oh, God. Glen, I didn't mean… I forgot. Honey? You okay?"

"Yep. Sorry. I forgot where I was, just for a second. Then I saw this sexy naked lady and realized… yep, I'm okay."

She kissed him once, then twice. "You're sure? That was stupid of me."

"It's fine, Katie. Fine. Let's get out of here, or we won't have time for a sandwich before we go down to the studio."

Even though he recovered, she had frightened him, almost sent him back to that cage where they kept dunking him in the water. God, how could she have been so thoughtless? They were having so much fun, and she had to ruin it, yet he'd bounced back with no animosity whatsoever.

Lately, she had been comparing her love for Stan with what she felt for Glen. Love with Stan had been like the coziness of a fireplace on a winter day. Simple, pleasant with no surprises. No experiments. She'd certainly been a prude, but then so had Stan. One position suited him fine. Maybe that was why she'd broken free of all restraints with Glen. All those years she had missed the excitement and glory of a great sex life. With Stan she never had to wonder what would happen next, until a tractor turned over on him and showed her how foolish she'd been to think God had forgotten her. She was sure the old fart had plenty in store for her yet that she wouldn't like one bit.

EIGHT

SPENCER CALLED THAT evening, told her someone would be out later in the week with equipment for Glen's therapy. While the VA wouldn't furnish it all, they had agreed to install a few of the more expensive items. She and Glen could either rent or buy the rest after they met with the therapist who would arrive as soon as the delivery had been made.

"That was quick." All afternoon she had argued with herself about whether to tell him about Glen's reaction to Ellie's visit. Terrified Spencer would yank Glen up and put him back in the hospital, she held her tongue. At least for now.

"I explained how important it is he get started. He's been neglected too long, and when I told them about how far he's come in just a few months, they agreed to hurry it up. Surprised me. How is he?"

She swallowed, ready to tell some more lies. "Well, he's moving his legs. Crazy fool thought that meant he could stand up and took a fall, but he's okay. Not even a bruise to show for it."

"Katherine, that's fantastic. How much movement does he have?"

She told him, then said, "And you'd be proud of me, too. I'm letting him do everything he can himself and asking more of him each day. Oh, he drove this morning. We went out on the mountain and took some pictures. We had an argument, and he got pretty angry without losing his temper, then we made up. I think he's doing just great. And he's eating me out of house and home. I love cooking for him 'cause he likes everything I make. And you know I've never been the best cook in the world."

"She is, too," Glen yelled into the extension in the sunroom.

"Are you eavesdropping?" she said into the phone.

"Shamelessly. Didn't want you telling him any lies. Besides, it saves you having to repeat everything he said."

"Hello, Glen, good to hear you so chipper."

"Hey, Doc. I got it made. Good food, a beautiful woman—what more could a man ask for?"

"I'm pleased. When are you going to come in for a session?"

"This was our session for this week. Can't you tell? I'm well adjusted."

"All the same, we need to talk about stuff, you know. Get your butt in here. How's Friday, three o'clock?"

"I have a class until four." Katie congratulated herself for not mentioning Ellie with Glen on the extension.

"Well, you said he's driving. Let him come in on his own."

"Oh, I don't know…."

"I can do that," Glen said.

"Okay, I guess he can do that," she said faintly.

Both men laughed.

"Now that wasn't so hard, was it? You'd better watch her. She likes to be in charge," Spencer said. "You two take care of each other. See you Friday, Glen."

He hung up before either of them could say anything.

"Go to sleep, Glen."

"Yes, sir," he said and hung up the extension.

She grinned, remained in the living room for a while, straightening pillows and stacking magazines they'd been paging through.

When she went into the sunroom, he was in bed, the light out. She undressed and joined him without making a sound.

He startled her by speaking. "Want to have an orgy?"

"As in Roman orgy?"

He rolled over and grabbed her. "Or the rape of the Sabine women." He nuzzled her breasts and laughed. "God, it feels so good to be able to do that."

"The boobs or the rolling over?"

"Well, if I know what's good for me, I'll say both, won't I?"

"You damned well better."

"Love you." He said no more and was soon asleep.

Odd. He must be worn out from the long day. Still, she couldn't help worrying about him. Not like him to fall asleep getting ready to make love.

He remained in bed asleep long after she rose, dressed, and started breakfast. Rather than awaken him when it was done, she set his plate in the refrigerator. She could always warm it for him in the microwave. By ten o'clock she was worried and slipped into the sunroom to check on him. His forehead was cool, his breathing regular, no sign of an ongoing nightmare. Just flat out sound asleep. She moved her lips from his skin and his eyelids fluttered. He shot up, bumping her nose with his head, scooting backward on the bed until his back was up against the headboard.

"What the hell is going on?" Panic ridden, his eyes darted back and forth, his gaze passing over her like she wasn't there.

"Glen, what is it? What's wrong?" Clearly, he heard her, but either didn't see her or didn't know who she was.

"Turn on the damned lights. Who's there?" He reached out, and she moved forward, took his hand like always. He jerked away.

"It's me, Katie. What's wrong?"

"Ellie? You get away from me, you bitch. Leave me alone." He spread his arms, grabbed the top of the headboard, and pulled himself to his feet, stretched as if peering into the distance. "The bastards are coming again." With that, he rolled into a ball in the nest of pillows.

Though her heart hammered in her throat, she took a deep breath to settle her own frantic emotions. He was having a flashback. It would pass, and he'd be okay.

She sat on the bed, kept an eye on him. When he didn't begin to improve, she moved closer to drag a blanket over him. He was slick with a cold sweat and had begun to shiver.

The moment the blanket touched his skin, he swung one arm to push it off. "Get away. Leave me be. Why don't you kill me and be done with it?"

Enough. This was enough. She couldn't let him go through this any longer. She locked both arms around his quivering body. "Glen, honey, it's Katie. Stop, you're okay. Everything's going to be okay. No one is here but you and me."

He bucked and fought, but she wouldn't let him go. Kept talking to him, holding him, telling him it was okay. After a while, he muttered, "She left me long time ago. Katie left me. I saw her go. Down the driveway. She drove away. Never coming back."

"Stop this, stop it now. I'm Katie, and I never left you. I never would leave you. Feel my arms around you? I love you. You love me."

"Can't be. Can't anyone love me. Never."

"Ssh, baby. It's okay. I do love you. Always."

This time he waited, listened, stopped struggling. "Katie?"

"Yes, sweetie. I'm here."

"In that cage? So damn dark. Can't see. Why did you come here? They told me you left. I believed them. Where are we? You didn't come over here, did you?" He leaned toward her. "Don't let 'em get you. They're mean sons a bitches."

She hugged him closer, tried to comfort him, make him realize where they were. He kept insisting he was blind, couldn't see where he was. Saying things like she was lying. He wanted her to go before they came and found her. She wasn't ever going to stay with him. He knew it. Nonsense like that went on for so long her arms and legs tired of their position, crouched over him on the bed trying to subdue him.

It must have been an hour or more before he stopped the babbling and fighting her and uncoiled himself, let her move him back down in the bed and pull the covers over him. He still didn't acknowledge her or his surroundings. She would have to call Spencer if he didn't come out of it soon, but it was the last thing she wanted. They'd put him back in the hospital, away from her. How could she stand it? How could he?

Instead, she crawled under the covers, took him in her arms, and held him close, wondering what had happened to cause this. Would he never be free of such torture?

NINE

WHEN SHE DECIDED to take another look at him a bit later, his golden eyes gazed at her.

"You okay, sweetie?"

"Where am I?"

Her heart nearly stopped. He couldn't see her. God, had he gone away entirely? Left only a shell of himself, one that had no idea who or where he was?

"In bed with your Katie, that's where," she said.

"No, no. She's gone. My Katie is gone. Why is it dark?"

She took his face in both hands. "Glen, I'm not gone. Can't you see me?"

"Can't see someone who has left."

"But I haven't left. Touch me." She reached under the covers, pulled his hand up and laid it on her breast. "There, your favorite place. There's my boob. You surely recognize that." It took every ounce of her strength to remain casual. She had to talk him out of this. Joking around might be the easiest way. He'd gone to sleep joking with her.

"If you think I can jack off with that, you're crazy. I can't get it up, so stop fooling with me. Can't see a fucking thing, either. What have you done to my eyes?"

"Your eyes are fine. Want to sleep?"

"No."

"I could get you a pill."

"No. It's okay."

"The dreams, will they come back tonight, do you think?

He sighed, shuddered.

"Want to tell me?"

He hesitated. Breathed in a controlled manner, then spoke in a flat monotone. "I see her standing in a dark room. I look down at the forty-five in my hand. I think of what she did to me, how much I hate her, how much I loved her." A sigh for fortification. "She laughs and just keeps laughing. She stops when I bring the gun up. I hold it in both hands, aim, and slow and careful like I squeeze the trigger, and I just keep doing that until it's empty." There was no emotion with his words, and that frightened her.

Through tear-filled eyes, she searched his features, the view misty as if in a dream in which nothing and no one is recognizable. Something she wanted to remember but couldn't quite do fingered through her like ripples in still water. She let it go when he began to speak again.

"As each bullet hits her I watch her jump, see all the blood, but I can't stop firing even after she falls down. I don't feel anything but a heavy darkness. All of a sudden, I'm washed clean, free of her at last. I'm empty of all that hate, but the love is gone, too, and that's hideous." A pause, a moment in which neither breathed.

She wanted him to stop, but dared not say so.

He went on. "I soar above the clouds in a glider with only the sound of the wind whistling around me. I want to stay up there forever, even believe I can. But the sun goes down, and it gets dark so I can't see. Now I'm afraid because I don't know how to get down, then I realize I don't even know which way is down."

He clutched at her a moment, as if in pain. She let him go on, because it was all she could do.

"I hear you then, calling my name, pleading with me. God, in that moment how much I love you, and everything is sweet and clear again. But then I realize I can't find you, can't even hear you anymore. What will I do if there's nobody left to love me, nobody I can love? I remember you promised me you'd never leave me, and I just keep shouting your name, calling for you over and over." His breath blew hot against her skin, and the litany subsided.

"I'm here, right here." She soothed him, kissed his eyes, the tip of his chin, quieting him for a moment.

Enough. Enough. She pulled him close, kissed him. "Sorry, sweetie, I'll have to call Spencer. Maybe he can talk you down if I can't. You may have to go back in the hospital. I'm so sorry."

"Sorry don't mean nothing. Ain't no hospital around these parts. You dreaming, chickie?" Terms and words he would never use.

"Yes, that's right, that's what you told me. Sorry don't mean nothing. Remember, we went for a drive yesterday? You drove your new red car."

His hand climbed from her breast, to feel of her face. "I dreamed about that. How did you know my dream? And you took pictures and stuck your tongue out at me. I talked about… oh, Katie, I miss you so. But, hell, I don't blame you for leaving me. Ain't nothing left but bone and bleeding scars. I coulda told you so."

"Oh, Glen, darling. I'm right here. Can't you see me? Please say you can see me."

He opened his mouth, screamed like she had never heard a man scream before, then shuddered and wrapped his arms tightly around her. "I got away, didn't I? I got away."

"Yes, sweetheart. You got away. You're here with me, and you're going to be okay. I promised you that. Can you see me now?"

He gave her a sickly, twisted grin. "Yes, I see you, Katie. You sassy redhead. Sassy redhead."

"Oh, God." She wrapped her arms around his waist, holding him so tight he grunted, squeezed her back just as tightly.

"I've got you, got you," he sang.

"Yes, you do."

He acted like he was drunk or high on something. Her heart skittered. She'd left him alone, alone in here the day before when she went to turn on the shower. What if he'd taken something out of the drawer? She kept some pain meds there and the sleeping pills she'd taken after Stan died. She'd never forgive herself if her carelessness had caused this.

She had to call Spencer, tell him, see what she might give him to counteract this mad reaction. What if it turned out Glen wasn't any safer here with her than with that Mason Harrington? She thought she could take care of him, keep him safe. And look what she let happen.

"Glen? Are you awake?"

"Yes, I think so. Goddamn. What the hell happened? That was a bad one. Damnation, I thought they were going to go away. I was back in the cages, and I was blind and—"

She put her fingers over his lips. "Ssh, you're okay now. Right? You can see me?"

His smile was tired. "Oh, yes, I see you. When are they going to stop?"

"I can call Spencer, get you back in the hospital. That was a really bad one."

He alerted, grabbed her arm. "No, don't do that. I didn't hurt you, did I? Try to? I didn't, I know I wouldn't."

She wrapped her arms around him. "Stop, Glen. It's okay. No you didn't hurt me, just scared me, but that's okay. Right? What is it you pilots say? I've got your six? Well, I have."

He relaxed, was silent for a moment, then said, "Is there anything to eat? I'm starved."

TEN

THE EQUIPMENT ARRIVED Thursday morning and was installed in a few hours. After Katie signed all the paperwork, the men left. Glen sat in his chair, at one end of a ramp leading to a walkway with bars on either side and another ramp.

"This is where I'll learn to walk? Maybe I should just try it now." He rolled up the ramp, took hold of the bars and pulled himself upright before she could stop him. Lifted his feet and swung back and forth, muscles bulging in his arms. "Well, that's half the work, right there." He swung back and dropped into the chair. "It's the rest that'll be the booger."

She walked past and smacked him on top of the head with a newspaper. "Could you behave for five minutes?"

"Not a chance. Besides, you'd hate that me."

Leaning down, she kissed his cheek. "You betcha, big guy. I think you have to begin over here on this table."

"When is this fella coming? Or is it a woman? A woman rubbing my legs would be much more fun."

"That wouldn't last long," she said. "You'd be so horny in five minutes I'd have to kick her out."

"Oh, is that right?" He laughed, rolled past her and pinched her behind. "What if I'm horny right now?"

"That's no great surprise. All that testosterone penned up so long, you'll be horny every five minutes until you're a hundred and five."

"Sounds about right to me."

He'd been making light jokes about the past and liked it when she did, too. Had to be another natural step in his healing process. She was trying, but it made her nervous as hell. He could switch to not liking it that quick. But going with his moods had become such a habit she fell into it without a problem.

"Hey, it's so pretty outside, how about a picnic?" He flashed his please grin more and more often, an expression she could not resist, no matter the request. He probably could ask her to hang upside down in a tree and she would do it.

"Sounds like fun. I'll put something together. You find us a blanket to throw on the ground, and we'll be ready."

He rubbed his hands together in anticipation. "Ah, a blanket on the ground. Sounds good."

In the pantry she filled a basket with a small canned ham, some crackers, and a bottle of Chardonnay, glasses for the wine, along with paper plates, napkins, and a sharp knife, then added a couple of apples and some cheddar from the fridge.

He showed up with a blanket folded in his lap and two sweaters. "Thought we might need these in case it gets chilly. Hope you got lots of goodies. I'm hungry."

"When aren't you hungry? I better throw in a package of cookies for your sweet tooth."

"I know something else my sweet tooth would like, but you won't fit in the basket."

"Calm down, buster. You gonna drive?"

"Love to, ma'am. Are we ready?"

"Look out, World, here we come."

She helped push the wheelchair up the graveled incline to the carport, then left him to the rest. He opened the door, laid the folded blanket in the back seat, swung into the front, folded the chair, and leaning forward, slid it behind his seat. She pretended not to pay any attention, but always had an eye out for any slips. He hadn't made many since he'd begun to move his legs around freely.

"Where we going?" she asked.

"I don't care. Just want out."

"I know the perfect place."

He followed her directions up the mountain to the south, driving fast and efficiently, as if they were flying off into oblivion together, windows down on both sides. She loosened her hair and let it blow free.

Probably because he had been a pilot, he drove as if he were an extension of the car, never took his eyes off the road, yet conveying that what he did was absolutely the easiest task he could perform. Using the hand controls had become natural to him. Must be because he'd flown a helicopter. Considering that he hadn't driven for a lot of years, she was amazed at the easy skill with which he carried out the job.

"Does it scare you... going fast?" He seemed to worry a lot that something he did might frighten her.

She understood why. When they first were together, he'd often asked if she was afraid of him because he was crazy.

"No, it's wonderful. The turn-off is about another mile or so, maybe twenty seconds down the road. Look for rock pillars on the left."

He laughed. "That would mean we're going a hundred eighty miles an hour."

Her nod was serious. "I thought we were."

He slowed a bit when he spotted the pillars, slotted between them and onto the narrow dirt road that dropped precariously into the valley far below. The rear tires spat dust, digging into the surface. From the sunlit mountain peak, they plunged into the dark shadows of a canopy road, and the air cooled.

"You're awfully quiet, Katie. Say something."

"Having a good time here. Traveling at the speed of light."

He chuckled. A bubble of happiness burst inside her, filling her with a fresh taste of mint and ice. She laid her hand on his knee.

"I can feel that," he warned, "and you know what that means. But I want to know things about you you've never told me. We talk about me all the time. Poets. Who's your favorite?"

"I don't know. I guess Rod McKuen." How many men would want to discuss poets?

"Rod How-much?"

"Don't you go highbrow on me. Just who do you like, Mr. Smarty?"

"Let's see. To prove I'm not a highbrow, I like country music, detective novels... I used to read Mickey Spillane avidly, and of course, poets, who but Emily?"

"Mickey Spillane? And you made fun of Rod McKuen." She pinched playfully at his bare skin beneath the loose shirt. "Now it's my turn. Emily who?"

"Oh, no. Don't tell me I'm going to have to educate you. I can't believe it. I've been sleeping with a woman who doesn't know and love the dark and mysterious Emily Dickinson." He only slowed a tiny bit to make the hairpin turn at the bottom of the long incline.

Beneath the jocularity, she read his message. He seriously wanted them to begin over right here, this day, and deny all that had gone before. The nightmares, the flashbacks, everything wiped out. Not that she could blame him. Dealing with memories had to be bitterly painful for him. She'd go along with that. Begin a brand new life together, neither of them having a past. Now if only he could stop reliving his in the dark of night.

After the hairpin, she guided him through a series of turns that forced him to brake. "Hard right here. Don't go there, someone lives there."

"I know where we're going. I'd forgotten all about this place. We used to come down here at night for catfish, at least a hundred years ago. Me and Mark and Luke. They loved it when I brought them here."

The canopied road narrowed, dipped through a few small streams.

"Tell me some Emily," she said.

He paused a moment to think, then quoted,

If all the griefs I am to have

Would only come today,

I am so happy I believe

They'd laugh and run away,

They could not be so big as this that happens to me now.

She caught her breath. "Lovely, but tell me why doesn't the last word rhyme with anything? Listen to this: But if you stay, I'll give you a day, like no day has been, or will be again."

It was his turn to catch his breath, and they rode in silence through the last turn that brought them to the spillway of the lake, which he drove across, dust spinning wildly into the air behind them. The warm weather had stirred the hearts of many a frog. As the sun dropped behind the western peaks, their gay chorus filled the valley. At the end of the bridge was a small picnic area that sat on the precipice of a gash blasted out of the side of the mountain to form the spillway for the lake. Near the single table, a giant cedar clung precariously to one side of the drop-off, the top twisting its way into the blue sky. Clusters of jonquils performed a golden ballet in the dying breeze.

Together they sat at the table and ate and listened to the cascade of water tumbling from the lake past boulders big as houses and into the creek far below.

"Someone once lived here a long time ago before this lake." She gestured around her. "A mother planted those flowers, watched her children play in the yard. Do you ever wonder about all the people, where they went, what they're doing?"

"I guess. Those were tough times, back then. People just went, somewhere, anywhere, to keep from starving. Does it matter now?"

"Everything matters. You and I matter. Our love matters. Our future matters. The past does, but we have to let it go to get to our future."

He finished his sandwich and picked up the wine glass, sipped and gazed out across the water, shimmering in the dusk, the surrounding mountains stark and bare, anticipating spring. "It's a lot like 'Nam here. Beautiful, deceptively serene. A lot of danger hiding out there."

More danger hiding within themselves, but she didn't want to talk about it. She wanted to go on from here, as he'd hinted at earlier. But she sensed that wasn't going to happen and was frightened for both of them.

He was about to bring out the memories, despite his vow not to do so. Spencer was full of crap when he talked about that therapy of his. Forget the past, think only of the future. It wasn't possible. It had to be talked about, listened to, understood, then perhaps it would settle into dust. She moved to the bench beside him where she could touch him, to sense what would happen before the monsters that lived in him got the upper hand, to stop, if she could, any rash or hurtful thing from happening to him.

Lately, all she could think of was keeping him safe.

"A bunch of us flew med-evacs. There was me, and MacArthur M. MacKenzie. We all called him Mac. He was killed coming in over a lake a lot like this one on an evening very much like this. These bastards just reached up and jerked him out of the seat right beside me. I asked for hands on, and he was sitting there in his own blood. I didn't even know he was dead. He didn't make a sound, just died. No good-byes, nothing."

Eyes closed she swayed, and grasped his hand. This should be their time to laugh, not cry. She swallowed painfully and rose to get their sweaters from the car. He was quiet until they both put them on. She hugged him from behind, and he pulled her hands to his mouth and kissed the palms.

"No one ever hit me in anger or tried to hurt me in my entire life," he said. "On the football field, or even in war, it's give and take. They do to you, you do to them. But 'Nam was different and then what they laid on me after, Jesus Christ. What we did, died for, was all for nothing."

A waxing moon hung in the sky that purpled along the eastern horizon, illuminating the lake and shoreline in a golden hue. She kept her hands on his shoulders, felt them heave in a sigh.

"Why didn't they save us from that? Year after year of rising above the pain to dare hope. We got nothing for it, not care or concern. Nothing. Hundreds of us in camps. Still some there. I'll always wonder why I was chosen and they were left behind."

"But they finally got you out," she said.

"The hell they did. A bunch of mercs got us out. I... they.... Shit, I can't remember anymore. I'm sorry, I didn't mean to bring this up. It just spews out of me sometimes before I can stop it." He rubbed her hands, went quiet.

His silence relieved her, but in a strange, unfulfilled way. She'd heard the story from Spencer, didn't need to hear it again. Except that Glen had to tell someone, and she had to listen. She could do no less for him. The love she felt for him was like nothing she had ever experienced. Though she had loved Stan, it was not the same as this all-encompassing sensation. She had always laughed at the term, soul mate, but this was that and even more. She was a piece of him, as he was a piece of her. She would die for him, die if she no longer had him, kill anyone who hurt him. So she would keep him safe and happy and healthy until he could do it for himself.

He swung around on the bench, dropped his feet to the ground, and patted his lap. "Sit here for a minute. I need to hold you, need you to hold me."

She lowered herself onto him, looped both arms around his neck. "Okay? I'm not too heavy?"

"Oh, you are so fat." He raised his face so the moonlight touched his cheeks, shadowed his golden eyes that caught the glow. Somewhere deep down the edge of panic hovered.

She lowered her lips to his. The kiss was at once tender and filled with desire. It went on and on, with neither pulling away. When it finally ended, she laid her head against his shoulder.

"Don't ever go away and leave me," he whispered. "I think I'd die if you did."

"You don't have to worry, cause I'd die before I would leave you." She shivered. Promises made by lovers in each other's arms on a chilly evening beside a lake reflecting a moon. Who could resist making such vows? But why did dying always come into theirs?

"You're cold. Let's go home." He rubbed her shoulders.

"Home. I'm so glad to hear you call it home. It is our home, isn't it?"

He didn't reply for a long while. "Sometimes I worry that it's your home, yours and your husband's, and maybe we ought to be somewhere else. Then I see you walking through the rooms and know I don't want to see you anyplace else but there. You fit there. As long as it's okay with you that I'm there… rather than him."

"He's gone, Glen. I'll always keep a little piece of his memory tucked away, but I love you, wherever we are. I like it there and hope you do, too." She touched his cheek. "We could get married, you know."

"For now, let's just be together. I like it as it is. Let's go before you freeze."

A bit disappointed but not surprised, she nodded and moved from his lap, gathered the leavings of their picnic into the basket, and took it to the car. She glanced back to see him struggling to move from the bench to the wheelchair. After watching for a moment, she went to him. "Could you use a hand, sailor?"

"I believe I could."

Back behind the wheel, he sped through the switchbacks of the mountain road.

"Look, it's the ghost light." She pointed off to their right, high above the peaks. Strobing lights here and then over there, sped across the sky.

"What is that?"

"It's just the television booster tower on Sunset Mountain. With the constant curvature and rise and fall of the highway the tower appears to shift to the left, then the right, then behind, then above and below. Soon after the tower was built the truckers driving Seventy-one spotted it and dubbed it the ghost light. For a couple of weeks it caused quite a furor on CB channels until the mystery was cleared up. Some of them actually thought they were seeing a UFO. Others swore off Coors and Bud Light for at least two weeks."

He laughed as she told the story. "No fucking shit." One of his favorite expletives, something she'd had to get used to, having once been a prudish old woman where swearing was concerned.

"We didn't use the blanket," he said when he turned up the lane to the house.

"It'll be much more comfortable in the bed."

"Yeah. It's not too early to retire, is it?"

She rubbed his thigh, let her fingers linger between his legs. "No, not too early at all."

"They installed bars in the bathroom, didn't they?" he asked.

He knew they did, but she played along. "Shall we go see?"

"How about a shower where I'm standing up, too? You can do all kinds of kinky things to me and I won't be able to do a thing about it but hang on tight for the ride."

"You are impossible. That sounds like a winner to me." Could he do that without falling? She didn't know, but was willing to let him try. It was past time for him to get on his feet, whatever it took to get him there.

ELEVEN

HE SAT ON the toilet seat to undress, used the rails to support his weight, and moved into the large shower stall, turning his back to the showerhead. They had never stood toe to toe, and she stepped in with her heart hammering in her throat, eyes scanning up his scarred body and into his face. She hardly noticed the scars there anymore, for they did nothing to mar his good looks.

"You're taller than I imagined," she said.

He gazed down at her, smiled. "You're shorter than I thought. Would you turn on the water, please?"

She was suddenly attacked with a desire for him so strong her knees wobbled. Her nipples puckered, between her legs a fire blazed. This man, standing here smiling down at her was not the man she had first laid eyes upon so many months ago. A painfully thin man slumped in a wheelchair slapping paint on a canvas filled with bloody, suffering figures. A man who did not know how to smile or how to love.

For a moment mesmerized, she just stared up at him.

"Honey? The water?"

"Oh, sure." She adjusted the spray, waited until it was hot. "I'm aiming it at you now. Okay?" She always feared a flashback to the water tortures he'd endured.

He sucked in a breath, nodded.

Steam surrounded them, rose like mist off a lake. She stepped in front of him, a twinkle deep in the black pupils of his golden eyes. Moving closer so his erect penis touched her stomach, she kissed him on the mouth. Pulled back and flicked at his hard-on with the tip of her finger.

"Want me to wash your back?"

"Not really, not right now. Couldn't we take care of that first?"

"Oh, you mean do kinky things to you when you can't fight back?"

"That's exactly what I mean. Dammit, Katie, do something."

"Hang on, big boy," she said and dropped to her knees.

"Holy fucking shit." He groaned, the muscles tightening in both arms. She grinned up at him. "Still hanging on?"

"Barely."

"There's a drop down seat. Why don't I lower it so you can sit?"

"I'm okay. Do something else."

She grabbed a bar of soap and a cloth and began washing him, starting between his legs. She took her time, lathering her hand and bringing his erection back full blown before soaping his legs, stomach, chest, and back.

"And you're going to leave me like that?" he said, while she spent lots of time scrubbing him.

"Well, you're really dirty, and I want to make sure and get you clean."

"You are a mean and evil woman, my Katie. Mean and evil."

"I know, sweetie. Just hang in there. I'm going to take the shower head down and rinse the soap off you. Water everywhere. You still okay?" Do not imagine they are hosing you down, shoving you under water until you almost drown, shutting you in a cage, stomping your clawing fingers. Do not imagine that.

"Other than Johnny there, yep, I'm fine."

Finished with the rinse, she circled his waist with both arms. "Time to sit down now, and I can finish that off for you, if you've a mind to."

"Oh, I'm of a mind to, all right. You're gonna pay for this. Wait until I get you in bed. You'll beg, woman. You'll beg."

"I can't wait. Besides you asked for it." She lowered the seat and positioned him. "Turn loose now."

He did, and she straddled his lap.

"Dammit, woman, you're something."

He closed his eyes, and she did, too.

In bed, both their bodies warm from the shower, they went into each other's arms and fell asleep that way. Her last thought, let the nightmares stay away, it's been such a wonderful day.

And they did. Sometimes they did, but not often enough. He slept deeply all night.

She awoke, and as usual, he was lying there staring at her. "How do you always wake up before me?" She kissed his nose and threaded her fingers through his curly hair.

"Like to watch you come awake. Your pupils go from wide to small, and the first thing you see is me. I know 'cause I see me in your eyes. Two mes."

"Two yous, huh? That is indeed scary."

"Yeah, in case one isn't good enough."

"One is absolutely good enough. Want to get up?"

"Not yet."

"God, you're insatiable."

Later she fixed breakfast, and he dressed, which took him a while. He came out wearing another pair of the jeans she had bought him and the red shirt she'd first seen him in. "You know, that was what you wore the first time I saw you dressed when you left the hospital."

"I remember. I remember every single thing about being with you."

"And I do you, too. Now how about we stop throwing compliments at each other and get busy? I want to call Spencer about this therapist who is going to come out here every single day. I've seen how some of them yell and push their patients, and that ain't gonna happen. No more like that Harrington bastard."

"Aren't you the tough one?"

"Never mind. I just have to let him know that."

"Katie, don't—"

"Don't you *Katie* don't me. I've got a job to do, and I'll do it my way."

He held up both hands. "Okay, okay. I'll let Spencer handle you. He's better at it than I am."

"Indeed." She glared at him and picked up the phone, grinning a bit so he knew she wasn't mad. He picked up on the third ring. "Spencer, I want to talk to you about this therapist."

"Now don't get all up in arms. He'll be competent."

"That's not what I'm concerned about. I know some of these guys think they're running a boot camp or something. I've heard them in there, yelling, bullying to get what they want out of their patients. That isn't going to happen here, not in my house, not to Glen."

Glen hollered, "She thinks she's got to protect me, Spencer. This wasn't my idea."

"Tell him I know that. And it's a good thing you *do* feel that way."

"Well, he's had enough assholes mistreating him to last a lifetime, and you just let this fella know he's going to be polite. This is going forward at Glen's pace. He says stop, he stops. Got it?"

"I'll send a kinder, gentler therapist. Don't worry, Katie."

"Smartass." She hung up on his burst of laughter.

Glen rolled up behind her, chuckling. "Guess you told him, huh?"

"Don't you make fun of me, Mister."

He rolled away fast. "Love you, sweetheart."

A card Spencer had given Glen explained the sessions. The appointment was for 9 a.m. until noon. Mornings were for exercises to strengthen the muscles. After a few weeks, at the therapist's discretion, work would begin on the bars in the afternoon. Walking. Depending on Glen's strength and ability at that point, they might put braces on his legs.

And to quote Spencer, "By God, we're going to get this boy walking."

Some afternoons she had art classes, but if necessary she would give those up. When she mentioned that to Glen, he exploded. Said he didn't want her giving up something she enjoyed for him. She told him she guessed she would if she wanted to. He was much more important to her than teaching art to women who had little talent and too much time to spare.

"What about the paintings for the exhibit? You'll not give those up. I won't let you. Please don't do that. I would feel fucking lousy, guilty, and pretty damned mad to boot."

She agreed. "After I'm sure this guy isn't going to drive you like a slave or yell at you."

He grumbled, "I don't need a keeper," and disappeared in the sunroom, slamming the door behind him.

Of course, they had made up, but a line had been drawn in the sand, as he put it. As far as Katie was concerned, what Glen wanted, he got. Thankfully, he was mostly easy to please. His only demands were not for himself but for her.

By the time the therapist knocked on the door, breakfast was over, the dishes in the dishwasher, and the house straightened. Having the equipment in their bedroom was a bit dicey, but she had found a plain spread for the bed and tossed colored pillows all over it.

"So it won't look like it's where we make love," she'd said. With a big smile, he'd hugged her tight and told her he adored her.

The therapist wasn't a very large man, not like Mason Harrington at all. She greeted him at the door. He introduced himself as Martin Clark, Marty would do, and they shook hands. From his grip she could tell he was steely strong, and she approved. His eyes were caring.

"Glen is in his room. After you finish, if you feel we need more equipment, would you give me a list so we can arrange to get it?"

"Yes, ma'am. I will."

She led him to the sunroom, opened the door, and let him in, then closed it, determined to give Glen his space. That is if Marty didn't start yelling at him. For a while, she stood close, listening, but only heard the low hum of conversation, and once in a while a chuckle from one or both of them. Finally satisfied, she went to her recliner and started reading *The Shining*, which she'd wanted to get to for a while.

TWELVE

GLEN AND MARTY came out of the room promptly at noon. Glen's hair was wet on his neck and curly. Marty shook his hand, smiled, and said he'd see him tomorrow. He told her he could bring the few things he wanted Glen to use, as the VA had done a pretty good job of providing everything. She could pay him then.

"How did it go?" she asked after Marty left.

"Fine." He shook his head. "Weird to imagine doing all that to my legs will make them stronger."

"Want lunch or a shower?"

"Had my shower. Guess that's part of the therapy, sending me in there to manage it alone." He grinned and tapped her on the nose. "Rather take one with you, though."

She put lunch on the table, poured iced tea, and sat down.

"Are you going down to the studio after we eat?"

"Yes. Want to come?"

"Yes, please. I need to watch you work and do some myself. Funny how I miss fooling around with charcoal. Prefer it to painting. And watching you create something on canvas is fascinating to me. You do it with such ease."

"I just make it look easy. It really isn't. I like you being with me when I paint."

He grimaced and rubbed his thigh.

"What?"

"It's nothing. Marty said I might have some cramps for the first few weeks. Said not to worry about it. Told me that pretty lady in the other room probably wouldn't mind rubbing my legs for me."

"Oh, he did, did he? I guess he'd be right. Just say the word."

He hadn't seen the large painting, tagged, An Immortal Hero, which she kept covered when she wasn't working on it. It was time she showed it to him, got his take on it.

After she whipped the cover off and stepped away from the two-foot-by-three-foot painting, he studied it for a long while up close, then moved back away from it a few feet. Nothing was finished. On the muted background, swirls of cobalt and pearl gray, were the faded portraits of Glen as a football hero, standing hipshot, helmet hanging from one hand, long hair blowing in the wind, a wide smile, probably aimed at some girl. Then as a young naval lieutenant and pilot, stance mocking the first one, uniform different, man the same. Another as a faceless man with hands that fisted bars of a cage hanging in a tree. Lastly the portrait of his gaunt face, an image of what she remembered the first time she'd walked into the hospital to meet him. The center focal point left blank for the final study of him on his feet and smiling.

The figures formed an elusive life-chain within the hushed monochromatic tones, yet their virility and despair exuded a wrenching physical force. Within the flow of innocence, of danger, beauty, strength, and finality, hope shown through to lift the heart even as it plunged to its lowest depths. Barely sketched into the background, so one had to look twice to make sure they existed, were fleeting images of boys on a football field, a helicopter, misty mountains, a camp somewhere in Cambodia.

"Dear God," was all he said. At long last, he slowly rolled the chair right up to the painting and the portrait of the gaunt man who had returned home. "Can you take that one off?"

Mutely, she nodded. "But I want people to see what war does to a young, hopeful, and handsome boy."

"I understand the message, Katie. It's alive. The goddamned thing is alive with message, with despair, with hope. Can you take it off? I don't want that to be the me people remember. It's like I'm seeing someone else I never really knew existed." His hands kneaded painfully into her back, and she accepted the pain as deserved punishment.

"Oh, sweetie, that won't be the you they remember. All these will be misted into the background and see that spot I've left in the center? There will be the you everyone will remember. The journey climaxes with your recovery, your new life, leaves behind all this."

He still wouldn't look at her, but kept staring at the huge canvas. "On my feet?"

"On your feet. Of course, on your feet."

"Jesus, this is something, Katie. Something. You are truly an artist."

"Thank you. May I leave the portrait of the first you I knew? It's up to you."

He came to her. "Of course, I didn't mean to say it. I didn't know I looked like that the first time. My God, why didn't you turn and run?"

"I almost did, but I'm sure glad I stayed."

"Me, too. Finish the painting the way you need to. It's heartrending but the message is promising."

He settled down near a window with his charcoals and large pad. She went to work on the painting, hoping to finish it in time to send a photo of it to qualify for an individual showing in The Art Gallery on Dickson Street next year.

"When does it have to be finished? He rubbed shadows into the gaunt face he'd drawn.

"March first. I've already been accepted for the first exhibit."

"Can you finish it in that length of time? What? Just three weeks?"

"If I work on it every day, yes. It's all in my head, so it's just a matter of executing those images from my brain to the canvas. And a lot is already there, just needs finishing."

"But I thought there was a showing in May."

"Yes, and my work has been juried and accepted for that one. All the artists who are accepted will show five of their best paintings then."

"Then you get a show of your own later? When will that be?"

"If I qualify, then there's a lottery to choose the month. Nine artists will get individual shows, one each month of the school year beginning in September. The gallery is open to the public, and we get a featured opening. That's a big deal." She dusted a large brush all but free of pale cadmium blue, dipped it in linseed oil and lightly moved it back and forth over the football hero. Stepped back and nodded. "It's a major undertaking for the art department at the university. The first time they've sponsored something like this."

"The May showing. Is it for a month?"

"No, there's a grand opening on Saturday evening, then the paintings will be there all day Sunday. Everyone who is anyone will be invited for the Saturday event, an invitation only affair, plus it will be open to the public on Sunday."

"This is very exciting, Katie. I'm so proud of you."

"Thank you. Yes, yes it is exciting."

He was quiet for a while, the faint scratch-scritch of his charcoal rubbing over the rough paper the only sound in the room. Then he said softly, "I don't want you to miss out on any of this, Katie."

She paused, glanced over to see him gazing at her. "I won't. Don't even think that, Glen. I mean it."

He shook his head. He turned and stared out the window, then back at her, and down at his sketch.

"Stop it, stop it now. You are part of my life. I love you. You come first, and you always will."

"That right there is the problem. If I do… do something crazy that keeps you from meeting these deadlines, I'd be devastated."

"You won't."

"You can't know that. I don't know it. Hard as I try, this stuff just fills my brain sometimes, and it spews out all over our lives, messing things up. Sometimes I don't know it's going to happen, other times I can't remember if it did or didn't."

"I don't want to talk about this, anymore. Besides, talking about it is keeping me from painting, so let's just talk about something else. Okay?"

He didn't reply, and they both went back to what they were doing. By five o'clock, she was ready to quit. Glen had stopped an hour earlier and retired to the office to sit on the couch and read.

She poked her head in, wiping her hands on paper towels. "Ready to go, sweetie?"

"Yep." He laid down his book, moved into the wheelchair, and retrieved the book. His eyes studied her, told her he was still mulling over their conversation about the art exhibits. He didn't trust himself. How could she help him with that?

That evening they watched The Blue Lightning with Sam Elliott before going to bed, and he was unusually quiet, wrapping her in his arms and falling asleep without making love. She feared a nightmare coming on, but he slept quietly. If he did dream, he didn't awaken her.

The next morning she told him she was going to town to buy groceries while he had his therapy.

He grinned. "Oh, so I guess you and Marty have come to an agreement about how mean he can be to me."

"Something like that. How do you feel about him?"

"You mean, are we in love?"

"Doofus. I mean it Glen. If he hurts you I want to know about it."

"He hurts me, I'll pop him one. You see the size of that guy? I wonder if he could catch me if I fall."

She glanced at him. "You worried he'll let you fall?"

"Nah, just being silly."

"Would you rather I didn't leave you here with him?"

He came to her while she fiddled with her purse to make sure she had her list and checkbook. "Katie, stop stewing about this. Everything is fine. Everything is going to be fine. He's no Mason Harrington. That was a major blunder I doubt will ever be repeated."

She dropped her purse in the chair, knelt beside him. "I was so terrified and at the same time angry that night. When I found you like that, I wanted to take someone out. I mean it."

"Aw, sweetheart." He kissed her, rubbed his knuckles over her cheek. "I appreciate how you feel, but you've got to let up. Relax. Don't worry so much about me. I'm fine, feeling better all the time. That's all because of you. I don't want you to stress out so. Marty is a nice kid, he knows what he's doing. We'll get along fine. He can take a lot of the pressure off you."

"Okay, I'm being silly. Just so long as we talk and are honest with each other, everything will be all right. So I'll go buy some food before you starve. See you when I get back."

He sat in the doorway watching her go down the driveway. She glanced back before pulling onto the road, and the door was closed. She met Marty in his little car before she got to the highway and gave him a wave. He waved back.

They would be all right, the two of them, without her help or interference. In town, she drove to the hospital and ran in to see Spencer.

He was alone in his office, and she went in. He rose, kissed her cheek. "How are my two favorite people doing?"

"Fine, we're doing just fine." She would not tell him about the horrid incident with Ellie or the night Glen suffered a severe flashback. He had recovered well, and that was all that counted.

"And Martin. Do you approve?"

"Yes. Glen likes him, and they're getting along."

"So you must trust him. You left the two of them alone. I'm shocked and pleased."

"Go ahead, make fun of me. Glen is happy. So am I. That's the result you wanted from your grand scheme, isn't it?

He chuckled. "Sit, Katherine."

"Don't have time. Have some shopping to do. I wanted to see your face when I told you my work has been accepted for the art show at the university in May."

He beamed. "Good work, my dear. Congratulations."

"Thank you. I'm pleased. I'm working on a large painting I hope will qualify me for a one-woman show later. I'm excited about it."

"What's the subject?"

"*The Immortal Hero* is the title. I was calling it *The Returning Warrior*, but he admires Emily Dickinson, and I thought that more fitting."

He tilted his head, studied her seriously. "Glen, I take it?"

"Yes."

"Be very careful, Katherine, how you portray him. Has he seen it yet?"

"It isn't finished, but yes, he has."

"And how did he react?"

"He wanted me to remove the one of him like he was when I first met him."

"Understandable. And did you agree?"

"No, I explained how important it was to the piece, and he agreed when I explained that an image of him fully recovered will represent the main focus."

"And how will he be then, my dear?"

"Glen asked if he would be on his feet, and I said yes. He was pleased."

"And that's how you left it?"

"Spencer, what's going on?"

"It's one thing for him to have lived through this, quite another for him to watch how it came about and how he changed during that time. We never see ourselves as others see us. We see a composite of what we suppose we are. Most everyone is startled to see how others perceive them. Glen may have a hard time when he realizes the difference in his beliefs about himself and how you see him."

"I'll... I'll discuss it with him some more. See if I can learn what he really wants."

"He won't tell you. Not when he knows how important this show is to you. He does know that, doesn't he?"

She nodded, miserable, glanced at the clock. "I have to go. I want to be home before Marty leaves, and I have to buy some food. Glen eats like a fullback. You should come out soon. I think you'll be pleased at his physical progress. He's beautiful, Spencer. Thank you for getting us together."

When she came out with her groceries, she quickly learned how plans can go awry. All the damn van would do was click. Crap, now what?

Cursing under her breath, she got out and lifted the hood. The damned battery terminals were corroded. Why hadn't she bothered to check them? The weather had been humid, and ugly white stuff had grown all over the metal. In the back of the van in a small toolbox, she found a screwdriver and a brush. By the time she had removed each connection, cleaned it well, and put them back on, along with turning down help from three different men kind enough to offer, it was noon. Why had she spent that time with Spencer? She should have simply bought the groceries and gone back home. Now she wouldn't be home until after Marty left for another appointment.

He might still be there. Near the grocery store were two public phones. She dug out some change and went to ask Marty to stay or at least, if he had gone, to tell Glen not to worry. The phone rang a long time without an answer. Heart in her throat, she hung up, ran to the van, ground the engine to life, and took off. He would be alone, which might be okay if he'd expected her to be late. He suffered from what a lot of men returning from war suffered from. The expectation that nothing was permanent. That whatever or whoever they loved would disappear without warning. That they'd be left alone… as they deserved. Glen had it big time because he had been abandoned for so many years by a country he thought loved him and by a wife who divorced him when he needed her support the most.

All these things ran through her head as she raced home, hitting sixty-five all the way on a highway built for fifty-five or less. The van yawed on the curves, tires screaming, sometimes leaving the pavement, but she couldn't slow down. Why hadn't he answered the phone? What was he doing?

Martin's car was gone. Slamming to a halt next to the door, sacks of groceries sliding all over the place, she jumped out and hurried inside. No sound, no signs he might have had lunch and gone to bed for a nap. She could scarcely breathe, her chest ached, her head swam. She called his name, no reply. The rooms were empty and silent as one by one she moved through those on the main floor. He couldn't have gone upstairs, could he? Just in case, she ran up there. Her old bedroom door was closed. Odd.

She took hold of the doorknob, pushed it open a crack. "Glen, you in there?"

"Go away," he said.

"Honey, I'm sorry I'm late. The van wouldn't...." The room was empty. "Where are you?"

No reply. She sagged against the wall, literally coming unglued.

What now?

THIRTEEN

HIS VOICE AGAIN.

"The only one who can hurt me now is me." The muffled voice spoke from the big walk-in closet. What was he doing in there?

She tip-toed to the door. "Glen? Can I come in?"

"Who is that? Katie is gone. She's not coming back."

"Glen, this is Katie. Okay if I join you? Maybe sit on the floor and contemplate our navels or something?"

"Do as you please, but she's not here." She eased the sliding door open, glancing at her reflection in the full length mirror, her eyes wide with fright. All she saw were his bare toes, feet flat on the floor. Sweeping some of the clothing aside, she peered into the shadowy corner. He sat, knees pulled up to his chin, gazing beyond her.

"Oh, I see, we're going to count our toes." The words barely came out, she was so frightened yet relieved to find him in one piece.

"Git on in here before they see you. How'd you find me? You have to leave. They'll hang you up by your wrists. Please leave."

"Glen, you're in our bedroom closet."

He shook his head frantically. "Nuh-uh."

Down on her knees, she crawled to him, snuggled in beside him. "Let's talk about this. Look around, see the clothes? This is a closet in the bedroom. Honey, how did you get up here? Crawl?"

Confusion colored his voice. "I don't know. Katie, how did you get up here? Crawl?"

"No, sweetie, I walked, but you can't, so I'm wondering just how you managed it. 'Cause I'm going to have to get you back down the steps."

"What are you doing, Katie? What happened? Why are we sitting here in the dark?"

He'd had a flashback, and in terror had managed to hide away up here. "I'm so sorry I was late." She put an arm around his shoulder, pulled him close. "I won't do that again."

His arms enclosed her and he sighed. "Do what? What did I do now? What?"

Struck silent by guilt, she settled against his neck.

"Aw, dammit, Katie. Why are we sitting on the floor? Please stop crying. I thought I heard gunshots so I hid. What in the hell happened here?"

He pried at her hands, trying to get her loose, struggling to rise, but she could not release him. Fright knotted her stomach, kept her holding him down in case he fell into the flashback again. How terrifying to be somewhere like that and not know why or how it happened.

"Katie, I'm sorry. So sorry."

"No, don't. Don't you be sorry. It's the sons of bitches who sent you there. Bastards who left you behind. Monsters who did this to you. They are the ones who ought to be sorry. Don't you dare be sorry."

"I… okay, if you say so."

When she began to talk, she couldn't stop. Neither could she let him go.

"It's all my fault, Glen. You didn't do anything. I did it. I showed you how you looked when you didn't know. I never thought you could come up here. You could have fallen. Never thought about it at all. If I'd taken care of the battery in the van, it wouldn't have quit working. I'm so so sorry you thought I had left you. I will never leave you, I promise, cross my heart and hope to…." She cut off the rest of the childish promise. No one would die here. No one. She would see to that.

"I need up off this floor. Could you please let me go?"

She laid her head on his shoulder. "Just another minute." She was making too much of this, yet she couldn't stop, imagining what could've happened to him all alone in this big house, his mind going crazy with fear and worry.

"You're not afraid of me, are you?"

"I am afraid. Afraid you'll hurt yourself. Please, Glen. Promise me you won't ever do that again."

"Wish I could. I have no idea how I got up here, what I was doing before I came up here, and I don't remember anything else."

"Did you lay down to take a nap and maybe have a nightmare and walk in your sleep?"

"Huh?"

"Well, you know what I mean. After Marty left, what did you do?"

"Hell if I know."

"Do you remember what you and he did all morning?"

He thought about it a minute. "Well, yeah. Same as we did yesterday, then he brought a big ball and had me sit in the wheelchair and kick it to him, he'd kick it back, I had to kick it again. Silly game without scoring or anything sensible like that. Then he had these wooden rollers, looked sort of like Julia's rolling pin. I rolled them back and forth under my feet, then he rolled them on my calves and thighs. Hard. And-uh, that's all I remember doing. Oh, I took a shower before he left, but I don't remember anything after that."

"Not anything that could have caused a flashback? The shower? You might have thought it was a cage. The water and all closed in. Only when I got here you knew it was me, got on me for leaving you. You mentioned how terrible you looked when we met. That must've been because of showing you my painting. Spencer said that wasn't a good idea to let you see that."

"Katie, I—I don't remember any of that. I swear I don't. I'm so damned sorry—"

She held up a hand, stopped him. "Huh-uh, none of that."

"But what if I'd found a knife or something else? I might have used any weapon at hand. I might've slit my wrists with a knife. I know how to do that. I've done it before. The thing is, you don't cut straight across, you go up from the wrist toward your elbow. Slash deep and wide."

She cupped her hand over his mouth. "Stop that. Right now. No more. Let's get you downstairs and fix some lunch."

He shook his head. "I don't think I could eat anything. How are we gonna get me down there?"

"I guess you can sit down and scoot to the steps and go down that way."

"Yeah, that'll work." He scooted out of the closet on his butt, using his hands and feet to propel himself.

Would this never end? How long did he have to endure going through such awful experiences? Would his mind always create ways for him to escape imagined threats to himself? One day they'd have so much fun and the next he sank into terror. Had those nine years of torture been more than his mind could handle? She couldn't face that, could not let herself admit the possibility that he might never heal.

At times like this she felt him slipping away. Like fine powdery sand running between her fingers in spite of her clutching fist. Should she open her hand, the wind would blow away the last few grains, leaving just a touch of grit against her skin. A memory.

She had to convince him to see Spencer at least once a week and talk some of this stuff out. Not that she had a lot of faith in Spencer's brand of psychology, but talking was always good, wasn't it? Unless Spencer decided to hospitalize him.

She walked beside him down the stairs, let him get in the wheelchair without touching him, though it was difficult.

As if reading her mind, he asked, "Are you going to tell Spencer what happened? Maybe you should. Maybe I should be locked up. Julia is right. I'm crazy, loony."

"Couldn't we talk about something else? I need to go down and work on my painting. Please come with me."

"So you can keep an eye on me?"

"Frankly, yes. I'm worried sick. All I care about is you getting well, physically and mentally. I will give up this show if that's what it takes to care for you."

"No, dammit, I won't let you do that. I'll go down there with you so you can work. Hell, I'll do anything you want me to. You are my keeper, aren't you?"

His anger was aimed as much at himself as anyone. Why he didn't aim it at those responsible was a mystery. Those who did this to him or caused it to be done. But God forbid he decided to take vengeance on them. It was one thing he'd never ever do. He abhorred killing to the point that she believed he would not kill to save his own life. Maybe to save hers, but not his own.

Sitting there gazing at him, a horrible truth began to dawn on her. She had come close to it with her previous thoughts, now it hit her between the eyes. In reality, he wanted to die. Believed he should have died in that crash instead of being the only survivor. Still, if that were true, why had he hung on so long in the prison camps? Spencer had said it was to come home and kill his ex-wife, which he could never do. If he couldn't walk, he couldn't get to her to kill her. It was indeed a conundrum and not one she could ever solve.

"Okay, then," she said brightly. "I'll put together some sandwiches, and we'll eat down there. Right now I have to bring in the groceries."

"I'll help."

"Good, I could use some help." Still shaking, she made an attempt to get back to normal.

She carried two bags from the van, set them in his lap, then went back for two more and followed him into the kitchen. Together they put everything away, her working in the pantry, him in the cupboards in the kitchen and the refrigerator.

"I saw some sliced ham and cheese. Could we have that?" he asked. "And some sweet pickles. They looked good. And cookies."

"I'm glad you're finally hungry. I was getting worried what I might do with all this food if you decided to go on a hunger strike." She started past him, and he reached out, grabbed her around the waist.

She turned into his embrace, let him pull her down into his lap. "I don't mean to snap at you," he said into her ear.

"I know you don't. This had to be hard on you. I'm so sorry it had to happen. Let's leave it behind."

"That's what I wanted to hear you say. My little keeper."

"Glen, don't."

"Well, you are, aren't you? My keeper. My guard. My caretaker."

"Your lover."

"Yes, well, that, too. Keeps me docile, fucking does."

"Glen, I don't blame you for being upset."

"Upset? Who's upset? Hell, I'm used to hiding out to keep someone from slicing some more of my skin off. That's some nut case who lives inside me, isn't it? Comes out to play when I least expect it. What do they call that? Sociopath? Psychopath? Split personality? Schizophrenia?"

He tightened his arms, so she couldn't turn around and look into his face, see his expression. But that was probably a good thing. She sucked in a breath. Relaxed in his grip.

"Time to go down to the studio, sweetheart. Let me up so I can fix us something to eat."

"Sure. Anything you say, sweetheart." He mocked her and threw his arms out to both sides.

He would get over this, surely. Go back to being his own sweet self, once he got all this out of his system. She sure as hell hoped so. He'd never reacted to her like this before.

In the studio they ate in silence, then she went to work on the painting, while he remained in the office reading a book he'd carried down with him. None of her brush strokes suited her, so she picked up the charcoal to begin her sketch of the focal point, the healed and happy Glen. Not pleased with anything there either, she picked up her camera and went into the office.

"Could I take a few head shots so I can begin the sketch? Nothing is working right for me."

He raised to peer at her, and there in his eyes she saw the man she had met at the hospital. The futility and sorrow he'd felt and then it was gone. Like that.

"So we're thinking this is the new me? All I'm going to get."

"No, sweetheart. All I'm doing now is your bone structure, the shape of your face. The rest will come later."

"You going to leave in the scars, or take them out?"

She set the camera aside and lowered herself beside him on the couch. Took the book from him and placed his hands on either side of her face. "Look at me. I love you. This is the face of the woman who will do anything in the world to make you happy. I love you. Touch me, feel me, kiss me, but stop punishing me. I know I made a terrible mistake leaving you alone, and I'm so sorry. What can I do to get you to forgive me?"

During her speech, his eyes filled and his features softened, let go the stiffness, the ugly mask he'd hidden behind all afternoon. "It's not your fault, Katie. I'm just angry that I couldn't return and be the man who left here all those years ago." He broke then, gathered her into his arms. She wrapped hers around him. He didn't say anything, just held her in silence, rubbed his hands up and down her back.

"Help me, help me," he finally whispered in her ear.

"Anything. Anything you need."

"I don't know what it is I need. You, I need you, but I'm afraid."

"Do you know what you're afraid of?"

"I'm afraid something is stealing my mind. When it goes, I won't have you, I won't have a life. Just the terror that lives in there. It likes the dark. That's why I have nightmares, so it can come out and play."

He'd used that expression earlier, and it sent chills up and down her spine. "All I can do is love you, hold you close. I wish I knew how to stop the nightmares, the flashbacks, but I don't. I do know how to love you."

"Yes, I know you do. Guess that'll be enough till we can figure something else out. Now, you want to take your pictures and get back to work? I think I'll do my sketch of Mac. I can't quite get it right, but when I do I'll know it's him."

They spent the remainder of the afternoon till almost dark on their respective projects, he on the couch, her at her easel within sight of him.

While they were packing up to go to the house, he said, "I'd like to make love to you tonight, if you're not afraid."

"I've never been afraid of you. I won't start now."

"If I were you—"

She covered his mouth with her fingers. "Don't you say it, don't you dare say it."

His failure to rise, get in the wheelchair, frightened her.

"You're tired."

"It seems I'm worse than tired. I can't get anything to move."

"Well, then stay there on the couch. Are you sleepy? I'll get the pillows and blankets, turn on the electric heat so it'll be warm all night. If you're okay here. There's a window, but the room is small."

"It's fine. I'll be comfortable, but what about you?"

"I have big fat pillows, I'll sleep next to you, on the floor."

Wearily he nodded.

She brought everything to him, lifted his legs, placed them on the couch, and tucked a pillow under his head. He took her hand, said her name softly, pushed a lock of loose hair back out of her face, ran fingertips over her cheeks, lips, down her throat.

"Don't tell Spencer about this. He'll take me away, put me in one of those awful places. I wouldn't make it. I feel safe with you. I know I'm supposed to be stronger, but sometimes… I just can't find the strength. So please don't stop caring for me because I shoot off my mouth. I love you."

"I won't. I'll be more careful, I promise."

He pulled her down and kissed her, his lips tender against hers. The kiss was long, and then he relaxed. She moved her head to his chest, listened to his breathing, his heartbeat.

Please let him sleep. Please.

With no idea to whom she spoke, she remained there a long time, then made her bed beside the couch and curled up beside him in a blanket. She toed off her shoes as an afterthought and closed her eyes. Behind her lids all she saw was him holding something sharp against the inside of his wrist, looking up and smiling before he slashed his arm open and the blood shot out. Over and over.

It was a long time before she went to sleep.

FOURTEEN

A MAGICAL HEALING occurred during the next few weeks. Over breakfast the last day of February, after she finished the painting and sent the photo off to Endlebeck at the art department, they tried not to discuss the matter. But they couldn't help themselves.

"It's so peaceful inside there." He tapped his temple, took a sip of, coffee and attacked a large western omelet. "Maybe things are looking up after all."

"Don't tempt fate." She held up a hand, smiled to show him she was kidding. Halfway. "Let's not talk about it. Think of something else to talk about."

Laughing, he said, "How about last night? We could talk about that, but probably better not or we'll be back in bed."

"What we'd better do is finish eating before Marty shows up. We can't fool around half the night and expect to get up at a decent hour. How's it going inside there?" She tilted her head toward the sunroom where she'd never ventured while the physical therapy sessions were going on.

"Only fair to middling. It's almost spring, and I'm losing hope I'll be walking in time for your exhibit in May."

Fork poised in mid-air, she glanced up. "That's a whole two months away. You'll make it. And so what if you don't? We'll just keep at it."

He grinned. "We, huh? Haven't seen you in there lifting fifty pounds with your legs."

"Well, I just might try it sometime."

"Hah. I'll tell Marty to expect you first thing."

"Well, since I'm taking this week off after working so hard to get those paintings done, especially the big one, I just might take you up on that. It's almost nine. You'd better get dressed, and I need to clean up this kitchen."

Marty had him barefoot and wearing shorts and a tee shirt for the workouts. He took a last bite of the omelet and, mouth full, said, "Very good stuff."

"Thanks." She stood there, dirty plates in one hand and watched him wheel away. His increased upper body strength continued to amaze her. Marty spent a lot of time on that, and it worried her. Was he preparing Glen to spend his life in that wheelchair? She should ask, but was afraid to. How like her to think that if she didn't know a bad thing, then it wouldn't happen.

She spent the morning cleaning closets and washing windows. The extent of what she deemed spring cleaning. Marty was there all day three days a week now, and the afternoons were devoted to getting Glen on his feet. Marty had finally been talked into eating lunch with them, so she quit cleaning about eleven and prepared a cold lunch. Ham salad on beds of lettuce, a plate of raw veggies, deviled eggs, sweet pickles, crackers, and iced tea with brownies for dessert. Glen ate a lot. He might never get over going hungry for so many years, but with all the exercise, his weight continued to remain a bit under what it should be. Marty said not to worry. When his legs muscled up, he would be right on the money.

Both men came from the sunroom about ten minutes before twelve, chatting away in a friendly fashion about yesterday's basketball game. She found that funny since she and Glen had spent much of the game wrestling around on the bed. Playing, he called it, but it always ended up in some serious love making. Playing had become a weekly Sunday afternoon pastime after they read the newspaper and ate something gooey and drank coffee in bed.

He rolled to his place at the table and held up his hands. "We washed." Then poured several teaspoons of sugar into his tea and filled his plate. "I could eat a bear, unless it was chasing me."

Happiness blossomed on his features, his smile popping dimples and sparking his golden eyes. His light brown hair was tousled, lying on his neck in damp curls. He was absolutely gorgeous, and she couldn't keep her eyes off him. How this beautiful man had sprung from the achingly worn out, torn up one she had first seen in the hospital, she would never know.

"That rag you got tied around your hair, I'll bet you been cleaning," he said between bites. "Spring has really sprung when a woman puts a rag on her head and starts pulling stuff out of closets and washing windows and batting rugs on the clothesline."

"We don't bat rugs on clotheslines anymore. And you'd better be careful. I'll tie a rag on your head and put you to work scrubbing floors."

"At your service, ma'am. I'd make a heck of a good floor scrubber, being close to my work." He took another bite of salad and popped a deviled egg in his mouth, washing it down with half a glass of tea.

Contentment seeped from her pores like the sweat from her morning labors. Even if she had dreamed her life would ever be like this, the dream wouldn't have been as completely blissful as she felt at this very moment.

"Glen tells me you'd like to see what we're doing in there." Marty pointed his fork toward the sunroom.

"Yes, I would, but only if you menfolk would feel comfortable having me look on."

"Actually," Glen said, "she challenged me to a weight lifting contest." Both men laughed.

"That's not polite," she told them. "Making fun of a frail woman."

"Frail. Don't let her fool you, Marty. She hefts me around like a dock worker loading a tramp steamer. She could probably out-press both of us."

"Whatever that is, you're right," she said. "What would we be pressing? Surely not ironing clothes in there."

She knew better, but thought it would give them a good laugh, and it did. Let them think she was dumb about working out in a gym. When she was a kid she was darn good with weights and even did some boxing with the boys for fun. That had been a long time ago. Working out with Glen sounded enjoyable, though, so she hoped they'd let her have a go at it.

She was cleaning the table when they headed back toward the sunroom.

"Join us if you'd like," Marty invited.

"Heck yes, come on in." Glen left the door open behind him.

"Be there in a little bit then. I'm going to kick some butt."

From inside, another round of explosive laughter.

Changing into shorts and a tee shirt, she joined them about an hour later. Long streams of afternoon sunlight splashed across the gleaming floor. Glen sat within a framework of metal bars, weights and springs, both legs extended before him. She had no idea what they called the machine, didn't even care as long as it strengthened his legs and got him on his feet. He glanced at her, pulled his knees up and said, "One thousand and one," and took a deep breath.

"Fool." She stared at him without shame. Muscles rippled across his stomach, bulged in his arms and back. His skin was the color of wild honey. She leaned down, kissed his sweaty cheek. "Looks like I've got you where I want you now."

"The way I smell, doubt you'll keep me for long. Anyway, it's right where I want to be. You come to show us your stuff? By the way, I like the outfit. Makes you look like a teenager."

"Oh, now you've done it. I'm not sure whether you're trying to insult me or compliment me."

"Take your pick, sweet cakes. Hop up on that table over there and lay hold of those bars. See if you can smack 'em together in front of you."

Marty strolled over. "Better let me adjust the weights on that. Make it easy on you."

He helped her get seated in the apparatus and lowered the weights behind her. Placed his hands over hers. "Okay, now, the object is not to hurt yourself. Do it right, and you'll only be a bit sore. Do it wrong, and you can pull a muscle and be laid up for a week or two."

While Glen continued to do what she decided to call leg-pushes, she let Marty guide her two or three times, then told him she thought she had it. He turned loose, and, arms extended, she tried to press the two bars together in front of her. Tried again. Found she couldn't stop looking at Glen's graceful movements long enough to concentrate.

"Keep your eyes off the man candy, ma'am," Marty teased, "and concentrate. How do you expect to expand those puny muscles?"

He turned, went over to Glen and squatted down beside him, said something she couldn't hear, and Glen stopped, announcing in a loud voice, "Two thousand and two."

"There's something wrong with this thing," she said. "I think I broke it. I can't make it move at all." She kept her gaze pinned on Glen. A bar hung above his head and he reached up, grabbed it, and Marty pushed a button, raising him to his feet.

How clever. That piece of equipment probably cost a fortune. She was glad to have the stuff on loan. He stood there for a moment, looked as if he could let go and step out of the contraption, but Marty swung him around and guided him down into his chair.

"It's time for him to walk on the bars," Marty said, coming toward her. Closer, he leaned over and said, "He's not comfortable with anyone watching him. It's a difficult and awkward workout."

She swallowed hard and nodded. Pretended she understood, when in reality she had hoped to remain and see just how well he was doing. "Okay, I guess I showed you guys who's queen of the gym, didn't I?" To Marty she said, "Don't you yell at him, or you'll have me to face."

Hoping down from the table, she waved her fingers at Glen, blew him a kiss, and got one in return. Then she left them to it, pulling the door closed behind her.

A week or so later, Spencer called, said he wanted to talk to her. Reluctant to leave Glen, even though Marty would be with him, she dressed for the appointment. Nervous about what Spencer might want, she summoned Marty while Glen was doing one of his exercises.

"He hasn't had an episode in quite some time. Only a few nightmares, but that doesn't mean he won't. I hate to leave him. Have you ever been with one of these guys during a flashback?"

"A couple of times at the hospital, but never in a one on one situation. I watched how they handled it there. Believe me, I won't let him hurt me."

How naïve he was. "And you'd better not let him hurt himself either. He doesn't like me to leave him. To understand that you have to know his history. Do you?"

"Some of it. Look, I'll take good care of him. We get along well. He's a hell of a guy with the courage of a grizzly. Believe me, I'll not let him get hurt."

She glanced at the closed door. "I'd better go tell him I'm going."

"If you didn't, he might not even know you were gone."

"Nope. That dog won't hunt. I don't do that to him. Sneak off? Huh-uh. Do you feel comfortable doing this? I won't be gone very long. Spencer thinks it's okay, so I'll trust you if he does."

"Sure, we'll be fine."

She went into the sunroom. Glen heard her coming and stopped his leg pushes. "Hey, hi babe, come back for a rematch?"

"No way, you guys are too good for me. Spencer wants to see me, said it would be fine if I left you in the care of Marty. I won't be gone long." She watched his expression as she explained the reason for her trip to town. If he showed the least bit of worry, she would not leave. Spencer could just wait till they could both come in together. He told her to have a good time, and she held his hand a moment. But he seemed okay about it, told her to be careful.

"I'll call when I get there and when I leave. Okay?"

"Sure, that'll be fine."

Deep in those eyes panic stirred like a great snake awakened from hibernation.

She kissed his hand, but that didn't help.

"Katie?" He pulled her down close, said in a husky voice, "Don't tell him about the flashbacks. He'll take me away, put me in one of those places. I couldn't make it. Not after... after what we've had."

She kissed his hand, then his sweaty cheek. "I'll call him back, tell him I'm coming in with you Thursday, anyway. If he wants to talk to me he can do it then."

The panic slithered away, and his expression softened with relief. "Thanks."

"And I won't tell him about anything. That's between you and me. Now get back to work before Marty gets out his spurs."

He held her hand tightly for a moment, then put it to his lips, and glanced up at her. "Do you know how much I love you?"

"Yep, I do," she said. He smiled and turned loose of her hand, went back to work, pushing his legs out straight, then pulling them up until they nearly touched his chest.

She went to tell Mary she'd changed her mind and wouldn't be leaving after all. He shook his head. He thought she spoiled Glen, and she did, but for good reasons. And they were none of his business.

The following Thursday Glen settled in the small waiting room outside Spencer's office with a book, and she sat fidgeting in a chair near the psychiatrist's desk, feeling like a kid called to the principal's office.

"Okay, why did you want to see me? Glen tell you something that worries you?"

"Nope, not that I can think of."

"Marty, then."

Spencer chuckled. "Figured you'd want to know how I think Glen's coming along."

"That wouldn't do me any good. You never give me a straight answer. All you tell me is to be patient. I have to tell you, though, that emotionally he's doing exceptionally well. Happy, content, filled with mischief, and he hasn't had a flashback episode in weeks. He's still having a few nightmares, but we handle them."

"What do you think about his physical advancement?"

"I know he's disappointed. Wants to walk by May, and he's killing himself trying to accomplish that."

"Does he ever mention Ellie?"

"God, no. Not a word about her. Why? Is that still an issue?"

"I've been talking to Marty. As you know the pain Glen perceived during his recovery had no medical basis, and now what he wants to do pulls him one way, while what his mind tells him he has to do pulls another, and he stands in the middle, as if he's watching to see what will happen. He gets on his feet, he has to carry out his vow to pay Ellie back for what she did. He doesn't, well, then he can't do it, so everything is fine. Because you'll support him, be by his side, no matter what happens."

"Of course I will. I won't threaten to leave him, I won't try to force him to do something he's clearly not ready to do. I know Marty thinks I spoil him, and he's right. The situation calls for that. Is that what you're trying to tell me now? Dammit, this was your idea. If you didn't want me to protect him, stand up for him, then you should have picked someone else. You make me so mad sometimes."

"Now Katherine, I'm not saying that at all. You're right. If we push him, he'll fall, and he might not get back up. Problem is Marty says he's ready for the braces and walking. Glen refuses to take that step. Says he's not ready."

"What is that scar behind his left knee? It appears worse than some of the others."

He stared at her as if trying to make up his mind about something. "The bastards tried to cripple him. Hard to know why. He may have attempted an escape at one time. At any rate that injury will cause him problems walking. He'll probably limp, have some pain there, have to use a cane. It's a miracle under those conditions that he didn't lose the leg."

"Why didn't you tell me about this before?"

"One thing at a time. We worked on what we needed to work on, then moved on. Now we are at this point, we need to work on this. But the thing is, we can't force him into situations that he can't cope with. Marty wants to get him on his feet, Glen is balking. I thought you ought to know. Perhaps you can talk him into trying. You know him so very well and have worked miracles with his emotional problems."

"I'll see what I can do. Is that all?"

"No. How's your sex life?"

"That's none of your business."

"Yes, it is. He doing okay with it? And you?"

"Ask him, he's your patient. And I still say it's none of your business. Spencer gave her a patient grin. "I have. Now I'm asking you."

"What did he say?"

"That it's none of my business." His grin widened. "Sooner or later he has to become his own person. That doesn't mean leaving you, but it does mean getting along in certain situations without you there to catch him. Yet, I have to tell you, considering what he's been through, that may never happen, and I can't see you dealing with that the rest of your life."

She stared at him hard, rose from the chair, so angry she could barely speak. "You go to hell." She rushed from the room, slamming the door behind her.

P A R T
FOUR

...And when the hand that plucked it,

ONE

THE FIRST WEEK of March offered warm, sunny days and cool nights. Frogs made so much noise it took some getting used to to sleep. At night Katie kicked off their blankets, and they slept under a sheet. Still Glen was unable to take those first steps, though Marty deemed him ready. She had a big job ahead of her convincing him to try, but not nearly as big a job as Glen's.

Then, one day leafing through Time magazine he found an article that caught his interest. "Did you see this?" He handed it to her. Marty had brought him a stack of back-dated issues so he could catch up on some of the news he'd missed.

On the page, partially covered in black, were names. Names and more names. The story told of a monument built in D.C. to honor those who fought and died in Vietnam and of a man who left his medals there and cried. Through tears, she tried to read further, but Glen interrupted her reading.

"They built a memorial and put all the names on it. The ones who died. MacArthur M. MacKenzie and Herman Franks, all the others, men I couldn't save, nearly fifty-eight thousand of them." He stared so deeply into her eyes she shivered. "Do you suppose my name is there?" he asked.

Her heart dropped into her stomach, her throat burned, and she turned away to hide a gush of tears. The tears he hated so much to see, tears she hadn't shed for over a month now. A month of struggles and mostly good times. When she reached to touch him, he was shaking.

"Oh, honey. Oh, no." She moved to sit beside him on the sofa where he usually relaxed at night, anything to be out of the hated wheelchair. She pulled him close and held him until he quieted, took a deep breath.

"Read it, read all of it, Katie."

So she did and broke down crying so hard she couldn't finish. He took her in his arms, his tears mixing with hers. It turned out to be a time for comforting each other.

"But look at it, so ugly, so dark," she whispered.

"It fits the war." He rubbed his fingers lightly over the photo. "I have to see it. I have to go and say goodbye. See if I'm there… where I belong."

Oh, dear God. It was going to be a bad night. All she could do was hold him, tell him she loved him, that he was alive and well, all the while knowing that being alive while the others were gone was the problem. Would this never be finished? She swallowed painfully, vowed to stop crying, make this as easy as possible for him. She never told Stan good-bye and would welcome the chance, even for a symbolic farewell, but damn it all… what would this do to Glen?

As he so often did, he sensed her thoughts. "I'll be okay if you'll go with me." He rubbed at her back awkwardly, as if embarrassed to ask.

"Of course I'll go with you." In her heart, she knew that would not make him okay.

He hugged her so tightly she gasped for breath, his heart pounding against her chest, his hot breath flowing over her neck.

"I'll tell Marty tomorrow."

"Okay." Because he would be gone a while? More reason than that, though surely, and there was.

"I'll want to be out of that damned chair before we go. If I can even use the arm braces, then it will be okay, won't it?"

Perhaps this was the miracle she'd been looking for, and he'd found it for himself. But how much blessing and how much curse?

"Yes, it would be okay. When do you think we can go?" she asked.

"During Easter? Before your art show. That will be my target."

"And how will we go? Can you fly?"

His expressions closed down, so he was no longer looking at her but into a distant past, and she prepared for a flashback, but he only said, "I didn't think about that. I haven't flown since… but of course, that's what we'll have to do, but it won't be the same, not like… will it?"

Tracers in the night sky, explosions, blood seeping from the body sitting next to him. The cold rush of air through the gaping door where the gunner hung exposed to death. Harsh burring as he pulled the trigger and swung the weapon in an arc. The sharp ping of shells hitting the chopper. Jesus, his memories had begun to haunt *her*.

Amazed at how quickly the waking nightmare had taken over and transported her, she jerked away from it. Suppose he couldn't handle the trip and flew apart while they were on the plane? She hugged up close to him, fisted his shirt into one hand. They held on to one another without speaking for a long while. His fears had to be so much worse than hers. Dark and foreboding.

They went to bed, and he made long, slow love to her until every inch of her body tingled and glowed and pulsed and she hammered him for more. After he came, he held her close, whispered in her ear over and over, "You're my love, my life."

"And you mine," she whispered. "Please don't leave me again. I couldn't bear it."

For the first time since they'd met, those words frightened her. Suppose, in the end, she couldn't be enough? He wanted his name inscribed on that monument. One of the KIAs. Dear God, how could she stop that yearning?

She held him close all night, dreading and fearing the worst, but he slept against her, scarcely moving until sunlight brightened the house.

Spencer motioned for her to come in to his office for a moment after talking to Glen on Thursday. Glen waited outside the door, staring at her with a pleading expression, still concerned Spencer would take him away from her. She nodded imperceptibly to let him know she understood, would not allow that to happen. He trusted her so much it frightened her. Spencer glowered and told her to sit.

"Glen tells me he wants to visit that monstrosity they built in Washington. Would you mind telling me why in God's name you encouraged him, agreed to go with him?"

"Easy to see you're not pleased. I'm going with him because he'll go alone if I don't. And he plans to walk through the mall there to see it. If this will get him on his feet, believe me I'll endure any reactions he may have. If he's willing, I am, too. What's your problem?"

She'd dreamed up all the scenarios she could imagine and how she would handle them. Perhaps Spencer knew a few more.

"What do you and Glen do? Where do you go?"

Where was he going with this? He had a knack for changing the subject. "Well, we go to the lake. He goes to the studio with me. We drive to new places when the weather is nice."

"And do you mingle with people any of these places?"

"Well, no. He doesn't... he can't."

"My point exactly. So the two of you are happy with this solitary life? No friends, no parties, not even an occasional visit to the movies or out to dinner in public?"

So this was where he was going. Before she could reply, he said in a thunderous tone, "Then how in God's name do you expect him to deal with the crowds you'll encounter on a trip like that? Worse, what in the hell do you suppose he's going to do when you get to that airport and start to climb aboard a plane?"

Struck dumb, she stared back at him, at a loss for words.

"The man is unstable. And that monument. The most negative statement ever made by men for his fellow man. Stresses the worst of that war, black and cold and ugly."

"Wars are black and cold and ugly," she managed, but he wasn't through, and she might as well not say more until he was.

"And you're kidding yourself if you think just because he can deal with you and Marty that he's well. I'm his goddamned doctor. Why didn't you ask me if he's ready?"

"Damn you, Spencer. Do you realize he thinks his name belongs on that wall? Do you know what it's like for him and me to struggle through all this? No, you don't know a thing about that. You sit here once a week and roll out your pathetic little diagnostic bullshit that you read in some book. You don't live with him. You don't love him. You don't want him happy above all else in this entire world, so don't you go criticizing me for how I handle living with him. If he wants to see that monument, then by God I'll see that he does. And then we'll handle the results as best we can together. I'll be the one who holds him at night when he's sweating and screaming and going through a hell neither you nor I can ever understand. And when we come back, I'll report to you so you can tell me all the reasons he acts the way he does."

Glen pushed the door open. "Katie, what's wrong? Are you all right?"

She smiled at him. "I'm okay, sweetheart. Just a mild misunderstanding."

"Doesn't sound mild to me. What'd you say to her?" He aimed a hard glare Spencer's way.

"It's okay. You know how I get," she said. "We were arguing, and I got carried away. I'll be out in a few minutes."

"Well, okay." He pulled the door closed slowly, as if not sure he wanted to leave her in there.

"You have to promise me if he gets dangerous to himself, you'll let me know."

"Damn you. You gave him to me, said save him, and so I'm doing my best. Helping him has given me what I'd lost. A purpose in life. I didn't expect to fall in love with him, but I did. So, yes, he is with me and I'm with him. Where we go, we go together. He is as much my life as I am his."

His sigh spoke volumes. "Always in charge, huh, Katherine. All right, you have to prepare him for this and keep me updated on how it goes."

"Well, that's better. What do you suggest?"

"Take him out where there are crowds. Start small, someplace you have some control if he gets out of hand. Do you have a friend, someone who owns a small restaurant or public gathering place? Not a bar. Where there's drinking, the ambiance is too much on the edge of violence. Or go to an outdoor park in town where children play and people mill about, not off out where there are only two or three people. Keep him in control. You don't want to end up in jail. Nobody understands how these men can react, especially not cops. So be very careful. Go easy. You've only got a few weeks."

She nodded. This made sense. She would try.

"This weekend take him out in the world, but be prepared for any reaction. Be ready to explain his behavior and get him out of there safely. I trust you to know how best to handle him by now. So far, you're doing one helluva job. Just be careful."

"You have to see he's doing so much better. I don't want this to ruin all the progress he's made." She rose, went to him, and leaned down to kiss his cheek.

"You call if you need help at all. Will you do that? And watch his behavior closely. Before you leave, I'll prescribe a sedative you can give him that will help get him through the stress without giving him any side effects."

"I always watch him. Believe me, sometimes I drive him to snapping at me for it."

Glen moved quickly away from the door when she opened it. He'd been listening, but what he'd heard she couldn't guess.

"Eavesdropper," she teased and lay her hand on his shoulder. He moved away from her and stopped at the windows, staring out over the back garden where they'd first been together. She joined him, remembering that day and him.

After a short silence, he said, "You said to him, 'you gave him to me.' What did you mean by that? Did he give me to you like a gift or what? Here's this loony, see what you can do for him. When you get done, just give him back? What, Katie?" The muscle in his jaw rippled, and he whirled to stare at her.

"No, my God, no. It wasn't… it's not like that at all. It was just a figure of speech, sweetheart."

"I don't remember, you know, not until the day we went out there to sketch together. Before that, what did you do? How could you have looked at the pathetic creature in your painting and agreed to go near it?

Unless there was a bribe or a dare, an experiment. Something like that. Is that why you're with me? Goddammit, Katie."

Her chest ached for him. How could she fix this? She touched his shoulder, and he jerked away. "Glen, please. It was no such thing. You only listened to that and nothing else. If you're going to eavesdrop don't take one sentence out of context. Stay and hear it all."

He wheeled away down the hall, and she trotted to catch up, finally grabbed the grips and tried to stop him. His strength overpowered hers, and he jerked into motion. "Let me go, Katie. Just let me go. I can't look at you now. Not right now."

Dejected, she slumped, filled with regret so bitter her stomach rolled over, and she fought gagging. Could only watch him roll away.

Harry came from down the hall at a run, caught up with him. "Hey, Glen. Good to see you, man. Could I give you a hand?" He was able to halt the furious forward motion. "The little lady wants to talk to you. Why don't you just wait here a minute?"

She hurried to them, touched Harry's arm. "Thank you. He's upset with me. Where can we go for some privacy to talk?"

"Should I tell Doc?"

"Not yet, but if you could stand by. If I can't fix this and in a hurry, we'll need him."

Harry nodded. "Anything for you two." He led the way, pushing the wheelchair. Glen didn't fight back. His silence was as frightening as his outburst.

Inside an empty room with the door shut, she dragged a chair over to sit beside him.

"If you'd listened to everything, you'd have heard I didn't expect to fall in love, but I did. That loving you and caring for you gave me a purpose, something I hadn't had for a long while. I told him where you go I go, where I go you go. Always. What I said about him giving you to me was just a figure of speech and nothing more."

He twisted away, refused to look at her when he spoke. "I've never known why you came here that day, what your reason for coming back was. I've always been so glad you did that I refused to wonder about it for fear it would be something I wouldn't like. And I didn't want to lose you. But now I'd like to know just what in the hell motivated some-one like you to hang around long enough to fall in love with someone like me. If you truly did, and you aren't just taking care of me for your good friend, Spencer, to complete his experiment. Because he sure as hell doesn't know what to do with me."

Oh, God, this was a mess. Hard to know where to start, how to ex-plain her actions without making him feel like a bug in a jar.

"Well, what's wrong? Can't think of anything to say? Maybe I ought to move back here and let you have your freedom so you won't have to go everywhere I go."

In his mood, he would take everything wrong she could possibly say by way of explanation. Better if she told him how she felt about him, rather than how the whole thing came about. Starting there would be easier.

"Glen, please look at me. Darling, please." He refused, so she moved where he was looking, knelt beside the chair, cupped his angry face in her hands. "I've loved you since that first day you remember being with me. You touched my hair with such reverence, with such a wondrous look on your face. It showed me the man hiding so deep inside he dare not come out. Showed me that beautiful young man who played foot-ball, a brave pilot who saved so many lives, whose courage kept him alive through hell and back. And then you ran your fingers across my cheek and down my neck, and you unbuttoned the top button of my blouse. In that moment, I wanted you to touch my breast, and I saw in your eyes what you were feeling, and I felt it, too. Blessed by something beyond my understanding. Then you asked me what my name was, like knowing it would make you better. And when I told you Katherine, you asked if you could call me Katie. I never allowed anyone to call me Katie because that was Stan's name for me. His and only his. But I wanted you to call me that because in that moment I knew we were going to be together. I know, sounds impossible, but I knew we were torn from a single piece. You were, you still are, the most beautiful man I've ever known, all the way to your core. I loved my husband, but with you, I discovered the kind of love most people never find. You hurt, I hurt; you're happy, I'm happy. I will do anything, anything to help you get what you want. I am so sorry for hurting you back there. Do you forgive me?"

The entire time she spoke he'd kept his gaze locked on her. When she finished, tears streaked his cheeks, and he touched her hair, as he had done that day. "How do I know this is the truth? And not that the two of you were conspiring to see if you could make the loony well. If one thing doesn't work, why then, tell him you love him. Take him to bed if you have to. Was that the way it was? I can't stand this, Katie. I feel like I've been tossed back in a cage, a larger one, but a cage nevertheless, where you and the Doc in there can find out what works and what doesn't. Go away, leave me here. I can't stay with you until I sort this out. How could you do this to me when I love you so damn much?"

"Sweetheart, you're just angry and justly so. I don't know what I can say to you, except, if you stay here, so do I. I'm not leaving you. Not here or anywhere else."

His laugh was bitter. "Obviously, I can't leave you, either. Do what you please. Get Harry in here. Tell him I want to see Doc about checking back in. I'm not feeling so hot."

She rose from her cramped position, tried to kiss him, but he turned away so her lips landed on the side of his head. She tried once more. "I don't want to lose you. One of the first things Spencer told me was never to lie to you because you would sense it immediately. Well, I never have, and I won't."

"And that is a bald-faced lie in itself. You lied to me about Ellie."

He might as well have hit her. She had lied. "Ah, yes, I remember. I didn't tell you about her, and that's the same as lying. I thought I was protecting you. Spencer said you were unable to deal with her, and so I did it for you. For that, I'm sorry, too. I didn't want to hurt you, but from now on, even if it's going to hurt, I'll be honest with you. But it'll be hard, cause hurting you is the most difficult thing I could ever do. You know that, don't you?"

A tap on the door, and Spencer entered. He didn't say anything, went to sit on the edge of one of the empty beds.

"He wants to come back to the hospital."

"Dammit, let me take care of this myself," Glen said. "I'm sick of you knowing what's good for me and providing it without even asking. Tell her to leave, I don't want her here. Would you do that, Doc? I don't feel well, and I want to go to bed."

Spencer rose, took her arm. "I'll get you registered, and someone will be here in a minute to take you to your room," he told Glen.

"What the hell is wrong with this one? I'm here, and it's empty. I'll just hop up on this bed, and you can take care of your records." He removed the arm of the chair, leaned forward a bit. "I can't... I can't move my legs." He hammered on his thighs, his gaze caught hers as it darted around the room.

"No, no," she cried and ran to him, bent and tried to put her arms around him.

He'd grown very strong working out in the sunroom, and he easily lifted her off and away. "Leave me be. Just leave me be. It's over, your little experiment. Over. I want a different doctor, too. Both of you get out of here."

Spencer took her elbow and practically dragged her from the room. He sent Harry in to help Glen get undressed and in bed.

"I can't leave him here. I won't. What can we do?" She collapsed against Spencer, and he assisted her to his office and closed the door, then lowered her onto the couch. Numb all over, she stared at him through tear washed eyes. Repeated, "What can we do?"

"For now, leave him alone. Let him settle down. We'll keep an eye on him. Once he has time to think, I'll have Dr. Swift see him, decide on a course of treatment. But face it. He's liable to lapse back into the man he was when you first saw him. We don't know what might happen because we've never dealt with a man who has survived what he has survived. It doesn't look hopeful."

She wouldn't give up, she couldn't. But she simply stared across the room and let Spencer think she agreed with him.

TWO

HOW LONG SHE lay on the couch, Katie had no idea. The day to night business of the hospital was muted beyond Spencer's door. He had left to make arrangements for Glen's admittance and to add his name to Swift's schedule. She sat up, dug tissues out of her purse, mopped her face, and blew her nose. A grown woman didn't settle anything by crying about it. She couldn't go home even if she wanted to. Glen had driven his car in, and she had no idea how to work those controls. Spencer would take her home, but she couldn't expect him to leave his normal duties with the patients.

Could she actually leave Glen here? She had become so attached to him, to filling his every need, to loving him and being loved by him, that leaving him in someone else's care wasn't an option. She wasn't qualified to take a nurse's position, but maybe she could have a volunteer job that would keep her here where she could look in on him once in a while.

What she hated the most was that he would not continue his therapy, get on his feet, and visit the Vietnam Monument in D. C. this spring, as he wanted. If his not being able to move his legs was permanent, then the therapy would have to begin all over. If he would even submit to further treatment. He was destroyed by those few words he'd heard through Spencer's door. She wanted to bite her tongue off.

When Spencer returned, it was nearing six o'clock. "You might as well go home, Katherine. There's nothing you can do here."

"I can't go home. I didn't drive, but before you offer to take me, would you consider letting me do volunteer work here? I know you can always use the help. I took care of all his needs at home, I can do the same for other patients here. Or I can do any other kind of work you think I'm qualified for."

He raised his brows. "Katherine, you need to go home. Stay away from him for a while. You both need that. This spat or argument, whatever you want to call it, will blow over. You can't hover over him. Let him come to his own decisions about this."

"You're wrong about what we both need, but I don't want to argue the point. He thinks we betrayed him. Spencer, think how that must have hurt him, thinking I was only loving him, caring for him, because we had some bright idea we could begin a new type of treatment, experiment on him like a guinea pig. At this point, he doesn't even believe I love him. I can't let him continue to believe I betrayed him. Let me stay. I'll get a motel room. I'll do any kind of volunteer work you have for me, just let me be close by. He'll need me, sooner or later he will. I know it."

Spencer's eyes held a deep sorrow, for surely he blamed himself for the conversation that had sparked Glen's relapse. "It's time we both faced it. Glen is broken, and I'm afraid he can't be fixed. There's something torn apart inside his brain by all those years of torture and captivity. He may never be able to face life."

"I refuse to believe that. I don't want you to give up on him. I won't.

We—*he* was functioning very well. He was happy. We were happy. This is just a setback. Something we should've expected. He's had them before and snapped out of it, but I was with him to help him. He relied on me. This is terrible. Why did he have to listen to us? Why did I say such a stupid thing? We have to help him. I won't allow you to institutionalize him. He won't make it if you do. He's said as much. Right now he thinks he doesn't want to make it, but I can get him back to where he was if you'll give me a chance. I know I can. Just let me sit with him, read to him, talk with him. What can it hurt if you're not going to treat him, anyway?"

He rolled his eyes, sighed, and sat down. "You are undoubtedly the most stubborn woman I've ever encountered. Do you really love this man enough to give up your life for him?"

She went to his desk, pounded on it. "Don't you listen? He is my life. Give me a chance to help him. Please."

"Christ. I know I'll regret this, but all right. Fine. I'll get a paper for you to fill out to become a volunteer. They'll give you a job to do you may not like, but you asked for it. They certainly won't assign you to keep Glen's room clean, so you'll have to arrange your visits around the jobs they give you. We'll see how long you last."

"Can I get some scrubs? I don't have anything with me except for what I have on."

"Yes, I'll have them issue you some."

She rose. At last, she was doing something toward her goal of getting Glen back home with her where he belonged. "I'm going across the street to that motel and get a room. I'll be back to pick up some scrubs and say goodnight to Glen, if that's not forbidden."

"Good Lord, I wouldn't dare forbid you to see him. I know what could happen then. You kidnapped him once from this very hospital. I hope you don't have that in mind this time."

"If I had a car, it might be an option, but only if he agreed."

It was nearly seven when she crept back into the hospital and down the hall to the room they'd given Glen. Supper would be over; he might be sleeping, since there wasn't much to do. Or he might be in the rec room, but she doubted it unless Harry had insisted. He'd never cared to mix with the other patients. It depressed him.

The room was lit only by the light on the headboard of his bed. He lay there on his back, eyes closed. She couldn't tell if he was awake, so she padded to his side, sat in a chair close to him, and took his hand from outside the sheet. It was limp and unresponsive, so he must be sleeping. She watched him for a long while. His long lashes curled on his cheeks, eyes only minimally moving beneath the lids. No sign of a nightmare.

"What do you want?"

She jumped at the hoarse sound of his voice. "Just to make sure you're okay."

"There are nurses here for that."

"I don't see them. How would one of them know you were having a nightmare, that you needed to be held, loved, soothed?"

"Don't you get it? I don't want your holding, loving, soothing."

"I know. Not right now, at least. What if I told you I need to be held. I need a hug. How would you feel about that? Maybe you owe me a few hugs."

"Huh. Get your hug from your good friend, the doc. You did what you did for your own reasons, whatever the hell they were. Doesn't make me owe you for it. I didn't ask. Not for any of it. Not even the fucking. You weren't raped."

Inside, she hurt so badly she squeezed one arm over her stomach. Instead of continuing the heated discourse—she refused to call it a fight—she kissed his hand, which he yanked from her grasp.

"Go to sleep, darling. I'll just sit here a while and not say anything." Before he could guess her intention, she leaned forward and kissed him. His lips remained nonresponsive, but he didn't turn away. She deepened the kiss, and his mouth opened a bit, but then he shifted from her touch.

She sat quietly until sure he was asleep, then lay her head on the mattress next to him and fell asleep there. In the night he began to moan and toss. She stood, felt his forehead. Sweating. Jaws clenching. Moans. Helpless in a dreamer's paralysis. He was walking through hell. As she had always done at home, she waited until he awakened on his own. He threw his arms out to his sides, rolled his head, muttered a few curse words, and she sat on the bed beside him, leaned over, and put her arms around him.

"It's okay, you're okay. I'm here."

"Katie?" he murmured and locked his arms around her.

She pulled him to a sitting position, like he preferred when coming awake. Where he could look around, make sure none of the horrors of the nightmare had followed him into the room. When he came fully awake, he released her, pulled back, and gazed into her eyes. "You're not leaving, are you?"

"Nope. I told you once I would never leave you; in fact I promised, crossed my heart and hoped to die. So, here I am, whether you want me or not. I can't stop loving you or caring for you just 'cause you say so. It won't happen. Go to sleep, sweetie. You're safe now. I'll be around somewhere, just in case you need me." She sat back down in the chair and lay her head beside him.

Sometime in the night, he spread his hand over her head. When she awoke, he was staring at her.

"I can't move my legs, Katie. What happened?"

She brushed a curl from his forehead. "It's just from being so upset.

Just a minor setback. All you need is some time with Marty. He'll set you right. Get you ready to go to D.C."

"Yes, D.C. I'm not sure yet I can go home with you, so maybe I'll have to go alone."

"No, you can't do that." His sharp gaze cut her short, and she took another tack. "I'm so sorry I hurt you. I would never ever do anything on purpose to hurt you. A slip of the tongue because that's the way Spencer and I talk sometimes, with sarcasm that can be misread too easily. We both honestly wanted… want to help you recover. You're not an experiment. He gave you to me in the best way he could possibly have given you. 'Save him', he said, on the verge of crying because he'd failed you. And so I tried. It was the art, the pictures you were drawing that caused him to think of me. I needed saving as badly as you. He knew it and did the best he could to help you and me both. And you saved me. You saved me from a dark depression of grief. Not once did I think of faking love to save you. I would never do that. Love is too precious to play around with it."

Calmer than earlier, he did at least listen to her without turning away. "I'll think about it some more. Is it true what you said last night that you are staying here?"

"Yes, I took a volunteer job so I could be near you." She chuckled. "I may be cleaning puke up or something equally revolting, but at least it'll be a new experience for me. And I'll be here. You want me, send word by a nurse." She kissed him on the forehead. "I love you, and I always will."

He watched her leave in silence.

At the nurse's station, they gave her a cart that held magazines and books to take around to each room. The patients could check out what they wanted, and she had to keep track of who had what. Some magazines were to give away and she could distribute those to anyone who wanted them. The nurse, Lydia was her name, told her often the patients would return the giveaways and tell her to share them with others. It was a much easier task than cleaning up puke.

She made her first rounds on a wing with female veterans. Some were up to visiting, and she took her time, as Lydia said she should. Patients needed visitors more than anything else, and some of them had very few. She found WW II veterans, and one, an elderly man so wrinkled she could not make out his eyes, had fought in France during WW I. This hospital was small, and patients often had to go to Little Rock for surgeries. It didn't take her long to make the rounds. She saved Glen's room for last. It was a bit past noon when she peeked in to see him sitting up, eating from a tray on a table across his lap. The bed had been cranked up.

"Looks good."

He didn't so much as glance up, just kept eating. Between bites, he said, "Not as good as your cooking, but I'll survive. I've definitely had worse."

"At least you're eating. That's good. How are you feeling? Are they going to get you up so you can go outside? It's a lovely day."

"I expect they will. Doctor Swift says I'm fit for wheelchair duty. Had nothing to say about the legs. Where's Marty? Do you suppose I could see him?"

"I'll find out. Better than that, I'll make it happen."

He grinned in spite of his effort to remain stoic. "I'll just bet you can, too. Were you here all night?"

She nodded. "Yes."

"When do you plan on sleeping?"

"I slept. When you did."

"Dammit, Katie, you make it hard for me to—"

"To keep being stubborn. I want you to come home with me, sweetheart. This is ridiculous."

After washing his hands and face on a wet cloth from the tray, he pushed the table away and studied her.

"Find me Marty, and after I talk to him, I'll tell you what I want to do. Okay?"

"Of course it's okay. As long as you're coming home with me." She left before he could answer that. Went in search of someone who could find Marty for her. When she found him, he agreed to go to Glen's room for a visit. He hadn't been assigned to him for therapy at the hospital, was upset to learn about his setback and the fact Doctor Swift hadn't gotten in touch with him.

Marty moved off down the hall, and she sat down to wait for him to come out so she could talk to Glen. If he didn't come home with her, she didn't know what she would do. But if she had to throw him in a laundry cart and sneak him out, then she could do that, too. But only if he wanted it.

THREE

WHEN MARTY CAME out of the room, he appeared stricken.

"What? What is it?"

"He's shut down. I tried to convince him we could get him back to where he was with some hard work on his part. Said he's been thinking about it, and it's best this way. Time to throw in the towel. Said he can't do this anymore. Those were his exact words. He's not the hopeful man I was working with, and I don't know what to do to get that man back."

"This is my fault, and I don't know what to do, either. I failed him. He may not be able to forgive me or come back from it. He doesn't want to begin therapy with you again?"

"He asked me what was the use. He has no place to be, nothing to do. So why should he bother. I brought up D.C. and he said he couldn't go alone and could think of no one who would go with him. That it didn't matter anymore, anyway. He wouldn't go into detail, and I guess what happened is none of my business. I ran out of things to say. Who is this Doctor Swift? I've never worked with him, but he's not addressing Glen's emotional link to the physical problem. Who is his medical doctor?"

She choked, unable to swallow past the knot in her throat. She had failed Glen.

Marty took her arm. "If you'll excuse me, you look like hell."

The room swirled, and his face receded into a long, dark tunnel, mouth moving but no sound reaching her.

She opened her eyes to see Spencer, Marty, and Glen, all peering down at her. A nurse had a stethoscope at her chest, Spencer was taking her blood pressure, and Marty stood near Glen's wheelchair. Glen had her hand in his, eyes sorrowful.

"Palpitations, doctor," the nurse said. Spencer glanced up. " BP is 190 over 140. Let's get her off the floor and into a bed until we can get that blood pressure down and the heart settled."

When they lifted her, Glen refused to let go her hand. Marty pushed the chair to keep up with moving her into a bed, the closest empty one, which was in the room Glen was in. She tried to say something to him, but the words wouldn't come out.

The nurse leaned toward Spencer, said something she couldn't hear.

He waved a hand at her. "I know, I know. We'll get her stabilized first, then worry about whether she can take up bed space here when she's not a veteran."

"Doc, she's going to be all right, isn't she?" Glen asked, then to her, "I'm sorry. I didn't mean to upset you. What can I do?" He glared at Spencer. "What's wrong with her, dammit? Tell me. Don't you let anything happen to her, you hear me."

"She's going to be fine. It's not serious. Too much stress is all. She just needs to rest and sleep and stop worrying over things she can't do anything about."

"That's me, isn't it? Katie? I'm okay. Don't you worry about me. I'm okay, you hear me?"

Marty wheeled him from the room so she could be undressed, gowned, and put to bed with an IV connected.

From outside the door she heard him shouting. "I want back in there as soon as she's settled, you hear me? Marty, dammit, I need to see her." His voice broke, and she struggled.

"Settle down, Katherine. Take it easy." Spencer held her wrist, fingertips on her pulse.

"Please let him come in, Spencer. Please." She grabbed his arm.

"Okay, okay." He threw his hands in the air. "You two must be joined at the hip, or think you are. I'll go get him. But you stay in bed, relax, don't get excited."

"I will, I promise. Just bring him in."

Spencer left, and in a minute, Glen wheeled in on his own. The nurse glanced at him, nodded, then slipped out.

Rolling up against the bed, he took her free hand and pressed it to his lips. "Katie, darlin'. I didn't mean… looks like our roles are reversed, doesn't it?" He tucked a lock of hair out of her eyes. "I'm so sorry, Katie, so damned sorry."

"I'm the one who is sorry, but why don't we just call it a tie and stop saying that. Okay? It don't mean anything, anyway. Right?"

He gave her a weak grin. "When I heard what all the ruckus was about and made Marty take me out into the hallway, I was terrified to see you laying on the floor, looking all white and still. I almost crawled out of the chair to get to you, but Marty held me back. I had some idea of how you've felt, tending to me when I'm in trouble. Mostly I realized how much I love you. Even if what you said was true, I can't be separated from you. I can't. We've got to settle this. But not now. Now you need to get some rest, some sleep. When I threatened to lock the doors and organize a sit in, Spencer decided it might be wise to let me stay in the room, sleep in the other bed,

"Oh, sweetheart, surely you didn't."

"Yep, I did. Now, I'm going to sit here until you fall asleep, then I'm going to bed and get me some sleep, 'cause tomorrow we're going to get together and work this all out." He kissed her hand again. "I love you, Katie."

They must've put something in her IV. He faded away while her lips formed the same words back at him. The next thing she saw was the sun streaming through the windows and him lying in the other bed, staring at her, solemn and waiting.

Activity revved up, and the day shift arrived. A nurse came in the room, stopped dead when she saw him in one bed, Katie in the other. "One of you is in the wrong room."

Katie threw back the covers, grabbed her IV pole, and hurried to the bathroom. "I'll explain when I get back." She shut the door behind her.

The nurse was gone when she came out.

"I explained, and she went to get one of the doctors. I get the feeling one of us is going to get kicked out. Let's both get dressed and escape this place before that happens."

"You're coming with me?"

"Don't think I can do anything else. We go together, Katie. No matter what."

She grinned at him. "Yeah, we do, don't we? Only one thing. I have to tell Spencer or he may have me arrested for kidnapping his favorite patient for the second time."

"That would be funny, wouldn't it? Probably have to wait until they take out that IV."

"Let's eat breakfast. I'm starved and I won't feel like cooking when we get home." She stopped, studied him for a long moment. "You're truly coming home with me?"

"Yes, it beats the hell out of sleeping under a bridge."

"Is that the only reason?"

"Bring that thing and come over here." He reached a hand toward her.

She padded barefoot to his bed, and he took her free hand, his lips twitching. "Love your outfit. So stylish." He raised his other arm. "Come here, babe. Be careful of that thing in your hand.

She went into his arms, lying across his chest.

"Get me up from here so I can hold you properly."

"There's a bar over your head."

"I don't want to turn loose of you. I just need a little help, not much."

She pulled him to a sitting position, and he wrapped her up properly. His familiar smell, his warm skin, his breath against her neck was all she wanted. She was where she belonged. Neither said a thing for a long while, just held each other. She would not cry, would not. Tears leaked from beneath her lids.

"You're getting me wet."

She snuffled. "I know."

Behind them, the door opened, someone said something, then the door closed.

"Hate to interrupt you two," Spencer said in a low voice. "Looks like you've made up. Glen, how are you?"

"Fine, now. I'm going home with her."

"Katherine?"

"He's coming home with me." She didn't turn around, just kept watching Glen. His golden eyes glistened in his beautiful face, which she kissed more than once.

"We've got a lot to talk about," she said. "But one thing's for sure, we love each other, so something's got to be worked out."

"Glen? You sure you're going to be okay?"

"Don't know. But she's the best one to be with when things go wrong."

"That's putting a lot on her."

"Don't I know it. But she... that's the way she wants it, and what Katie wants, Katie gets."

She played at smacking him, then turned toward Spencer. "That's enough. Nothing bad is going to happen to him. You know how I feel and what I want, so leave it alone. I want him out of here. Today. See if Marty can continue coming to the house. We've got places to go and things to do."

A few hours later, both dressed and released to leave, he grabbed her hand tight. The fear in his eyes alerted her.

"Everything will be fine, sweetheart," she said.

"I need a hug really bad," he said.

She bent and put her arms around him as best she could and held him for a long time. "When we get home and get you out of that chair, I'm going to hug you so tight all your broken pieces will stick back together."

"That may not be possible, but it's sure a fine thing to imagine, isn't it?"

"Yes, it is. Now, let's go home."

She walked beside him down the hall and out the door into the warm March sunlight.

In bed that night, he remained quiet for a while, and she feared he might still be angry with her. He waited until she turned out the light and was settled, then he moved so close they touched from head to toe.

"Remember about that hug you promised me? The one that will put all my broken pieces back together. I come to collect 'cause some of my pieces need mending."

"You come here, then, and I'll see if I can fix them."

He smelled of soap and shampoo and minty toothpaste that reminded her of walking in the woods in the spring. Tracing the scars on his back, she placed her arms tight around him and hugged him up so close nothing could come between them. His muscles, firm and warm, rippled in her embrace. She recalled what Julia had said about how hugging him when he came home was like hugging a gunny sack filled with straw. How close he had come to dying and how many horrors he had survived.

"I am so proud of you," she told him. "So proud. I love you so much I could just eat you up."

"Sounds good to me. Come here." He lifted her across his lap.

"Whatcha got there?"

"Something special, just for you."

FOUR

A WEEK LATER, on a rainy Friday afternoon, Marty peeked out of the sunroom and gestured to her. "Come and see," he whispered.

She ran to the door and peered through the open slit. Glen was halfway along the bars, moving first one leg then the other in fierce concentration.

"He's not putting his weight down yet, but this is the first time I've coaxed him into doing that much, and he's been back and forth several times. I need to go stop him before he hurts himself, but I wanted you to see first."

If it weren't so undignified she would've jumped up and down and shouted, then run to him cheering like one of those girls at a football game.

Marty held a finger to his lips. "Let him tell you what he did, okay? He needs that."

She nodded. He closed the door.

The panels pressed to her back, she cupped her hands over her mouth to muffle her crying, then hurried to the couch, grabbed some tissues and dried her eyes, plopped down, picked up a magazine, and tried to look as if she'd been there all along. Some fifteen minutes later, he came out showered, dressed in jeans, a tee shirt and white socks in his chair. His grin wide, eyes shining.

She could scarcely contain herself. "Well, you look happy. Must've gone well." Rain pelted the windows, the room so gloomy she'd turned on the lights. But it might have been a sunny day the way she felt.

"Pretty good," he said casually. "I made three round trips between the bars on my feet. Three times. Actually counts as six, across and back, doesn't it? Would've gone more, but he wouldn't let me."

"That's wonderful. That's so wonderful," and she burst out crying. Blubbering was more like it. She could only hold out her arms to him. He came to her side, levered himself out of the chair to sit beside her. They went into each other's arms. It was just her way and he understood.

The closer Easter loomed, the harder he worked. Sometimes he was so beat up when they went to bed he fell asleep when his head hit the pillow. She would snuggle over close as she could get and close her eyes, listening to his heartbeat, his soft breathing. And the nightmares receded to one a week, then not even that. He marked the days off until Easter on a calendar he'd hung in the sunroom.

She took to praying, though it surely wasn't right to pray only when one wanted something. So she added thanks at the end every night. It was so easy to believe in a benevolent God these days.

At lunch on a Tuesday, when Marty wasn't with them, she said, "Isn't it time we had a trial run? Find a bit of a crowd and wander through, just to see how things go?"

He kept eating like he hadn't heard her.

"Glen?"

"Heard you. Thinking. Okay, done thinking. No, don't need a trial run yet. Wait until I can walk, then we'll see."

"Okay. So let's go somewhere where there aren't any people and you can practice walking with the arm braces. Maybe down to the lake."

"Too rough."

"No, the old lake. There are sidewalks and parking lots and not many people this time of the year. And there are stretches of smooth, soft grass."

He glanced up, took a sip of tea. "You're gonna keep at this, aren't you? Until I say yes."

She smiled sweetly at him. "Probably. You know how I am."

"Come on over here and let me see how you are. I'm feeling randy and we haven't had a good romp in a while."

She put down her fork, rose. "Leave it to you to change the subject. Don't you want to finish eating?"

His gaze roamed up and down her body. She wore a short sundress that showed off her shapely legs. "I guess not." He put down the sandwich and reached out. "Come on, pretty lady."

"You're just trying to get out of going to the park."

"No, what I'm trying is to get you out of that dress."

And so another day went by without him giving in and going out in public using the arm braces. She refused to force him, and he well knew it.

It was another week before he gave in with a great deal of reluctance. Katie drove them down to Lake Fort Smith State Park on a warm sunny day. The highway was a bustle of truckers, and she dared not take her eyes off the traffic, yet she sensed terror beneath his thin coating of courage.

"I've changed my mind," he said. "I don't want to do this. Not yet. Katie, please."

Her heart melted, but she remained stern. "Do you want to go to the monument?"

Silence, then a sullen, "You know I do."

"Okay, then. Hang in there. I'm with you all the way." She slammed on the brakes to miss a passing car that crowded back in front of her to avoid colliding with an oncoming tractor trailer.

"Why don't we just go for a drive today? Maybe over to Oklahoma. That would be nice. We could stop for buffalo burgers."

"Okay, if you'll get out in the parking lot and walk all around it on those damn things."

Silence.

After a few more miles poking along the dangerous curves of the highway with nothing more from him, she said, "You still with me over there?"

"No, I got out a ways back. We were going so slow I thought I'd just walk a while."

"Well, that could work. How's it going?"

"It's hell."

"Aw, honey. I wish this wasn't so hard for you. If you truly want to go back, we will."

"I don't know. I... hell, keep driving. We'll give this a try, anyway. If I can't cut it in a park with people, I sure as hell can't wander around D.C., can I?"

"Did you bring the camera?" she asked. "Buddy, where'd you learn to drive?" she muttered at the weaving, braking car ahead.

"In the basket with the food. Why do you want it?"

"I want some pictures of you and me. To start our own album."

"Do you ever wonder what people will think when they see us together? Will they wonder what a woman like you could ever see in someone beat up like me?"

"Don't you say that. Don't you ever say something like that." She turned on the blinker and pulled off the highway at a wide spot, nosed in under some trees. She stared through the windshield for a minute before taking a deep breath and turning toward him. He gazed over at her intently. Expectantly.

She scooted over on the bench seat and cupped his face in both hands. "First place, what other people think has never concerned me. You are the best man I've ever known. You're brave and kind and so, so beautiful." She traced his features with a finger. His eyes, nose, along one cheek, his chin, the other cheek. The scars were almost invisible, pale lines where the monsters had sliced his face when they ran out of other ways to torture him. She didn't even see them anymore.

"If anyone thought a thing, they'd probably feel sorry for you having that old lady on your arm." She laughed. "Give me a kiss. We're going to the park."

He laughed. "Okay, old lady." He kissed her and said no more, though he continued to fidget with the metal crutches propped between his legs.

Parking the van against the split rail fence that bordered the circle drive, she hopped out. "I'll take the basket to that empty table over there, then come back, and we can carry over the rest of the stuff."

Motionless as a stone, he remained in the seat until she claimed a table and returned, came around to his open window. "Ready?"

He sat there a moment, then lifted his shoulders in a sigh. "Ready." She opened the door and he twisted in the seat, put his arms through the cuffs of the crutches, placed them on the ground. "I'm going to get you for this, you wait and see."

She laughed. "I can't wait to find out my punishment. Now, come on."

He inched away from the door, and she closed it. "I'll get the ice chest, and you wait right here until I come back."

"Yes, Mother," he said.

She hurried back to him, desperate to help him. God, would she ever get the strength to make him stand on his own when she wanted so much to prop him up? They had to walk a ways to find an opening in the fence she had climbed over with the basket. She carried the cooler in her left hand and placed herself between him and the slow traffic meandering through the picnic area. How terrifying it must be for him, the cacophony of noise, people shouting, doors slamming, children crying and squealing. Cars starting up, a motorcycle revving to life.

He staggered toward the rail, and she reached for him, then the damn bike backfired twice. Glen shouted and hit the ground on his face, arms folded over the top of his head, those infernal metal sticks at odd angles. She didn't have time to do anything but fling the cooler and dive after him, skidding through the gravel on her knees.

"Honey, you okay? Sweetheart?" She crawled to him on knees that were scraped raw and burning, covered his hunched figure with one arm and leaned close.

Several people watched, apparently unsure how they could help or if they should try. Then a burly young man in jeans and tee shirt approached from the other side of the road.

"Hey, man. Out of sight. Shit, can I help you up, man? Lady, he okay or what?"

"Could you help me, please?" she asked in a voice that trembled so she could hardly speak.

Glen raised to his knees and half turned toward her. "Dammit, Katie, just get me the hell out of here."

"We are. We will." She held on to his arm.

"Should I, like, grab on to his other arm?" the kid said "I could just pick him the hell up if you like. Fucker don't look too heavy to me."

The young man was kind of grungy and appeared tough, but he had an expression of such concern on his unshaven face that she wanted to hug him. And he was the only one helping her.

The small crowd discussed the problem amongst themselves. One asked if she needed an ambulance. An old lady kept shouting, "Call the cops, call the cops." A younger fella retrieved the cooler. Most of the crowd didn't seem to know exactly what they should do, stay and stare or go on their way and ignore the problem.

Glen managed to push himself into a sitting position and leaned against one of the round posts of the fence. "What the hell is everyone looking at?"

She attempted to shelter him from the crowd. "It's okay. Calm down. Are you hurt?"

There was a bit of blood on his chin, but it looked like a superficial scrape. Her knees were more damaged. She stood and helped the kid, who wasn't the least put off by Glen's hollering. Together, they got him to his feet, let him lean against the fence while they repositioned the crutches. Most of the crowd had wandered away.

"Look at your legs. God, Katie, doesn't that hurt? Jesus, I'm sorry. What the hell was that?"

The kid who'd given them a hand hovered nearby as if expecting Glen to fly off again and he'd have something further to do. He replied to his question.

"It was my son-of-a-bitching bike. Fucker's out of time. I kick the son-of-a-bitch, all hell breaks loose. I'm sorry as hell, man. Thought you was being attacked, I guess. Got me a buddy, he's the same way sometimes. Some scene, that shit, huh?" The boy, whose shirt read, Shit Happens, backed up with fly-away hand gestures, then trotted off before Katie could thank him.

"Kind of enjoyed that, didn't he?" Glen remarked dryly.

"Maybe, but he did help. No one else knew what to do." She limped slowly along beside him. "Okay if we go ahead and have our picnic?"

"Sure. I'm not hurt, but your knees could stand a tending to. Besides, the worst has already happened. Hell, look at me walking along like I don't have good sense. If you brought some water I'll clean your knees for you."

"Oh, sure, any excuse to get your hands on my legs."

"You bet, babe."

He had put a pretty good face on the entire affair, and she was proud of him. He sat her down then dropped beside her on the bench at the table, cleaned her knees with napkins and cold water from the Thermos, then rubbed her thighs.

"Look out, buddy. We're in a public place."

He laughed, but she could see the apprehension in his eyes. "Need bandages on those. Maybe we ought to go home."

"Nope, we're here, we're staying. I'll survive. Let's eat."

After they ate, they walked in the grass under the trees, strolling like any other couple. He just had a bit more trouble than some. Once he jokingly offered her the crutches and managed to laugh with her. She watched him closely, his features clenched in concentration. That was good, better than panic.

"Say when you get tired, you can sit at a table, and I'll go get the van. No sense in overdoing it."

"I'm fine, Katie, it's you that's wounded. Let's just go back together. I'd rather not wait alone, if you don't mind."

"Okay, then, let's start back."

They were halfway home before she remembered they hadn't had anyone take their picture together. Maybe she should've handed the camera to someone in the crowd around her fallen hero, had them get a photo of that.

During the following two weeks they spent Tuesdays and Thursdays in places more and more crowded. The mall became Glen's favorite place, which surprised her because of the crowds. He said he liked the windows filled with Easter decorations and clothes and the benches where they could stop and rest, and with few surprises. No backfires or unexpected noises. No shadowy places where monsters could hide. Most of all he liked that no one stared at him. Laughed because he was the one staring at all the pretty women. Everyone was busy with their own lives and didn't have time to poke into his. One thing he could not do was be alone in those crowds. He did not trust himself. Suppose he went crazy and hurt someone? A child. They did not belong in the world he'd created, the one that kept him sane. The world that belonged solely to him and Katie. She would not allow that to happen. She was with him.

Odd that she belonged in the world he'd created, for he'd never mentioned it before. So she asked him about it.

His reply frightened her more than she could say. "Only if you can stay without being hurt. If I should ever hurt you or keep you from being happy, then I'd not want you there anymore, Katie. Or me, either, for that matter."

For that reason she vowed never to get hurt. What he meant, of course, had nothing to do with scraped knees. It went much deeper than that. And she got it. She really did. Even though sometimes his reasoning didn't make sense, for when she had passed out in the hospital was when he took her back into his world. She refrained from arguing with him about stuff like that. How could he be expected to reason properly when he had been mistreated for so long by people who, he must have thought, had no reason to do what they were doing to him?

Anyway, she was happy because he was preparing for the trip and doing so well. To hell with worrying about his small misconceptions.

FIVE

SPENCER DIDN'T LIKE it one bit, but he finally stamped a reluctant okay on the trip to Washington, D.C. and prescribed a heavy sedative that Glen should tolerate. Katherine didn't tell him they would go anyway, because Glen claimed he was ready, and he was who counted, not the doctor who sat in his safe office with only good memories.

The drive to Tulsa for the flight out to D.C. proved uneventful, probably because Glen was too terrified to talk and simply stared out the van window at the scenery. Probably imagining God only knew what. At the airport, he was allowed to board first and she accompanied him. They had opted to use the wheelchair to get him on board and off and to the hotel in D.C. He didn't want to, but admitted she was right. He vowed to walk during his tour of the monument, but she would be his backup with the chair, much as he hated the idea. In the dark of night, lying in bed with her arms around him, he'd told her he loved her for making sure he did the safe stuff, even when he grouched about it. She smiled in secret and whispered in his ear she loved him back.

Inside the 727, he began to shake. Close quarters plus the impending flight unnerved him. He asked her to take the window seat so he could sit on the aisle, all the better to make an escape. To where she had no earthly idea. After stowing the chair, she returned to climb over him and sit, immediately taking his arm and draping it around her shoulder. His tension was palpable and he gripped her tightly. Bits and pieces of him threatened to fracture from the whole, and she vowed to give him a hug to stick them all back together when they arrived at the hotel.

In the meantime, she dug in her purse and found the pills Spencer prescribed, shook one out and offered it to him. He frowned, shook his head.

"We talked about this. You need to take it. It's perfectly safe, it'll help you relax. Sweetheart, you're terrified and rightly so. Please take it. I don't want you going off in here and you don't either." She continued to hold it in her palm until he plucked it up between his forefinger and thumb and stuck it in his mouth. She kissed him on the cheek. Wished like hell she could take some of his burden on her own shoulders.

What she hadn't counted on was belting him into his seat. They hadn't either one thought of how he might react. Spending nine years often strapped down and tortured had naturally made him a bit leery of the seat belt thing, and when the stewardess came along and told him to please fasten his seat belt, panic flew through his eyes. He snapped a worried stare between her and Katie, shook his head, and it was up to her to manage this.

"Okay, sweetheart, now lean back and relax. I've got this, okay?"

He managed to grin at her, uttered a few words. "I know you have."

"Okay, I'm going to fasten it for you. No danger, no worries, and I'll hold on to you tight. Will that work for you?" She spoke in a low, nonconfrontational voice, and he shook his head frantically. "Tell you what, sweetheart. Put your hand over mine and you can help me get this done.

All right?" Again that shake, but he did place his trembling hand over hers. She wanted so badly to yell he didn't have to do this. That, they weren't going to crash, so just leave him the hell alone. Instead, she smiled at him, kept eye contact, and slowly lay the belt over his lap. Like a skittish pony never broken to ride, he trembled all over, but he didn't balk. Not until he heard the click, felt it tighten across his thighs.

"Fucking shit," he said, breath hissing in and out.

He was going to come apart, tensed under her touch, started looking all over the airplane like he might find a way out. "Glen, look at me. I'm here, you're here, and we're both okay." She cupped his chin in one hand, turned him so he was again looking at her. "I love you, and you're going to do this. Hang on to me." And he did, dear God, he did, his grip so tight she'd carry bruises, but she didn't give a damn as long as he made it without flying to pieces.

He never let go of her arm during the takeoff. By the time the seat belt sign went off he was feeling the effects of the pill. Still, he fumbled for the buckle, released it, and relaxed.

A young, attractive flight attendant bent over him and flashed her toothpaste-ad, brace-corrected teeth in his face and asked if he wanted something to drink.

His tentative effort to smile had the girl fluttering her eyelashes.

"No, thank you," he said.

"Your dinner will be served in a few minutes," she told him coyly, effectively ignoring Katie. Glen leaned out into the aisle and watched the delicious figure ripple slowly away.

Relieved he was acting more like himself, Katie pinched him playfully through his thick sweater. "You're drooling."

"Fine stuff," he replied and kissed her on the tip of her nose. The pills were definitely doing their work.

"Maybe," she said, "but if she doesn't leave you alone, she won't have anything to stuff."

He grinned big time, displaying those dimples. "Well, well. No sooner drag me out in the world until your secret comes out. You're jealous. I wouldn't have thought it."

The attention the attractive girl had paid him pleased him to no end, and he couldn't help showing it. That was a fine thing for his self-esteem, and she certainly wasn't worried about the girl getting anywhere with him. Still, the young thing did make her painfully conscious of her forty years, of wrinkles and no more smooth complexion, pert breasts, or tight little butt.

"Hey, darlin', don't look so glum. You don't have anything to worry about. I was just horsing around."

"I know that. Don't mind me. I was wishing I was a little bit younger, that's all."

"With nothing on your mind but how you look in your tight jeans? No, thanks."

"Now, that's not really fair. Plenty of pretty young girls are intelligent and mature."

"Maybe. It so happens I don't want any of them. Besides, what would that frail little thing do the first time I started climbing a wall? Probably leap out the nearest window or beat me with her high heeled shoe."

The stewardess kept up a running flirtation with him during the entire flight. Her swift patter laced with double entendre made him squirm, but he was flattered nevertheless. What man wouldn't be? The episode served a valuable purpose by keeping him occupied with something he didn't comprehend and giving him little time to contemplate his fears.

None too soon the ribbon of silver that was the Potomac River reflected rays of afternoon sunlight in brilliant flashes on their approach to Arlington airport. His hand tightened around hers when she quickly fastened his seat belt and the big jet touched down. The airport made Tulsa look like a backwater bus stop. In the noisy rush of humanity she struggled to get him safely through. They couldn't communicate over the hubbub, so she simply moved him along, watching him for any frantic body movement. Given enough impetus he could bail out of the chair. After what seemed like a mile and might have been for all she knew, she spotted the rotating luggage rack and their one bag.

He took it in his lap, and she headed for the doors that would take them outside and into another frightening world. Horns blared, tires squealed, voices demanded. Exhaust hung heavy in the surprisingly cool air, and she moved to the first cab in the queue lined up at the curb. The driver hopped out, took the bag and set it in the front seat, then opened the back door and stood aside.

"Does he need help, ma'am?"

"He does not," Glen replied.

"Thank you," she said, and waited while Glen moved out of the chair and into the cab, taking the braces with him.

She went around and climbed in the other door, and soon the trunk slammed down and the driver climbed behind the wheel. She gave him the name of the hotel, then leaned back. A loud whew escaped through her pursed lips.

Glen patted her knee. "Everything will be okay, just relax."

She laid her hand on his and laughed, and so did he.

"We made it, babe," he said. "We're here."

"Indeed we are. We'll have some supper sent up by room service, get a good night's sleep—"

"Well, that's debatable. After a little healthy exercise, we'll sleep."

"And then it's on to the monument."

The driver maneuvered in and around the heavy, slow moving traffic. "You folks come to see the Vietnam monument?"

"Yes, how'd you know?" she replied when it seemed evident Glen wasn't going to.

"Educated guess, I suppose. You over there, buddy?

"Yep."

"For how long?"

His tension ratcheted up until she thought he might spring from the seat, and she put a hand on his thigh. "Long enough."

"Ain't that the God's honest truth?"

"You, too?" Glen asked, relaxing a bit under her touch.

"Yep. Hell of a lot better here, even with all this." The driver gestured toward the four solid lanes of slow moving traffic. "Even with all this."

"Fucking A," Glen said and leaned his head against hers, taking a deep breath. It was time she got him into the hotel and to bed. The day had been grueling for her, no way to imagine what it had been like for him.

"Just a little while longer, sweetheart. It's not far now."

As if he had overheard her, the driver said, "I'll make it short as I can," and began weaving in and out of the traffic. He pulled to the curb at the hotel, hopped out, retrieved the wheelchair and brought it to the back door, opened the front door, and grabbed their bag.

She dug in her purse, paid him and gave him a good tip. "Thank you so much."

When Glen was in the chair the driver shook his hand. "Good to meet you, buddy. Take 'er easy."

"Same to you."

Checking in, she kept one eye on him, the other on the man behind the counter, who took too long to process and get her a key. Time continued to drag when they boarded the elevator, rode up four floors, residue from the pill holding him down a little, though he looked as if he wanted to hit the deck. Out, then down the hall to the room.

By the time they reached the door, he was a man pursued, flashing worried glances in both directions, checking no doubt for those monsters that slithered out of the dark to bedevil him. The key finally worked, and she pushed him inside quickly. The lights were on, and the room was airy, clean, and ordinary. The king-sized bed was covered with a burnt orange spread, a color she abhorred. She dragged it off and wadded it into a corner.

"I'm not hungry. Think I'll just crawl in the bed," he said.

"I'm going to take a shower."

He watched her for a minute. "Could you leave the door open?"

The heebee-jeebees. Dear God, don't let him fly apart now. "Sure, sweetie. No problem. Peek if you want."

He didn't answer, and she saw he had turned down the covers on his side of the bed and was perched on the edge taking off his shirt. Removing her blouse, she went around to him, knelt on the floor, and pulled off his shoes.

"I can do that now, you know," he snapped.

"I know, but I don't want to feel completely useless."

When she started to rise, he reached down and rubbed her shoulder. "You'll never be useless. Never."

"Good to know. I'm also good at taking your pants off."

Tired as he was, he laughed. "In that case, be my guest. I'm so tired I could have gone to bed in them."

Rising to her knees, she unbuckled his belt, unsnapped his jeans, and ran the zipper down. "Ready? Lift your butt."

He did, and she slipped them off.

"You're right, you are good at that."

For a brief moment she rested her head on his bare thighs, rubbed a thumb over a jagged scar above his knee, kissed it, and raised her head.

He stared down at her. "Come here," he whispered, and when she moved to sit beside him, he said, "Do you know how much I love you?"

"Yep." She nodded her head. "'Cause it's how much I love you. Now I'll tuck you in, and you can go to sleep. I'll keep watch."

He'd told her once he liked how she tucked him in, it left him feeling protected and safe. That was a long time ago when he was so very fragile, but she kept doing it. It left her feeling she had shown him how much she cared for him.

She pulled the covers up under his chin, sat beside him with her hand on his stomach until he closed his eyes and relaxed in sleep. Then she went to take a shower and left the bathroom door open.

Some hours later, she knew not how many because she hadn't looked at the clock at all, he awoke, shoving her aside because she was spooned against him. Shaking, panting, sweating. By now she knew the drill, took him in her arms and let him wind down and hug her back. By then they were both wide awake. The next step, though, the one where he said something like, "I'm coming," and then proceeded to make that happen, didn't.

She rubbed his belly, let her hand trail lower. Nothing.

"I can't do it. Not now, not in this place with what we came here for hiding in the closet, or maybe lurking under the bed. I can't do it tonight. I'm sorry, so damn sorry."

"No worries. It'll wait." She lay there, holding him close and safe until the throbbing went away and left an empty, aching hole inside her. When he spoke again, she steeled herself.

"I had fantasies of lying in bed with a beautiful woman. I never forgot it 'cause it kept me going. Morning after morning I'd wake up sure that was the nightmare and the fantasy was real. After a million years, I had to admit I'd wake up in that cage for the rest of my life. There'd be no beautiful women." He paused, toyed with a lock of her hair that stranded over his arm like silk. "I still wake up like that. This world has become the unreality, that other is so real I can't get rid of it. Somehow I have to get rid of it, Katie. I can't go on and on living like this, believing I'm dreaming when you and I are together and that the nightmares of that place are real. Jesus." He was quiet a long time, but she did not fill the void, just waited. There was more yet to come.

"That's why I wanted to come here. Say goodbye to all of it, like those other guys, leave the remnants piled at the feet of that monument. Maybe then this will become my real life. Do you think it matters my souvenirs are invisible? I guess I never earned any medals."

That cut a hole right through her, and she leaned against his shoulder so he could snake an arm around her.

He didn't wait for her to reply, but kept going. "I can still see him, you know? We called them dinks or slopes, but I suppose that's out of fashion now. This bastard would stand over me—they strapped us where they could tower over us, the shrunken little shits—and he'd stare down at me with the most ugly revulsion. I never did figure out why he hated me. He sure did like to hurt me, though. Push me right to the brink, then pull me back. He kept me bellowing in agony just on the verge of passing out for hours at a time, like he didn't want to lose his new play-toy before he got all the good out of it he could. Eventually he went away, but another took his place and then another and another. And after a while, I knew it would go on like that into infinity.

"And then one day there was you... a new fantasy, one I hold on to but still, once in a while, I'm afraid of slipping back into that real world that waits in a dark corner."

Oh my God. She shivered in his embrace, didn't quite know what she could say, was devastated that he still lived these horrors as if they were real when all along she'd thought him all but rid of them. Prayed she could think of something more to say, but only came up with, "I love you, and that, my sweet, is real. Believe me, this is your real world."

She eased him back down on his pillow and snugged into his shoulder, hand on his chest, feeling his heartbeat.

"I'll never hurt you, Katie, I promise."

"I know, sweetheart, I know. Go to sleep." She said a silent prayer that she would never have to hurt him again.

The next morning they visited the eternal flame at the John F. Kennedy gravesite.

"Do you suppose it would have been different if he'd have been allowed to stay around and get us raised?" he said.

"Oh, yes, I do." Some things she'd never ever forget. The election after Kennedy's death would have been her first to vote. She didn't. The man she idolized had been shot down on a Dallas street. Nothing would ever be right again. And in truth, it never had been.

"The whole world went lopsided after that," he said. "What was once insanity is now normal, while sane people are treated like fools. Maybe I'm not the only one who doesn't know what's real anymore."

They walked slowly away, him managing to support himself on the crutches quite well.

"I know one thing that's real," she said.

He darted a silent query in her direction.

"Us. You and me are the only real things I know."

"Are you absolutely, positively sure?"

"Oh, yes. Want me to pinch you?"

"Better not," he said.

The grass in the stone garden glistened a bright and shiny green from an early morning shower. Crosses marched symmetrically in long lines, here and there broken by a solitary tree. Everything so neat, precise, and white that it seemed to deny the lost hopes buried there. Monuments for the dead.

But what about the living? Where were the monuments to ease their torture? She wasn't sure but that this visit wasn't going to be as hard on her as on him.

"I want to go now."

"I think I do, too."

Neither looked back as they walked away under the bright sky and praying trees.

The visit to the Vietnam Veterans Memorial could be delayed no longer. Anxious as he had been, he had postponed it with other detours. Coming into sight, the black slabs slashed deeply into the earth, cut a wing-shaped scar across two acres of the mall. It pushed its way out of the ground like a frozen ebony berg, each end stretching at an angle toward a ten-foot apex. The warm day couldn't dispel the sudden chill that slashed through her on seeing it. His emotions were so strong they emanated over her in waves. Pain, fear, regret, guilt, bled from his eyes.

Take him home, now. Take him home. Drag him kicking and screaming from this dreadful place.

Still she shuffled on behind him, pushing the chair because he would never make it out of here when this was over.

"My God in Heaven," she breathed. "Look at all the names." Who could even imagine what 58,000 names would look like? She stared down at the shiny tips of his boots, not wanting to look anymore.

She had to stop him. Prevent him from joining the others who stood, sat, or knelt there. Screaming, crying, gnashing of teeth. That was her imagination, for in actuality it was eerily quiet, and those who suffered did so with dignity and reserve.

She was invaded suddenly with a vivid flash of memory. A trip to Shiloh with Stan. A stroll through the battlefield on a hushed, peaceful afternoon. Peering among the trees at the sunken road down which troops had dragged their wagons of death. None of the visitors spoke, so caught up were they in the ghostly screams of those long-ago battles. Another in a series of never-ending wars producing dead and damaged heroes, on and on and on.

Horses straining against impossible loads snorted white plumes into the morning mist that rose off the river. The deep boom of black-powder rifles filled the air with odorous sulferous charcoal. Deep thumps from cannon jarred the ground. Visions were like remembrances which, should she close her eyes, would transport her back there to feel the fear and see the death and taste the ashes of despair. Lead balls were buried deep in the trunks of the mammoth trees, trees that stood patient and indestructible as silent witness to the carnage. She reached out and touched them and felt dizzy and not of that world.

Wounds healed, destruction ended. And peace had come at last to Shiloh, the common grave of the enemy finally removed, and the Confederate remains given an honorable resting place near their Union brothers. Hate and revenge a live remnant for years to come.

"How will we find their names?" Glen asked, jarring her back from those long ago memories into the present and a quite different place honoring war. "I don't see how we can...." he trod the path, one single halting step at a time, eyes on the black slab.

"They have lists, we can find out," she told him.

Mesmerized, he moved slowly toward the information table where he could find where his buddies' names were engraved. The man in uniform, a boy really, helped him look up MacArthur MacKenzie and Herman Franks.

She remembered their names so well.

Dear God, don't let him ask for his own name.

After he got the information, she helped him find the proper panel, then stepped away from him. Fists bunched at her sides, she raised her head so the mirrored images disappeared from her view and she saw only the tops of far off trees against a blue, blue sky. And across that cerulean slate, a miniscule, far away plane trailed a white streak that broke into tiny puffs and vanished in the wind. She lowered her head and closed her eyes. Her heart ached fiercely, and the quiet around her pulsed with threats of impending doom. Frantically, abruptly, she searched for Glen in the line of mourners.

She found him, standing near a man in a wheelchair. Caught her breath as he removed the braces from his arms, let the crutches drop to the ground, and placed both hands flat against the monument. For a while he concentrated on tracing the letters of his best friend's name with one finger. *MacArthur M. MacKenzie*, the man he'd flown beside and loved. Then he rested his head there.

She tumbled into the deep void of her soul, blacker, heavier and colder than the slab that stretched across the mall. Somewhere a child's small voice, a mother's anguished cry.

How could he stay here any longer without vanishing into his past? She raised her shoulders, intending to fetch him, move him on. Beside him stood a short husky man, his long hair held down by a bandana. He wore a shabby army jacket, jeans cut off above the knees and scruffy leather sandals on unbelievably dirty feet. He watched Glen, so she waited a moment, gave them time to commiserate.

Would this place ever stand for peace? The conflict lived on like a writing beast in his soul. Meanwhile 2500 MIAs, left behind, hovered as accusing ghosts asking where they belonged? Was their common grave to be forever unmarked?

Who will leave them flowers?

Who will bring them home?

She stepped forward, for whatever reason she wasn't sure. All she knew was she had to stop something bizarre that was poised to happen. The man's heavy body odor overpowered the fresh scent of spring flowers. The man in the wheelchair breathed heavily and harshly, then moved away. Why didn't the other man leave, too? Let Glen grieve alone? But he remained, and she retrieved the crutches, moved in under Glen's arm, darted a swift glance at the intruder. He watched her with small, marblely eyes that jolted her like a charge of electricity.

"You oughta get him outa here," he said in a piercing voice. "I come here all the time, I see 'em all. I can tell you, you better take him on home. Sooner the better. There ain't nothing here for him but hell." He eyed her, and she was reminded of a rat's gaze. "I can getcha sumpun for him, you want."

She pretended not to hear for fear of what she would say, raised her gaze, and saw herself and Glen reflected beyond the names like beings sucked into its ebony essence. Their faces stared back from the jet mirror, expressions bewildered and tightened in mourning. She had a wispy vision, a fearful thought that each visitor was somehow captured in the reverse image and stored away within the pure stone slashed from some faraway mountain. It would forever hold the names of the dead and their tortured souls as well as a piece of all who came to lament their passing. The fury of the place burned like a fire, names of the slain marched forever across the black headstone against which lay flowers, pictures, letters, and medals, all spotted by salty tears. It was as quiet as if the world had ended.

Glen's ragged voice filtered through her thoughts. "I wanted to find all their names, all the men who died while I tried to save them, and the guys left behind in the camps. Are they on the wall, along with mine? But I can't remember all the names."

She shuddered, could not allow him to look for, and possibly find, his own name, carved out there as if he had died, so he could be dismissed from their guilt.

"Come away now," she pleaded. Supporting him, the weariness of his mind became a ponderous weight. She coaxed him into sitting in the chair, knelt to lower the rests for his feet. "Let's go, sweetheart. It's time to go home now."

How long did he have to suffer for that stinking, useless war that had gained nothing but shame and shattered lives? She wanted to climb to the top of that shard of stone and shout that he wasn't to blame. That suffering and war would go on and on and on, just as it had for the eternity of mankind, so how could he possibly be to blame?

She could not shout at him. Instead she offered him all she could. A promise that she would always love him and would never leave him. At the moment she feared that might not be nearly enough.

S I X

KATIE HAD ALWAYS held a deep-seated distrust of drugs that deadened the senses, so she was engulfed in dread when she dosed Glen with the medication Spencer had provided. But he was a zombie with eyes that snapped at every sound and no voice to express his needs. She drugged him to sleep that night, drugged him so he could fly, drugged him for the long drive from Tulsa, and tried to see to him as best she could. Prayed he would not have to pay later.

Spencer was right about the trip and its effect on him. Still he had needed to go. If she hadn't gone with him, he might have attempted the trip, ended up in some dirty alley with a needle crammed in his veins, put there by a helpful friend such as that dirty man at the mall.

Somehow, she got them both home, but when she awoke the next morning and saw they were safe in their bed, she couldn't remember how she'd managed it. Their clothes were scattered all over the floor. They both lay naked beneath the covers, him curled into a fetal position. She touched a finger to the throbbing pulse at his temple. He twitched and muttered something that sounded like go away or don't touch me. Before she could decide what to do, he began to tremble and make a dreadful humming sound down in his throat. To what horror would he awaken today?

Fearful he was having a nightmare from which he might emerge swinging, she moved out of his reach, but couldn't stand his suffering for long and curled around him, whispered in his ear. He could hit her if he wanted to. He tensed up, muscles hard as rocks.

"Baby, baby," she crooned. "No one is hurting you. This is Katie. We're home, and everything's okay."

God damn those who did this to him. Setting her jaw, she spoke low to him. "Turn over so I can hold you. Come on. It's Katie."

He jerked again. What had she done to him? Spencer said the drugs would be okay. Suppose she had sent him back to the way he was the first day she saw him?

Please, please, please. A silent prayer. "Ssh, my darling. I'm here. Come on. I want to hold you."

So quickly she couldn't dodge, he twisted over, straightened his knees, bumping her hard in the shins and hooked his arms around her. Dragged her so tightly to him she lost her breath for a second. He uttered her name under his breath, over and over and over.

Relieved, she touched his face with the tips of her fingers, rubbed his temples, continued to croon to him. Without opening his eyes, he settled into a relaxed sleep. She remained there stretched out against him a good long while until sure he was okay. The best thing was to let him sleep and make some coffee. Soon enough they could both use it. Once the pot was dripping, she wore a path between the kitchen and sunroom, making sure he was sleeping peacefully.

The phone rang while she watched the coffee drip into the glass pot, and she picked it up quickly so it wouldn't awaken him.

"Well?" Spencer's voice grumbled.

"Bad. He's drugged and finally resting. Happy?" She had no patience with the man. He'd called to gloat over being right, the bastard.

"But you're both back and still functioning."

"That remains to be seen. He's not coming down off the drugs well. I'll handle it. What do you want? I'm not in the mood for banter. Haven't even had coffee yet."

"Call me back when you're in a better mood, and let me know how he is. I'll need to see him."

"That's debatable." She hung up without waiting for him to answer that one, so angry she wanted to kick something.

Unable to wait for the last of the coffee to run through, she pulled out the pot and poured herself a cup, catching the final drips in another cup, then carried it back into the sunroom and sat cross legged next to him on the bed, watching him sleep. Deep down inside, she ached so much she could scarcely control her need to touch him, check on him.

Damn, where had this need to nurture this man come from? All the years with Stan he had taken care of her, only wanted her presence, and she had accepted that even though she missed nurturing. Perhaps all women had that instinct built in, and having no children, she'd missed using it. Stan was too strong, too stubborn, too sure he was always right in his attitudes and judgments. Hated her giving him backrubs or washing his back in the shower. All that made him sound like an awful tyrant and bore, but he hadn't been. Not at all. He was fine and kind and generous, and she'd loved him, still missed him. Yet she was so totally consumed by the needs of this damaged man that she no longer felt Stan's loss like she had.

Now she was caught up in the love of a man who needed all the nurturing she'd saved up. Sometimes she feared it wasn't enough to help him heal. And she had never once resented that, rather understood and gave of it willingly.

His eyes popped open and he stared at her for a long while as if confused.

"What the hell? How did we get here, Katie? I feel like hell, worse than a hangover. Jesus, what did you give me? My mouth feels like it's full of cotton, and there's a goddamn cannon firing in my head. Whatever those pills were, could you please throw them in the toilet? I don't even remember coming home. I thought I was back there, someone was coming to drag me away to the torture chamber."

"I've already tossed them. I hardly remember it myself. It was the only way I could get you back without help. You want a cup of coffee?"

"Hell yes, or a gallon jug of the stuff." He pushed himself up on his elbows. His hair was standing on end.

"Wow, the room just flipped upside down. I feel like I'm falling. Fucking shit is that stuff?"

She handed him her half-full cup and scooted over to steady it in both his hands while he took a few sips, shaking so hard he slopped some out.

"Just stay still for a while, get your bearings. Don't want you getting up and falling flat on your face. We're home and safe, you're in one piece."

"Not so sure about that." He drank down the rest of her coffee in one long swallow. "Could I maybe get some more of that? I'd go get it myself, but the floor won't stop rolling around."

"I'll never feed you those pills again. I promise. You stay where you are. I'll bring us both another cup, and we'll drink it right here."

"Don't think I have a choice, unless this galloping bed dumps me out on the floor."

When she returned from the kitchen, relieved that he sounded pretty good considering, she set his cup on the table beside him, lowered herself on the edge of the bed and patted his leg. "Sit up."

He did, then reached for the cup and missed. "Drunk as a skunk."

"Here, let me before you sweep it off onto the floor."

They finished their coffee, her guiding his to his mouth so he wouldn't get burned. When the cups were empty, he rubbed a hand over the other side of the bed. Her side. "Come here."

She grinned. "I'm coming," and crawled past him.

"Me, too, though it may be a bumpy ride."

Sunlight poured in the window and crossed the bed where they lay snuggled together. He ran a finger up her belly and between her breasts. "Oops, missed. Was it bad, Katie? Really bad?"

"Nope, it was fine. Really."

"Don't lie to me. I remember parts and they were awful."

"It's okay though. We're home in one piece."

"You're a hell of a piece, too."

"Those pills are making you plumb silly."

He lay still for a long while holding her close. "Can't seem to get it up, darlin'. Can you wait an hour or two?"

"It'll be hard, but I can try."

"Glad something is hard."

"I think you ought to close your eyes and sleep off your drunk, don't you?" And pray God no nightmares. She'd kill that Spencer if she ever spoke to him again.

Some doctor he was.

"A damn fine idea. Don't go far, though, sweet...." He was asleep that quickly, and she lay there content to be in his arms, just in case he had some after effects and had another nightmare.

Surprisingly, she awoke from her own sound sleep a couple of hours later, stretched languidly, and turned to be greeted with a kiss.

"Mmm, you taste like coffee."

"And other junk, I'm sure. I could go brush my teeth." He flashed his perfect bridge.

Sometimes he used sex to blot out the horrible nightmares that awoke him with a surge of adrenalin. She understood, but enjoyed it more when they made love out of a desire for each other. This was one of those times.

When they finally got out of bed, the sun was far to the west, and he was begging for food. "When was the last damn time we ate anything?"

"I can't remember, but I think it was before we left. I don't remember eating anything all the time we were there. Oh, yes, we did have a meal on the plane."

"Must've been a doozy, 'cause I don't remember it."

"Best if you don't remember anything about the flight."

"That bad, huh? I'm so sorry to put you through shit like that."

"Not your fault. Let's get up, and I'll fix us something to eat. You know, I think there are some T bones in the freezer. I'll thaw them a bit in the microwave, then grill them. How about that and a baked potato and salad, then some of that leftover pie I froze before we left?"

"Oh my God, I'm drooling." He smacked her on the bottom. "Get your fanny in the kitchen, woman, and now."

"I'm going, I'm going. I was going to take a shower first, but that can wait until we eat."

"Darn right, it can. Otherwise I'm liable to chew something off here." He grabbed her foot and nibbled on her toes until she hollered.

Maybe a small dose of whatever was in those pills would be good for him. She immediately took back the idea. Not good at all. If she had her way, she'd never allow him to be drugged again for any reason.

They did nothing but eat and sleep that evening and night. She thanked whatever entity was responsible for him sleeping deeply. The next morning dawned rainy, so they took another day off for some more of the same. If she held him close enough, loved him enough, perhaps he would recover from his devastating visit to the monument.

"Tomorrow for sure we have to get busy choosing the paintings for the exhibit and packing them. I can't do it on my own, 'cause I've looked at them so many times I think they're all lousy."

"Okay," he agreed. "I'll be a critic if you'll promise I won't get in Dutch with you for my opinions. You don't have to worry, though. I like 'em all."

She laughed. "That'll be no help, then. Maybe I'll have to put them up for a vote with some of my students."

"I promise to do my best, ma'am."

But that evening came a knock on the door that tossed their plans all over the place. Glen was shaving after they'd showered, and she was in her robe reading in the living room, a small fire burning to chase away the dampness of the day.

The knock startled her for she hadn't heard anyone drive up. Peering through the oval glass, she didn't recognize a tall, angular man with graying hair. She opened the door, thinking he might be lost.

"Yes? Could I help you?"

"I'm Lowell Francis. You don't know me but Julia said you could tell me how to get in touch with her brother." He had a pronounced accent that told her he had lived in hill country all his life.

"What is this in regard to?" She would never let a stranger with any connection to Glen's sister near him.

"Julia and I are planning to marry this summer, and she would like to get the business of selling the farm over and done with before that. I think that he has to sign some papers, if that's possible."

Glen came in from the sunroom using the crutches. "Who was at the door, honey?"

"Someone who wants to see you about selling your farm. Says he and Julia are getting married."

"No shit?" Glen came across the floor until he could see the visitor. "Well, I suppose you should let him in."

The surprised look on Lowell Francis's face turned to puzzlement when he stepped in and saw Glen. Muscles well defined by the tight fit of his white tee shirt, he wore jeans and white socks, no shoes. Except for the cuffed crutches, the picture of a robust and healthy man.

"You're Julia's brother, Glen?"

"Yes. How is my sister?" He didn't blink, and she joined Francis in staring at him.

"I'm sorry, I think I must have misunderstood her."

Glen turned to Katie, lifted an arm, and put it about her waist, using the other crutch to hold him steady. "Ah, I'll just bet she told you I was a drooling loony." He actually smiled, but it wasn't pretty.

"Not her true words, but close enough," Lowell said. "I'm plumb sorry for what I been thinking."

"We haven't gotten along lately, I'm sorry to say. Mostly my fault, I'm sure." Glen paused and pinned a steady gaze on the man.

"That's not true," Katie said, no longer willing to let this ruse go on. "Julia was entirely to blame for what happened out there, and I won't let you blame yourself. I can't."

"Let's be polite to the man, Katie. Do sit down. Would you like a cup of coffee?"

Katie peered up into his face, and mouthed, show off, at him. He smiled down at her.

"I'll get the coffee." She guided the cuffed crutch and his arm from around her back and set it down smartly next to his leg. "Be careful, now, sweetheart."

"Indeed." He grinned, moved to the couch and sat. "Please sit. So you and my sister are getting married? I'm happy for you. These papers I need to sign for sale of the ranch, do you have them with you?"

"Why, no. No. She… Julia said you wouldn't be able to sign, and Katherine could give me the name of your power of attorney, if it wasn't her. I figure there's been a downright awful mistake. But I can get you a copy. I reckon you're willing to sell the place. Julia can't sell it without you sign—and of course Mark and Luke Tanner."

Katie returned with a tray containing three mugs of coffee, cream and sugar, and cookies. Glen's favorite. She didn't give a rat's ass about Lowell's favorite anything. Anyone who loved Julia was either a fool or in worse condition than that woman was. His to-be wife might hang him by the rafters in the barn if she didn't like the way he buttered his toast. She had better sense than to voice the thoughts that ran through her head. To keep from doing so, she sat in a chair opposite the two men, leaned back, sipped her coffee, and peered at them over the rim of the mug. No telling what might happen, so she was ready for anything.

"Tell me," Glen said, his voice sharpening until her ears pricked. "Did she tell you just what happened out there at the farm the night I was hauled off in an ambulance? Or perhaps that other time when she had me dragged away in handcuffs?"

Francis gulped loudly and set down his cup. Clearly he did not want to reveal what Julia said, but couldn't see an out other than to lie. Katie shifted her glare from Glen to Francis and tilted her head, as if expecting him to lie. He finally managed a "not exactly."

"Well, exactly, Mr. Francis, was she put me in a cold shower, hid my wheelchair, and shut off the power to the house as well as disconnecting the telephone, all in the middle of the winter. So even had I been able to make it out in the dark, I couldn't have called anyone. Of course, I didn't make it. I tried to climb the wall instead. A misconception of mine when I imagined I was confined in a concrete cage."

The longer he talked, the more brittle the words. His anger turned to fury. Though Katie did not blame him at all, she feared for him, so she rose and went to sit beside him, placing a hand on his quivering thigh before he could try to rise. Had he been a violent man, he could have beaten Lowell to death with one of those crutches, but he only sat there smiling that deadly smile and watching the fear bloom on Lowell Francis's face.

"I won't go into details on the first time. You may tell my sister that when she wishes to sell the farm, she will first ask me if I intend to buy her share before she does so. Would you take her that message? And I am indeed sorry for you."

He removed Katie's hand from his leg gently, struggled to his feet, and left the room, the sound of the crutches thump, thumping in the silence that followed his pronouncement. The door slammed behind him, and her shoulders twitched.

Face red with embarrassment, Lowell Francis stood. "I sure am sorry, ma'am. I will carry his message to Julia."

She nodded without saying anything, accompanied him to the door, and let him out into the pouring rain. He'd be better off to drown out there than to hook up with Julia.

SEVEN

THE CLOSED DOOR of the sunroom didn't bode well. Time ticked by, and she listened at the door. From inside came the steady swish of the machine he used to strengthen his legs. Back and forth, back and forth. Best to leave him be for a while, so she picked up a book and settled on the couch to read.

After more than thirty minutes, she couldn't help but peek in and make sure he was all right. Getting out of that thing was tricky without someone to help balance him.

He sat in it, unmoving, staring across the room.

"Need out now," she said, "or are you gonna sit there contemplating your navel all night?"

"I wanted to hit him, Katie. First time since I came home I've actually been so angry I wanted to hit someone."

"But you didn't. No harm in getting angry, in fact it was probably good for you, because your anger is really at Julia, isn't it? I'm proud of you for not hitting the son of a bitch, but I kind of wish I had."

He grinned and held out a hand, beckoning her to him. "Crap, isn't one psychiatrist plenty enough without you psychoanalyzing me?"

His hand was sweaty in hers, the tee shirt soaked back and front. "Guess you took it out on the machine, huh?"

"This means another shower. Wanna come?"

"I'm about to do just that, looking at you all sweaty and sexy."

"So you like men who stink?"

"I like this one man whether he stinks or not. Can I give you a hand out of there?"

"Please."

They went into the bathroom and showered together, then crawled into bed and into each other's arms. After a long while of holding each other he said, "Ever get tired of… you know, helping me?"

"Nope. Why would I? You're such a grateful man."

He shifted his hand, moved it between her legs. "Oh, yeah, is that what you call it?" His finger moved slowly inside her, searching out the swollen nub, rubbing until she burst into bright shiny pieces that floated down around her. Taking her arms, he lifted her on top. "Here's a grateful man," and planted kisses over every inch of her.

"That's my grateful man," she teased when she could breathe again.

The next morning they took the van down to the studio to spend the day readying her paintings for the May showing. Hard to believe they had first laid eyes on each other seven months ago. And immediately knew it would be forever.

The room was a shambles, paintings propped against walls and table legs and lying on the worktable. Boxes of several sizes were scattered around on the floor.

He halted just inside the door.

"What on God's green earth hit this place?"

Ankle deep in boxes, she said, "It's impossible. None of them are good enough. I can't decide on anything and they have to be in Saturday for hanging. Why did I say I'd do this? Why?" She ran fingers through her hair, tumbling it about in disarray.

"Come here," he said. "Come on. I don't dare try to make my way through this mess to you."

She poked and stumbled about in the disorder and stopped in front of him like a small child. He leaned the crutches against the wall behind him and put his arms around her.

"First thing is," he said, playing with long strands of her hair. "They're all good, so we have to decide what kind of display you want. How you want the paintings arranged. We can make a sketch if need be. Then we'll know where to start. How many are you to take?"

She dragged a stool over to the long work table. "Here, if you want to help, sit. We'll go through them. I'll have to pack the smaller ones in boxes, and pad the larger ones so they don't get scratched." She started dragging out some prospects, studying them with the knuckle of her thumb in her mouth.

"Don't do that, Katie."

"Hmm, don't do what?" She glanced at him, then back at the small painting of an old mill.

"Give me the menial jobs. I can help with the heavy stuff, too."

"Sorry. Of course you can. I didn't mean…." Ashamed because she had meant exactly that, she wasn't sure how to get out of this without digging a deeper hole.

"It's time you quit treating me like an invalid. It's not that I don't appreciate all you've done for me. Shit, you dragged me out of hell, but I'm out now. Let me help you with this as if I were whole instead of the leftovers of a man who can't button his own shirt." He stopped, got off the stool, and using the crutches, swept a path into the storeroom to fetch some boxes for the smaller paintings she had stacked in front of him. Piling them on the floor, he kicked them over to the worktable and followed along.

"Lowell Francis got to you, didn't he?" she asked.

"I guess, but dammit, I'm tired of not being able to do anything. Being helpless… of you watching me like I'm going to come unglued any moment."

"I'm sorry I've made you feel that way. I don't mean to."

"Aw, hell, I know you don't." He leaned his butt on the stool, discarded the arm braces so they dropped to the floor with a clatter. "I'm worried about this situation with Julia and Lowell and the farm and what the hell we're going to do. Please don't take my words to heart. I wouldn't hurt you for the world. Hell, for a thousand worlds. You're all I know, the only person I trust."

She kicked her way through the pile of boxes around him. "I know that."

His face, his wonderful, loving face. Those eyes that revealed so much of himself, looking up at her, probing to her very core. She cupped both hands around his cheeks, lowered her mouth to his, and felt a caring so deep emanate from that kiss. He spanned her waist with his hands, opened his mouth to her. He kept her there for a while, touching, moving the kiss to nibble at her throat, her ear lobe, eventually pulling back with a husky laugh.

"Probably ought to get on with this before we end up on the floor rolling around in the boxes."

"Sounds like fun to me."

"Yeah, but it doesn't get the work done. Now, go on, get busy, and I will, too." He paddled her fanny. "We can worry about the farm stuff after we deal with all of this."

"I don't see a problem. You want to keep the farm, buy her out. You don't, then sign the damn papers and be done with it. I don't want her anywhere near you… I mean, I didn't mean… it's up to you about whether you see her or not. But like it or not, you aren't going alone."

He grinned. "Hard to give up being the boss, ain't it honey?"

"Crap, yes. I guess I just grew to like being in charge these last few months. Taking care of you, keeping you out of harm's way. So afraid something bad was going to happen to you. Stan took care of me for so long, I liked the feeling of having someone to care for. To love." Her voice broke.

"Aw, Katie. Without you I'd still be that stick of a man with no hope. Just let me do what I can do. Trust me to know what that is. Can you do that?"

She nodded fiercely. "I'll surely try, but don't you go climbing trees and stuff like that. Okay?"

He held up a palm. "You think I'm crazy?" He stopped abruptly, stared at her, then they both laughed. "Let's get to work."

"Good idea. We'll start by eliminating the ones I absolutely refuse to take. I should've asked your advice in the first place. I dragged them all out before we left for D.C. and this was as far as I got."

Still propped on its easel, the large painting of The Immortal Hero held a prominent place in the room. Once they had cleared out some of the rejects and arranged the smaller ones on the table, she moved to it. "I want to show this one. In fact, you know I hope to make it the center of the exhibit. It's the best thing I've ever done. Do you mind?"

He took a long time to study the work, moving from scene to scene following his adult life from football hero to recovering veteran. Finally he faced her. "You're right —it is your best work. But how could it miss with such a model?"

She let out a sigh of relief, for all along she'd been fearful he couldn't accept his life being put on display in such a way.

They worked on the sketch of the arrangements, placing his painting center stage and others that ranged from still-lifes to portraits to abstract and photographic scenery where they fit.

"Fun to work together. Feels good." She peeked at him, and he nodded and smiled.

His demeanor lapsed into a brooding silence.

"You okay?" She paused in her work.

He glanced up. "Yeah. Sure, just thinking about stuff."

"You worried about the farm deal, seeing your sister?"

"Let's not talk about it now. This is your show we're working on."

She studied him for a moment, then nodded and went back to work. At last both agreed they had a viable exhibit, and he glanced up. "We can take this sketch with us for whoever will be hanging the paintings. I'll start getting some of these smaller ones in cartons. I can pack them right here on the end of the work table. No sweat."

"No sweat," she replied and let him have his way. He could handle the job without her constant supervision, something she had to let go of. His physical and emotional improvement called for more independence. Her worst fear that he had programmed himself to carry out his vow to kill Ellie stirred its way to the surface. Spencer insisted that sooner or later he would have to conquer his savage feelings about his ex-wife. On the other hand, Katie would just as soon her name was never brought up. Glen had only done so once and then without any dire repercussions. It was probably foolish to worry about it. No one had heard from her since her drunken visit to the house when Glen had tried to throttle her. Surely that would be the end of it, and he could continue to improve and leave all that behind.

While caught up in those rambling thoughts, she padded the corners of the last large painting, strapped it into its cardboard carton, and stood it against the wall. "Done here," she announced, rubbing her hands together.

Glen worked on his final box. "All done here, too. Now what?"

"Let's go up to the house, and I'll fix something to eat and we can discuss this deal with Julia and Lowell and the farm. Whatever you decide to do, I'm with you. Just please don't shut me out."

She approached him, and he looped both arms over her shoulders. "Never happen, darlin'. Never happen."

Together they left the studio, crawled wearily in the van, and headed for home.

EIGHT

THE ROOM IN Walton Hall where the joint art exhibit was to be held was large, the walls off-white, the carpet wine red. There were low, white-cushioned benches and track lighting movable in all directions to spotlight the series of exhibits. No plants or fancy decorations distracted from the paintings. While she went inside to find her assigned area, Glen remained with the van to supervise. Her section had her name displayed. A young helper unloaded the paintings from the van and onto a cart and brought them in.

"You tell me where each one goes, and I'll hang it for you," he said. "And anything else you need, I'll see to it."

Glen handed him the sketch. "We've drawn this out. I'll hang around if you have any questions or problems with deciphering it." He wandered off. When he returned he was shoving a chair ahead of himself, using one crutch then the other.

The boy went running, and she watched with good humor when Glen waved him away. "I can handle this, but thanks, anyway."

The one of Glen, which she had titled *The Immortal Hero*, from an Emily Dickinson poem he liked, was placed directly opposite the entry to her exhibit. Once it was hung, she walked to the doorway, turned and caught a first glimpse impression of the entire display. Glen studied it from his vantage point and gave her a thumbs up. She blew him a kiss. Silly old woman, acting like a teenager in love. Why not? That's how she felt.

Ivy Delacourt, one of the main supporters of the show, approached. A tall, thin woman dressed impeccably in an ankle length flowing black dress, pearls around her neck, white hair swept up and back off her face, she was the epitome of the moneyed social set of Fayetteville. "My goodness, dear, that's indeed impressive. The images are so real I expect them to speak. Who is that lovely young man?"

Katie smiled and pointed. "He's right over there."

Ivy turned. "Oh, my dear. Your model is actually here? How fabulous. We must arrange for him to attend and be with you during the showing. Do you think that would be possible?"

"Oh, he plans on being here. Why don't you ask him? I'd be happy to introduce you."

"That would be delightful. When the models attend, we find our audience so appreciative."

She led the woman across the shiny marble floor. When Glen spotted them coming, he fetched the crutches and rose to his feet, smiling that dimple-flashing smile that lit his beautiful eyes.

"Glen, this is Ivy Delacourt."

"But you really did… I mean, I thought you simply posed for her, but I can see you are real… I mean, I'm so sorry. I just wasn't prepared. I would absolutely love to have you come speak to our Ladies Society, Mr. Tanner. Your story must be so intriguing."

He darted a quick, amused look at Katie. "I'm pleased to meet you, ma'am. You might not want me to speak. I'd probably get my tongue all tied up and say some dreadful things that would make your ladies society blush in unison."

She touched his arm with long, graceful fingers. "Oh, I doubt you could say much of anything that would make us blush. We've all been around the block a few times."

"I should try very hard not to. Do you like my Katie's paintings?"

"They are lovely, aren't they? Your Katie? Are you two...? Umm, well, I mean...."

"Yes, we are," Katie said. "Very much so."

Glen's glance slid toward the boy hanging a painting. "Honey, you'd better go supervise, I don't think you want that one there."

"And I must go see if I'm needed," Ivy said. "A real pleasure to meet you, Mr. Tanner."

"Glen, please. And I enjoyed talking with you, ma'am."

"Call me Ivy, dear, won't you?" and she was gone.

He raised his eyebrows in Katie's direction, and she laughed before hurrying to assist with the arrangements of the remainder of her paintings. He had certainly charmed the socks right off that one.

Back home, Katie stretched out on the couch, and Glen took her feet in his lap, massaged them gently. "I'm tired, and that feels heavenly."

"Well, my dear," he mimicked, "let me see what I can do about that."

"You were a hit with those society dames. Are you going to the exhibit with me?"

He rubbed his thumbs over the balls of her feet. "I wouldn't miss it for the world. You may put me on display anytime you want."

She studied him closely to make sure he was sincere and not upset.

"I do believe you enjoyed those ladies fawning over you."

He kept rubbing, a smile dimpling his cheeks. "You know what? I did. It was fun. They were so, so polite and… I'm not sure what to call it. Above it all, seems to fit."

She broke into laughter. "Perfect. I actually think Mrs. Connover thought you were a professional model playing a role. Oh, right there, that feels good." He massaged her arch a while longer, then lifted one foot, then the other and planted kisses.

"I want to call this Lowell person tomorrow and arrange to meet with him and Julia. Will you come with me?"

"Yes, indeed. You know I will."

"I'm trying to think of a good place. I can't go out there. I get the shudders thinking about it. Odd, huh? I was raised there, but since that night trapped in the shower, the idea of going through the door terrifies me. And I don't want her here. This place is ours."

"And just in case she wants to make a scene," Katie said, "a public place isn't a good idea. I see your dilemma."

He trailed a hand up her leg, rested it on the curve of her hip. "On the other hand, perhaps a public place would prevent my sister from acting out." He tilted his head, said too seriously, "You don't suppose it runs in the family, do you?"

She stared at him, but he wouldn't look at her. "What runs in the family?" She knew damn well what he meant, but wanted to hear him say it so she could box his ears for him.

"Some of the guys at the hospital, I heard them discussing Post Traumatic Stress Syndrome. They said only men who had an unstable home life came home torn up like that. Called some of them malingerers. Katie, Spencer said what I have is PTSS, so maybe it—"

"No, no, no. Don't even think that way for a second. You went through trauma so extreme it would've messed up anyone. You don't listen to that kind of talk. You had a normal childhood, you were a nice boy, everyone liked you, a strong young man, a football star, you made good grades. No."

He held up his other hand, rubbed her hip. "Whoa, didn't mean to start something. I concede. While my sister is a bubble off center, I have a legitimate reason for being the way I am. Hell, for all I know she does, too. I don't remember my parents. You don't suppose they... well, they abused us when we were small."

She swung her legs around and sat up, leaned into him. "The way you are is sweet, kind, lovable, beautiful. And I suppose abuse is possible. You'll never know unless she remembers and tells you. Still, you are so very thoughtful and sweet and the best lover in the world. So don't go thinking that way, not at all."

"Okay, okay. Enough. You're embarrassing me."

She planted noisy kisses all over his face. "Can't help it. I love you. Know what I want to do right now?"

"Heh, heh, heh, I can guess, wicked lady."

"Oh, no you can't. I want to give you a back rub in return. After being on your feet so long it must hurt."

"That sounds so good. Last one to the bed is an egg-sucking hound." He grabbed the crutches off the floor and hopped away.

By the time she found the lotion, he was lying down with no clothes on. "You took your pants off," she squealed.

"Hell, yes. I can put 'em back on if you need to take off my pants yourself, in order to get in the mood. Think they call that a fetish."

"Doofus." She poured her palm full of the lotion and slapped it on his back.

"Fucking *shit*, that's cold woman. What're you trying to do to me?"

"Hold still. Don't be such a baby." She chuckled and worked her thumbs into the muscles on either side of his spine, then used the heels of both hands to rub in circles over his muscles. He moaned. Down and over his bare behind, the thigh, past the scars that always distressed her, especially the large slashes behind his right knee and down the calf. Remembered what Spencer had said about the monsters trying to lame him so he couldn't run away. He might never regain full use of that leg, was lucky he hadn't lost it while lying unattended in that cage.

Stop, stop, Katie.

"What's up, babe? You stuck in one place? You okay?"

She opened her eyes, came away from her dreadful imaginings, and rubbed that leg with special care, then on down to his foot and up the other leg. To lighten the mood, she smacked his left butt cheek smartly.

"Ow, woman. Don't damage the merchandise."

"I'll give you merchandise. Now turn over."

"I don't think I can."

"What's wrong?"

He laughed. "Nothing too serious. I'll show you." He rolled over to reveal a quite healthy erection.

A chaotic dance pounded inside her, the beat intensifying with each breath. She tantalized him by rising and humming a stripper tune, undressed slowly, one garment at a time until she came to her panties and bra, wiggling and squirming, dancing closer to him the less she wore.

"Holy fucking shit. I never had a back rub like this before. Do something else. Quick."

She hooked her thumbs in the panties, wiggled them off, arched her back, and unfastened the bra, let it drift to the floor.

"Get yourself over here right now, woman, before I have to come after you."

And so she did.

NINE

KATIE AND GLEN spent a couple of anxious days after scheduling a meeting with Julia and Lowell following the gallery showing that coming weekend. By the day of the opening, Glen had worn himself out on the exercise machine, and Katie had turned into a vexed woman.

He sat on the bed watching and shaking his head while she tried on one outfit after another. Finally, she threw down a navy blue pants suit, jerked a dress off its hanger, held it up under her chin and threw her hands up in defeat. Nothing looked right.

He chuckled, but said nothing.

"Don't you dare say a word, or you're toast," she warned. "For two cents I'd wear jeans and boots."

"Wahoo, and nothing else. Sure like to see those fancy ladies' faces if you did that."

"Okay, that's it. Out. Go."

He rose, stood there a moment, then limped slowly over to her, curled her in his arms.

She dropped the dress she was holding. "You, uh, left your crutches over there." She pointed, breathless and close to speechless.

That heartbreaking smile. She squeezed him so hard he grunted. "Are you sure? Be careful, don't fall. Oh, honey, my God, that's wonderful."

"Yeah. Doesn't last long, but… with a cane I think I'm good to go." He leaned heavily on her, and she supported him back to sit on the bed. "But I can do it for a minute or two before needing something to lean on."

"And you kept it a secret. How long?"

"This morning, you were in the bathroom, and I'd dozed off, half asleep, not sure where I was. I got out of bed and walked, well tottered actually, toward the window. Surprised the ever-loving hell out of me. There I was, waking up to a world where I stood upright. Had to be a dream. Felt so damned good, then I staggered back. Almost didn't make it. If I'd sprawled out on the floor, you'd a had a fit. But I kept doing it while you were in the shower."

She hugged him some more, kissed him some more.

"Baby, you'd better find a dress to wear, or we're gonna be late. I've got to dress, too. What in the world should I wear?"

She punched him on the arm. "We bought you a suit, so what do you have to worry about?"

"A tie, oh, my goodness. What color tie? Which shirt?"

"If you don't behave, I'm going to make you think what color tie."

"Now, Katie darlin' you know you don't like it when I behave. Please pick a dress and let's get cracking. You look so sexy in a dress."

The day stretched out before them with new promise. A gallery showing and his exciting surprise were enough to satisfy her forever. Time to forget all her doubts about what might lie ahead for them, her worries about the demons he fought in the nightmares that continued to plague him, and that ever present dread about Ellie.

Sooner or later the ex-wife's existence had to be faced, but not this day.

She settled on a pink frilly dress and a pair of high-heeled sandals she hadn't worn in years. Makeup hid the tiny crow's feet at the corners of her eyes and her hair swept up, then flowing to her shoulders succeeded in making her look a bit younger.

"You look ravishing."

She twirled. "Didn't know sailors knew such refined language."

"Oh, we know tons of stuff, simply tons."

He appeared relaxed for a man who preferred solitary confinement to a crowded affair. All he ever wanted was the two of them, and no one else. Yet he had done quite well with the society ladies. She prayed the crowd wouldn't upset him. She was nervous enough without worrying about him. What if no one liked her paintings?

Shaking off the jitters, she looked him over.

The gold shirt with pearl buttons, a pale blue western style suit and the Stetson she had bought him all fit together nicely set off by a leather and turquoise bolo tie.

"By the way, you look pretty spiffy yourself. I love you so much." Too bad she couldn't speak all her thoughts to him so he'd know what he meant to her. Perhaps she could. One day.

"Scared?" He followed her out the front door and pulled it closed behind him.

"Who me? No. Yes. My stomach hurts, my eyeballs feel like they're lying on my cheeks, and I'll probably fall and break a leg in front of everyone when I walk across that gallery in these shoes. Otherwise, everything's jim-dandy."

"I want you to remember something there in amongst all those artists and hoity-toits. You are the best there is, and don't you forget it, not for even one second."

At that moment she would have done anything for him. No ands, ifs, or buts, no conditions. If he needed her this instant to get in the bed and hold him safe forever, forsaking all her life, she would do it. He meant more to her than her own life. The knowledge was terrifying, yet there it was smacking her right in the face.

"Okay, looks like we're ready." He dragged in a deep breath. "You wait here in those fancy shoes, and I'll get the car. Bring it down to you."

"Appreciate it, sir. Thank you so much." She wanted so badly to tell him no, she'd go with him, make sure he didn't fall, but she kept her mouth shut. Watching him make his way awkwardly up the rough incline to the carport would break her heart if she let it. When she allowed herself to remember all he'd gone through, her heart did break, but each time he mended it with one smile.

He backed the car around and pulled up so the passenger side was in front of her, leaned over and swung the door open. As usual, he drove expertly with an ease that told her nothing could happen that he couldn't handle. She had an urge to go flying with him, challenge gravity and loop through the air in childish abandon. But of course, they never would. Not good to think of what they couldn't do, but of all the things they could do. All the happiness that lay ahead of them.

The parking lot was already full. "I'll let you out at the door. You don't need to have to walk in those shoes," he said.

"I'd rather we go in together."

He glanced at her with a stern look. "Katie, I reckon I can handle coming into that place on my own."

"Maybe you can. I can't."

"Dammit," he croaked, but found a parking place with no further debate. He knew she was lying, ever his protector.

When he started to get out, she saw what he'd been up to. He reached over the back seat, and instead of the metallic crutches he'd come to hate, produced a beautifully carved wooden cane. Where or when had he managed that? He gave her a smartass look, climbed from the car, and twirled the cane, then set the tip firmly on the pavement.

"Courtesy of the craft shop on the mountain."

Tears in her eyes, she waited for him to come around and open the door, just as she knew he wanted. Seeing the pleased expression on his face was more than she could take. Some days were too full to hold any more, and she clasped a hand over her mouth and swallowed harshly several times before the door swung wide. Now she'd have to repair her lipstick, but she didn't care.

"Katie, don't make a big deal of this. And don't you dare cry. This is your day and I wanted to surprise you. Walk in there with you on my arm. Now, get out of the damned car and take my arm and smile. Okay?"

"Yes, it's more than okay. Thank you."

At the large double doors that opened into the light and airy building, she paused and took a deep breath, nerves jangling. She was never going to make it.

"Easy, sweetheart. Don't come apart now."

"I'm shaking so bad I can't... suppose they don't like my work? Suppose they laugh out loud."

"No one will laugh. Now, here's a kiss for luck and in we go."

She accepted the kiss, gave him one back, then he opened the door, and they were inside, amidst the babble and laughter of the growing crowd.

Several people were gathered in front of The Immortal Hero, discussing it in low tones. No one was laughing. They were as quiet as if worshiping in church. Why hadn't she thought to have copies of Dickinson's poem available? Perhaps the message would be obvious without it.

In the center of the group stood a thin woman with artificially black hair bunned severely. She wore a cream suit with a single red rose pinned at her lapel. Mrs. James Edgar Jones, President of The Art Association. Perfection itself until she opened her mouth. Every word she spoke gave the impression someone was standing out of sight, pinching her. But she was studying Katie's exhibit, not that of any of the other twelve artists who made up the showing for this weekend. Katie also spotted Ivy Delacourt at the edge of the crowd. The woman nodded in their direction and smiled. Glen waved gaily at her. He had removed his hat and left it at the door, his curls dented in a circle where it had rested.

"Oh, dear, everyone. Here's our artist now... and isn't that...? Yes, it is her model."

A television cameraman who had been wandering about turned his attention in their direction, then came over, pointing the camera at the painting, then at her and Glen. A well-endowed young woman who introduced herself as Penny Adams, Channel 27, studied a paper held in one hand and poked a mic in Katie's direction, and read off a few standard questions she had no trouble answering.

Then came one that stunned her.

"Why have you shunned the more modern techniques in favor of stark realism, such as The Immortal Hero?"

Glen nudged her when she stared at the woman in silence. "Oh... I suppose... like all artists, I paint what I see, so I guess that's how I see things. In a mirror starkly, if I might misquote."

"A mirror? Not a glass? And starkly. How interesting," Adams remarked. "Are they perhaps then reflections of your own soul, rather than how you see the world?"

She hadn't really thought much about that, hadn't anticipated such probing questions, and was thrown off guard. She glanced at Glen, and he nodded, eyes sparking. "I think my soul is entwined with the world's."

"I see," Adams murmured. Obviously she didn't, for her pale blue eyes shifted to Glen. "And this is your model for *Immortal Hero*? You are?" She poked the mic under Glen's nose, and Katie winced.

He didn't blink. "Yes, I am," he replied, eyes twinkling. "If you'd care to visit Katherine's studio, she has some lovely nudes there. I posed for all of them."

From somewhere in the cluster of observers, laughter trilled, and she could have sworn Mrs. James Edgar Jones was the guilty party. It spread through the crowd, some of the men laughing outright.

Adams blushed, and Glen began an outrageous flirtation with her until she became totally disoriented. The camera man panned the room while she pulled herself together.

The young, boyish Governor entered about then, a masterpiece of illusion who dealt words like cards from a stacked deck. When Adams finished his interview, he headed for Katie's exhibit. Shook her hand.

"I've been hearing some good things about you." He turned and glanced at the painting, "This in particular. Quite a story there, huh? Tells so much with such simplicity."

"I wish it said more than it does. But there's no way to show what those men have gone through, what some of them are still going through."

He batted his eyes, but recovered quickly. "Yes, well, we're going to try and remedy that. You know, we've built a memorial in Little Rock to all the Arkansas boys who fought and died in Vietnam. Actually, it's a miniature of the one in Washington." He paused, glanced around at the crowd to a scattering of applause.

She tensed. Glen stood nearby, his eyes turned toward her. Adams remained beside him.

The governor said something, and she turned her attention back to him. "We'd be interested in more paintings like this one."

"I'm sorry, what?"

"I said, we'd like to purchase *The Immortal Hero* for a small museum we are planning. It will stand in an adjacent park near the memorial. Perhaps you'd consider doing a few more along that line?"

"Buy it?"

He patted her hand with his soft one. "Of course. Don't you think it's time we did something about that Vietnam thing? Do what's right so we can put it all behind us and go forward together."

Glen's breath on her neck alerted her, and she hurried to introduce him to the governor.

"Is that the popular opinion now? About that Vietnam thing?" Glen's voice remained controlled.

So far.

A wary flicker passed over the man's face. "Well, it's been coming for a long time."

"Tell me," Glen said. "You'll have this 'thing' put before the public right away, in time for the elections?"

"How long were you there?" A blunt way to send the conversation in a different way.

"Somewhere around twelve years, give or take a month or two. I lost count along toward the end." His voice remained even, but she didn't know for how long.

"That's impossible."

Glen ignored that and went on. "What are your plans for the men still over there? Perhaps you could build an addition to your memorial, a monument to the abandoned ones. Or is deserted a better term?"

Finally, the governor showed a desire to escape, but they had drawn a small audience, and Adams continued to practice her sleight of hand with the mic. As any politician, the governor was aware he had to say what the majority of his voting public would feel was right. The waters would be tested.

"The government is doing its best for all MIAs, son. As they always do for any citizen of this country. Of course, I'd be glad to talk to you further about it. Call my office, and make an appointment. I'll see you anytime."

"I'd rather talk about it here, if you don't mind. That shouldn't be a problem. I realize most of the guys who went to 'Nam were just ordinary men, no one important. Only a few sons of doctors or lawyers or senators... or governors. But you go ahead and build your museum, and you'll sleep nights and stop worrying about your constituency judging you badly. You'll have done the right thing."

By then the governor was frantic to get away, but the crowd made it all but impossible.

Glen continued. "Their blood and their suffering is on your hands and every son of a bitch right on up to the President is guilty of murder for every one who has died since the first goddamned shot was fired over there."

Katie reached for Glen's hand, got a firm hold on it, and continued to stare blandly at the governor. Considering the spot he was in, he was behaving rather well. Taking the beating without anger or embarrassment. There wasn't much else he could do.

Glen was also doing fine. He'd never even raised his voice. Now he slipped his hand from hers. "I think I'll go get some air."

The governor approached her, turning his back on Adams. "Mrs. Kelly, I'm sorry if I upset your husband. It was not my intention. I had no idea he... I do hope you'll consider doing the paintings for our memorial. It really is an honest effort at reparations for all the wrongs we've done these men, and I hope you can see your way clear to join us." He tilted his head. "Twelve years? My God, I'd like to hear more about how that happened."

"Ask Lyndon," she snapped, then smiled at him. "I'm sorry. Of course I'll think about it. Now, if you'll excuse me."

"Of course."

She found Glen standing on the lawn near the parking area, leaning heavily on the cane.

"Sweetheart, you okay?" From behind and out of his reach, she waited until he acknowledged her, then curled her arms around his waist and rested her cheek against his back. His muscles were bunched, his heart hammered, and he trembled.

"God, I hope I didn't mess things up for you, Katie. I'm sorry."

"No, it needed said. Perhaps he'll carry the message back where it will do some good. He's too young to have been involved. He's just playing catch-up to a cause he never thought much about. You must realize none of us thought much about it. I'm guilty, too. We watched it on television every night. It was like it was taking place on the moon or perhaps it was only another show we watched on television. Not real. Not like anything we'd ever experienced. Besides, the governor was a teenager at the time."

He sagged a bit.

"Honey, let's sit down on this bench. Please." Though she expected him to object he didn't.

After they were settled, he had to go on. The words spilled out of him. "Yeah, he might've been nineteen or twenty, like most of the guys in 'Nam. Oh, shit, forget it." He swiped over his face with both hands. "I can't expect the world to care. I just get all fucked up over it sometimes. I'll go back and apologize to the asshole if it'll make you feel better."

By the tone of his voice, he was forcing himself out of the black mood, but only for her sake. This was her day. That made her appreciate the effort even more. "You don't owe anyone an apology. Don't you dare."

He put his arm around her. "Come to think of it, I feel one hell of a lot better."

"You should. You got a lot off your chest in front of a politician, an audience, and a television camera and crew.

"Oh, Christ. I completely forgot about them. You don't suppose they'll splash it all over the tube?"

"I expect they will. Just the kind of thing they thrive on."

"Well, you can't say you won't get publicity for the show. Stick with me, kid, you'll go a long way," he said out of the corner of his mouth, but there was a hint of irony despite the attempt at humor. "You going to do the paintings? Sell him mine?"

"Yours isn't for sale. I won't do the paintings if you don't want me to."

"Hold up, now, just a damn minute." He leaned back to get a good look at her. "Lately I've been getting the distinct impression you've endowed me with some God-like powers. I can't say I like it. What does what I want you to do have to do with this little deal?"

"It was your life, something you'd just as soon forget. For me to paint versions of it for all to see might not be okay with you."

"Hmm. Possibly, and in spite of my fat mouth, I can't think of a better place for those sorts of paintings to hang than in a place paying tribute to all those guys. That's not exactly what we're dealing with here. I don't want to dictate any of your actions. Damn, I have enough trouble figuring out what's best for me. That's not to say I don't care, just that—"

Adams came around the corner, interrupting him. "Good, I found you. I was wondering if you'd both care to appear on my Sunday afternoon show? We do in-depth interviews on what should motivate the movers and shakers. You know, what made you paint that haunting Immortal Hero, what it represents, and what should be done about it."

She stopped, turned her eyes toward Glen. "You don't really pose in the nude, do you?"

"Why? You want me to join her and perform on your show? That would be a real motivator. Katie is good at taking off my pants."

She poked him. "Glen, stop that, right now."

Adams's bubbly laugh matched her size to perfection, and she reverted to the southern belle when she said, "Why, Mr. Kelly, you're just a mess."

"I'm not Mr. Kelly," he said when the laughter died down. "Name's Tanner, Glen Tanner."

"Oh? You two aren't married then. Oh, my." Penny was obviously disconcerted. "Well, still, would you and your friend be interested in coming on the show?" Penny asked Katie.

"I don't know about my friend, you'll have to ask him, but I suppose I wouldn't mind talking about the importance of what my work stands for. Nothing personal, though."

Adams turned to Glen. "Would you be available?"

"Depends," he said with a showy flash of teeth and dimples.

"On what?"

"On what you have in mind."

Katie poked him again and covered a smile, but he was on a roll and couldn't be stopped. She had never seen this side of him, and she liked it. This was probably what he was like as a young man, before all the horrors of war and its aftermath ripped out his soul.

"I really don't think you want me to appear nude, though," he said. "You see, I have this terrible mole." He reached for his belt buckle as if to bare the horrid mark.

"My goodness," Adams squealed, but then a look of understanding crossed her round face. "You are purely a caution. Shame on you."

After another healthy round of laughter, Katie offered her hand. "I'll call you in a couple of weeks, and we'll arrange an appearance. He really won't act that way on the air if you think you still want him to come along. Maybe I'll put him on a leash and gag him."

"You might ought to do that, Mrs. Kelly. Frankly," she leaned closer to whisper, "if he were mine, I'd keep him on one, anyway. Someone's liable to steal him right away if you don't. If I weren't happily married, I'd consider it myself. Bye-bye now." With a flutter of white fingers, she was gone.

"Well, what do you think of that?" Glen asked.

"Aren't you purely pleased with yourself?" Katie stood. "I think it's time I went inside and mingled. Are you coming with me? I'd like to introduce you to Professor Endelbeck and see if Spencer is here."

"Sounds like I'd better come then. And I'll try to muzzle my remarks. If I don't, just tug on my leash. One of these young ladies is liable to steal me right away if I don't stick close to my handler."

They could not find Spencer in the large crowd that milled about, checking out all the art work. The Immortal Hero continued to attract the most attention.

Glen echoed her thoughts. "I'm really impressed."

Katie spotted Endlebeck at the back of that crowd and led Glen to him.

The man could have played a part in a Mickey Rooney movie. Tufts of graying hair poked crazily around a shiny bald spot on top of his pink head. A fine specimen of a handlebar mustache quirked and bright hazel eyes glittered when he greeted her.

She shook his pudgy hand. "I had to come thank you, for making that recommendation to Doctor Spencer."

"I always wondered if that was wise. I take it things worked out well for you."

Katie took Glen's arm, urged him forward a bit. "Worked out well for both of us. This is Glen Tanner."

The professor fixed him with a puzzled frown. "I understood you were—well, incapacitated."

"I couldn't paint, either." Glen shook hands with the man.

"Ah, yes. Very good, mmm, very good, I should say."

"Very good indeed." Glen patted her hand on his arm.

"He's really a fine artist as well," Katie said. "I'm so grateful to you for having such faith in me and my talents, whatever they might be. You are the cause of all this, you know."

"And of this, too," Glen put in, staring down at her with that look he sometimes got in his eyes that melted her like butter.

"I'd say it was a faith rather well placed, in both instances. And you've really hit your stride with this work. Of course, I always knew you had the talent. I'm very proud indeed you were a student of mine."

The praise sustained Katie for the remainder of the festivities. Glen found a chair in a corner and lowered himself carefully into it. She leaned over him. "You okay?"

"You bet I'm okay. Don't fuss. Go. Mingle. I want to see if I can attract some more pretty girls."

"Mr. Kelly, you're a mess." She kissed his cheek while he laughed. "Love you."

"Right back atcha."

Through all the hand shaking and the shock of two substantial sales besides the governor's request, she held up pretty well, though her feet hurt like the very devil. The exhibit would remain up all day Sunday open to the public. The artists weren't expected to attend. Tonight was the night, and at long last it was over and she and Glen could escape. She had been told she would have her own showing in November at The Art Gallery on Dickson Street.

Glen shoved the key in the ignition and started the car.

"Want to go somewhere and eat?"

"Are you sure?"

"Of course. Wouldn't ask if I wasn't. Where to?"

It was as if she had awakened to one of those rare spring days when the air is so clean and pure, the sun so warm and soothing that nature's grand plan is revealed in all its glory. It was hard for her to speak for a moment, but she finally did.

"I would love a big thick steak and a baked potato that weighs at least a pound. And I would like to leap from this car and scream and yell and shout my happiness to the whole world."

"I'll second that." He grinned. "Where do we go to get steak and potatoes, though? McDonalds?"

Their gaiety filled the car all the way to the steak house. It had been a day to tuck in her secret place. She wished she could keep them all like photographs in an album, for they had been few and she feared they'd come to an end. Glancing over at his profile revealed in flashes and shadows from lights of the passing cars, she admitted it was way past time she let go of that anxiety and enjoyed this feeling of wellbeing.

TEN

BECAUSE AN ATTORNEY and real estate agent should be present when the farm deal was completed, the four involved had decided to meet at a local real estate office. Even though Glen was doing quite well emotionally, Katie worried about putting him and Julia in the same room. It might bring on a flashback. He hadn't had one in weeks, so she crossed her fingers and trusted he could control himself. If not, she'd handle it, and so would he. She had to believe that and refrain from mentioning it ahead of time as if he were a child told to be on his best behavior.

On the way up to the car, she took his hand, as pleased as he that he was free of the cuffs and metal walking sticks, as he had called them. He had problems on rocky inclines, and they went slowly to accommodate his use of the cane. She didn't mind, for with her hand in his, a trust passed between them that she treasured. Because he insisted, she allowed him to open her door, then cringed when he made his way around the car.

The most difficult adjustment she'd made since he became mobile was to back off helping him. It annoyed him, and she did understand. It was just so hard after seven months of being his helper and protector at every turn. That it made her feel useless was something she denied, but only to herself. They were slowly becoming equal, and she did not resent that, not at all. It was just that he didn't seem to need her so much. Oh, God, what a selfish thought. She was so proud of him, so happy for him. Loved him so much.

"Where you at?" He slammed the door and adjusted the seat belt.

"Right here. Just thinking."

"Worried?"

"A bit. I'll have to refrain from slapping her, that's all."

Head tilted, he gazed at her, then started the car, worked the hand controls and backed into the turnaround. "Me, too. Let's make a pact. I won't slap her if you won't."

On the highway headed up the mountain to the real estate office, he said softly, "Seriously, I'm a bit nervous about this myself. I love her, she raised me, gave up a lot to do it, too. Hard for me to forget that, until I remember how it felt in that cold shower, believing this had all been a dream, and I was back where I belonged."

"I don't blame you one bit for feeling that way. Whatever you want to say to her, say it. She needs to hear how that made you feel. In essence, she abandoned you when you needed her, just like—"

"Just like my country," he finished.

She let out a long breath, afraid he was going to bring up his ex-wife, the wife who sent him the letter he received the day before his final, fatal flight. Those cutting, cruel words would remain with him for the nine long years he spent as a prisoner of war. A man tortured beyond endurance who only survived to kill her. Spencer said it was normal for those who managed to survive to focus on one reason to live. All he had to think of was his hate for her. It was part of his training.

"I think it's that driveway there. Yes, see the sign."

The office was situated in a grove of oak trees with a spacious gravel parking and five steps up to the front deck.

"Oh, shit. I didn't know about the steps. I'm sorry, I should've checked." She lay a hand on his thigh.

"Hey, no sweat. Gotta learn to live in this world. I can make 'em."

And in truth he did. One hand on the rail, the other on his cane, he made it to the top step with her beside him, refraining from helping him. At that moment Lowell's truck rattled into the parking, tires crunching on the gravel.

"They're here. Keep going until we get away from these steps so you don't fall."

With fondness he smiled at her. "Yes, Mother."

"Oops, couldn't help myself. I am trying, honestly."

"It's okay, Katie. I do understand, and I thank you for caring. Let's get this shit over with, then I want to go to town and get some ice cream. Chocolate, if you don't mind."

She was transported back to the day in the hospital, her third visit, when she took him chocolate ice cream, and they shared it, eating from the same spoon. "Sounds wonderful."

The big door to the office stood ajar, and he pulled the glassed-in outer door open, stood back to let her pass through first, then followed, still without looking at his sister and her husband-to-be. This had to be painful, and she hated that he had to go through it. The husband and wife team who ran the real estate company had arranged for one of their agents to be present along with an attorney they had recommended.

The agent introduced herself, a forty-something woman in a two-piece brown suit and sensible shoes, her dark hair cut short. "I'm Amy Sanderson, and Clark Brown will be here momentarily. I take it you're

Katherine Kelly and Glen Tanner." Smiles and nods all around, and she showed them into a small adjacent private room with several chairs around a table. "I see the other parties have arrived, so I'll get everyone some coffee while we wait for Clark."

Before she returned with coffee, Julia and Lowell were sent in. Julia slashed a quick glance toward Glen and Katie, said nothing, and let Lowell seat her then himself across the table from them. Clark Brown bustled in carrying a briefcase and took a seat at the head of the table. He looked to be fourteen, but of course he was at least eighteen. Katie covered her smile with a fist and glanced at Glen, whose expression matched that of a wooden Indian. Not good.

Before the attorney could speak, Amy returned with a tray of coffee, creamer and sugar, placed it on the table and sat next to Julia. Everyone took a cup. Katie studied each in turn while spoons tinkled against cups, and someone coughed. Her gaze moved lastly to Glen. He sipped black coffee and peered over the rim straight at his sister. Julia did everything she could to avoid meeting that stare, but finally connected, only to dart off.

The attorney spoke with a deep voice that did not fit him at all. "I understand that the party of the first part—that would be Glen Tanner—wishes to buy out the party of the second part—Julia Tanner—in her part-ownership of the farm, legal description listed here."

He passed the paper work around to Glen and Julia and gave them a chance to look over what he had drawn up. Katie contented herself with staring at Julia until the woman began to fidget.

"What about Mark and Luke?" Glen asked when he'd finished reading.

"I have been informed they were offered the ten acres that contains the poultry houses and their home, and they were satisfied. That was a separate agreement, unless you contest, Mr. Tanner."

Glen gestured across the table. "Of course not. If they are happy with that, I am, too. I just want ownership of the remainder of the farm, and I will pay whatever is fair at today's prices."

"What if I don't want to sell my half?" Julia said, her voice harsh.

"Then why did you come here today?" he asked, just as harshly. "You wasted all our time to say no. How like you, Julia."

Lowell intervened. "I thought you had decided to sell him the farm, Julia. I don't understand what the problem is."

"The problem is he's living in sin with this hussy. She'll end up getting the farm when she decides she can't put up with his violence no more."

Glen stiffened, and Katie laid a hand on his leg. Their eyes met, his flashing with anger, and she grinned at him.

Brown pulled the paperwork back and straightened it and put it in his briefcase. "I'm sorry, I thought this was settled, and we were here to sign the papers and finalize everything. Who shall I send my bill to?" He shoved back his chair, made to rise.

"Could you wait just a moment?" Amy Sanderson took Julia's arm and leaned close to say something Katie couldn't hear. Neither could anyone else, it appeared. Apparently the two women were friends or at least acquaintances, for Julia nodded and turned back toward the others.

"I will agree to sell my half of the property to my brother, provided her name is not on the deed. She doesn't look like a stupid woman, so surely she wouldn't marry a madman just to get the farm. I still don't approve of her living with him, but he's out of my care now, though I raised him as best I could and welcomed him home from the war… until he tried to kill me."

Glen shoved his chair back, but couldn't rise easily and so remained seated and silent.

Brown cleared his throat. "This is no place to air personal problems, Miss Tanner. Shall I finish with the paperwork? We have listed the suggested price of the entire value of the farm without the ten acres that includes the poultry houses. The deed shows it was owned jointly by brother and sister after the death of their parents." He stated the price of half the value, showed them where to sign, and Glen made out a check, his hand shaking so badly he could hardly sign everything, but he got it done, laid down the pen, and closed his eyes, obviously fighting hard to control his emotions. Katie put her arm around his shoulders and placed his hand in her lap.

"Miss Tanner, with Amy's suggestion, we have given you sixty days to completely vacate the property. You may take your personal belongings, but you must leave all farm equipment. We understand the animals have been sold. Is that acceptable?" He fiddled with the paperwork, handed Glen and Julia each copies, and she nodded.

Julia grabbed the check and paperwork, wadded it into her purse, and rose. "I'll be going." She looked at Glen for a long time, then said, "I am truly sorry, truly. I did the best I could." She was crying when Lowell put an arm around her shoulders and guided her from the room.

"Let's just sit here for a moment, Glen," Katie said.

His shoulders heaved, and he covered his face. The attorney and Sanderson left the room without saying anything further.

She leaned close, whispered, "Everything's okay. It's finished." She lay her head against his arm, and they sat that way for several minutes.

"I'm ready to go now." He gathered up the papers, folded them, and handed them to her. "Could you put these in your purse, please?"

She took them and tucked them away.

In the main office, Sanderson smiled grimly. Katie thanked her, then took Glen's arm, and walked out with him.

After they managed the steps, he glanced at her. "Well, neither one of us got to slap her, did we?"

"In my mind, babe, in my mind. Let's go get that chocolate ice cream."

PART
FIVE

...Hath passed beyond the Moon.

ONE

THE STUDIO WAS a cluttered mess when Katherine unlocked the door the following Friday. After a week of classes and private students and taking no time to straighten up before quitting for the day, it was no surprise to find several hours cleaning awaited her.

She got busy storing the paintings from the exhibit so they would be ready for her private showing in the fall. No sense unpacking them. Glen had remained at the house, saying he had some things he wanted to do. She refrained from asking what, smiled, and said she'd be back up to fix them some lunch after she finished.

Friday continued to be his afternoon at the studio in what he called his private lessons from his very own private teacher. So she went about her work with a light heart. Things were going so well, but she didn't dare tempt fate by thinking too much about it.

Wednesday's newspaper lay on the worktable, and she folded it open to the *Ozarks' Scene* section. Some enterprising photographer had managed a close-up of Glen at the opening, and it ran next to a color photo of the painting, *Immortal Hero*. The effect was uncanny. Beside it, she and the governor shook hands. Accompanying the photos was the story of Katie and Glen and the purchase of her future paintings for the Vietnam War Memorial and Museum in Little Rock. The governor had managed to get his political message in, despite it being an article about a local artist and her work.

The pot in the office stopped gurgling, and she went to pour a cup. The clock showed 11:30, and she gulped down the coffee. Stowing the paintings had taken more time than she'd anticipated. Time to go up for lunch.

At the house she ran in, only to find Glen standing in the middle of the floor, an expression on his face told her immediately something was badly wrong. Her throat dried out, her limbs refused to move.

"What is it, sweetheart?"

He made his way carefully toward her, his limp pronounced without the cane. It took him a while to get to her. Unfocused eyes gave him a sleepwalker's look. She reached out and took his hand. Cold. He did not yield to her caress or her kiss, but moved on past, stumbling so she caught at his sleeve. He jerked away.

Dear God, please stop this torture, let him have some peace. "You look so tired. Is everything okay?"

He dropped into the recliner next to her. She smoothed his hair back. He twitched at the contact, flashed a dark glare in her direction. She pulled away and chewed at her lower lip.

"What is it?"

"I'm sorry, just had a bad night."

"Why didn't you mention it? I would've stayed up here with you."

"No sense in ruining your day."

She lowered herself onto the arm of his chair. "Doesn't ruin my day to spend it with you."

"I'm hungry. What's for lunch?"

Something really bad was going on. He didn't usually shut her out like this. They had shared so much it was natural for him to tell her whatever his problem was so they could work it out. Together.

"What would you like to eat?"

"Don't much care. Surprise me."

She patted his leg, felt him tense under her touch, and studied his features, trying to read what might be going on. No luck there, so she went into the kitchen and put together a cold salad from some leftover macaroni, a few raw vegetables, and chopped ham. Adding some crackers on the side and pouring two glasses of iced tea, she took the tray to the table and turned to tell him it was ready.

He had started toward her, limping badly.

"Sweetheart, where's your cane? You'll hurt yourself."

"Goddamn it, Katie, lay off, would you? I know how to walk, for Christ sake." He staggered, tried to catch himself on the arm of the couch, but slid to the floor.

She went to her knees beside him. "Are you hurt? What is wrong?"

"She called today. I wondered how long it would be before she showed up."

"Who?"

"Who the hell do you think? That bitch of a wife of mine, that's who." His expression told her everything. Ellie had finally surfaced, and it was time to deal with the fallout. With dread she took him in her arms.

"She's not your wife. She's your ex-wife. Why did she call?" Here we go again. She'd been preparing for his reaction ever since she learned the woman was trying to get in touch. Didn't she understand what divorce means? Separation. Leave him the hell alone. In all their time together he had never taken his problems out on her, never snapped at her or blamed her for what was happening. She'd always been his anchor. Why now was he so angry with her?

"Who the hell knows? I hung up on her."

Though he remained stiffly opposed to her touch, she helped him up and managed to get him seated on the couch. His gaze took her in with such disdain, she could hardly believe he was her Glen.

"Time for you to leave me now, isn't it? Go on, Katie. I'm way too much trouble." He propped his elbows on his knees and buried his face in his hands.

"Ssh, Glen. You know I'll never leave you." Threading fingers through his hair, she searched for a way to reassure him. She wanted to roar a protest. Hey, God, hey you. Don't do this to him. You cruel, vicious, unfeeling, sadistic God. I hate you, hate you.

"She's coming here, coming here. Can you believe that? I need to do something. Something. What?" He gazed at her with despair.

"Well, she won't get in. I won't let her. I promise I'll stay with you." What if he actually tried to carry out his vow to kill Ellie?

He turned glistening eyes toward her, a plea that squeezed her heart. "Please. Don't promise something you can't deliver. Let's go down to the studio. She can't find us there. I won't see her. I can't. Do you understand why?" It was as if he heard nothing she said in that world to which he had retreated. He grabbed her wrists, pulled her close, his face a twisted caricature of himself.

"Yes, I do understand." And she did, knew from Spencer what Glen felt he must do to Ellie. He'd blamed her for the past nine years and had to kill her for causing him such pain. It was logical, and in his mind it made perfect sense. On the other hand, because of his experiences, he could not bring himself to kill anymore, for any reason. It was tearing him apart.

"If you want, we'll go right down there. I'll take our lunch with us. Then, when she arrives here and finds no one home, she'll have to leave."

Still clutching her wrists in a painfully tight grip, he said, "Make sure you lock the doors so she can't get in and hide somewhere until we come back."

"I will. Where's your cane?"

He looked all around, head turning like an automaton. She studied him closely. Worried that he was going to flash back to his prison days at any moment.

"Do you remember where you last had it?"

"The phone. When I answered the phone."

"Honey, turn loose so I can get it for you, and we'll leave right away."

He kept hold and pulled her so close his breath washed over her face when he said, "Katie, I can trust you, right? There isn't anyone else. Please don't abandon me like the others. I don't know what to believe."

Despite the pain of his grip, she leaned into the few inches that separated their lips and kissed him softly. "You know you can trust me. We're in this together. I will not leave you. You know that."

"Yes. No. I don't know why you would stay." he said. "Let's go. Now."

Her heart thundered. What should she do? He looked on the edge of madness, a man she did not recognize, and for the first time she was frightened of him. If he thought her to be Ellie, it was hard to imagine what he might do. Still, in her heart of hearts she did not believe him capable of violence. Especially against her.

Not as himself, but the animal that had come at her, at Ellie, that day was not Glen, and IT was capable of violence.

"The van's out by the door. Can you make it okay?"

He nodded hard, fast. "Hurry, we'd better go now. They'll find us."

She almost lost it then. They? Dear God, help us both.

Leaving lunch on the table, she helped him stand, looped his arm over her shoulder and supported him out of the house and into the van, making a show of locking the front door. The others were all unlocked, but he didn't think of that, and she didn't mention it.

Down at the studio, she again supported him inside. Breaking away, he held on to walls and the backs of chairs and staggered into the storeroom before she could stop him. Then he cried out, a pathetic wail that would haunt her the remainder of her life. For a moment she couldn't move, was frozen to the spot.

Drifting seconds of eerie silence followed that scream. Her senses probed the heavy air, past the odor of oils and turpentine, beyond the waves of fear, and through dusty shafts of sunlight and detected only shadowy phantoms that swayed and beckoned. She tossed her head, squeezed her nails into sweaty palms, the pain rousing her from wherever she'd been. Stumbling the few steps into the storeroom, she called to him.

In the gloom, the overhead light swung slowly back and forth, creating cavorting ghosts, then smothering them in darkness. An unmoving mound lay tumbled into a pile of empty boxes. Terror stricken, she crept to within a few feet of the object and sank to her knees. The light reflected a pair of eyes staring, not at her but into endless horror.

She cried his name, reached to comfort him, touched him with a shaking hand. He swept away her hand and grabbed her shoulders in a vice-like grip.

"Got you," he spat and dragged her close.

A yelp burst from deep inside her, leaving behind a quivering mass of terror, like she'd been plunged into an icy pond.

Underwater.

Unable to breathe.

His breath blew hot on her face. "I'll break your goddamn neck.

Snap it in two." He confirmed his intention by locking his arm around her throat.

She choked, gagged, coughed. Struggled to breathe.

He released the pressure slightly allowing one small puff of air, said in her ear, "You got the keys? Sure you have. Give them to me. Now."

"Yes, I will. Yes, yes," she gasped.

"Get me out, then." He struggled to climb to his feet while maintaining his choke-hold, but couldn't rise. With a thigh-tightening heave, she managed to help him lift them both until they stood with his back against the shelves, one arm around her neck, the other forcing her wrist up between her shoulder blades.

Waves of darkness, jagged shards of yellow light slammed through her vision, and she fought unconsciousness. She had only enough air in her lungs to call out his name weakly.

"Shut up and move. Move." He pushed her forward ahead of him. She was able to breathe a little better while they stumbled toward the open door into the office. The telephone on the desk. Grab it. Somehow get a hold of it. Even if she could, she'd never make it to dial, wait, get out the words. What good would it do if she did? No one could get here in time help her. He would kill her. Then when he learned what he'd done, he would go screamingly insane, exist forever locked up in a land of raving madness. There'd be no one left to care, to trust.

Dear God, save me, she prayed, save us both.

Why hadn't she strapped him into the van when she had him there, driven to the hospital? The answer to that was obvious. What seemed like an eternity ago, he'd told her she was the only one he trusted, and she would not break that trust.

He sucked in a noisy breath, moaned, and his knees buckled, dumped him to the floor, taking her with him. She lay on her side half under him, excruciating pain pounding through her shoulder and hip where they'd struck the concrete floor. She shoved feebly at him and was surprised when he slid away. Using the arm of the couch, she struggled to stand. His hand snaked out, closed around her ankle and toppled her back to the floor. Under her clawing hands, nothing to catch hold of, only air. Closer and closer, he dragged her. Skin scraped from her hands, fingers digging at the rough floor. His strength was overpowering. With no defense against it, she collapsed into dead weight. He fisted handfuls of her hair, the pain paralyzing, forced her face close to his. Her mouth filled with a bitter taste that choked her.

"You know what slopes do to cunts like you?" he snarled in her ear. "Stick it in you in every hole, maybe even cut you some new ones." His fist tightened in her hair. He was tearing it out, shaking her, bending her head back until her neck curled into a rigid arc. The bones crackled.

His features twisted, distorted, and wavered until she could see nothing there of the man she loved. He was lost, gone. A vile, insane stranger assaulted her. The monster from their nightmares had finally come out to play. She perceived that with dumb acceptance. Readied herself to die in the arms of the man she loved.

His face went slack. "Katie, help me," dribbled from clenched lips. He collapsed onto the floor where he rolled into a tight ball, breath ragged.

Scrabbling toward the telephone, she stopped. The mournful plea tore at her heart. Make the call or go to him? She sobbed, spared him a quick glance. Knees drawn up under his chin, arms clasped around them, he remained where he had fallen. Rocking, rocking, harsh sobs jerking his chest so violently she couldn't stand it.

One last look at the phone. Dear God, what would they do to him?

What would he do to her? If she lost him, it didn't matter what he did to her. Tamping down any fear of the danger to herself, she crept toward him on her hands and knees, tried to take his head in her lap, but he was stiffly frozen in a fetal position, so she wrapped herself around him from behind. Sweat-drenched hair brushed her face, his dear and familiar scent smothered by the stench of fear enveloped her. Where he had gone, she could not go.

She crooned to him, calling him baby and love and sweetie. Tears flowed while she waited for his terrible keening to stop. At last, he went limp and shifted position, as if he craved their touching. Her body ached, and her limbs were stiff. The agony of lying on the floor in such a position became unbearable, still she held him, afraid to move. At last, when she could take it no longer, she asked softly, "Honey, do you think you could get up? Please, let's sit up."

His torn voice uttered her name.

"Yes, sweetie, it's me. Could you help me?"

He straightened his legs, raised his head, and peered around the room. She inched away and tried to stand, staggered and tried again.

"Goddammit, don't go away," he screamed, startling her into immobility. "Don't you take her away from me, you fucking bastards."

A cold understanding that Glen had dragged her into the nightmarish flashback with him and was using her to bring himself out dazed her. How bizarre, impossible. Had she gone insane? No, hold it together. Take care of him. Keep him safe from this threat. Scrabbling back to him, she lay a hand on his shoulder. "I'm here. I'm not going anywhere."

"You stay with me, don't let them take you away," he whispered. "They'll hear you. Shhh. Be real quiet." He pawed at her, huddled around her as if to hide her within himself.

"Glen, please listen, darling. You're here with me. Me. We're not there in that awful place. Please, we're here together. That place doesn't exist anymore."

"Next time they come, we'll hide." He bobbed his head up and down. "They won't find us."

He wasn't hearing her at all. She couldn't handle this alone. She had to get him some help. This was Ellie's fault, and she'd strangle the bitch with her bare hands. Now that made no difference. What mattered was that she could save him. She held trembling hands over her ears and fought a scream. Damn them all for forsaking men to this.

Damn them all to *hell*.

She caressed his cheek, looked into eyes so bright with anguish they threw her frantic reflection back at her. No other way, she had to do this.

Taking his hand in hers, she dragged him to his feet. "Come on, we'll hide. Come with me, I know a good place where they'll never find us. Come on, sweetie. Come with me."

As if his leg were torn and bleeding, he leaned heavily on her. Glancing down she expected to see a crimson stain wetting his pant leg. Legs and arms that belonged to someone else finally reacted to her efforts, and she managed to wrestle him into the passenger seat of the van and buckled in. Where the hell was the damned key? In the ignition. Hands trembled so bad she couldn't get hold of the thing. There, finally. Numb fingers could barely grasp it, turn it, start the engine. For a moment she collapsed across the steering wheel. Her pounding heart quieted. Pull the shift into drive. Bleary eyes so she could barely see. Okay, get moving. Take him to a safe place, the only place where someone could help him. The place neither wanted him to be.

"Where we going?" he asked.

"Somewhere safe where no one can find us." The sound of her own ragged voice shocked her. A sob tore from deep in her gut. One last chance. She put on the brake, said his name. If he replied, coherent, she'd take him up to the house and put him to bed. Let him sleep it off.

"Don't stop, Katie. They'll get us. Run. Run." Frantic, pawing at the seat belt.

Okay, the hospital it was. But stay with him. Don't give him over to anyone else. Tuning the radio, she found soft country music and locked herself into automatic with a great deal of effort.

"You still here, Katie?"

"Yes, darling. I'm here." Where would I go, where could I go with your love holding me prisoner? There was nowhere for her but next to him.

A pickup loaded with hogs, hairy snouts poking through slats of rough oak, tiny eyes peering between the boards, swayed back and forth ahead of her, doing a dashing forty miles per hour. Her patience ended before the double yellow line did, and she floored the accelerator to roar around the laboring vehicle. An oncoming car hurtled to the shoulder to get out of her way, and she swerved back into her own lane.

It might have been best if she'd just.... "No, no, no," she said under her breath. "We mustn't die now."

She hadn't meant to utter that thought aloud and glanced at Glen to see if she had frightened him. His lips moved soundlessly, his fingers plucked in an absent minded gesture at the seatbelt. He was no longer there with her, but lost in a savage, dark place where she couldn't go. Or could she? Perhaps she was already there with him. After all, he'd taken her with him earlier.

By the time she pulled into the drive at the hospital, she was nearly hysterical. She leaned on the horn button and stayed there until someone came. They had to pry her off after taking Glen from the van. He screamed her name over and over, growing hoarse and distant when the doors closed after him. So weak she couldn't stand, she watched helplessly. She had betrayed him, and she wanted to die.

An attendant took her inside where she collapsed.

TWO

KATHERINE CAME TO on a couch in Spencer's office with a nurse holding her wrist in firm fingers.

In one motion she jerked loose, came to her feet, and headed for the door, dizzy and staggering.

"Where is he? I have to see him now."

The astonished woman made no attempt to stop her.

Outside the door, she peered down the corridor at Spencer talking to an orderly and headed for him. The psychiatrist spotted her. "Calm down. You can't help him right now."

"Spencer, so help me, don't you try to stop me. Don't you understand, I have to help him. Oh God, why did we do this to him? I want to see him this minute, right now." Her voice was so shaky her words were nearly unintelligible.

"Katherine, look what he did to you. You're covered in bruises, your knees and hands are scraped raw. And you want to see him?"

"Yes, right this minute."

"Okay, calm down. But you might keep in mind we didn't do this to him. Now come with me."

"Oh, but we did. We could have left him in that other world he was living in. We could have done that much for him." She allowed the psychiatrist to drag her by one arm to a room where he inched the door open a crack so she could peek in.

A nightlight burned in the darkened room. Glen lay very still on the bed, mussed hair sweat-damp under the glow. Straps at his wrists, ankles, and upper and lower body restrained all but the slightest movement. She let out a sigh and slid down the wall to the floor. She wouldn't budge from the spot, and Spencer finally left her there. Minutes or hours later, body stiff and aching, she wandered the hospital like a waif waiting for him to awaken. He was drugged, and she hated that nearly as much as the alternative, except that it must be giving him some peace from the madness.

Spencer sought her out again. "I thought we had him on his way this time," he said. Shrugged. "Well, it's just a setback, after all. You'd do well to remember he suffered in that other world where you think we should have left him. Stop being so egotistical as to take all the blame. If you're ready to quit, I'm sure we can arrange it."

In his expression, frustration warred with anger and something else, too. An expectation that she had gone the limit.

"My God, Spencer, you want me to quit, don't you? You of all people, who believed in him best. You think he belongs locked away, don't you?"

"Goddammit, I don't know. Can't you see I don't know, and the responsibility if he does something godawful is mine. He could very well have killed you. That eats at me." He slammed his fist against the wall. "There's so much we don't know, so damn much."

She tried to tell him about Glen thinking she was with him in his nightmare and that she could somehow save him, but a sharp rap on the door interrupted her before he could get the gist of her conversation.

Harry poked his head around the jamb. "Doc, he's awake and you'd better come." He indicated Katherine. "Her, too, I think."

She followed Spencer, but he ordered her to wait in the hallway and shut the door in her face. She flattened her hands there and rested her cheek on the cool metal to wait. Inside, Glen was saying something, but it took a moment for her brain to understand he was rasping her name as if he had never stopped. Mouth set grimly she shoved the door open, dodged Spencer, and headed for the bed where Glen strained against the straps. Tendons bulged on his neck and at his temples, and his face was red. His torn screams were only her name, over and over and over, until she couldn't bear it.

"Katherine, dammit, stay away from him," Spencer roared.

It was too late, and she didn't care, anyway. She grabbed at his tense body, threw herself across him as if she could somehow protect him, spoke soothing words in his ear. He stopped screaming immediately, and the eerie silence halted even Spencer's actions. He glanced at the hypodermic he'd filled, then motioned Harry, who had started toward her, to wait.

Glen could barely speak, his voice was so spent, but he choked out a few words. "I knew you'd come back. You said—"

"Oh, God, sweetheart. You're okay, I promise." She buried her head against his shoulder.

"Listen to me," he whispered. "I don't know what's happening." He gasped out short sentences, leaving great spaces between, and she strained to understand him.

"I made all the tapes, said the things they wanted, even did the television stuff, but they won't stop. You've got to help me. Tell them to take these chains off. Please. I can't stand them. I'll be good. God, tell them I'll be good. Don't let them cut me anymore." The gritty voice faded, and he rolled his head back and forth ever so slowly.

A pleading glance at Spencer confirmed what she'd supposed. They wouldn't take off the restraints.

Tapes? For television? What had gone on in that godforsaken place? Just how much did the military know about this? Or the government. No time now to think or consider the implications of his ramblings. Her only concern was the man she loved who lay suffering before her.

She took his face in both hands, his cold clammy skin flushing hot. "Honey, it's all right. You're not chained."

He lifted his head and nuzzled into her caress.

God, she was so tired. She closed her eyes and took in several deep breaths. An unbidden memory teased at her senses. A darkened hospital room, her crawling into bed with him, how he told her later she had saved him.

Her head drooped, and she jerked awake. How much longer could she remain awake?

"Spencer? Go away. Let me stay here with him."

"You know I can't do that."

"But look at him. He'd be okay if I just stayed with him."

"Don't be ridiculous. I can't let people sleep in bed with the patients. I'm going to give him a shot, and he'll go to sleep. Then you're going to go home and get some rest yourself. Everything will look better in the morning. We'll figure something out." He moved to the bed.

Glen took a deep breath and turned his head on the pillow. She rubbed his neck, watched the closed eyelids flicker ever so slightly when Spencer slid the needle easily into the pinioned arm.

"It'll just take a few minutes. You can stay until then." He left, but

Harry remained just inside the door. In the dim light she could scarcely make out his hovering presence.

Glen's voice startled her. "You still here?"

"Yes, I'm here, sweetie. You can sleep now, you're safe."

"I feel like I'm going away, falling. Flying, far away. Come too, please?"

"Yes, I'll come with you." She lay her cheek against his, kissed him gently and repeated her words close to his ear. "I'm coming with you, my darling."

His head rolled lifelessly away from her, and his muscles relaxed. At that moment, a numbness crept up from her toes to cover her like a shroud. Harry caught her by one arm, and bearing her sagging weight, led her from the dim cubicle. In the waiting room he lowered her to a couch, and she announced she would sleep right there. She knew nothing until Dee Dee the receptionist shook her and offered her coffee, the hallway awash in morning sunlight.

After she drank that first cup, she tried to get off the couch. Her arms and legs were weak with pain. Raw, scraped flesh on her palms, elbows, and knees. She was a mass of bruises. She rose and walked slowly in small circles until she could move more easily.

"Is Glen awake yet?" she asked the receptionist.

"No. I'm so sorry, Mrs. Kelly. What happened? He was doing so well. We all hoped—"

"I have to walk some more. I need a bathroom and a comb. My purse, I guess I left it home." She was about to come apart and struggled to maintain a hold on rationality.

Dee Dee accompanied her to the ladies room, produced a hairbrush and some fragrant cream, stayed with her to help. After they had settled for what little they'd accomplished, Katie said, "I think another cup of coffee might make me halfway human again. I'm going to peek into his room."

"Gee, I don't know. You really shouldn't." The young receptionist hesitated a moment, then motioned conspiratorially. "I'll just go get you that coffee."

Rushing before someone could catch her, Katie eased the door to Glen's room open, squeezed through, and let it close softly behind her. Aching arms hugging her chest, she approached the bed. He breathed lightly in a slow, even rhythm. Except for a tic under one eye, his features appeared relaxed and calm.

"Where are you, my darling?" she asked.

His eyes snapped open. She jumped and let out a choked cry. Immediately he began to twist his hands, chaffing his wrists with the bonds.

"Help me, please, Katie," he husked in his used-up voice. The plea cracked like ice splitting across a frozen lake.

With a sob she worked at the straps with stiff fingers. "Hold still, honey," she whispered, ripped and tore frantically at the unyielding pads. At last, she controlled her frenzy enough to study the fastenings and then free one of his arms. With lightning speed, he wrapped it around her waist. A spasm of fear shot through her, but he was holding her, rubbing the flat of his hand around on her back. She leaned across his chest and undid his other arm, collapsed into his embrace.

Letting out small, detached moans, he touched her hair, ran his palms up and down her arms, as if checking to see if every part of her was there. She cupped his face, kissed his dry lips until she assured him of her existence.

"Where are we?" he asked in a gravelly voice. "I dreamed I tried to hurt you. Not true."

"Hospital. Not true."

He croaked out a few impatient expletives. She put two fingers over his lips. "Sssh. I'm not supposed to be here."

To that he managed a crooked grin, and she silently cheered his courage. Then he asked cautiously, "What did I do?"

He was back. Relief flowed through her like the touch of a spring breeze. Kissing him on first one eye, then the other, she said, "Nothing, you did nothing."

THREE

THE NEXT MORNING, she perched on the edge of the couch in Spencer's office, exhausted and drained.

"Well," he said and raised his hands from the file on his desk. "He seems to be completely rational this morning. Damn good thing for you, Katherine, since you saw fit to diagnose his condition and carry out your own treatment."

She submitted to his criticism in silence, waited for him to go on.

"The last thing he remembers is leaving the house to go to your studio."

"He told me he talked to Ellie."

"He didn't say, but from the reaction, we can assume so. It triggered a psychotic episode."

Katherine looked up sharply. "That sounds ominous."

"It is. I won't soften this. It is indeed very serious. As yet I haven't told him he nearly killed you. God knows what that will cause."

"Please, don't tell him. Please."

Spencer shook his head, let out an explosive sigh, and said nothing.

"I won't leave him," she told him harshly.

"Fine, but the hospital will take care of him for a while."

Katherine pushed herself out of the chair and leaned against his polished desk. "No. I'll not let you tie him up in some room so he thinks he's still in one of those bamboo cages and someone is coming to torture him. No, no, no. He'll lay there and scream until he has no voice left, no sanity at all." She glared at Spencer, who watched her pensively with burnt umber eyes. "You will not do that to him."

He broke contact with her intense stare. "Calm down. You're doing no one any good, certainly not yourself and not him."

She slumped back down in the chair. "You're not going to do that to him. I'll take care of him."

"Don't be ridiculous. You look like you've been through a meat grinder. I think a few days for all of us to cool down, then we can discuss this more rationally."

Katherine fingered the angry red marks across her throat. He acted as if it were settled, and she struggled to keep her voice level. "You saw him when I went in that room. He needs me. I tried to tell you before, and you didn't listen. He took me with him into that hell, used me to come out of it. His violent reactions only happen when Ellie is involved." She slapped both hands flat on the desk. "I want him to come home with me. He'll be all right. We'll both be all right. I will not let her near him. Here he'll just suffer more, and so will I. Spencer, please."

"Forget it. As his doctor, I cannot condone such a thing. It's too dangerous. And don't think for a minute you can pull a stunt like you did before and whisk him away."

"What's dangerous is keeping him here. You'll turn him into a zombie. Shoot him full of drugs or strap him to a table and try one of your fiendish little experiments on him."

"Oh for Christ's sake." Spencer bolted to his feet.

She'd broken through his professional veneer, but went on stubbornly, hammering away at his stubborn resolve. "If I were his wife and I wanted to take him out of here, I could do it legally, couldn't I?"

Spencer stared at her. "Don't tell me you're thinking about marrying him? I won't allow that. He isn't capable of making such a decision."

"I am getting him out, one way or another. I'll find a legal way to do it, or failing that, I'll do it illegally. You know I can and will."

"Dammit, Katherine. He's no worse than a lot of people who are walking the streets, but my better judgment tells me, no, warns me...." He stopped, studied her expression of determination. "I can't guarantee you anything."

"I know that. You're no better than a damn witch doctor."

"I don't suppose it's possible I'll ever understand women, especially one in love."

Sensing victory, her voice took on a cajoling tone. "He'll come back every week, twice a week, whatever you want. And I'll call you if anything happens. He'll be with me. At peace."

She paused and stared out the window at the early summer rain that showed no promise of letting up. "I need him with me. He needs to be with me." The statement hung solemnly over the sounds of their breathing, and she let it lie there a while.

At last, when no one seemed to have anything more to say, she came to her feet, glanced down at the wrinkled shorts and tee shirt, the dirty sneakers. "I know I look disreputable, but I want to take him home with me today. As soon as you can release him. I know all about 'against medical advice.' Do that so you won't be to blame."

Spencer sighed and tapped a finger on the file lying on his desk. "If he does this again, I'm putting him on drug therapy. You understand that? No ands, ifs, or buts. And you'd better pray he doesn't kill you the next time." He expelled a puffy breath and wagged his shaggy head. "Take him home, then. I'll get the papers ready. I want to see him twice a week. You bring him in, don't send him. I hope you know what you're letting yourself in for."

"You let me in for it a long time ago, and it's been too late for me to do anything ever since. He told me once I'd be sorry one day I ever set eyes on him." She placed the statement out carefully for examination.

Culpability clear on his lank features, Spencer gazed at her sadly. "And are you?"

For a long while she was silent, watching rains drops cry down the window panes, then looked back at him. "No. No, I'm not," she whispered. "I'm going in to get him ready. Please don't make us wait. He doesn't need the stress."

"Katherine, please be very careful. I don't want to see either of you hurt any more. That's the only reason I'm allowing this."

She rose on tiptoe and kissed him on the cheek. "You won't be sorry."

"I hope to God I'm not."

Harry wheeled him out in the chair, dressed in the clothes he had on when he arrived, a bit the worse for wear. The rain had let up, but a mist still fell, shimmering on Glen's hair. At the van Harry assisted him into the passenger seat and buckled the seat belt, then turned to Katie.

"I know what you mean to each other. Don't forget I was there the day he saw you for the first time and reached out to touch your hair." He shook his head, eyes bright. "I never thought I'd see him with that look on his face. It was like he'd touched an angel. You're right to take him home. You need anything, day or night, you call me, and I'll be there. You hear?"

Her eyes burned and she wiped them. "Thank you. Thank you so much. You come see him… us… whenever you want to. I'm going to see no one hurts him again if I have to barricade the house." She hugged him, leaned into the van, and kissed Glen on the cheek. "I'm going around to the other side. Be right there."

After she backed the van up, she glanced in the far side rear view to see Harry standing there in the rain watching her pull away.

"Katie?" Glen said when she stopped at the highway to wait for a break in traffic.

"Yes."

"Do you intend to follow me into hell?" How alert he sounded, enough to surprise her.

He very well might be right, but not if she could help it. "There and back again, sweetie. But I'll do my best to keep you from hell."

"What about your life? All the things you could be."

"None of it means anything without you. I won't be without you. I won't wake up every morning and know you're somewhere suffering and not with me where you belong. I won't wander through an empty house or paint my dreams out on a blank canvas, only to have them mean nothing."

She touched his stubbled jaw with the tips of her fingers, saw an opening in traffic, and pulled out.

"You told me once you'd die without me," she said. "I've never been much good at telling you how I feel. Just saying I love you seems so pale a thing. I've never loved anyone like I love you. Without you, my only worry is I might not be able to die. I'd live in that hell you talk about, and I'd never recover, never." Tears leaked down her cheeks. "Dammit," she said.

He pulled some tissue from the console and handed them to her.

"Thank you, Katie, for this. I love you."

Images of the earlier terror he'd experienced receded. For the first time since he'd come into her studio in a rage, he sounded calm. But he dropped off to sleep soon after and didn't move again during the long ride.

F O U R

BONE WEARY, KATIE wasn't sure how she kept the van on the highway. The hills and valleys peeled away on either side, so it appeared she was driving through a tunnel into an unknown—and slightly frightening—future. Again.

Would anything have been different if she hadn't fallen in love with Glen? Could she then have simply walked away? When you got right down to it, life offered only one escape, and the nature of most wouldn't allow that. The ultimate, cosmic Catch 22. As soon as they arrived home, she would cancel all her classes and go to bed with him for at least a week. Keep him warm and sheltered, safe, and most of all peaceful. Spencer had stressed that above all else, humans needed food, shelter, love, and safety. And those she could give Glen. She'd feed him and love him and steal him away from his demons when they weren't looking. Keep him safe. To hell with everything and everyone. He was going to make it, dammit, and so was she. There was a certain restful serenity in the silent declaration. And hope, too.

The moment she pulled up near the front door, and he raised his head, she recognized a problem. She could not get him in the house without the wheelchair, and it was inside. He could not remain inside the van alone without going wild. Yet he had to somehow. Even as she left the driver's side and ran around to the passenger side, he began to shout for her, pound on the window. His fear she would abandon him had doubled and tripled since Ellie's call. All she could do was try to explain it to him. When the door swung open, he saw her and quieted. She took his wrists in her hands, held them until he aimed his eyes at her.

"Listen to me, sweetie. Can you hear me?"

He nodded, squirmed.

"Yes, I know you need out of there. I have to go inside and get your chair. I can't carry you inside. If I try to help you, we might both fall." No, too much information, keep it simple.

She began again. "Glen, we're home. I'm going to leave you here and get your chair. You wait, and I'll be right back. Yes." She nodded, relieved she couldn't see his expression. The moment she released him and took a step backward, he grabbed for her, began that litany of saying her name over and over.

"Sweetheart, I'll be right back. I'm so sorry. I'll be right back." The drugs, those damned drugs, were having exactly the reaction Spencer had feared. So why in hell did he give them to him? Because he thought he'd have him strapped to a bed, that's why.

Ignoring his anguish, even the repeated sound of her name, she pushed the van door shut in case he managed to unfasten the seatbelt and hurried inside as fast as she could go. The chair was in the sunroom, and she stumbled through the house, grabbed it, and headed for the front door. Opened it and heard him, beating on the window, screaming her name.

Dear God. Trundling the chair out, she yanked open the door and threw herself into his lap to keep him from bailing out. "I'm here. I'm back. I'm so sorry. Let me get you out of that seat belt."

His body shook as if he had the ague, his hoarse voice wound down. She fumbled for the release, finally got it. He lunged forward, tossing her against the dash. Throwing her arms up, she blocked the door with her body. If he leaped out he could be badly hurt.

"Okay, it's okay now. You're safe. I've got you. Take it easy. Help me, sweetie. Help me get you into the chair."

The unearthly sounds silenced, and he appeared to understand. "Come on, baby. Put your hand here." Placing his left hand above the door and wrapping his fingers around the bar there, she whispered softly. "Now you just hang on, and I'll do the rest. You trust me, don't you? Easy."

With the chair outside the open door, she was able to lower him from the van seat so that when she had him let go, he dropped gently into the chair. "There now. That wasn't so bad."

A kiss planted on his cheek calmed him, but didn't help her much. He was breathing heavily, wringing wet with perspiration and trembling hard. Frightening him was the worst thing in the world, and she wanted never to do it again.

With the chair and its precious cargo safely inside, she locked the front door, unplugged the telephone on the way through the living room, took him to the bathroom, then the bedroom, where she turned down the bed covers and coaxed him into moving to the edge of the bed, and pulled off his boots and jeans and tee shirt. Still suffering from the heavy dose of drugs given to him in the hospital, he lowered his head and submitted to everything. She straightened him onto the bed, covered him, bent over onto his chest, and took some deep breaths. His heart pounded in her ear, one hand patted her head.

"Let me get you some water."

"Yes, yes." Yet he wouldn't let go her hand.

Her heart ached for him. So frightened, so confused and mistreated for so long. Could she manage to get through this once again, help him heal his wounds and become whole? They had almost made it once, and she damn well planned to get him back. One more time. She kissed him. "Sweetie, let me go get you a drink. Just there. See the light on? You can watch me, and I'll be right back. Okay?"

Again he nodded, and finally released her hand. She hadn't made it to the bathroom door before he cried out her name.

He's terrified of losing you, Spencer had explained. Because he's lost everyone else in his life.

She replied to Glen's shout. "I'm coming right back. Just a minute."

With the glass still dripping water, she hurried back, raised his head, and put it to his lips. He gulped the entire contents, tried to get more.

"Oh, sweetie, I'm so sorry. I should've given you water first. I never thought. Those drugs dry you out. Want some more? I'm going to get another glass and set it here on the table for later." Again she went through the same regimen. Kissing, whispering, loving. Fighting tears, she fetched another glass and put it on the table, almost spilling it when he grabbed her other arm.

"Katie?"

"Yes, darling, it's me."

"Are we home?"

"Yes, we're home." A long sigh, as if the declaration comforted her as well as him.

"Come to bed with me."

"Of course. There's no place I'd rather be. I'll just come around to the other side and—"

"No," he shouted. "Here, get in with me here." He lowered his voice. "You'll get lost in the dark, and I won't be able to find you."

"Yes, yes. Okay." Toeing off her sneakers, she climbed over him, shed her clothes, kicked them off into the floor, and crawled under the covers while he fought to keep a hold on her. Dear God, would she be able to do this? Surely she didn't know enough. And her so cocky about being able to help him when Spencer couldn't.

"Come here," she told him, pulled his arms around her, wrapped hers around him. "See, I'm right here with you. I won't leave. Close your eyes, and go to sleep." She placed a kiss on each of his eyelids, buried her face against his chest, and stretched out tightly against him.

If anyone or anything tried to come near him with drugs or stories or anything else that might hurt him, she would clock them. He would find peace here with her and heal. She would see to that or die trying.

In her embrace, he relaxed. "Thank you for bringing me home. I will be good." He took a deep breath and succumbed once again to the drugs.

For a long while she lay awake, tears flowing so hard she could scarcely breathe.

Thank you for bringing me home.

Such a humble statement, yet it touched her more than anything else he could have said. It frightened her, too. Could she truly keep him safe, or was she, like Spencer suggested, a fool? She could not prevent the nightmares, but she could keep at bay anyone who threatened his peace. That had to be enough.

When she awoke in the early light of dawn, he was lying there staring at her. "You always wake up first, don't you? Did you have a good night?"

"Please tell me how I got here. I was strapped to that bed in the hospital. I wake up, and we're here. Which is the dream, Katie? Am I awake now or dreaming? And what happened to your face, your neck?"

She touched the bruises. Had forgotten all about them. "An accident, that's all. I brought you home from the hospital last night. I couldn't leave you there like that. Did you have a good night?"

"Yes, I did. I feel grungy. Could we take a shower before breakfast?"

He appeared free of the drugs this morning, but it would be hard to tell until he got up and began to move around.

"Whatever you want, sweetheart. We don't even have to get up."

"Oh, can we take a shower in the bed?"

Amazing that he could regain his sense of humor, considering the memories churning in his brain.

She laughed. "No silly, I mean, we can come back to bed and stay here all day if you want."

He nodded, revealed a spark of dimples. "I'm tired of being in bed. Let's go outside in the sunshine, walk around in the yard. I'm feeling stiff."

Before she could stop him, he threw back the covers, swung his legs around, stood up and went down, all in one frightening moment.

Across the bed and to the floor, she scrambled to his side.

"Are you hurt? Wait, don't move yet."

"Dammit, what happened? Dammit, Katie. My leg is killing me."

"Hold still, please." With both hands, she felt up and down his legs and body. "Do you hurt anywhere?"

"My leg hurts like hell. They cut it so I couldn't run."

Oh God. "Glen, where are you?"

"I can't walk. I thought I could walk, but I forgot they cut me up. I can't escape, can I?"

"Dear Lord." She sat there beside him, arms around his shoulders rocking him and crooning to him. When he quieted, she took his face in both hands. "Honey, look at me. You're with me and safe." What if she couldn't do this? She'd made mistakes already, letting him get up unsupervised, forgetting last night about getting him water, and she should've taken the wheelchair from the hospital to bring him inside.

Dammit, dammit.

He lifted fingers to stroke her bruised cheekbones and jaw. His hand clasped her arm, and he turned it. "Where did you get those bruises? Did I do that?"

"Those were an accident. You didn't do that, not really. You were terrified of something."

"I hurt you. Are you afraid of me?" Soft trembling voice.

Her hand only shook a little when she caressed his cheek. "No. Never." She kissed him. "Let's get you up off the floor. I'll see if I can find your cane."

"I think you'd better get the wheelchair. I don't think I can walk."

Surely this was only temporary. With a heavy heart she brought him the chair, and they finally got him up and into it.

"Still want to take a shower with me? I'm really grungy, too."

"Sure," he said.

Together they went into the bathroom where she adjusted the spray. He pulled himself up by the rails, and she soaped up a sponge and washed his back.

"Fine tight butt you've got there," she said, then knelt to wash his legs before moving around in front. He grabbed the sponge and lowered himself to the bench.

"Better let me do you before you get that far, or there'll be an orgy right here, and you won't get washed for a long time."

"Does that mean you're horny?"

"I wish I were is one way to put it."

"What's another?"

"I want to make you feel good." He soaped her back. "Okay, turn around." It didn't take long before he dropped the sponge and used his hands to finish the job, rubbing between her legs until she wiggled.

"Talk about starting an orgy," she joked.

"My turn," he said, pulled himself up by the bars and waited while she washed his chest and his belly.

"Don't forget my horn." He laughed.

It was so good to hear him laugh, she paused and gathered his happy features together in one hope-filled long gaze.

For a moment he went stone cold silent, looked all around wildly. "My God, get me out of here. Now. Please."

She opened the doors of the shower. "Look, Glen. You're not shut in." He'd always liked this bathroom because it was open to the outdoors and to the bedroom, but his claustrophobia had kicked in for some reason. Those damned drugs again. He eyed the opened doors and settled down, but his breathing and heartbeat remained elevated for a while.

Summer moved slowly, each day filled with lazy, serene moments. Though Martin hadn't returned, Glen worked out every day on the equipment in the sunroom. Soon he was once again walking with only the aid of the cane.

He continued to have other problems that angered him, though, mystified her. Their sex life had dwindled to nothing. She fully understood how he felt when he couldn't get it up, or worse, when he did but he couldn't climax. It was a problem she felt they could overcome, but he wasn't so sure.

He was unhappy she hadn't resumed her art classes, felt he was stealing her life. She repeated that he was her life and wasn't stealing anything.

One evening they sat on the deck watching the setting sun bleed shades of carmine into the purpling sky.

"Can't you think of something you'd like to do?" he asked.

"Mmm, we could go down to the lake when the moon is full and make love on the picnic table."

"Wow, that's a good one, considering my current problem. But that's not what I meant, and you know it. If I weren't here for you to baby all the time, what would you do?" He appeared determined to take the blame for what he felt was wrong between them.

She refused to give in to him. "I guess I'd have to find someone else to baby, but no one as cute as you. Besides, I'd be so lonely I'd want to die."

"Okay, I give up. When will the moon be full again?" He kissed her hand and held it for a long time against his lips.

She marked the date of the next full moon on the calendar, pleased it was the middle of the week. Less chance someone would have the table. To her it was simply a matter of setting the mood, and he would be fine. Back to his old horny self.

The evening of their full moon date was clear and warm. The fates co-operating. She folded a thick quilt around a bottle of wine and curled up next to him on the couch. "Come on, let's take a drive down to the lake."

He glanced up from the magazine. "It's almost dark."

"Yeah, but it's going to be a beautiful night. Let's do something fun and crazy."

"Okay, if you really want to."

"I do. Come on."

"I'd like to drive if you don't mind," he said.

"Sure. I like it when you drive."

"Brave, aren't you?" He grinned.

"Where you're concerned, I am." She made a mental note to plan more excursions in his car.

He switched on the lights going down the driveway, though it wasn't quite dark. He enjoyed driving like mad over the mountain, brakes squealing around the tight curves, the little car holding on like it was built to do.

At the lake, he pulled up to their favorite table. "Was this what you had in mind?"

"Smart ass, you knew all along, didn't you?"

"Yep, saw it on the calendar." He was quiet for a moment, then reached over and took her hand. "I appreciate this, Katie, but I'm afraid it won't make a difference."

"We'll see. Positive thinking. Have faith. Oh, look at that." She pointed out the window toward the upper end of the lake. A red-gold moon emerged slowly as if out of the water, trailing a shimmering path over the glassy surface toward them. "Looks like we could walk right out there and touch it, keep right on going beyond the moon into the velvet blackness and touch the stars. Park the car so we can see the moon from the table, would you?"

He backed up until the front cleared the view. "Ready? Isn't that beautiful?"

"Yes, come on."

Quilt in her arms, she covered the table and set the wine bottle on one of the benches. He rattled around through the rough gravel, and she remained where she was, letting him handle it. Anticipation stirred between her legs like the beating of her heart, and she slipped off her panties from under the short dress.

"Sit," she directed, removed the cap, took a swig, and handed the bottle to him. "Drink."

He turned it up and drank deeply, then drank some more, eyes glittering in her direction. He wiped his mouth. "One more time? Get me drunk, maybe this will work."

She waited while he slugged it down. "Okay? Ready?"

Moon glow lit his features, turned his hair a pale bronze.

She sidled over to him. "Ever had a lap dance, good looking?" She straddled his thighs and swaying her hips, slowly lowered herself into his lap. Reaching for the buttons of her shirt, she undid them, taking her time, and thumbed down one strap of her bra. "Want to take it off or want me to?"

He held up a hand, playing her game, a goofy look on his face. He never drank, and the wine was hitting him just enough to loosen him up. "Pick me, teacher. Show me how, put my hand where it goes."

She placed his palm over her breast. "Oops, missed. Are you drunk, sailor? Up a little bit." She leaned into his touch, and when he loosened the strap, her breast filled his hand.

"I have another one if you'd like it." She kissed his mouth, ran her tongue over his lips, tasting the wine. She wanted him desperately, hoped this was affecting him the same way. His eyes were a bit glazed, but that could be the wine.

"Why don't you put those gorgeous lips of yours right here." Hand on the back of his head, she guided him to her breast, let it fill his mouth. "Touch me," she murmured, placing his hand between her legs.

Desire stirred while his fingers massaged deep inside her. His lips, his warm tongue, the gentle suckling, popped goose bumps all over her. She slid one hand to his zipper and pulled the tab down. Pressed against his rubbing fingers. Watching him for a reaction, she slipped a hand inside his pants and cupped her palm over his growing erection. His closed eyes opened, glittered in the moonlight, and she ran her tongue across his lips.

The moon spread light along his dreamy features. She removed her hand and his, then swayed her hips ever so slowly, swaying hard against him.

"Oh, God," he moaned, made tiny little grunting sounds and clutched at her waist, while she continued to move against his growing erection.

"I need… I need."

"Not yet, baby. Not yet."

"Yes, please. Yet."

"First, take my skirt off. Up over the top of my head. Give that guy a little practice at standing tall."

He groaned, then slowly removed her skirt, touch lingering over her bare flesh. The moonlight slashed across her bare belly, leaving a dark shadow in the V between her legs. He dragged in a harsh breath.

"Kiss me there," she said, shoved his head down. His hair tickled her tummy, and she let him know she was ready.

"Can you stand up?"

He gulped. "I seriously doubt it."

"Okay, then we'll do it right here." With practiced ease she skinned his pants and shorts off, climbed back onto his lap and took him deeply inside in one swift push.

"Oh fucking A." Distantly an owl answered his low cry.

"Amen," she moaned and wiggled to settle fully.

Hanging onto her, he matched her rhythm, and she led him toward a climax that sent them to the ground in a heap, both laughing and hanging on to each other.

After a long while, she said, "Well there you go."

"I reckon as how."

"Must've been the moonlight," she teased.

"Yeah. Couldn't have been the company. Good Lord, woman. I think I'm broke."

"Aw, sweetie. Let's get you up off the ground. Did I hurt you?"

"Not so's you'd notice, but I do need to get up. Want to lend a hand?"

She stood, waited while he propped one arm on the bench, then helped heave him up to a sitting position.

"Can you get on the table? Lay on your back?"

"I suppose. Why?"

"Why? Because I want to do it again, and you'd better get comfortable. I think we're in for a long haul." She waited a moment. "All fixed?"

"I… yes, I think so. The thing is, is he ready?" He glanced downward.

The moon climbed slowly across the sky.

He wrapped both arms around her, held her close, and grew to fill her again. Murmured her name over and over. Deep inside her moist warmth he climaxed, breath hissing in and out, in and out, until at last he lay back.

"Look at that, I can see beyond the moon all the way to the stars."

A long while later, with the silvery orb hanging high in the sky, she slipped from his arms and gathered up their clothing. She caught him watching her dress and smiled. What did he see when he studied her like that? A woman ten years his senior who sometimes felt too old for him and other times felt he was much too old for her. If she could keep him from harm, he might live as long as she did. But after all he'd endured, she couldn't count on that. So much damage to his body and mind. And each time he eased away from the precipice toward a normal life, something happened to put him teetering back on the edge.

"Whatcha thinking, honey?" he asked, his bare butt shivering.

"Thinking maybe I ought to give you your pants." She tossed them over to him and pulled her shirt on without putting on the bra. Saw he watched her, said, "All the easier to get naked fast."

Laughter emerging from him so easily gave her renewed hope. Give us the summer, she prayed. Then the winter. Just one season at a time. "Get into those pants. I can see goose bumps on that good-looking butt of yours."

"Katie?"

"What?"

"Come here."

She grinned. "I'm coming."

The months slipped by, her marking them off by the day, making great black Xs on the calendar. There was, of course, the Fourth of July fireworks lighting up the sky and sending him into tremors he tried to hide. Eventually he gave up, crawled into bed, and coiled into a ball. She joined him and wrapped him up tight within her embrace. And then that marvelous day in late July when he told her he was ready to chase her through the fields, holding up the cane and walking with only the vestige of a limp.

"Next March, darling, when the spring beauties are in bloom. Then we'll have a blue carpet to lay on." Because he hid the pain well didn't mean he was ready to endure it while running.

In retaliation, he'd padded across the floor, grabbed her around the waist, and tossed her onto the couch so easily she was amazed at his strength. "Just so you know." He stood over her, eyes sparkling, dimples flashing. If Spencer could see him now.

But Glen had stopped going to see the psychiatrist because something had happened between them he wouldn't talk about. Probably a clash about their differing beliefs regarding the flashbacks. Though she believed Glen bore a great resentment against Spencer for strapping him to that bed and dosing him with drugs, she didn't really blame him. At any rate, she didn't press him. He was doing so well, protected by her tender loving care. Harry called occasionally to see how things were going. She figured Spencer put him up to it. Her reports were good. How could any of them be worried? How, indeed.

Yet as summer faded into fall, it was as if Glen climbed one steep hill after another, only to slide down the other side into darkness. She refused to believe nine years of destructive torture had permanently damaged his mind. That he was broken so badly no amount of hugs could stick the pieces back together.

FIVE

NOVEMBER WOULD BRING not only Thanksgiving, but her month-long showing at The Art Gallery. Meanwhile, she had managed to finish two paintings for the Little Rock Vietnam Museum and she and Glen had been invited to be guests at the grand opening. He did not want to go, but would not say so outright. She could not leave him alone.

"That man is an asshole," he said of the governor.

"No, he's not, sweetie. He's merely a politician."

"What I said. One in the same."

"Okay, you win that one. But we can manage to be polite for an hour or two, considering the money he's paying for the paintings."

"How easily you are bought," he said, hugging her and resting his forehead against hers.

His exquisite eyes that had beheld such terrors could gaze at her with so much love it made her ashamed to ask more of him than he might be able to give. "Sweetheart, let's not go. I don't want you to be upset by this."

"Of course, we're going. I'm so proud of you and your paintings, so proud those particular ones will hold such a place of honor."

Worried he was faking it, she took him to bed early the night before the event to make sure he had plenty of rest. Went to sleep holding him as if she could keep away the night terrors. Once in a while it worked. This night it did, and he awoke early to lie and gaze at her until she opened her eyes, smiled, and touched him. Their daily morning ritual. To prove this was reality, not the nightmare of the cage.

At breakfast he asked, "What time does this shindig start? And what should I wear? I'm just so confused. Maybe I should begin trying on clothes now."

She punched him on the arm, and he feigned pain, then laughed at her. "What are you going to wear?"

"Oh, I don't know."

"Well, then, I guess we'll be late."

To prove she could, she pulled out a dress at random, laid it on the bed, nodded her head, and began to dress. It was blue like her eyes and complimented her streaked hair, hugged her figure to the waist, then flared softly to just below the knee. She looked damned good in it if she did say so herself.

A perfect choice, he told her.

They arrived in Fort Smith in time to stop at a small local café and eat something before the ceremony. "Just in case you drink too much champagne, it won't be on an empty stomach," he told her when he suggested they order some southern fried chicken.

"I'm onto you, Glen. You're not fooling me one bit. You don't be careful, you're gonna get tubby." She patted his hard, flat belly. "Right there. A paunch is growing. I can feel it."

"I'll go on a diet right after I eat some of this fried chicken," he told her over his plate piled with mashed potatoes and gravy, corn, two rolls, and of course three pieces of fried chicken.

"I'll just eat some of his," she told the waitress with a wave, and both women laughed.

"I love a good-looking man with an appetite, don't you?" the pretty redhead remarked, and he blushed to the roots of his wind-tossed hair.

"Don't go away, Red," he said. "I'll have pie. What kind do you have?"

It was her turn to blush when he turned his golden gaze on her. Women did that around him. He had a look about him that said take me home with you, I'm a lot of fun. Plenty of them would be glad to do just that. Of course, he had no idea he had that effect on women. He laughed at Katie when she said so. She loved him for that. Damn, did she ever.

She ate a piece of his chicken and a few bites of potatoes. When a big slab of cherry pie with ice cream arrived, she took one look and groaned. "Where in the world do you put it all?"

"I'll show you when we get home." He fed her a couple of bites before digging in. There wasn't a crumb left when they got up to leave.

The ceremony was laid back and just right for those it honored, the Arkansas men who had not returned from Vietnam. Not much glitter or glitz on the society people who attended with quite a few veterans. The speeches were short and touching. She held onto Glen's arm the entire time. Then something neither of them had been warned about happened.

The governor stood up and said he had a medal to award to a man who had survived that conflict and was with them tonight. The thing was he should have told her and Glen. Though his intentions were good, his method was not.

"Could Glen Tanner please come to the podium?" He may have thought what a nice surprise this would be, but he hadn't thought it through.

Glen remained seated, staring at her as if she could fix this. She didn't know how. Everyone was looking at him because they all knew about the presentation. Everyone but him and Katie.

"Mrs. Kelly, perhaps you could escort your friend up here to receive his Purple Heart with three stars. We made a special effort to get it here in time for this opening ceremony."

Glen leaned against her. "Did you know about this?"

"Of course not. I wouldn't have let them surprise you like this. Can you go up there if I go with you?"

"Katie, I don't… I can't… shit." His frantic gaze took in the room, and she felt him panicking, took his arm, and tried to soothe him. "Sweetie, I'll go with you out of the room. It's okay."

Tears poured from his eyes, his breath came in gasps. "Help me get out of here, please."

She rose with him, and that might have worked just fine had not everyone in the room stood and began to applaud. He stumbled, kicked a couple of chairs trying to get past her, away from the noise and all those people staring at him. He pushed her aside. She caught at a chair and lost her balance, went down to her knees. Watched with dismay as he shoved his way through the crowd and out of the room.

Where would he go? What would he do? A man next to her helped her to her feet.

"What the hell is wrong with him?"

She glared at him and hurried after Glen, but when she got outside, he was nowhere in sight on the well-lit street. Panic set in. What might happen to him out here? He was probably having a flashback episode by now. The scene was right. As if to add insult to injury, the skies opened up, and it began to rain, a cold hard rain that soaked her instantly. She took off her high-heeled shoes and started walking, looking for him. He couldn't have gotten far. The blue dress was sodden, clinging to her body.

The governor caught up with her. "Is there anything we can do? I'm so sorry, I thought he would be pleased."

"Just see if you can get me some help to find him. He could be having a flashback, so they need to be cautious approaching him. He won't hurt anyone unless he feels threatened. Please help me."

About then she heard her name being called. It was Glen. Rain poured over her face, practically blinding her. She followed the sound of his voice, found him crouched behind a Lincoln Town Car in the nearby parking lot, soaked to the skin and terrified he was being shot at.

The governor sent a couple of younger vets with her, but she signaled them to stay back. She knelt beside Glen. "Honey, it's me. Come on, let's get out of the rain. You're freezing."

"Katie, there's someone over there. He's got a gun."

"No, there's no one with a gun. A couple of the guys from inside are here with me. They'll make sure no one has a gun."

After a few minutes of persuasion, he let her lead him to the van, which she was glad they had brought. He was in no condition to drive home. She thanked the two men who stood by the entire time, disregarding the rain to make sure she got him to the van.

"That's okay, ma'am. I was in the Marines in-country," one of them said. "He's got a bad case of stress. Is he in a group? We have one over here if he'd like to come talk about it sometime." He handed her a card. "This here's my name and a phone number he can call."

"Thank you so much. Please tell your friend thanks, too. And let's all get in out of the rain. I don't want to leave him alone in the van."

"You call if you should need anything."

"Yes, I will." Now all she had to do was get him home in one piece. Little did that fool governor know the Purple Heart should've had a thousand stars on it.

SIX

GLEN WAS IN the sunroom exercising when the governor came to the door a couple of days later. Katie was so surprised to see him she gaped in silence for a moment.

"Mrs. Kelly, I come with hat in hand, so to speak, and a request. May I come in for a moment? I won't stay long."

She glanced beyond his shoulder at the black car, a driver behind the wheel. "Yes, of course. I'm sorry. I was just so surprised to see you. I mean, it isn't every day the governor is at my door."

He chuckled. "I understand how you feel. Especially after my thoughtless act last week. Is your... is Glen here?"

"Yes, he's in the other room. Could I tell him what you want, prepare him, more or less?" She tried out a smile that didn't quite come off.

"Again, I am so sorry. If I had known... or at least spoken to you ahead of time we could have avoided that embarrassing situation. Embarrassing for me, of course. I've since learned some of his history. A lot of it is classified."

"I'll just bet it is. If you were embarrassed, imagine how he felt when he remembered what had happened. Would you like to sit down?"

Together they perched on the edges of two chairs in the living room, each looking as if they might leap to their feet at any moment.

"Now, what brings you to this part of the state?"

Before he could reply, the sunroom door popped open, and Glen came in wearing jeans, a sweat-stained tee shirt and no shoes. His face was glowing from activity. "Katie, do you know where—"

He hauled up short when he saw the two of them perched on chairs, mouths hanging open.

"Uh, sorry. I didn't know we had company."

She rose and went to him, interlaced her fingers in his. "You remember the governor?"

"I certainly do. Sir?" He let her squeeze his fingers without flinching or turning his gaze from the visitor.

"Yes," the governor said, rising. "I came to apologize for my thoughtless behavior last week."

"You came all the way up here from Little Rock to apologize?"

"Well, my actions merit a bit more than a written apology or even a telephone call."

"Your apology is accepted, sir." Glen eased from her grip and limped back toward the sunroom.

"I'd like to ask you something, if you don't mind."

Glen stopped with his back to them. He turned around and flashed that million dollar smile he kept for special occasions, and she couldn't help but smile back at him. "I don't mind."

"I'm sorry. What?" the governor said, obviously taken by surprise.

"You asked if I minded if you asked me something."

"Oh, yes. I still have that Purple Heart. And I would be most honored if you would allow me to present it to you at Mrs. Kelly's opening at The Art Gallery next week."

Katie beamed at Glen. Maybe he'd get the message without her butting in too badly.

"No, I won't take her day away from her." He rubbed his thumb absently over the back of her hand.

"Glen, sweetheart, it would do my heart good if they gave you that medal at my gallery opening. That is, if you wouldn't mind accepting it."

Glen stared at the governor. "Sir, I thought a member of the Armed Services was supposed to present medals to servicemen." He let his gaze rest fondly on Katie. She winked at him, and his dimples flashed.

"Well, you may be correct, but this is very special to me, as is that memorial down in Little Rock. And I would most certainly feel honored to present it if you wouldn't mind. So many of our Vietnam vets have been shortchanged when it comes to ceremonial presentations of what they so richly deserve."

Glen cleared his throat and took Katie's hand. "If Katie thinks it would be okay, and you need to do this, then I'd be glad to take part."

"I really appreciate that."

"One thing, though," Glen said. "I won't make a speech. Just a thank you and handshake."

"That's just fine. I can't tell you how much this means to me. There will be reporters there for the opening, I'm sure, and they'll want to take photos. Will that be acceptable?"

"I suppose. Please remember this is Katie's opening. I won't have this ceremony take that away from her. Especially not for political reasons."

"Of course not." The man flushed and reached out to shake Glen's hand. She had to grin, knowing Glen had worked up quite a sweat and would have damp palms.

The governor didn't blink or wipe his hand, at least not in their presence, but said his goodbyes, thanked them both, and left.

"Means he'll get his face plastered all over the newspapers and on television again," Glen said.

"But you'll get what you deserve."

"Fucking shit, what I deserve." He stared out the window, refused to meet her gaze. "Reckon I've already got a boatload of that."

"Honey, hey," she whispered and turned his face toward her. "Let's forget this whole damn thing. You don't want to do it, and I don't want you doing it to please me or that asshole."

"Sometimes I wonder just what I do want, Katie. Besides you, that is. I'll do what will please you because I love you. You've given me everything I have. Everything I'll ever have, including memories."

"Then we're okay? You're okay with this?"

He grinned and hugged her tight, his chin resting on top of her head. "Fucking A, darlin', fucking A."

She wasn't sure, yet did not want to push the matter further. "I hope you'll let me go up there with you. I'm so proud of you, so damn proud."

"Of course, and if you hold on to me real tight, maybe I won't make a fool of myself."

"One of those hugs that glues back all the broken pieces?"

"Yeah, that. I gotta get back in there. Haven't gotten to two thousand pushups yet."

"Doofus."

She watched him limp back to the sunroom. Those moments broke through, moments that showed her the man he once was, could hopefully be again, touched her to the core. Made her wish to God she could rain down a miracle and heal him.

SEVEN

THE ART EXHIBIT opened the first weekend of November. Katie and Glen spent Thursday and Friday at the gallery, making sure all the paintings were exhibited the way they wanted them. She asked his opinion on the placing of every one, and he patiently gave it, making helpful suggestions. Turned out he had a good eye for the overall décor.

Both days they ate dinner at George's, a small bistro down the street, then came home for a light supper of soup and sandwiches. Through the entire preparation he was laid back, not nervous at all, giving her new hope. Even with all the street traffic, he remained calm. They strolled the half block to eat Friday as they had the day before, arm in arm, talking about the upcoming show.

"Are you nervous?" he asked when everything was coming together, and they were eating a mid-day meal.

"More so than you appear to be." She grinned at him.

"Not my show. I'm calm as can be. See?" He held out a steady hand.

"You're going to be okay for the presentation?"

"Yep. You know what, Katie?"

"No, what, my sweet young thing."

He laughed. "Sweet young thing? Damn, you nearly made me forget what I was going to say. Oh, yeah. I'm going to make you a promise." Looking serious, he held up a hand, as if taking a vow. "I hereby promise not to fly apart and ruin your opening, so help me God."

Her throat burned, and she turned away so he wouldn't see the tears glistening in her eyes.

"Katie?"

"It's okay, sweetie. I just had this overpowering desire to leap across the table and kiss you. Had to control myself. Do you know just how much I appreciate you?"

"Hadn't thought about it. The way you have to keep rescuing me from my screw-ups. Just don't want it to happen this time."

"Okay, that's fine. I'd be happy if you don't screw up, as you put it. Happy for you. You do understand that, don't you?"

"Think so." He finished off his dinner and asked the waitress what was for dessert. She brought him a big slice of chocolate cake, and he gave Katie a few bites, both of them laughing when the frosting smeared onto her nose.

It was the finest day they had spent together in a long while. She treasured it and prayed for more.

Saturday morning dawned with clear skies and one of those warm southern breezes that occasionally breathed in late fall in Arkansas. While she dressed, Glen made a big fuss of putting on a tie with the Western suit after spending a long time in the bathroom shaving.

"With or without the Stetson?" he asked, put it on, struck a pose, took it off, another pose, had her giggling like a girl.

"Wear it," she finally managed. "You look so blamed cute in it. You can leave it at the door if you don't want to have it on for the presentation. Do you know what time the governor is going to show up?"

"Cute?" He stared at her and tried not to laugh. "Cute? I had absolutely no idea. Wait, he didn't tell you when he'd be there?"

"Nope. Guess he wants to surprise us." She moved past him in her underwear on the way to the bathroom to put on her makeup.

He reached an arm out and circled her waist.

"If anyone's cute, it's you." He held her close and kissed her. Then glanced down at his tented pants. "Now look what you did."

It was a good thing they had started dressing early. He shed his pants, backed her up to the bed, and pulled down her panties.

In his arms, held close while he made tender love to her, she felt so blessed to have this man. When they finished and lay tangled together on the bed, she said, "Do you remember once you said to me that one day I would be sorry I'd ever laid eyes on you?"

He went so still it frightened her.

Then, in a soft voice, "Yes, and...?"

"That day will never happen. You are the sweetest man I've ever known. I am so happy to have found you. When you hold me it's like we have our own world. I love you so very much, and I will always treasure the day I first laid eyes on you. Don't you forget it, either."

He pulled her against his chest, cleared his throat. "Damn, Katie. Well, damn. I don't know what to say."

She wiggled back so she could look into his face. "I guess damn is okay, sweetheart, long as you say it with such gentle inflection. We'd better get dressed and get going, or we'll be late."

He turned her loose reluctantly, followed her into the bathroom where they both cleaned up and finished getting ready to leave.

She wore a new cerulean blue, floor-length dress with a V-neck that gave a peek at the swell of her breasts. A filmy shawl around her shoulders glistened when she moved.

"That's beautiful," he told her. "Correction, you're beautiful in that. You gonna be cold before we start home. I'll throw in a coat for you."

"Thank you. Probably a good idea. You look pretty damn good yourself." She smoothed her palms over the front of the suit jacket, kissed him on the tip of the chin, and they went to the car. He had already told her he wanted to drive.

If anything did happen, she wouldn't be able to get them home, but she only nodded it would be fine. Trust him, damn it. Trust him.

And, indeed, she could, for the day went perfectly. Even the governor didn't act like a politician, but instead came off as their best friend. Though, come to think of it, politicians could make people believe most anything. He even teared up a bit when he presented Glen with the Purple Heart in a black-velvet lined box. He didn't pin it on his suit, which Katie decided must be regulations, since the governor wasn't in the service.

The ceremony was held after lunch, and long after Katie had been introduced and her paintings discussed for the television cameras. Everyone clapped and cheered. Glen stared out over their heads, standing stiffly at attention and holding the box at his side. That took all the willpower he had, but he pulled it off. A young man covered the showing this time, and that reminded Katie she had promised Penny Adams they would appear on her show and had never gotten back to her. Just as well.

She waited nearby for Glen, who was surrounded by visitors after the cameras left and things settled down.

"Fine turnout, Katherine," a familiar voice said at her shoulder.

"Spencer." She turned and gave him a hug. "So glad you could come."

"Me, too. Sorry I missed the one in May, wanted to make sure I came to this one." He peered over her shoulder. "He looks good, doesn't he?"

"He looks fabulous. It's been a lot of work for him to get this far, and I feel like I'm walking on eggshells. He still has horrible nightmares, almost more than he can stand sometimes. They frighten him so much he fears when he wakes up he'll be there, not here. He's not absolutely sure which one is reality. Is there nothing we can do to help that?"

Before he could answer, his expression changed. "Doc," Glen said from behind her. "Good you could come. I know Katie is pleased." He put an arm around her and kissed her cheek. "Isn't she beautiful?"

"Yes, she is. Good to see you looking so well. I'm pleased. And about the Purple Heart, too. You deserve much more than that."

Glen shrugged. "Ah, well, you know. The guys who really deserve them aren't up and walking around. They're gone."

All three stood there in silence for a long moment. Then Spencer broke the spell. "I'm going to check out this wonderful artist's work. Good to see you two again."

"Come see us sometime, Doc," Glen said, then he leaned on her heavily. "Gotta sit down, babe. You go ahead. Meet and greet. I'm fine, super fine."

"I know you are. You're still cute, even without the hat. I'll walk with you until we find a chair."

"Yes, Mother." He grinned, put an arm around her shoulder, and let her help him to a chair. "Next time tell me not to be such a show-off and bring the damn cane, would you?"

"Huh. You know how you are about being told what to do."

"Yeah, how am I? Did you see that girl in the short dress? If she took a long step you could see her under britches."

"I didn't notice. Not surprised you did, though. Here's a chair. I won't be much longer, then we can go home."

"No hurry, cupcake."

Cupcake, she mouthed and raised her eyebrows. He wiggled his fingers at her and gave her the smile that sparked his eyes and popped dimples in his cheeks. All the time she visited, she looked his way every few minutes to make sure he was still there and looked comfortable. The last thing she wanted was for him to start wandering around and get in trouble.

By the time they left, the gallery owner told her several of the paintings had been purchased, two by a prominent attorney and another by a member of the art council. She walked out beside Glen, his arm over her shoulder, hers around his waist.

"Well, we've had quite a day, haven't we, sweet cheeks?" she asked.

"Yes, indeed we have, cupcake, and I'm beat. Is that cheeks as in these?" he pinched her face "or these?" and then her butt.

"Doofus. Let's go home. I'll give you a back rub, and you can rub my aching feet. Then we can figure out the cheeks."

A motorcycle roared down the street, and she tightened her hold.

"No worries, I'm fine. Gotta admit, there for a minute I was gonna hit the deck, but it didn't happen."

She still didn't manage to relax totally until he drove up to the house, and they were both inside, shedding their clothes on the way to the bed. He fell asleep in her arms as soon as they crawled under the covers. For a long time she lay against him, first listening to his heartbeat, then counting his breaths. Finally, she tucked her head against his shoulder, closed her eyes, and drifted off.

EIGHT

THE NEXT MORNING, crossing the room, he caught the cane on the corner of one of the exercise machines and nearly fell.

"Let's move into the main bedroom," she suggested. "We don't have to remain in this makeshift place now that you get around so well. You can do the steps, can't you? There're only four."

He stared at her. "Yours and Stan's room? Are you sure?"

"If it wouldn't bother you, I'd much rather. The bath is larger with a tub and shower, the bed is near the east windows so we can watch the sun come over the mountain in the morning. You don't have all those machines to fall over. The room itself is more comfortable with recliners, and the patio is just out the French doors. But it's up to you. Absolutely up to you."

"Let's talk about it over breakfast. I want you to be sure you can share that room with me after all your years spent there with your husband. More ghosts we don't need."

"Oh, Sweetie. Stan is not a ghost anymore. He's a good memory of my former life." Taking his arm, she strolled beside him into the large country kitchen, excited about the idea. "You could have the sunroom for the exercise equipment and a bright corner where you can do your sketches. We can have the bed taken out or left if you'd like to have a place to sleep in private. It could be your own place when you need to be alone."

He stopped midway through the room carrying plates. "Are you saying we should start sleeping apart? Not that I'd blame you, but—"

She turned from the stove. "No, no. I just thought you might… never mind, we'll have the bed taken out, give you more room."

While he finished setting the table, she took up the eggs and bacon, made some toast, and poured two cups of coffee. The shine in his eyes, his improved energy level, a smile that came more often as the days passed, gave her hope his emotional stability was on the mend. Even without Martin's presence, he continued to do his exercises each day. Sometimes she sat and watched him with sheer joy as he grew stronger and stronger. If only the nightmarish memories would stop haunting him.

Perhaps in time.

The leg would always give him trouble. The damage done to it by those monsters was permanent. He could do no more about that.

At the table, finishing the meal with more coffee, she lay her hand over his. "I love you."

He smiled, eyes sparkling. "I love you."

"So what do you think of moving? It wouldn't take much. Our clothes, some things from the bathroom is all."

"If you're sure you want to."

"I'm sure. Let's start over in a place away from all the troubles we've faced together."

"Okay, if you're sure. Shall we do it today?"

"Yes, let's. It'll give us a project for the day. No hurry, just a few things at a time, then we can put the sheets on the bed." She glanced up at him. "Perhaps we can christen the bed tonight, then. That is if you're horny."

"Katie, don't you know I'm always horny?" He lifted her hand, kissed it.

"Bragger."

"We'll see who's bragging."

By the time they put a meal on the table that evening, everything had been moved. Only the bed remained in the exercise room, and they would have to get someone to come in and take it down.

That night he proved to her he wasn't bragging at all. Afterward they slept spooned together all night without once awakening to deal with nightmares.

Before the next full moon, he awakened from a nightmare, sweating and gasping. She sat up, gathered him close and spoke quietly until he settled down.

"Tell me about it." While Spencer thought they should only look forward and forget the past, many other experts said it was best he talk about these dreadful memories. Since Spencer's method hadn't worked too well, they both agreed to try this.

So while she held him, he told her.

"I dreamt I killed her. The problem is, suppose it's you and not her when I get right to it? What if I don't know the difference?

She kneaded at the tight muscles across the back of his neck. "It's only a dream, only a dream." Her heart fluttered until it took away her breath. He was finally able to refer to his ex-wife without losing control. A good step, though she didn't like where he was going with this.

"Am I there when you kill her?"

"You're everywhere I go, Katie. If you weren't, I couldn't get back again."

Of all the things he said, that one frightened her the most. Suppose sometime she didn't go with him, and he didn't come back?

In the dark stillness of the night, long after he slept, the telephone downstairs rang, stridently and with fearful repetition. Nothing good could come from a phone call in the middle of the night.

NINE

WITH ONE QUICK glance at the bedside table and the silent instrument she hadn't thought to plug in, Katie grabbed a robe, eased the door closed behind her and ran downstairs to answer the phone so she wouldn't awaken Glen.

"Kate, this is Spencer. Is Glen with you?"

"Of course, but he's asleep. He—"

"Kate, they found Ellie's car in the river near the highway south of West Fork. She'd apparently run off an embankment into the creek. Must have been on her way to you."

"Oh, God. Spencer. Why? After all this time."

"Who knows? They called me at the hospital. She had the number in her purse."

"In her purse? Why would she carry around your number in her purse?" A crackle and rattle in her ear, and she hesitated a moment. "And Ellie? Is she okay?"

"Kate, Ellie's dead."

"But she was just… I don't—"

A jarring crash echoed through the static on the rural system. A berserk howl reverberated through the lines.

"For Christ sake, Kate. What was that?"

The sound was in the house with her, its fury assailing her senses. She dropped the receiver and screamed, "Oh my God. Glen." He'd picked up the extension, plugged it in. Heard what they'd said about Ellie.

Frantic, she bounded for the stairs, stumbled up them, toes catching, throwing her off balance. Terror stricken shrieks, animal-like bellows echoed through the house. She couldn't swallow, choked on her parched tongue. Breathing was impossible, her heart raced. No sound would come when she tried to call his name. Beating, pounding, struggling with sweating hands, she made the doorknob work, threw open the bedroom door. And plunged into hell.

The bulb in the hall sent pointed fingers of light across the empty bed, lit up the telephone lying on the floor, the open drawer of her nightstand table, a swath of red felt hanging from it like frozen blood.

Dear God in Heaven. He had Stan's gun!

The sound of her breathing was scratchy, raspy, and she stifled it with her fist to listen. All these months, something had pecked at her, and she didn't know what. If they died here it would be entirely her fault. She'd left the goddamned gun in the goddamned drawer. Absolutely forgotten all about it. How could she have been so stupid?

She had to do something. Fix this. Now. She leaned sideways to get a better view of the room and the doorframe exploded in splinters. In reflex, she covered her ears to drown out a thunderous roar. She fell to the floor, cracking her knees painfully. A deep breath inhaled the smell of gunpowder thick in the air, leaving a taste on her tongue.

"Son of a bitch, Mac," Glen shouted. "They're all around us."

Katie peered over the edge of the mattress, saw the .45 and his fingers clutching the grip. One curled around the trigger. A far-off voice chattered at her from the telephone receiver lying on the floor. Spencer. She fought a frenzied, instinctual urge to crawl away from the inferno, escape the madness.

But she couldn't leave him here with the gun she'd supplied for just this moment. All these months it had lain in wait in the drawer, and she'd forgotten, driven its existence from her mind. Admitting to her own stupidity made her sick.

Glen squeezed off a round that thunked into the highboy just above her head. "You bastards. Not this time. You won't get me this time."

Crouched within the stench of fear running rampant in the darkness, she breathed the heavy odor of gunpowder permeating the room. Lying flat, her cheek against the cold, hard wood, the bitter taste of gall gagged her. Paralyzed with panic, she swallowed it down, hugged the floor.

In a worn out, crackly voice, he rambled on. "I know what they'll do to us. Not this time. I'll fuckin-A die first."

No! She would not let him do that. Numbed by terror, she inched her way around to the foot of the bed. Another shot rang out, windows vibrated, the bullet smashed into the wall.

In a moment of frozen stillness, arms crossed over her head in useless protection, close, right on top of her came a slithering, sliding movement, harsh breathing.

"Move you fucking son of a bitch, I'll blow you away."

A whine bubbled from her throat, and she couldn't help but move enough to peer into the ashy shadows. Right into the black and monstrous eye of the .45. Glen lay on his stomach at right angles to her and against the foot of the bed. He clutched the weapon in both hands, aiming steadily.

She let out an audible hiss. They were both going to die, right here in this room, together. A flicker of insanity told her that wouldn't be so bad. But no, not this way. Dear God, not this way.

Barely aloud, she spoke fervently. "Glen. Glen, it's me, Katie."

He cocked his head, the barrel of the gun wavered minutely. "No," he whispered. "It's a trick."

For a brief instant the muzzle pointed at the floor. She touched the backs of his clenched fingers. He jerked spasmodically, throwing her hand away. With the movement the gun went off. Her ears pealed and she cringed from the gust of the deadly missile's passing.

Hysterical, she screamed at him. "Please, Glen. Help me. Save me."

"No," he whimpered, "I can't. You're gone. They took you away. Oh, Katie. Oh, God. Jesus, I wish I could die."

Well, I'll not let you. In desperation, she pleaded with him. "I'm here. They didn't take me away. It's me, Katie, and I need you to save me. I love you, please help me."

"A lie. She's gone. Where the hell is everybody?" he shouted. "Is everyone dead? Goddammit, I can't save everyone." He let the weapon rest on the floor.

"You can save me."

"Katie? I won't let them take me. I won't let them take us."

He'd heard her. She'd made it into that world. In wordless relief she dropped her head on her arms. Heat simmered from his body, a wretched, clinging steam that made her gulp for air.

He tugged and pulled at her so she was beside him. "Get behind me. Hurry, quick."

Relief made her dizzy. She scrabbled in a half-crawl around the bedframe. He jerked the gun up, fired again, and breaking glass crashed in the next room. Closing her eyes, her mind catapulted away from the mindless turmoil. She saw him in the glow of moonlight, gazing out across the still lake, his face transformed by happiness and joy. She touched his shoulder, and it was wet, as if he came from the depths of the lake. To touch him, sense his substance brought her a temporary respite from the pending loss.

His fear filled her, quavering in her stomach. The enemy, surely out there beyond that door, waited. Ready to spring on them both. A blare of gunfire, tracers arcing against the night sky, the whine and whump of incoming mortar, the whip-whop of chopper rotors. She reached beyond the battle, searching for another reality. On realizing it was just as bad, she huddled over herself for protection.

"Katie, baby. It'll be okay. I'll get us out of here. Don't cry, honey."

"But there's nobody out there." Is there?

He crabbed sidewise. "Come on, we've got to move. Hurry."

Keeping her head down, she went with him until they were deep in the bush. He cautiously lifted himself to a sitting position, keeping the downed chopper between them and the moonlight pouring through the thick foliage. She moved in beside him, grateful to lean against the rough bark of a tree.

He held the .45 in his right hand and put his left arm around her shoulders. "We'd have a better chance with an M-16, but I lost the damned thing."

She peered into the depths of the shadowed ground, searched frantically through leaves and grass, but found no weapon. With a trembling sigh, she collapsed backward.

"They'll hang us up by our arms until they pull out at the sockets. They've got these little electrodes they attach to batteries and then to tender parts—"

"Oh, God, Glen, stop it."

"You're not Katie," he accused brutally. "You're trying to fool me, help them catch me. But Ellie, she... Ellie?" He paused, breath whooshing in and out. "Katie, is Ellie dead?"

"Yes, darling. She's dead." For a while, she'd fled into the bush with him, but that had to be her imagination.

He laughed, a demonic chuckle sending chills through her. "I really loved her once. How could she do that to me?"

She held him, rubbing her palm over his sweating bare chest.

"That's why I killed her, you know," he said.

"No, darling. You didn't kill Ellie. You were with me."

"You're just saying that. I wanted her dead, wished her dead, killed her dead." A moment's hesitation, then, "And that's what I came back for. That and to pay. Haven't I paid now, Katie? Haven't I?'

He had paid all he should ever have to pay, but how to tell him that? His admission they were no longer in the jungles of his mind didn't relieve her. Reality might offer him a final solution. She had to stop him before he put that gun to another use. How many shots had he fired? She couldn't remember. Maybe, just maybe, it was empty, but she dared not take that chance.

Spencer would come soon or send someone, if she could just keep Glen occupied until they arrived. But would they have guns, shoot back? Such suppositions were pure nonsense. Spencer's pride wouldn't allow him to call in the law. He'd come for Glen himself. Even if it put him in danger.

Glen tensed. The quiver of his muscles sent fear ripping through her. Before she could react, he swung the gleaming black barrel around and fired a shot through the window, shattering the glass into noisy shreds. She cried out, buried her face in his chest, against his thundering heart. The last of the falling glass tinkled in melody with a host of night peepers. An unsettling quiet enabled her to reason with him.

"Remember when we first met? You said you thought I was an angel, remember? And the night at the pond, the first time we came together. Glen, we love each other, we always will."

"I know, but it isn't enough. I can't give you anything but that. What's love without hope?"

He wanted no answers, expected none, and it was a good thing. "Glen, would you give me the gun if I asked for it?"

"No. I might need it later."

"What for? There's no one here but us. We're in our bedroom, and there's no one else here."

He remained adamant, stubborn, and she returned to her original tack.

"But think of all our life waiting for us. We can get married and live happily ever after. We really can."

"Katie, when I was in high school, I believed that fairy tale, too. I thought there was nothing but endless days forever and forever. Life just went on, and I was immortal and could do nothing wrong. God, that was so long ago, and now there's nothing there at all. The only thing worth remembering is our time together. Now that's over, too."

"No," she cried. "It's not over. I won't let it be." She forced him to accept her into the curve of his arms, and he pulled her close, pressing the .45 against the flat of her back. Cold and immense and terrifying in its power.

A breeze ruffled the curtains above their heads, bringing in the sweet aroma of earth and damp leaves, of winter on the way, turned sour by the overpowering odor of sweat and terror. Her heart filled with a desire to run barefoot through wild, brown-eyed Susans while he held her hand, race along together within the freedom of wind and mountains.

Escape from this room and his destructive fantasy became an overpowering need that grew in intensity until it was only a raw and animalistic instinct for his survival. A matter of keeping herself between him and the gun.

Where was Spencer? It seemed like hours since the phone call. He would surely come soon, but would it be soon enough?

Glen spoke in an eerily calm voice, interrupting her wish. "I've been looking for something I must have left undone, some reason all those guys died over there in 'Nam and I was spared. 'It feels a shame to be alive, when men so brave are dead,'" he quoted from his favorite poet. "Was it only for Ellie and not a noble reason I was spared? God, oh, God. I can't think. I'm not making sense.

"I need to know I lived through those nightmares to do more than just come back and kill my wife. Make my life worth something, please. You, our love. I need to leave the best parts with you for safekeeping. You are all that will survive of me. I'll never die as long as you keep the memory."

With trembling fingers, she covered his lips. "I won't listen to any more. I can't stand it."

He shook her hand away. "Katie, you have to, and you have to forgive me. Love me enough to let me go."

"No," she cried. "No. I have loved you enough, enough for both of us. It's time you loved me enough to make my life worth something. How could I live knowing I'd let you die and did nothing? How? No, let's be fair with each other. At least that. You love me enough to stay and put up a fight, and I'll be there with you. Always. Please. Because, Glen," she said in a clenched voice on the edge of panic, "If you do this, I'll never forgive you, never ever." She could say no more and hung on to him ferociously with a strength she had reached for and found, but would never know from where.

He still held the gun, she knew it even though she could no longer feel it against her back. She saw him again the way he'd looked the first time she laid eyes on him, how he'd reached out from his own sorrow to comfort her in hers. How brave he'd been all these months, getting back up and fighting every time he was knocked down.

Would he ever be grateful if she managed to keep him alive for still more punishment? Or was enough indeed enough?

God help her, she understood his need to be finished with it all, had even said to Spencer perhaps they'd done the wrong thing bringing him back to this world. But she had to stop thinking that way, or they could both die. So help her God, if he died then she would want to as well, for she had put the gun in his hand. Would never forgive herself for being that thoughtless.

He was talking again, and she couldn't shut out the words. "Lying in bed with you in my arms doesn't stop it, anymore. I see the faces of those butchers, feel the flames, the blades slashing incessantly at my flesh, hear them coming, coming, and wonder what it will be this time. It never stops, and the pain is as real as it was then. And one night, Katie, when I can't stand it any longer, I'll think you're one of them, and I'll kill you. So, you see, it's time you let me go." He paused, and before she could say anything, added, "I've done what I came back for. She's gone."

The words tore at her, and she struggled to see his face in the glow from the nightlight. Gently she wiped away glistening tears from his cheeks.

"I love you more than life, I truly do. How can you want to leave me now when I love you so much?"

In that moment of silence, while he truly seemed to consider answering her question, the far-off wail of sirens bounced in eerie echoes across the mountains. She drew a deep breath. "Thank God."

He kissed her, held on a long while. "Yes, thank God that I've had you to love. You kept me safe for a very long time. I need to let you go, too."

Mesmerized, she watched him raise the automatic between them, regard it in an offhand way, and then uncurl his finger from around the trigger guard. Tears flowed down his cheeks.

The sirens moved from the highway and headed toward them. She fastened both hands over his, fingers wrapped over the .45, and held on.

The wailing floated up the lane toward the house and wound down to a spectral silence of flashing lights, and the blink, blink, blink of blues and reds at the windows. Spencer had called the police after all.

Screams split her throat, the release of such pent up anguish she had thought she might burst. Feet thudded up the stairs, Spencer's booming voice called, and she replied in a broken, mewling cry. He'd come in alone, as she knew he would.

Blackness closed around her, a remote wilderness in which she floated and beheld Glen emerging from a jade green pool of water, his bronze body breaking the icy crystalline surface to splash bits of rainbow high into the sky. His golden eyes beckoned, and she went to him, grasped him in her arms and held on.

TEN

"I DON'T WANT him on drugs. It's not helping." Kate moved away from the door to Glen's room where he sat staring out the window.

"It's not up to you, Kate. I can't keep him here any longer. I've pushed it already. He's being transferred to Little Rock to a Vet's Home there. He'll be kept comfortable."

She grabbed his arm. "No, I won't let you do that. I won't. I'm taking him home with me."

Spencer whirled, grabbed her arm, and guided her into his office. "That's insane. Do you know what that means? It means the rest of your life caring for a man who is not much more than a vegetable. Haven't you done enough?"

"No, I have not done near enough yet. You let me go. Now. He will never be a vegetable. He knows me every day when I sit beside that bed. He holds my hand and looks into my face and knows me. He's in there, I know he is. The man I fell in love with is inside there, screaming to be let out. I can do that much for him. Let him out. He'll be better off with me. At least he can have what he wants when he wants it. Not shut up in a box down there in Little Rock. For God's sake, Spencer, after what he went through to live, you want to sentence him to that?"

"Katherine, I care too much for you to let you do this to yourself." His eyes shone brightly, but she refused to let him sway her.

"I took him from here before. I can do it again, and I will. Release him to me now against medical advice. I'll take him home where he belongs."

Spencer shook his head. "You can't care for him. Not this time. It's too much."

"Then I'll get help." She fell to the couch, covered her eyes with one hand. "I cannot pass a day knowing he's trapped in some cubicle so much like that cage they kept him in. I'll never sleep. I can't live knowing I've abandoned him. Don't you understand? I did that to him. I put that gun in his hand. Spencer, please don't do this. Give us a chance. If you ever loved him, if you care for me as you say, don't do this."

He stood, stared down at her. "My God, if the gun hadn't been there, he'd have found something else. A knife to rip his arms open or cut his throat. Something. Stop blaming yourself."

"I can't stop. I'll never stop. I have to do this."

In his dark eyes, the look of surrender. He knew her too well. She would not quit. "Follow me. If you can get him to show he recognizes you, then you can take him, but only against medical advice. I will not be held responsible for what he might do."

Heart racing, she ran ahead of Spencer and through the door into Glen's room, went to his side, sat beside him and took his hand. "Sweetie, look at me. It's Katie." He didn't move for so long she thought she might have to kidnap him again. "Glen, it's Katie. I love you, sweetie."

He turned slowly, looked into her eyes.

She held her breath. Waited.

"Katie?" His hoarse voice echoed in the silence of the room.

"Yes," she whispered and kissed his hand. "It's Katie, come to take you home."

VELDA BROTHERTON writes from her home perched on the side of a mountain against the Ozark National Forest. Branded as *Sexy, Dark and Gritty*, her work embraces the lives of gutsy women and heroes who are strong enough to deserve them. After a stint writing for a New York publisher, she has settled comfortably in with small publishers to produce novels in several genres.

While known for her successful series work—the *Twist of Poe* romantic mysteries, as well as her signature Western Historical Romances—her publishing resume includes numerous standalone novels, including *Once There Were Sad Songs, A Savage Grace, Wolf Song, Stoneheart's Woman, Remembrance,* and this, her magnum opus, *Beyond the Moon.*

Facebook: Author Velda Brotherton
Twitter: @veldabrotherton
www.veldabrotherton.com

CPSIA information can be obtained
at www.ICGtesting.com
Printed in the USA
LVHW050824070119
602984LV00002B/211/P